"Simon? You're the only thing about this whole mess that I wouldn't change."

"Even though I brought this mess to your door?"

"You're not responsible for the truth being what it is."

He went to put the key in the front door.

And realized it was already open.

"Uh-oh," he muttered.

He held out a hand to stop Dina from entering with him. Who knew who had been there, or why, or if they remained?

"Call nine-one-one on your cell phone. Tell them there's been a break-in," he said quietly.

"Are you serious? . . . Oh, my God, Simon, don't go in there."

He pushed the door aside far enough for them both to see inside, enough to know that someone had done far more than simply paid a visit. . . .

Also by Mariah Stewart

LAST LOOK
LAST WORDS
LAST BREATH

COLD TRUTH
HARD TRUTH
DARK TRUTH
FINAL TRUTH

DEAD WRONG
DEAD CERTAIN
DEAD EVEN
DEAD END

UNTIL DARK

The President's Daughter

A Novel

Mariah Stewart

BALLANTINE BOOKS • NEW YORK

The President's Daughter is a work of fiction. Names, characters, places, and incidents are the products of the author's imagination or are used fictitiously. Any resemblance to actual events, locales, or persons, living or dead, is entirely coincidental.

2007 Ballantine Books Mass Market Edition

Published in the United States by Ballantine Books, an imprint of The Random House Publishing Group, a division of Random House, Inc., New York.

Originally published in mass market in the United States by Ivy Books, an imprint of The Random House Publishing Group, a division of Random House, Inc., in 2002.

ISBN 978-0-345-44739-5

Cover illustration: Vincent Ricardel/Getty Images

Printed in the United States of America

www.ballantinebooks.com

OPM 15 14 13 12 11 10 9

With love and thanks
to the incomparable Linda Marrow,
for having faith in me

Prologue

Washington, D.C.
December 14, 1971
2:03 A.M.

The woman stepped from the shadow of the stylish Art Deco apartment building, heels clicking on the walk as she strode with purpose toward the street. The light at this section of Connecticut Avenue was scant, despite it being a fine neighborhood. In fact, but for the lights at the intersection some hundred feet or more from the building, the lighting was scarce indeed.

At the end of the sidewalk, the woman paused, shivering. On this night, not even her fur coat and her cashmere gloves could keep out the cold.

The caller had said that a car would stop for her on the opposite side of the street at exactly 2:00 A.M. It was now a few minutes past. But she was certain the car would come. . . .

She continued toward the street. Such an odd time to be meeting someone, though of course she understood. There were good reasons for keeping their meeting a secret.

It was such a sensitive situation. And she totally understood the caller's reluctance to be seen with her in public.

She doubted if even the caller had any idea of just how sensitive the situation really was.

She hunched her shoulders, as much against a sudden gust of wind as at the prospect of what she was about to face, desperately not wanting to go through with this meeting but knowing there was no way to avoid it. To try would appear cowardly. And how could she have refused? The caller had pleaded, had seemed so truly in need of speaking with her. . . .

How could she have said no?

The light changed and she stepped off the curb, a full half block from the light. Turning up her collar against the sharp wind, she began to cross to the designated spot on the opposite side of the street where she was to be picked up. She'd taken but four or five steps toward the centerline when she first saw the car approaching on her left, had barely noticed it at all when it had been loitering at the light, hunkered in the shadows with its lights off. She had assumed it to be unoccupied and therefore had paid it no mind.

Until it began to move.

Rapidly.

Accelerating as it passed through the intersection until it was upon her in less than the blink of an eye. There had been no time to move out of its path, no time even to scream.

She was dead before the car came to a stop barely fifteen feet from where she had fallen and idled for a long moment, as if in reflection, then shot backward defiantly to run over the lifeless body a second time.

Three cars would pass through the intersection before one would stop on the nearly deserted street to investigate the still bundle that only moments before had been a vibrant and beautiful woman.

Chapter One

Early February 2002

The money paid had been money well spent.

The figure paused in the doorway, backlit by the dim glow from the hall, eyes flickering from one still form to the other. The patients were scattered about the room, here and there in their chairs, each wrapped in his or her gauzy haze, somewhere between the memories of the past and the vagueness of today. The object of the visitor's attention was in his usual place by the window that overlooked the wide expanse of lawn, where he could catch the changing of the seasons, year after year, for as many years as his advancing age and the whims of fate would permit.

And fate could be fickle, as everyone knew. Everything could change in a heartbeat. One moment of clarity, one memory recovered, and even the old man's now-simple life could so easily become nothing more than someone else's memory.

Crossing the room in a long-legged stride, the visitor took a seat in front of the old man's chair.

"Hello, Miles."

"Hello." The old man nodded.

"How are you?"

"I'm fine," was the automatic response.

"Did you have a good day?"

"Yes." A nod of the head.

"What did you do today?"

"I took the train to Chicago." The old man smiled. "With Dorothy."

"Did you?"

"I did." His smile broadened.

"And who is Dorothy?"

"Dorothy is . . ." The old man frowned. "Dorothy is . . . someone."

His face folded into lines as his brows knit together, as he tried to recall. Tried so hard to bring it back. He'd just had it, if only for a second. Now it was gone.

"Dorothy was your sister," he was reminded. "She died a long time ago."

"I see," the old man mumbled as he picked at a thread on his expensive sweater.

"Do you remember when Dorothy died?"

"No." The old man shook his head. "But I remember when she was in Chicago."

"What else do you remember, Miles?"

The old man looked out the window, as if perhaps something there might be familiar.

"Do you remember when you lived in Washington?"

"No."

"Do you remember when you worked in the White House?"

"We lived in a white house, once. It was near Newport. There was a pond out back. Teddy drowned in the pond. He was very small. . . ." The old man's gaze drifted back to the window, where the setting sun was beginning to send streaks of orange across a pale lavender sky.

"Yes, that was your little brother." A touch to the old man's face to get his attention. "I don't mean that white house. I mean *the* White House. In Washington, D.C. Where the President lives. Do you remember when you worked there?"

The old man's vague look was his only response.

"Do you remember Graham Hayward? President Hayward?" A studied pause. "Do you remember President Hayward? He was your friend. Your very best friend. You worked together in Washington."

"Am I supposed to remember?" the old man mumbled. "I can't remember."

"It's okay." A forgiving pat on the old man's hands reassured that all was well. "It's all right. It's okay that you can't remember." Another pause to reflect before adding, "Better for your sake, actually, that you don't."

The visitor sat with the old man for a few more moments, grateful that no memories had surfaced, that there would be nothing this day to be dealt with.

Finally, "Do you remember me?"

"No." The old man searched the face that was now so close to his own. A sharp but fleeting image flashed from somewhere in the past but disappeared before he could name it.

"No," he repeated warily, denying recognition even to himself.

His companion smiled for the first time since walking into the assisted living home, then stood and returned the chair to its place by the wall. In that brief time, the old man's gaze had drifted back to the window and the world beyond.

"Good-bye, Miles. I'll see you again soon." The parting remarks went unnoticed.

A pause in the hall only long enough to press a folded envelope into the hands of the white-jacketed orderly who awaited.

"How did you find your . . . old friend?" the orderly asked.

"Same as always."

The orderly nodded and served as an escort down the hall toward the now-darkened dayroom and the back door he'd unlocked earlier. In his pocket his fingers toyed with a corner of the envelope in which there was cash in an amount equivalent to his monthly salary. All for watching one old man and listening to his ramblings. The rich sure were different.

But why should he care, he shrugged, as long as that fat envelope came every month like clockwork? And it wasn't as if he were doing anything illegal or immoral. Hell, he wasn't hardly doing anything at all.

"Call me if there's a change." The figure paused in the open doorway.

"Of course."

"*Any* change." The emphasis was unnecessary. The orderly understood perfectly.

"Take it easy out there in the parking lot!" the orderly called through the double doors. "It's still a little icy there. . . ."

"Thanks." Hands tucked into pockets, the visitor headed out into the cold of the winter evening. Large, soft flakes were just beginning to fall, and they covered the brick walk and the parked cars like lacy leaves.

Humming, the figure walked through the pale shadows cast by the overhead lights to the car that waited at the back of the far lot, between a rusty Dumpster and a new red pickup truck.

The money had bought peace of mind. At least for tonight.

The old man's memories were buried and locked away in a place where, hopefully, they would remain for the rest of his natural life.

Which was a very good thing. As long as they remained so, the secret was safe.

And Miles Kendall—who once long ago had moved among the powerful, among Kings and Princes and senators, who had kept the confidence, and the secrets, of a President—would live to see another day.

Chapter Two

Simon Keller handed over the keys to his vintage Ford Mustang to the valet, then climbed the steps to the trendy restaurant that overlooked Baltimore's Inner Harbor. His curiosity piqued by an invitation to lunch with his favorite former college professor, Simon had been more than happy to make the drive across the Chesapeake to meet with Dr. Philip Norton. Onetime head of the journalism department at Georgetown University. Onetime White House press secretary.

It had been an unexpected pleasure, Simon reflected, running into his old journalism professor three weeks ago at the wedding of a classmate, after having lost touch for the last year or so. Time in which Simon's life had changed as surely as had Philip Norton's.

The maître d' led Simon to the table where Norton sat admiring the sweeping view of the harbor where water the color of dull pewter crested in whitecapped waves and a few hearty souls braved the winter winds for an afternoon sail.

"Philip." Simon smiled at the aging but still handsome slightly balding man who turned and leaned his tall frame half out of his seat to extend a hand in greeting. "I hope you haven't been waiting long."

"Not at all, Simon. I was just admiring the courage

of the skipper of that small sailboat." Norton gestured toward the water. "Those little yellow and red and white flags seem to lend it a bit of bravado, don't you think, considering the forecast?"

"I missed the forecast, but judging from the look of those clouds and given the fact that the temperature has been dropping all morning, I'd say we were in for a storm." Simon accepted the menu that was handed to him by a young waiter.

"While driving up from D.C., I heard that we could expect another half foot of snow, to begin sometime this afternoon." Norton sipped at his water, then set the glass down carefully and smiled. "I'm hoping to get back to the city before it starts."

"In that case, maybe we should order now," Simon suggested.

"I heartily recommend the crab cakes," Norton noted. "They're a specialty here."

"Crab cakes have become a staple of my diet, since I live so close to the bay. I think I'll have a salad and the steak sandwich this time around." Simon smiled and folded his menu, handing it to the waiter who had appeared to take their orders and to bring Norton a previously requested cup of tea.

Simon watched his old mentor's eyes as they followed the efforts of the small boat to fight back against the wind, and wondered for perhaps the tenth time what had prompted Norton's call. He wasn't the sort of man given to idle socializing. His contacting Simon had a point, and Simon was intrigued by what that point might be.

Finally, Norton turned and said, "How are your folks? Still farming?"

"Still farming." Simon smiled. "Still doing hand-to-hand combat with those northern Iowa winters."

"Any thoughts of going back someday?"

"Only for Thanksgiving, Christmas, and Mother's Day. The family farm is in the capable hands of my father and my brother. Steven never wanted to do anything but farm. I knew by the time I was eight that I didn't have a feel for it."

"Then your family is lucky to have Steven to carry on the family business." Norton folded his arms, one over the other, and leaned forward slightly. "So. Tell me how that book of yours is coming along."

"Still working on it."

"Have you been able to find an agent?"

"Still working on that, too." Simon shrugged.

"It's a difficult business, publishing."

"Are you speaking as an author or as a publisher?"

"Both, actually." Norton smiled.

"Who's your agent?" Simon asked, one side of his mouth edging into a half grin.

Norton laughed. "Actually, I do have an agent. I've only published a few, very select works of my own through Brookes Press."

Simon raised an eyebrow. "What would be the point of owning a publishing company if you're not going to publish your own books?"

"Brookes has the reputation—well earned, I am proud to say—of publishing only top-rate nonfiction. Last year's bestseller of former U.S. Supreme Court Justice Howard Rensel, for example." Norton stirred his tea. "Several years ago, I wrote a novel. I felt at the time that, had I published the book myself, it would have been viewed as unnecessarily self-indulgent.

Which, in truth, it would have been. I was afraid of undermining the reputation that I'd worked for over the years as publisher of a small independent press. The last thing I wanted was for Brookes to be thought of as a vanity press. So I took my novel elsewhere."

"Was it published?"

"No, it was not. Actually, I have the distinction of having been rejected by every major publishing house in New York." Norton looked momentarily amused, then sobered. "We did, however, publish a small volume of poems my wife had written shortly before her death. They were damned good poems, and I forgave myself that bit of indulgence because they were so damned good. Elisa deserved to have those poems published."

The death of Philip Norton's wife, the junior senator from New Jersey, several years earlier had been ruled a suicide. Simon knew that Norton never believed it. He could not accept that his beloved Elisa had put a gun to her head and pulled the trigger, regardless of the assurances of law enforcement officers that no evidence had been found to the contrary.

Norton's eyes drifted, then focused on the waiter who approached with a smile on his face and a salad plate in each hand.

"It's tough to sell a first book, especially one such as yours, that deals with a controversial topic," Norton continued after he and Simon had been served and the waiter turned his attention to the next table. "Especially one without corroboration. Some publishers might be afraid of being sued, should the story be challenged."

"You mean, should the story be challenged and

should the author refuse to reveal his confidential sources."

"Yes. That's exactly what I mean." Norton met Simon's eyes from across the table. "And I am assuming that you are still unwilling to reveal yours."

"You assume correctly." Simon leaned back in his chair. "I quit my job at the *Washington Press* rather than reveal my sources on that story. I will always do everything I can to protect them."

"It must have been very difficult to have walked away from the newspaper," Norton noted.

"I could not work for a paper that demanded disclosure—even to their legal department—of the identity of some poor sucker who was putting his life on the line by talking to me." Simon's eyes reflected the same dark pewter as the bay. "Or an editor who failed to back me up."

"I admire your sticking to principal, Simon, however difficult it might make life for you at times. But tell me, then, if I might ask, what are you doing for work?"

"Right now, I'm working on my book." Simon shifted slightly in his seat.

"Anything that's generating a little income?"

"Not at the moment." The fact was that he was pretty close to the end of his savings, a fact that Simon knew he'd have to deal with in the very near future.

Both men picked at their salads for a long moment; then Norton said, "I have a proposal I'd like to run past you."

"A proposal?"

"For a book that I have in mind. One I'd very much like to see written."

Simon looked up from his plate of greens, wondering where this might lead.

"Simon, what do you know about Graham Hayward?"

"The late President?"

"Yes."

"Well, I know that he's considered by some to be one of the great presidents of the twentieth century. That he had the reputation of being totally honest and ethical." Here Simon smiled and added, "As honest and ethical as any man with so much power could be, I suppose. And I know that, back in the seventies, when he was in office, you were his press secretary before you taught at Georgetown."

"And very proud to be. Graham Hayward was a man who was never touched by scandal. As far as I know, he kept his promise to never lie to the American people. Hayward set the moral standard that subsequent occupants of the White House have never been able to live up to."

"How did you meet him?"

"We were both from Rhode Island, both attended Brown, as you may know, though he was several years ahead of me. Our paths crossed many, many times over the years. I supported him in every way I could. I was thrilled to be able to work with him in the White House. Those days were some of the best of my life."

Norton sipped at his tea. "I suppose you're wondering where this is leading and what it might have to do with you."

"Yes."

Both men paused as the waiter placed the barely

touched salads to one side to make room for their entrées.

"President Hayward's son is being groomed to run in the next election; are you aware of that?"

"I'd heard some talk."

"He's the perfect choice. Mind you, I've known young Gray since he was a boy. He's his father all over again. So often that doesn't happen, you know. All too often, the apple falls far from the tree." Norton shook his head. "But not in this case. Gray is every bit his father's son. He'll make a fine candidate. A fine President."

"I've heard he's made a name for himself as a congressman. He's in his, what, third term?"

"Third, yes. He's done an excellent job on the Hill. The party's been working with him over the past few years, cultivating his image. You see him at least once a week with his wife, his children, often his widowed mother, at his side. Always, the family together, rock solid. The party honchos know they have a winner in this young man, Simon."

"You were going to tell me what this had to do with me." Simon was becoming antsy for the point to be reached. He couldn't possibly imagine what it might be.

"In an effort to . . . let's say, lay the groundwork for young Gray's run for the White House, I'd like to do a new biography of Graham Senior. Something that would bring him—and his accomplishments—back into the minds and hearts of the American people."

"And you're planning on publishing this book yourself?"

"Yes."

"Isn't that just a little self-indulgent?" Simon heard

himself say before tact kicked in, and he added, "I mean, you were just saying how you disliked using Brookes Press for personal reasons. If I understood you correctly."

"Oh, you understood perfectly. I did say—and mean—exactly that." Norton smiled to himself, pleased that Simon had not missed the point. "But I prefer to think of this book as being less a vanity effort than a timely exercise. It's the right time to do such a book. Someone will do it, sooner or later. I'd like to be that someone, and I'd like to do it sooner rather than later."

Simon was buttering a roll, still wondering what all this had to do with him, when Norton added, "And I'd like you to write the book."

"What?" Simon put the knife down. "You want me to . . ."

"Write a biography of Graham Hayward."

"Why?" Simon's roll sat forgotten on the side of the plate.

"Because I want the book done right and I know I can trust you to do the job the way it needs to be done. After all, I'm not totally unfamiliar with your writing, you know. All those papers you wrote for me at Georgetown." Norton grinned. "All those pieces you wrote for the *Washington Press*. You've made quite a name for yourself."

Norton studied Simon's face, then shifted to another tactic.

"I know that this would mean having to put your own book aside for a time. But if the Hayward book does well, it would certainly open doors for you. I think it goes without saying that Brookes Press would be first in line to see the finished product."

"Tell me what your interest is in this biography. Besides the obvious, that Hayward was your friend and, at one time, your boss."

"Simon, I do believe—*sincerely* believe—that young Graham can, that he will, bring integrity back into our government. I want to see that happen. I believe that he is the best person on the political scene today to do that. I believe that he can win. He's extremely intelligent, tough, energetic, handsome—he's the future."

"And you think that by reminding the public of just how good things were under the father, those good feelings will just flow over to the son."

"That's correct."

"A bit manipulative on your part, wouldn't you say?" Simon asked.

Norton chuckled. It was no less than he'd expected from his old student. "As I said, I believe that the time is ripe for someone to write this book. And someone will, sooner or later. I want that someone to be you, and I want it to be now." He hesitated momentarily when the waiter appeared with the check, which he took. "Manipulation would be if we were to present a scoundrel as a saint. Everyone knows what kind of man Graham Senior was."

"No dirt under the carpet, no skeletons in some long-hidden closet?"

"None. I'm not looking for a gossipy exposé. There is no gossip. The man's accomplishments speak for themselves. You'll talk to the family; you'll talk to a few friends. . . ." Norton watched the younger man's face.

"I don't do puff pieces."

"I'm not asking you to."

"What would the timetable be?"

"I'd like to see a rough draft in six months. I know it's not a lot of time," Norton added when Simon's eyebrows rose, "but I will be able to provide you with all the secondary material you need. I'll be sending you several boxes of old newspaper articles, interviews, film footage, magazine features that you can use as reference."

"I'll do my own research, my own interviews. If I do this, I'll do it my way."

"Of course you will. But I'll provide some background material for you to look over, just the same. And I'll make certain that the family is available to you whenever you need them."

"You've already discussed this with them?"

"Yes. Of course."

"Why?"

"Because I thought they should know what I was planning on doing. It wasn't a matter of asking permission, Simon. It was merely a courtesy."

"As long as we're not going for an authorized biography. I don't want the family—or anyone else—to have final say over the manuscript."

"It would be your book, Simon. Look, I realize this isn't a deep investigative piece—the man's life doesn't need to be reinvented. But I do want something new on the market that can capture the attention of the people. Something that will get you—and the future candidate and possibly the former First Lady—on *Good Morning America, Today, Larry King Live,* the usual. Don't overlook for a minute what that kind of exposure, those sorts of contacts, can do for your own book, once it's published."

"If it's published," Simon reminded him.

"I doubt that will be an issue, Simon." Norton appeared to be giving great thought to something, though in truth he'd had this part already thought out. He held out the carrot. "What if we make this a two-book deal?"

"Two books," Simon repeated as if he wasn't certain he'd heard correctly.

"The Hayward book and the book you're working on now. I will want the Hayward book first, of course."

"You'd buy my book sight unseen?" Simon's brows lifted.

"Well, of course, I would want to see the first hundred or so pages as soon as you can get them to me. If I don't like what you've done, well, we'll have to talk about it, once the Hayward book is finished. Though frankly, judging by all you told me about the book at Frank's wedding, I can't see how I could be disappointed."

"How much?" Simon heard himself ask. After all, before he agreed to sign away the next several months of his life, to put aside the book he'd been sweating over and living with for the past year, he had to know.

Norton took a pen from his pocket and wrote a number on an unused napkin, his eyes twinkling. Not for the first time, Simon was reminded of Sean Connery, tall and once brawny, albeit with a New Englander's accent.

Simon studied the sum for a very, very long minute and willed himself not to react. It was more than enough to fill up that on-empty savings account. Enough to keep Simon in food and shelter—if not some few minor trappings of luxury—while he finished not only the Hayward book but his own book as well. With enough left over for the first real vacation Simon had had in a very long time. Mentally, for just a flash, Simon pictured himself trekking across the hot sand of a tropical island. . . .

"I don't know what to say."

"Say you'll think about it."

"Yes. Of course I will."

"Give me a call after you've had a few days to mull it over. I understand that you'll have things to think about. Rest assured that I'll make certain your interests are protected. But to keep all aboveboard, I know of several fine agents that I'd be happy to refer you to—including my own."

"That's very generous of you."

"Just want to make sure that you feel comfortable with the arrangements I'm offering."

"I appreciate that. I'll definitely give your offer some thought."

Norton took a last bite of his crab cake and gestured to the open window, where fat flakes were beginning to fall and the small sailboat was heading for the marina. "Can I plan on hearing from you within a few days?"

"I'll be back to you by the weekend."

"I can't ask for more than that. Now"—Norton stood and straightened the sleeves of his well-tailored jacket—"why not send that manuscript along to me? Overnight it, if you would. I'm eager to have a look. . . ."

All the way back to his apartment in McCreedy, Simon tried to put his finger on just what it had been about Norton's offer that had kept him from turning cartwheels from table to table across the restaurant and accepting on the spot.

Perhaps it had something to do with the fact that the money seemed like a lot for a book that was only expected to take six months of his time and a second book that Norton hadn't even seen.

And then, it had struck Simon as odd that his former mentor—a man whose high journalistic standards were legendary—would be willing to use Brookes Press to promote someone's political agenda.

The money aside—and Simon readily acknowledged that the money was more than would have occurred to him to ask for—he wasn't fool enough not to recognize an amazing opportunity when he saw one. As he sat in traffic on the approach to the Chesapeake Bay Bridge, Simon ticked off the pros in his head.

For one thing, the book proposed by Norton wasn't expected to take much more than a few months of his time. And he'd been guaranteed publication by Brookes Press, something no previously unpublished author in his right mind would pass on. The book itself would have tremendous support from a respected independent press—support that he hoped would carry over onto *Lethal Deceptions*, a book even Norton had agreed would be a tough sell, though Norton hadn't seemed concerned about Simon's refusal to name his source of information. Of course, Norton knew Simon, knew he wouldn't have stuck by that story if he hadn't believed, heart and soul, in its verity. There was a trust factor there, something he'd been disappointed to have been found lacking in his editor at the *Press*, he recalled with a pang of annoyance. With luck, by the time *Lethal Deceptions* was ready for publication, all the wheels would be in motion to garner enough attention to propel it right onto the bestseller lists.

Who gets an opportunity like that? Who in his right mind would turn it down?

So why then, Simon asked himself yet again, had he not jumped at Norton's offer right then and there?

"I don't know," Simon said aloud as cars once again began to move over the bridge from Annapolis to Maryland's Eastern Shore. "I do not know. . . ."

But a glance at his mail once he arrived home—too many bills, too low a balance on his bank statement—was enough to convince Simon that Norton's was, in fact, a classic case of an offer too good to refuse.

Besides, hadn't he known Philip Norton for close to fifteen years? He'd never known the man to be less than forthright. And the book he'd asked Simon to write would, once it was completed, permit him to take his time while he finished *Lethal Deceptions*. . . .

Simon dropped the mail onto the counter in his cramped kitchen and sat down at the small table. The apartment had been the least expensive living quarters he could find at the time he'd first left the paper, a definite comedown from his apartment in D.C. that had overlooked the Potomac. He glanced out the kitchen window, which overlooked a narrow yard and a derelict garage that the landlord always kept locked.

Simon took off his jacket, then roamed into the living room, where he tossed it onto one end of the sofa while he sat upon the other. On the coffee table sat the latest draft of *Lethal Deceptions,* Simon's work on a money-laundering operation that reached far into the government and involved diplomats from seven other countries. While the individuals had hotly and sternly denied the allegations, Simon had spent too many nights in covert conversation with several members of the organization to doubt that the story was true. Unfortunately, his editor wouldn't print the story without clearance from the legal department, and the legal department wouldn't clear it without independent verification of the sources.

By the time Simon and legal had finished arguing, the bodies of three of Simon's sources had been found on a fishing boat in the Gulf of Mexico, their throats slashed.

Simon felt he owed it to those men to finish the book and to get it published. And the best way to do that—the fastest way to do that—was to put it aside for a few months and write Norton's book for him. It was a no-brainer.

So what was it, then, about Norton's offer that continued to prick unmercifully at the edge of his conscience?

Chapter Three

The late-afternoon sun slanted in through the windows of the greenhouse at sharp angles, casting thin splinters of light across the worn wooden tables that stood, end to end, down the center of the narrow room to form one long, continuous work space. In perfect precision at the end of the table closest to the door, peat pots awaited their allotment of specially mixed growing compound and carefully selected seeds. At the opposite end, clay pots had been readied for the small seedlings that would be transplanted, one of these late-winter days, and eventually hardened out-of-doors as preparation for sale in the retail shop out front.

Dina McDermott opened the wooden door and pushed it aside with her foot just far enough to permit her entry into the moist, warm confines of the greenhouse that sheltered much of her nursery stock. She back-kicked the door closed, dumped the large bag of perlite onto the floor, and snapped on the light, then glanced at the indoor thermometer that she'd nailed to the back of the door on the day the structure had been delivered. Satisfied that the temperature remained at an even sixty-eight degrees, she pulled off her old suede gloves and stuffed them absently into the pockets of her down jacket, which she shed and tossed onto a hook near the door. She snapped on the radio and jumped nearly out of her skin as the harsh staccato of heavy rap jolted out in a loud, profane pulse.

"Yow!" Dina turned quickly to lower the volume.

"William, my friend, I can see we are going to have to have a little talk," she muttered under her breath as she searched for her favorite soft rock station.

William Flannery, the young high school student Dina'd hired to take care of the odd jobs she often couldn't get to, had a penchant for loud music, fast cars, and Kelly, the pretty young blonde who helped out in Dina's shop on weekends during the busy spring through early fall seasons. He'd hung around so much last summer that Dina had ended up putting him to work.

If only his taste in music were a little more tolerable.

Dina tucked a long strand of black hair into the makeshift bun at the nape of her neck and leaned over one of the flats of annuals she'd planted the previous Sunday. The first little spikes of green had just pushed their way from the soil, and the sight of those thin featherlike leaves brought a smile to her lips. Growing all of her own nursery stock gave her total control over color and type, texture and fragrance, and ensured that she'd be able to meet the needs of her landscape and garden design customers. Already three shelves of heirloom plants—salvia, larkspur, dame's rocket, columbine, and poppies—had germinated, plants that were indispensable to the old-fashioned cutting gardens so in demand these days.

At thirty, Dina was the owner of Garden Gates, specializing in re-creating and restoring eighteenth- and nineteenth-century gardens. Such projects having been scarce those first few years, she'd focused her energies on building up her greenhouse and retail efforts. The business had grown solidly, and as time went on she'd managed to snag a few of those landscaping plums as gentrification sought out one after another of the small towns near Henderson, her home on the upper end of Maryland's Eastern Shore.

Over the past year, Dina had been tapped for the private restorations of several historic homes since building her reputation on the renovation of Ivy House, a local property that had been bequeathed to Henderson by two elderly sisters, longtime residents of the town. Dina also wrote an occasional column on heirloom plants for the local newspaper and served as the gardening consultant for the local television station. All in all, Dina was doing just fine.

"Pretty *damned* fine, if I do say so myself," she reminded herself as she debated on whether or not to plant another flat of hollyhocks, recalling that last year the double yellows, reds, and pinks had sold out of the greenhouse by the beginning of June. Everyone, it seemed, wanted to re-create their grandmother's garden.

And Dina's business was booming.

From a drawer in the center of one of the worktables she pulled out a pad of paper and began to sketch a flower bed she'd been contracted to design for a family who'd recently purchased one of those new executive-style homes that were being built out on Landers Road—McMansions, as the locals referred to the overly large homes on the postage stamp–sized lots—and lost herself in a dream of midsummer color. That's what the owners had wanted. Lots and lots of color . . .

"Garden Gates," Dina said as she lifted the ringing phone from its base on the small desk behind her.

"Hi, sweetie," Jude McDermott greeted her daughter.

"Oh, hi, Mom. You're home from work already?"

"Already?" Jude laughed. "It's almost six. Actually, I'm running a bit late today."

Dina frowned and looked out through the glass walls. Sure enough, while she'd been picking through plastic bags and vials and envelopes filled with seeds and plotting out beds of summer annuals the last bit of afternoon had slipped away and the sun had set, and now her stomach took the opportunity to remind her she hadn't eaten since eleven o'clock that morning.

"I didn't realize how late it was," Dina said. "I have a meeting at borough hall tonight with the volunteers for the new memorial park project."

"What time?"

"Eight. But I'm hoping to get there a little early to catch up with Don Fletcher. I want to speak with him about building some benches for the memorial garden."

"Oh." Jude's voice brightened. "Isn't Don that good-looking carpenter who worked with you on the gazebo for the park?"

Dina rolled her eyes. "You know perfectly well who he is. Don't get any ideas."

"Whatever do you mean?"

"Mom, you are about as subtle as a sledgehammer. But for the record, I'm not interested in Don. He's a good carpenter; he's a nice man. He's been very generous with donating his time and his talents to the community projects we've been working on."

"And . . . ?"

"And nothing. That's it. I really don't have any interest in him other than a professional one."

"Pity." Jude sighed. She knew her daughter well, knew when to give up. "Why not stop by on your way back home, if you're not too late? I'm thinking about making a cranberry apple cobbler."

"Bribery," Dina muttered. "Some mothers will resort to anything to keep their offspring tied to their apron strings."

"Whatever works."

"Unfortunately, I think tonight I'll have to take a rain check. I have a big day at the shop tomorrow and I'm beat. Polly and I worked day and night during the Valentine's Day rush."

Dina glanced at the clock. "Mom, I have to run. I need to shower and grab a bite before the meeting. I'll give you a call in the morning."

Dina hung up the phone, then, slinging the forgotten bag of perlite into a bin under the table she kept for that purpose, dusted her hands off on her jeans. She took one quick glance at the primroses that sat under the grow lights, then, satisfied that all was well, grabbed her jacket, turned off the overhead light, and locked up for the night.

Alone in the frosty air of late February, Dina paused between the greenhouse and the carriage house that served as her home. Against a darkening pink-and-gold evening sky geese flew in a precise wedge over the flat fields, and somewhere in the distance an owl hooted. Dina smiled. All was right with her particular world at that particular moment. She climbed the three steps leading to the porch of the carriage house, searching her pockets for the key, then unlocked the door and walked into the quiet of the small entry.

The clock ticked loudly from the wall, and she scowled as she passed it to turn on the light. She'd found the clock at a yard sale in town six months ago, and no matter how many times she changed the batteries, the damned thing still kept erratic time. Tonight it read 1:45. Dina sighed and made a mental note: *Buy new clock.*

She passed through the small dining area and slid her jacket onto the back of one of the four chairs. The table was cluttered with several piles of mail, magazines, and other assorted stacks of papers. Contracts for future jobs, bills relating to the business, household bills, phone messages, sketches, each had their own place on the table. It was the only way Dina could keep things straight.

In her all-white kitchen, Dina filled a pot of water and placed it on the stove to boil for pasta, then assembled all she would need for her dinner. While the water simmered, she went to the living room window and looked out toward the former Aldrich farm, which Dina had purchased the year before primarily for its acreage. The lights were on in the kitchen windows of the old yellow farmhouse where her assistant, Polly Valentine, was making dinner for her daughter, Erin.

That same old yellow farmhouse that Dina had purchased with an eye toward living in herself.

That had been her original plan. The fates, it would seem, had something else in mind.

When Dina had started looking for a property from which to run her business, the only suitable place available had been the seven acres with the carriage house in which she now lived. At one time there had been a farmhouse, but that had been burned to the ground by vagrants years earlier and since the owners, who lived in town, rented out their fields to a neighbor, the house had never been rebuilt. With money from a trust fund, Dina had purchased the seven acres with an eye toward eventually buying the adjacent ten-acre property when it came up for sale. Three years later, it had, and she'd successfully bid to purchase it from the previous owners' estate. However, squabbles within the sellers' family had held up the sale for almost eleven months. By the time the sale had been finalized, Dina had already turned the carriage house into comfortable living quarters and was just too busy to take on the restoration of the aging farmhouse.

It was just about that time that Jude had come across Polly Valentine and had suggested that Dina meet the fragile young woman with the sad past.

Polly, a refugee from a bad marriage, had taken a well-aimed swing at her abusive ex-husband with a baseball bat as he attempted to sneak into her apartment after repeatedly threatening harm to her and her child. Unable to make bail, she'd spent five months in prison, awaiting trial for assault. Though she'd been acquitted, she'd lost almost half a year out of her life, along with her job at a flower shop, her self-respect, and, most important, her nine-year-old daughter, Erin. Jude, a volunteer teacher at the county prison, had met Polly there and had seen something in the young woman's eyes that had drawn her to the courtroom when Polly's trial began. On the day Polly was acquitted, Jude waited for her outside the courthouse, and learning that Polly had no place to go, Jude had taken

Polly home. It hadn't taken much for Jude to talk her daughter into hiring Polly on at the shop and renting out the farmhouse to her. After all, Dina needed help, Polly needed a job and a home, and the old farmhouse needed painting. It was a given that Dina, already living comfortably in her carriage house, would never find the time to do it.

It was the best decision Dina had ever made. Polly was a natural with flowers, and she had become a huge asset to the business. She was also a good friend.

The water started to boil, and Dina unceremoniously dumped the pasta into the pot. A second, smaller pot of marinara sauce began to simmer as Dina went into her small office at the end of the hall and took a yellow file from the desk. She cleared a space at the table, then returned to the kitchen, the file under her arm, and, standing up, ate the leftover salad from lunch. The timer went off on the pasta, and she drained it absently, her mind on the yellow folder and the work order within. She prepared a plate, then headed back to the dining room, where she ate with her left hand while her right hand played with the sketches from the folder, landscaping plans for another of the new houses being built out along the river. This one was a beautifully designed redbrick Federal-style house from its roof to its windows.

And Mrs. Fisher, the owner, was insisting on what she termed a "wild English country garden." Despite Dina's gentle suggestion that perhaps something slightly more structured might be more appropriate for this particular home and property, Mrs. Fisher would not be shaken from her vision of oceans of waving delphiniums and phlox, hollyhocks and roses. The best

Dina could hope for was to plan the beds in a manner that would complement, rather than overwhelm, the architecture. To this end, she played with sketches of a walled garden with a patio and a bricked walk that would wind around a series of raised beds. Back against the walls, the tall perennials would appear more graceful, less serendipitous, than in smaller beds closer to the formal house. Those small beds were just right for an herb garden, the scale of which would be in better proportion to the back of the house, the function more in keeping with the era the Fishers were trying to recreate.

Dina downed the last now-cold bite of rotini just as the alarm on her watch alerted her to the fact that it was coming up on seven. If she was to be in town in an hour, she needed to get into the shower now. She closed her file, took the dishes into the kitchen to rinse, then locked the back door before heading up the narrow stairs to her bedroom, where she stripped off her work clothes. As she hastened toward the bathroom, she caught a blurred glance in the mirror of her tall, lean body, her robe slung over her shoulder. Even to herself, she appeared to be hurried and just a little haggard. She turned on the shower and worked the elastic and pins out of her dark hair and hoped that a few minutes under steaming water would revive her.

All too soon, the hot water started to lose pressure, and Dina knew it would take another ten minutes for it to get back up to speed. She turned off the shower and stepped out onto the thick cotton rug that covered the cold tile and dried her hair quickly. Dressed in khakis and a blue sweater, she grabbed her jacket, her purse, and the yellow file of sketches she'd prepared, then headed out the door. It would only take five or so minutes to drive into Henderson proper, but she did want to catch Don Fletcher as early as possible.

A light snow had started to fall, and the front steps were already beginning to slick. She climbed into her Explorer and drove past the greenhouse, then the shop, and finally through the small parking lot.

Dina passed by the ancient apple orchard, the acres of Christmas trees, accelerating as she passed the farmhouse, her thoughts focused on the reflecting pool she had in mind for the new park and who among the volunteers she might talk into digging it.

Dina's meeting with the volunteers took less than an hour, and she was anxious to get home and crawl into bed.

The whole drive home, Dina's mind was occupied with work. Perhaps, when Polly was ready to take on more responsibility with the shop, she might have a little bit more time for herself and the things she liked best about the business. The prospect of spending more time on the design end of the business cheered her. She pushed open the door and stepped into the quiet of the narrow front hall, the only sound the bubbling from the fish tank in the living room.

Less time in the shop would give her more time, too, maybe, to spend out at the trade school, where there were so many students willing to learn the basics of landscaping, as she'd discovered through her volunteer work there.

Less time in the shop would mean she could almost—maybe—have a life apart from her work.

Fancy that, she thought wryly as she locked the door behind her and hung up her jacket.

She toed off her boots and left them near the door, pausing to flip through the day's mail. A few bills, a catalog or two, and a card from a friend who'd just returned from a honeymoon in Hawaii, complete with a photo of the happy couple, who sat at a table in a restaurant, leis draped around their necks. The camera had caught them gazing into each other's eyes rather than at the photographer, and their love for each other shone so brightly in their eyes and in their smiles that Dina had the fleeting feeling that she'd somehow intruded into their privacy.

She slid the photo back into the envelope and tried to ignore the ache of envy that swept through her. She'd never looked at anyone the way Cara was looking at Tom in that photo. It was a subtle reminder that for all she'd accomplished in her business, she still went to bed alone every night.

Chapter Four

Within three weeks of having met with Philip Norton, Simon had found a furnished town house to sublet in Arlington, packed up his belongings, and bid adieu to the run-down neighborhood he'd called home for the past several months. He'd also viewed eighteen hours of videotapes and read mountains of newspaper and magazine articles relating to the late President Graham T. Hayward. Simon had made a tentative list of people he'd like to speak with, then, using the Internet, set about the business of figuring out who on that list was still among the living.

He'd positively eliminated seven of the names and was in the process of checking into yet another when the phone rang. Simon stepped over a pile of magazines and sorted through a stack of newspapers to locate the phone.

"Keller."

"Philip Norton here, Simon. How's it going?"

"Good. Fine." He managed to grab a magazine that was sliding toward the edge of the table and stop its forward motion.

"I wanted you to know that I've read the pages of *Lethal Deceptions* you sent me." Norton drew on his pipe. "I'm pleased with what I've seen. Your book has a lot of promise, Simon. It needs work, needs polish, but it has great potential."

"Really." Simon sat on the edge of the sofa, drinking in the news as eagerly as a dusty field drinks in the summer rain. "You really think so."

"Yes. I really do." Another puff on the pipe. "I have a few suggestions that we'll talk about when the time comes, but all in all, I think it is quite good."

"Thank you, Philip." Simon felt the slow release of a breath he hadn't realized he'd been holding.

"Now, how are you doing with the project at hand? Have you had time to look over any of the materials I sent to you?"

"You mean the fourteen boxes of documentary videos, newspaper and magazine articles, and interview transcripts?"

"Yes."

"I've been plowing through them since they arrived."

"And?"

"And I'm starting to develop a feel for the subject. Hayward appears to have been a man who had many more friends than enemies. I started making a list of people I'd like to speak with and was just trying to track them down through the Internet."

Norton cleared his throat. "Who's on your list, if I may ask?"

"Well, I suppose the dead ones don't much matter," Simon muttered while he shuffled a few more papers in search of his list. "Of the ones who I know are still alive, I'm having the most difficulty hunting down Aaron Follows, Mike Huntley, and Miles Kendall."

"The last I heard, Follows was living in San Diego,

but I can check that for you. Huntley I'd steer away from. And as for Miles Ken—"

"Why?"

"Why what?"

"Why steer away from Huntley?"

"Because he's a mean-spirited SOB who spent most of his time on the Hill starting feuds between other people. He won't have anything good to say about anyone, but of course, it's your call." Norton added, "It is your book, Simon."

Simon got that feeling again—that Norton was keeping something from him. He found it annoying. Of course, he would track down and interview Mike Huntley, whether Norton wanted him to or not.

"What about Miles Kendall? I can't seem to bring up an address for him, though Social Security indicates he's still alive. As Hayward's Chief of Staff, I thought he'd have some interesting anecdotes to share."

"Well, he probably does, but he won't remember any of them. Kendall's an Alzheimer's patient. From what I understand, he recalls nothing of his days in the White House."

"I'm sorry to hear that. Having been so close to the President for so long—he was a Rhode Island boy, too, I understand. . . ."

"And a Brown grad as well."

"Yes, I saw that someplace. You must have known him well."

"We knew each other, yes. We have lost touch in the years since the President died."

"You and Kendall weren't close friends, then?"

"We were both closer to the President than we were

to each other." Norton appeared to choose his words carefully.

"You wouldn't happen to know where I could find him, would you?"

"He's in a nursing home."

"Do you know where that nursing home might be?" Simon had the distinct feeling he was being played with, and he didn't like it.

"He's in Saint Margaret's, in Linden."

"Linden, Maryland?" Simon's brows rose.

"Yes. I think I recall hearing something about Kendall having been ill and living with a nephew for a time; then the nephew was transferred to Houston and he made arrangements for Kendall to be moved to Saint Margaret's."

"No children?"

"No. Kendall never married." Norton paused before asking, "I suppose you'll be seeing him as well as Huntley?"

Simon laughed. "With any luck."

"Who else do you have there?"

"The only other person I have on my short list is Adeline Anderson."

"The reporter for the *Washington Press* who covered the capital social scene back in the day." Simon could almost see Norton nodding his approval. "Good choice. She knew everyone in town back then, knew what they were doing and who they were doing it with. It was said that if Addie Anderson didn't know about it, it hadn't really happened."

"I thought she'd be helpful in setting the stage. The social stage, that is."

"She will be, I'm sure. Now, I think she's living out in—"

"Already found her, thanks. And I have calls in to Congressman Hayward and the former First Lady, as well as Sarah Decker, the former First Daughter."

"Well then, it sounds as if you're off to a fine start."

"I am, thank you."

"If you need my help don't hesitate to call me."

"I don't expect to." Recalling his manners, Simon added, "But appreciate the offer."

"Well then, keep in touch."

"Will do." Simon hung up the phone.

He'd no sooner put the phone on the table when it rang again.

"Mr. Keller? Sarah Decker returning your call."

"Yes, of course. Mrs. Decker, thank you for calling back so promptly."

"I understand that you're doing a book about my father."

"Yes, I . . . Excuse me, how did you know that?"

"My mother mentioned it. I believe she spoke with Philip Norton over the weekend—"

"Oh?" Simon frowned, vaguely annoyed by this news.

"Mother said that you'd probably be calling to set up an appointment to chat."

"Yes. I was hoping to schedule some time to spend with you, at your convenience, of course."

"I know that everyone in the family is excited about your book, so I certainly want to cooperate. Did you have any particular date in mind?"

Simon heard what sounded like pages turning softly in the background.

"The earliest date that you are available would be fine. Whatever works best for you."

"In that case, how does next Tuesday look?"

"Next Tuesday is fine." Simon didn't have to check his appointment book. Even if he had scheduled something previously, he'd have broken it to meet with Sarah Decker.

"Is one-thirty good?"

"Perfect."

"Great. You have our address?"

"I do." He read it off to her from a slip of paper he'd tucked into his shirt pocket after he'd placed the call to her earlier in the day.

"I'll look for you on Tuesday afternoon," she told him. "Now, don't hesitate to call if something comes up."

"Nothing will come up," he assured her.

Nothing was going to come up that would prevent his interview with Sarah Decker, former First Daughter and sister to the man who would be president. Simon would be there, come hell or high water. She could bank on that.

Simon was wondering how one might put a fresh spin on this well-known family as he drove the Mustang to Annapolis, then parked in front of the home of Sarah Decker and her husband, Rear Adm. Julian Decker. The newly retired Rear Admiral, Simon reminded himself as he followed the cobbled path to the front door of the handsome stone colonial home that sat on an impeccably landscaped lot.

The door opened before he even lifted a hand to knock.

"Mr. Keller?" Sarah Hayward Decker stood in the doorway, as perfect a creature as Simon had ever seen.

"Yes." Simon nodded and smiled almost involuntarily. Clearly, photographs of the former First Daughter did not do justice to her delicate beauty. Pale blond hair to her shoulders, eyes of palest gray-blue, Sarah, in her mid-forties, could have been mistaken for a woman ten years younger.

"You're right on time." She smiled pleasantly and gestured him to enter. "I appreciate that."

"Thank you," Simon said as he passed her and stepped into the foyer.

"Your coat?" She reached a hand for his topcoat, and Simon tried not to appear as awkward as he suddenly felt as he juggled his briefcase and attempted to remove his coat.

"Thank you."

"How about if I take that?" A still-smiling Sarah reached for the briefcase just as Simon managed to slip off the camel overcoat he'd bought the week before.

Instead of the briefcase, Simon handed her the coat, and said, "Thank you," for the third time in almost as many seconds.

Simon mentally kicked himself for sounding like an idiot.

"Come on in through here," Sarah was saying as she led Simon down the hall to the back of the house. "I thought we'd sit in the sunroom to chat. It's such a lovely afternoon, so cheery and bright. I've been dying for some sunlight after this gray winter, haven't you? And what can I offer you? Do you prefer coffee or tea?"

"Either would be fine." Simon followed her into a room that fairly burst with sunlight pouring in through windows that wrapped around three walls.

"Or perhaps something cold?" Sarah Decker paused in the doorway.

"Tea would be fine." He nodded.

"I think I'll have tea as well, and a few of the raspberry shortbread cookies the housekeeper made yesterday," she said brightly. "That is, assuming that our daughter and her friends didn't finish them off last night."

"This is a terrific room." Simon dropped his briefcase on the floor next to one of the high-backed wicker chairs that flanked a round table with a glass top.

"Isn't it lovely?" His hostess beamed. "It was an old sunporch, but it needed such repair when we moved in. I spend so much time in this part of the house now. I have lunch here every day, overlooking the gardens."

Clearly this was a woman's room, with delicate lace curtains tied back at all the windows, pale rose flowered wallpaper covering the one wall that wasn't windowed, and white furniture, all reinforcing Simon's first impression of Sarah Decker as a very soft, feminine woman.

Sarah returned in minutes with a tray that held a teapot, two blue-and-white ceramic mugs with small matching plates, a sugar bowl, two spoons, several linen napkins, and a clear glass plate upon which a small mountain of cookies was stacked.

She took the seat opposite Simon's. He had a feeling that the tray had been prepared and waiting in the kitchen.

"Here you go," she said as she placed the tray in the center of the table.

"Mrs. Decker—"

"Sarah," she said as she lifted a mug, poured the tea, and offered the mug to Simon with one smooth, practiced movement. "Please call me Sarah. I'm feeling enough of the years, with my oldest daughter turning twenty in February and my youngest turning seventeen next week. And unless you object, I'll call you Simon. Is that all right?"

"That would be fine."

"We're really quite informal here, as you can see." She blessed him with a smile and stirred a touch of sugar into her tea.

Simon had viewed countless film clips and photographs of the former First Family over the past week, but once again he acknowledged that none of them had really captured the beauty of the woman who sat across the table from him. Sarah Hayward had been a pretty teenager, but over the years she had grown quite lovely. Simon suspected there might be a bit of steel under all that softness, considering the sturdy New England stock she'd come from.

"My mother said she had a pleasant conversation with you yesterday," Sarah said.

"The pleasure was all mine. I'm looking forward to meeting with her. I'm guessing she was a formidable First Lady. In her own quiet way, of course."

"My mother has been quietly formidable in every aspect of her life." Sarah laughed. "In every role she's played."

"That's an interesting way to put it. Which do you feel was her best?"

"Her best?"

"Her best role."

"Oh, that's easy." Sarah slipped several cookies onto a plate and passed it to Simon with a napkin. "Mrs. Graham Hayward was definitely the job she did best. Both before and after the White House."

"And as a mother?"

"She was wonderful. Loving. Supportive. Always on our side, mine and Gray's. When we had a problem, she helped us to find a solution. She taught us both that there were few situations in this life over which we could not gain a certain amount of control if we tried hard enough. She was also very understanding, always put our needs and our happiness first, regardless of what anyone else might think."

"Such as . . . ?"

Sarah nibbled at the corner of her cookie. "Such as letting me stay at boarding school even after my father was elected."

"That was important to you?"

"It was at the time. I was thirteen when my father ran for his first term. My parents were gone for weeks at a time. After my father won the election, I begged to stay at school, to stay with my friends. My mother championed that for me, convinced my dad—and the Secret Service—that it could be done without taking any risks."

"Do you feel you missed anything by living at school instead of in the White House? That had to have been a pretty exciting place."

"Don't forget we had lived in Washington for twelve years. I started at Beaumont Academy when I was in grade school. School was a mere forty-five minutes—that's forty-five minutes in traffic—from Pennsylvania Avenue. I went back and forth whenever I wanted."

"So you had the best of both worlds."

"Exactly. I had a room there—after all, it was our family home—but really, when you live in the White House, everything happens *around* you." Sarah grinned. "There, it was never about me, you understand. It was always about my dad, which is how it should have been, of course, since he *was* the President. But as a teenager, I wanted to be the center of attention, too, you know. I guess everyone does at that age, at least to some extent. At school, everyone knew me and accepted me for what I was . . . whatever that was back then. So I stayed at Beaumont during the week, but I spent almost every weekend with my folks and often brought a friend or five home with me."

"I think I do recall reading something about slumber parties on the top floor of the White House."

"Many slumber parties." Sarah's eyes danced. "Lots of loud music and having pizza delivered in the middle of the night. Lots of lectures from my mother the next morning. Just like any other teenager."

"And from Beaumont you went to Brown?"

"What Hayward did not go to Brown? Other than Mother and Jen, of course, since it was still all men then. But our Emily, Dad, Gray, my grandfathers on both sides . . . how far back would you like me to go?" Sarah laughed softly.

"And your husband?"

"Julian's dream had always been to go to Annapolis, but of course he is from a navy family. He and his father both were in Vietnam, and his grandfather served in the South Pacific during the Second World War."

"How did you meet?"

"His younger sister, Carolyn, was a classmate of mine at Beaumont."

"Ah, that's nice. Did you know, when you graduated, that you'd be sisters-in-law someday?"

"Well, we didn't exactly graduate together. She, they—Carolyn and the others from my class—graduated a year earlier than I, since I took a year off in high school." Sarah hesitated slightly, then asked, "Had I mentioned that?"

"No."

"Oh. Well, I traveled a lot with my parents during what would have been my senior year—my dad had a lot of visits and such scheduled that year in Europe and several in South America, so we decided that I'd take that whole year off so that I could go with them. That was the biggest concession I made to being First Daughter."

She smiled somewhat wistfully. "Of course, by the time I got back to school in the fall, all of my closest friends had graduated. And after college, well, we all settled in different parts of the country. Got involved in our own lives, our careers, our children. It seems that the only time I ever see my old friends now is at weddings and funerals. The last time, happily, was a wedding."

"How long ago was that?"

"Three or four years ago." Sarah sighed. "It's really a shame, but it seems that once your children hit a certain age, your life is no longer your own, between this activity and that. Although with Kirsten getting her driver's license in another week, I will have a few hours each day when I won't be on call."

"Are you telling me that Sarah Hayward Decker, former First Daughter, is a soccer mom?"

"Lacrosse mom," she corrected him good-naturedly. "This is Maryland, you know. We carry sticks down here."

"I take it that both of your daughters play?"

"Every chance they get."

"And what is your husband doing now that he's retired?"

"Has Julian retired?" She feigned shock. "I hadn't noticed."

She laughed. "Actually, Julian has always been a bit of a secret scholar, so he volunteered to give a lecture class at the Academy this year. He's loving it to death. And he's busy writing, trying his hand at fiction. He's writing a mystery set here in Annapolis. And he is perfecting his golf game."

"And you?"

"I golf right along with him. I play tennis twice a week with friends. I joined a gym. Started lifting weights." She raised her right arm and pretended to flex a muscle. "Can't see much improvement, but then again, I've only been lifting for three weeks."

"You don't strike me as the weight-lifter type."

"Now, now, that is definitely not a PC remark, Mr. Keller." Sarah took a long sip of tea. "Though I admit that I only took it up because my doctor told me it was a good way to avoid osteoporosis and I thought, why not? I have no aspirations for bodybuilding, but I'm doing quite well. Gray's wife, Jen, is lifting now, too—she's becoming the real iron woman in the family. And I've even gotten Mother to lift a weight now and then, and though she won't admit it, she's building up a muscle or two herself. Not a ladylike endeavor in her circle, but there it is."

"What are your best memories of the White House?" Simon asked.

"Oh, the incredible food," Sarah laughed. "They had wonderful dinner parties and everyone would be beautifully dressed, long gowns and fantastic jewelry. Elegant people from all over the world. Ambassadors and princes. Movie stars and heads of state. It was like slipping into another world, those parties. And the White House at night, well, it was like a movie scene, only better, because it was real." She stood up and walked to a wicker armoire, opened the center doors, and scanned a stack of books. She withdrew one and tucked it under her arm.

"Come sit on the sofa with me and I'll show you." She took a seat and patted the cushion next to her. She opened the book and held it on her lap.

"See here," she said as Simon sat where she'd indicated. "Here's one of my old photo albums. Here's Barbra Streisand. And Paul Newman. An astronaut, I can't recall which one. Muhammad Ali . . ."

Sarah's index finger touched one photo after another.

"You're not in any of these," Simon noted.

"That's because I took them all."

"That was quite an opportunity for a teenager."

"You're telling me."

"It must have been fun," Simon murmured as she turned page after page of pictures of the rich and famous and important.

"Playing amateur photographer?"

"Being the daughter of the President of the United States."

"Most fun I ever had," Sarah said softly as she returned the album to its place on the shelf and lifted another. "I loved being First Daughter every bit as much as my mother loved being First Lady."

"Even though you preferred to live at boarding school?"

"One had nothing to do with the other." Her words were crisp, not quite a snap, but it was, Simon realized, the first bit of real emotion she'd shown since he had arrived.

"Do you have pictures from your trips abroad?" he asked, wondering what had caused the momentary pique.

Sarah looked over her shoulder and paused, then turned back to the shelves, tapping her fingers on the nearest shelf as if hunting for something in particular. Finally, she pulled out an album that looked almost identical to the first.

"I must have left that album at my mother's." She smiled warmly, the moment of tension having passed. "But this one has mostly pictures of my dad."

She eased back onto the sofa.

"See this one?" She turned the book toward Simon. "This is one of my most favorite photographs ever."

"Who is the woman with your father?" Simon peered at the white-haired woman who stood smiling in the embrace of Graham Hayward in what was obviously the Oval Office.

"That's Mrs. Carlyle, Dad's secretary. He loved this picture so much that he had it enlarged and framed and gave it to her when he left office. She was such a great lady." Sarah turned the pages, pausing to point out this dignitary or that celebrity she'd caught on camera so long ago.

"Now, is that Miles Kendall?" Simon turned the album into the light to get a better look.

"Yes. He was my dad's Chief of Staff." Sarah nodded. "And his best friend."

"I understand he's been ill."

"Yes. It's such a shame, really. He and Dad were best friends forever. And he was almost like a second father to me. Whenever my parents were out of town, he was the one I had to answer to. He stood in for my dad so many times." Sarah's smile was nostalgic. "He even taught me how to drive. It's just heartbreaking, the way . . . well, the way he is now."

"You visit him, then?"

"No. I'm ashamed to say it, but no, I don't. The last time I saw Miles was right after they moved him to this new home. We all went together—Mom, Gray and Jen, and I. It was clear that the man we knew and loved was . . . well, just not there anymore. He didn't recognize any of us, and never spoke a word while we were there. It was very upsetting. Not very noble of me, but I just haven't been able to face going back."

"Do you happen to know Kendall's nephew, the one who made the arrangements with the home?"

"It was Dan . . ." Sarah pursed her lips. "Dan . . . I can't think of his last name. My brother might know, though."

"I'll be seeing him soon, so I'll make a note to myself to ask."

"You aren't thinking about going to see Miles, are you?" Sarah's eyes widened slightly.

"Yes. After all, he was the confidant of a President."

"I doubt that he remembers anything from that time, Simon. It's terribly sad, but I'm afraid it's true," Sarah said. The pages of the book of photos made a sharp snapping sound as she closed it and stood up.

"Maybe I'll hit him on a good day."

"I'm not sure he has any, anymore. But of course, you should check that out for yourself. And you might want to call first and save yourself the drive."

"That sounds like good advice."

After an awkward pause, the former First Daughter stood up, and Simon realized she was bringing the interview to a close.

"Now, if there's anything else you need to know, any other questions you want answered, feel free to give me a call," Sarah said pleasantly, once again the charming hostess.

"I may need one more interview," Simon said. He folded his notes into his briefcase and snapped the lid before standing up. "And as we discussed on the phone, I'll be faxing over a short list of questions. You don't have to answer all of them—this isn't a test—but if you could just add any thoughts you might have, I'd appreciate it."

"Well, whatever you need." Sarah led him back down the hall to the front door.

"I appreciate your time." Simon had started to extend his hand to hers when her phone rang.

She startled, then laughed and said, "I'll bet that's Kirsten. I think I was supposed to pick her up after school today and it looks like I may be late."

"Then I'll get out of your hair and let you go." Simon opened the door and took one step out.

"Thanks for understanding. We'll talk again." She was still smiling as she closed the door and disappeared behind it.

Simon slid the Mustang into the first open spot in the visitors parking lot and stared at the handsome mansion that, five years earlier, had been converted into St. Margaret's, a care facility for well-to-do seniors who could no longer live on their own. Some of the residents required only minimal assistance, while others—those who lived on the newly constructed lower level—demanded the highest level of concern from their caretakers. And these, the Alzheimer's patients, also paid the heftiest fees for the privilege of living here on the old estate at the top of the Patuxent River, midway between the nation's capital and the Chesapeake Bay. Patients such as Miles Kendall.

Kendall must have seen it all back in the Hayward days, Simon thought, and if he could remember something of those days—even just the *flavor* of those times—Simon's book, newly titled *Remember the Time: An Intimate Portrait of an American President*, would be a fitting biography. The concept—to present the many faces of the man in the words of those who'd known him best—had come to Simon as he'd driven from Annapolis. After checking his watch and finding several hours left in the afternoon and realizing that St. Margaret's was a relatively short drive away, Simon decided on a whim to stop and see for himself just what the former White House aide did—or didn't—remember.

After all, how much richer the collection of reminiscences would be with a contribution from the man who had known the former President longer than any other living soul.

Simon opened the briefcase that sat on the passenger seat and took out the small handheld recorder. Chances were he wouldn't need it, but better to have it than not. There was but a slim possibility that Kendall could be having a lucid day, and if he was, Simon didn't want to miss a word. He slipped the recorder into the pocket of his tweed jacket and set off for the main entrance.

The lobby of St. Margaret's was all dark wood, worn Oriental carpets, and hushed voices. Despite the several large fresh flower arrangements and equal measures of disinfectant and air freshener, the lobby bore the distinct albeit faint trace of the old and infirm. An oak desk sat at the lobby's dead center, and behind the desk sat a young woman wearing a dark suit and a vacant smile who chatted softly into a telephone.

"Hi!" Simon called a quiet greeting even as he entered the lobby.

The receptionist returned the greeting in a voice that was nearly a whisper, though as he came closer Simon couldn't imagine whom she might be disturbing. As far as he could see, not another soul was present.

"I'm here to see Mr. Kendall," Simon told her.

"Is he expecting you?"

"Ah, no. Is that a problem?"

"Only if he's sleeping, or in therapy." She put her call on hold.

"Perhaps you could find out if he's available for company right now."

"Sure. Just a second."

Simon's eyes scanned the row of portraits that hung

from the walls in heavy frames and wondered if any of the subjects had ever been residents of the house or if their presence was a deliberate effort to give the hall the appearance of still being part of a family home.

"Mr. Kendall is in the dayroom."

"Where might that be?"

"It's through those double doors and down to the end of the hall to the new wing. But you'll have to wait for an aide to take you." She pressed a green button on the phone, then turned her back as if to preserve her privacy.

As if Simon couldn't hear every word she said.

"Someone will be out in a minute," she said as she swiveled around in her chair to face him again. "You'll have to sign in first, though."

She pointed to a notebook, opened flat with a pen cradled in the seam, that lay upon a small table to her right. Simon signed in—name, date, time, and destination—and looked up to find his escort coming through the double doors.

"You're here to see Mr. Kendall?" asked a pleasant young woman with thick glasses perched upon a wide round face.

"Yes, I—"

"Wonderful. Come this way." She gestured for him to follow as she quietly closed the doors behind them, then stopped to ask, "You've signed in?"

"Yes."

"Good. The dayroom is this way." She pointed to the left. "So nice that someone has come to see the old gentleman. Such a sweet man, most of the time anyway."

"He doesn't have many visitors, then?" Simon quickened his step to keep up with her.

"None," she told him. "At least, none on my shift."

"Which shift is that?"

"Eight A.M. to four P.M."

"How long have you been here?"

"Oh, since we opened five years ago. I was one of the first employees," she said with just a touch of pride.

"And Mr. Kendall hasn't had any visitors in all that time?"

"Oh, he hasn't been here all that time. Just since his nephew moved . . . the end of last summer, maybe? But I don't recall that anyone's come to see him. Shame, really, to live so long and have everyone forget about you, you know?"

She paused at French doors that opened into a spacious room with a wall of windows that looked out over a vast expanse of lawn divided by a fast-moving stream.

"There, in the rocking chair," she said in a low voice, as if afraid to disturb the occupants of the room. If any heard, none reacted.

"They're *all* in rocking chairs," Simon whispered.

"The gentleman nearest the window. Sorry. I thought you knew him."

"We've never met."

"Nice of you to take time to visit a stranger, then. I hope he's talking today. So often he isn't."

"Well, I guess I'll soon find out." Simon smiled and noticed her name tag. "June. Thank you."

"You can find your way out when you're finished?"

"Yes. I'll be fine."

"If not, there's always an orderly or two around. Take your time. Just remember to sign out."

Simon walked the length of the wide room on dark maroon carpet, though no one seemed to notice him at all. Even Miles Kendall didn't blink when Simon pulled over a chair and sat down facing the old man.

Pale blue eyes were set in a face grown narrow with age. Brown spots covered his hands, and as Simon drew closer he could see there were several similar patches on the man's bald head as well. Dressed in a plaid cotton shirt of navy blue, white, and brown, a navy cardigan, and navy slacks, Miles Kendall bore no resemblance to the man who, once upon a time, had been so close to the most powerful man in the world.

"Mr. Kendall," Simon said, and the blue eyes blinked.

Simon leaned a bit closer. "Hello, Mr. Kendall."

"Hello," the old man acknowledged him with a nod.

"Mind if I join you, Mr. Kendall?"

The old man smiled and nodded.

"It's a pleasure to meet you, sir."

"Do you have gum?"

"Excuse me?"

"Do you have gum?" The old man worked his jaws as if chewing.

"You mean, chewing gum?"

"That's right. Got any?"

"No, I'm afraid I don't. I'm sorry, Mr.—"

"How 'bout licorice, got any licorice?"

"Ahh, no, I—"

"What have you got?" The old man appeared perturbed.

"I . . . well, let's see . . . I . . ." Simon searched his pockets. In the inside pocket of his jacket he found a small forgotten mint wrapped in green metallic paper. "Seems the only thing I have is a mint, and God knows how old—"

Kendall reached out and took it with hands that

trembled. He brought it to his lips and Simon realized that he planned on biting into it, paper and all.

"Wait! The wrapper . . ." Simon reached for the mint.

"It's mine. You said I could have it. You can't take it back now." Kendall's hands disappeared behind his back as he sought to protect his prize.

"It *is* yours. And you're welcome to it. But you have to take the paper off before you can eat it. Here, bring it here." Simon gestured for Kendall to bring his hands forward. With a sigh of suspicious resignation, Kendall complied.

Simon unwrapped the mint and handed it back to the old man, who popped it into his mouth before Simon could change his mind and possibly eat the mint himself.

"How was it?" Simon asked when Kendall had ceased chewing.

"Small." Kendall frowned. "Got any more?"

"No, I'm sorry. That was the only one."

Kendall grunted his displeasure.

"If you like, I'll come back another time and bring you more."

"Bigger one?"

"If you like."

"Okay."

"Tomorrow maybe," Simon told him.

"Okay."

Kendall began to rock slowly in his chair, his eyes drifting toward the window and beyond. What, Simon wondered, did he see there?

"What did you do today, Mr. Kendall?" Simon asked.

"Went sailing," Kendall replied, his eyes never turning from the window.

"Who did you go with?"

"Jamey and Dan."

"Where did you sail?"

"In the bay, of course." Kendall turned and looked at Simon as if the question was a stupid one.

"Did Graham go with you?" Simon thought he'd throw the name out and see what happened.

Kendall shook his head.

"Doesn't he sail?" Simon asked.

"Doesn't who sail?"

"Graham."

"Of course Graham sails." Kendall gave him that look again. *Stupid* question. "Everyone sails."

"Why didn't he go with you this morning?"

"Because he's with Tommy."

"Tommy? You mean his brother, Thomas?"

"No one calls him Thomas," Kendall advised him.

"Where were they, Graham and Tommy, do you remember?"

Kendall gave Simon a withering look. "Of course I remember. I told you, it was this morning."

"Sorry, I forgot," Simon apologized. "Where were they, this morning?"

"Getting ready for Tommy's party."

"What party is that?"

"Graduation."

"High school?"

"Sure." Kendall nodded.

"Where does Tommy go to school?"

"Choate. We all go to Choate."

"So today is Tommy's graduation from Choate."

"Yesterday was graduation. Today is the party."

"Where's he going next year, do you know?"

"Of course I do." The look of annoyance crossed the old man's face again. "He's going to Brown. Don't you know anything?"

"I guess not."

"We're all going to go to Brown," Kendall told him. "Me, Graham, Steven . . ."

"Steven?"

"He's Graham's brother, too."

"The brother between Graham and Thomas," Simon said quietly, as if to himself. "The one who died."

"Why did you say that?" Kendall sat back in his chair, clearly startled. "Steven didn't die."

"Oh, I'm sorry. I was thinking of someone else," Simon covered. If, in Kendall's mind, Tommy Hayward had just graduated from high school, Kendall and Graham would be fourteen years old. And Steven, two years older than Graham, who died in a boating accident when he was nineteen, would still be alive.

"That was a dumb thing to say," Kendall muttered, and focused his eyes out on the lawn again.

Simon touched the man's arm, and when he turned back to Simon, Kendall said, "Got any gum?"

"No, sorry. Not today."

Miles Kendall rocked for a few long minutes, a distant look in his clouded eyes. Simon watched in silence, wondering just where Kendall's mind had taken him.

Finally, Simon stood and said, "Mr. Kendall, may I come back to see you again?"

"Will you bring gum?"

"I'll bring something," Simon promised, thinking about just what Miles Kendall might do with a whole pack of chewing gum. "Maybe more mints. Would you like that?"

"Sure." Kendall nodded enthusiastically. "Tomorrow?"

"Sure. Tomorrow," Simon told him.

"Mints," the old man said with quiet satisfaction. "Tomorrow."

Tomorrow, Simon thought as he patted his new friend on the shoulder, *perhaps we'll be in a different decade.*

He glanced over his shoulder just as Kendall turned back to the windows and went still.

Then again, maybe not . . .

Chapter Five

Her arms folded across her chest and a half smile on her lips, Dina watched as her mother first examined, then rejected, one dress after another from the display in a favorite store. By the time Jude reached the end of the rack, she'd found only two garments to her liking, and those she held out for Dina's opinion.

"The black?" Jude asked. "Or the gray?"

"The green." Dina reached behind her mother for a soft crepe dress of pale sage. "Definitely, the green."

Jude frowned.

"Not my style. That would look terrible on me."

"How do you know? You haven't tried it on."

"I make it a habit of not trying on things that I know would depress me. A dress, for example, that is cut lower in the back than the base of my spine—"

"It's not *that* low."

"—is probably not a good look for this middle-aged body." Jude took the green dress from Dina's hand and returned it to its place on the display. "Though I do appreciate the fact that you obviously are blind to the extra ten pounds around my middle and the fact that the skin on my upper arms continues to wave on its own long after I've said good-bye."

"Ten pounds? Nothing that a good workout program can't help."

"Remind me to have this conversation with you again on your fiftieth birthday. In the meantime, I'm leaning toward the gray. What do you think?" Jude stood in front of a mirror and held the dress up to her body. "Simple lines and a great color to set off that wonderful amethyst necklace that you bought for me in Mexico last summer.

"I think I'll try it on." Jude turned in the direction of the dressing room. "Why not take another look and see if there's something you may have missed the first time around? I'll just be a minute."

Jude's *minute* was actually seven, but Dina didn't mind the wait. A second look through the racks produced nothing that caught her eye, so she amused herself by trying to count the number of piercings on the face and earlobes of a young girl who was waiting for the elevator. Dina was up to eleven when Jude stepped out of the dressing room.

"The gray is perfect," Jude declared, smiling as she returned the black dress to the rack.

With a look of longing at the pale green, Dina said, "Mom . . ."

"Yes?" Jude was still smiling as she walked toward the nearest cash register.

"Nothing." Dina sighed.

As Jude searched her wallet for her credit card, Dina leaned over and whispered, "Mom, you're in a rut."

"I like my rut." Not bothering to whisper, Jude handed over the card to the saleswoman. "I'm happy in my rut."

The forty-something saleswoman chuckled as she rang up the sale.

"Besides," Jude continued, "I have lovely gray shoes that I barely ever wear—"

"Would it anger the gods so terribly if you were to buy new shoes *and* a new dress on the same day?"

Jude laughed good-naturedly. "Sweetie, you talked me into a dress. Take your little victory and be content with it." Jude took the dress bag holding her purchase from the saleswoman with one hand and signed the sales slip with the other. "If you weren't insisting on me accompanying you to this fund-raiser for the new park, I wouldn't have thought about what I'd be wearing until the morning of the affair."

Jude tucked the sales slip and her credit card into her purse and nodded thanks to the saleswoman.

"You're on the committee. You have to go," Dina reminded her mother as they walked toward the entrance to the mall.

"But I didn't have to buy a new dress, and I don't have to go with my daughter."

"You have someone else in mind you'd rather go with?"

"No, but I don't know why you'd want to go to something like this with me." Jude paused in the entrance. "How 'bout some lunch?"

"Great timing. They can probably hear my stomach complaining in Chestertown, I'm so hungry."

"The Plum okay?"

"Perfect. They have wonderful turkey sandwiches and they're only three stores away."

"So why do you?" Jude asked as they walked into the restaurant and waited for the hostess to seat them.

"Why do I what?"

"Why do you want to go to this fund-raiser with your mother?"

"Two?" the hostess asked.

"Yes. Nonsmoking," Dina added before the young woman could ask.

"This way."

Dina and Jude followed to a small table at glass windows overlooking the mall, from which they could see the constant parade, mostly, on this Saturday morning, groups of teenage girls and young mothers with strollers.

"You didn't answer my question." Jude decided not to let the subject drop.

"Which question was that?" Dina's eyes skimmed the menu.

"The one about why you want to go out with your mother on a Saturday night instead of, oh, I don't know." Jude frowned and pretended to search for a suggestion. "A young man, perhaps. It's not as if there aren't any vying for your attention. There's Jack Finnegan, and there's that nice-looking Don who's always building something for one of your projects. Those window boxes he made for the new library wing are just darling."

"Don and Jack will both be at the fund-raiser." Dina looked up at the waitress who had appeared at her elbow the second she began to close her menu and said, "I think I'll have the turkey and an iced tea."

"I'll have the same." Jude nodded and added after the waitress walked away, "Which one would you rather go out with?"

"Neither."

"What's wrong with them? They're both such nice men," Jude came to the defense of Dina's would-be suitors.

"Mom, there's nothing wrong with either of them. Yes, of course they're both nice men. They're also both fun to be around. But neither of them . . . how does one put this to one's mother?" Dina paused, then grinned. "Neither of them does much to speed up my heart rate."

"Oh." Jude slipped a straw from its wrapper and slid it into the glass of iced tea that the waitress set before her. "But maybe if you—"

"No maybes, Mom. The chemistry is there or it isn't."

Jude frowned and Dina laughed.

"Mom, what was it about my father that made you pick him out over every other man you met?"

"What?" Jude tilted her head, as if surprised by the question.

"My father. What was there about him that attracted you? What was so special about him that you fell in love with him instead of someone else?"

"Well." Jude cleared her throat. "He was . . . smart. And . . . good-looking. And . . . fun. He had a great sense of fun. And of course, we'd been friends for a long time."

Dina moved her iced tea glass to permit the waitress to serve her sandwich. "If you add to that, that he had short legs and a slightly swayed back, I'd think you were talking about Waylon."

Waylon was Jude's basset hound.

Jude stole a French fry from Dina's plate.

"Your father was just a very special man, Dina," Jude said, avoiding Dina's eyes. "Certainly he was a man of honor. He served his country proudly—in the end, he gave his life for his country. Everyone said he was a hero."

"Do you ever regret not marrying again?"

"No, of course not."

"Mom, don't say it like it's something disgraceful. Your husband died before I was born. You've been alone for thirty years."

"I've never been alone. I had you."

"But weren't you lonely?"

"Truthfully, honey, Frank and I hadn't been married very long. I grieved for him, but I was never really lonely." Jude smiled and repeated, "I had you."

"Yes, but I was a kid." Dina wrinkled her nose.

"You were all that I needed."

"Didn't you ever want, you know, a relationship with a man?"

"I never had much time to think about it. I was so busy raising you and working that I never missed having a social life, if that's what you're asking."

"But, Mom, now that I'm older and on my own, don't you wish that maybe you'd met someone to share your golden years with?"

"I loved raising you. Loved being your mother. More than anything else I've ever done, Dina, I've loved being your mother. I have no regrets. None at all." Jude grinned. "And I always figured I could count on you to pay a visit, now and then, when I finally hit those 'golden years.' "

"You can count on it, Mom." Dina smiled back, all the while swatting away the sting of nostalgia. Jude had never missed a school play or a parents meeting. She'd been Brownie leader and Halloween costume maker.

She'd stood on the sidelines for every tennis match, every field hockey game, through high school, had even tried her hand at coaching a club softball team just so that the team would let Dina play. Jude had been the best of mothers, the best of friends. If she felt she'd sacrificed for Dina's sake, she'd never let on. Still . . .

"I wish you'd take some of the money from my trust and treat yourself. Maybe buy new furniture. A new car. A fabulous trip." Dina sipped at her tea. "To France. Italy. Spain. Russia. Who knows who you might meet? You're still young, attractive—"

"That money was intended for you and you alone, sweetie, as we have discussed a thousand times."

"I'll never understand why Dad's parents didn't provide for you, too. It would have saved me the trouble of nagging you to let me do things for you."

"Dina, we've been over this so many times before. Your grandparents never really knew me, but you were their only grandchild."

"Well, they didn't know me any more than they knew you."

Jude stole another fry. "Frank died before his parents and I could make much of a connection."

"Their loss."

"Water under the bridge, honey. Besides, keep in mind that they'd never really had time to deal with the death of their son before they themselves were killed in that plane crash. Don't judge them so harshly."

"Still, I wish they'd set things up differently, so that it could have been easier for you while I was growing up."

"We never had things so very hard, if you recall. We had our sweet little house in our wonderful neighborhood in a wonderful town. And let's face it, neither of us ever wanted for anything, Dina."

"Still, some of the McDermott money would have gone a long way to—"

Jude held up a hand to stop her. "What would you have wanted that you didn't have back then?"

"Besides a car on my sixteenth birthday?" Dina grinned. "Actually, I can't think of a thing. But you wouldn't have had to work."

"Darling, I'm a librarian. I've hardly been out digging ditches in the hot sun all these years. I've loved my work. I have—*have* had—a wonderful life."

"Isn't there anything you want that you don't have?"

"Yes. There is one thing that I really, really want right now." Jude smiled longingly.

"Name it and it's yours."

"I'm about to do just that." Jude turned to the pony-tailed waitress as she approached their table. "I'll have a hot fudge sundae. Seriously heavy on the hot fudge. You can give the check to my daughter. . . ."

The wind had picked up and a fast rain had begun to fall by the time Dina dropped off Jude and returned home. The lights in the greenhouse assured her that Polly had kept her word and was checking the seedlings for signs of mildew, which could ruin all of the fledgling plants. Hoping to avoid a soaking of her favorite suede jacket, Dina parked as close as possible to the carriage house, then made a break for the front door through the deluge. Her keys were in her hand before she reached the shelter of the porch, and within seconds she had the door unlocked and pushed open and was dripping a path of fat drops of water from the narrow foyer to the kitchen.

"Damn," Dina muttered as she shook off her jacket and hung it carefully over the back of a kitchen chair, slipped out of her wet shoes, and left them under the table.

Then, "Ugh," as she caught a glance of herself in the mirror over the sink in the small powder room.

Her black hair was plastered to her head, her nose and cheeks red with the cold. She toweled off the hair and padded back to the kitchen in stocking feet. There she made tea and skimmed through the pile of mail she'd brought in earlier that morning but hadn't had time to look at. Dina left it all on the counter and went upstairs to change into dry clothes.

A vintage University of Maryland sweatshirt and a pair of well-worn sweatpants suited the day and the weather. On her way back down the steps, Dina paused at the small square landing and pushed the curtain aside to look through the window. From this vantage, she could see the entire expanse of fields that, on this miserable March afternoon, lay frostbitten and hard. Under a blanket of straw and last year's leaves that covered the frozen soil, the perennials she'd planted a year ago simply waited out the cold, withstanding heaving earth and enduring unpredictable changes in temperature. What was predictable was that, within the next few weeks, the daylilies would break through the ground and the peonies would appear seemingly overnight. The hiss of sleet that bounced off the window assured her that tonight would not be that night.

The teapot summoned from the kitchen, and Dina hurried to silence its annoying shriek. She made her tea and went into the den, where she studied the notes she had made for Monday's 6:00 A.M. appearance on the local news. Last visit she had talked about caring for shrubs through the winter. This week, she'd talk about pruning—which shrubs to prune in the spring and the best way to do it. The station liked to shoot these segments on location there at the nursery, which was perfect. Besides the fact that she'd have plenty of specimens to choose from, it was excellent publicity for her business.

While her tea cooled, Dina called down to the greenhouse, expecting Polly to answer, and was startled when a blast of unintelligible sound assaulted her unsuspecting ears.

Dina pictured William scrambling to turn down the music.

"Yeah, Dina, hi."

"Wow, William." Why, she wondered, was this child not deaf? "You know, you shatter the windows down there, you're going to have to clean it all up."

William laughed self-consciously, then turned the radio down even more.

"I thought *soothing* music was recommended for plants, William. What is that, anyway?"

"Mötley Crüe," he told her. "The hollyhocks like metal."

Dina rolled her eyes and shook her head as if to shake away the ringing in her ears.

"Now, the annuals, I think they like classic rock the best, but the perennials, they definitely prefer metal."

She could imagine her young employee, his brown hair pulled back from his face in a ponytail, his glasses etched with a touch of condensation, his quietly amused smile as he offered his theory on the musical preferences of plants to his boss.

"Is Polly down there with you?" As soon as she asked the question, Dina realized how unnecessary it was. If Polly had been there, the radio would have been tuned to golden oldies and the Crüe would have been replaced by the smooth sounds of Motown at a fraction of the decibel level.

"Polly went up to her place around one. She was here for a while, but she was sneezing and coughing a lot so I told her I'd finish up mixing the soil for the stuff you wanted to pot up this week." William paused, then asked, "Was that okay? I mean, she seemed really sick."

"No, that was fine. Absolutely. She's been coming down with that cold for the past few days. Thanks for taking over there."

"No problem. I like this part of the work, you know? I like the greenhouse and all. Planting up those flats and watching the little shoots come up. It's cool."

"William, you have the makings of a fine nurseryman."

"Thanks," he mumbled.

"You're welcome." She smiled, knowing that his adolescent face had turned scarlet, as it always did when Dina praised his efforts. "I'll be coming down in a while. If you leave before I get there, just leave the door unlocked."

"Okay. I'll probably be heading out after I finish with this mix. Unless you need me for something special."

"No, you go on whenever you need to. There's nothing that has to be done this afternoon. Just don't forget to fill in your hours on the calendar."

He was a good kid, she thought as she hung up the

phone. In spite of his dizzying taste in music, he was an all-around good kid. Hard worker. Honest. Dependable. A quick study. A raise was probably in order, she was thinking as she pulled on waterproof boots to prepare for her short trek to the greenhouse.

Dina stopped in the kitchen to call Polly, then chatted with Erin, who informed her that her mother was napping because she had a cold.

"Don't wake her, honey," Dina told her. "Just let her know that I called and that she can get back to me whenever she's feeling better. It's nothing important."

"Okay."

Dina was smiling to herself as she got a rain jacket out of the closet. Erin was such a sweet child. For the briefest of moments, Dina considered the special tie that held Polly to Erin, mother to daughter, that same tie that connected her to Jude.

Endless circles, Dina reflected as she trod on stepping-stones touched with a silvery glaze where sleet had turned to ice. Mother to child and child to mother, on and on, through time, a certain and necessary continuation. Dina wondered if it was in her cards to one day form a link of that chain with a daughter of her own.

Assuming, she thought wryly, that she'd find that man who could . . . what had she said to her mother? Raise her heart rate? A man who set her pulse racing and brought a smile to her lips and filled her nights with dreams.

He had to be out there somewhere.

She wondered what it was going to take to find him.

Chapter Six

Miles Kendall reminded Simon a bit of his grandfather, who, in spite of his frail physical condition and his own loss of memory, had lived to the ripe old age of eighty-six before succumbing to pneumonia five years ago. Simon had never quite forgiven himself for not making the trip back to Iowa during those last few weeks before his grandfather's death. The fact that he probably wouldn't have recognized Simon didn't matter. He should have made the effort and hadn't. He'd never ceased to regret it. That regret may have been at the heart of Simon's decision to pay a second visit to St. Margaret's.

On his way, Simon stopped at a convenience store where he filled up the Mustang with gas and stocked up on mints. Minutes later, he parked in the lot at the home, locked the car, and headed for the front door, mints in one pocket, his tape recorder in the other.

"You're back." June, the nurse's aide he'd met on his first visit, waved from a concrete bench that was set in a patch of sunlight to the left of the steps.

"I thought I'd stop in for a minute and drop off some mints for Mr. Kendall."

"That's nice of you. He's feeling pretty spunky today." June closed the book she'd been reading.

"Spunky?"

"Oh, yeah. He's been talking all morning about a trip he and his sister took to Chicago on the train. Sounds like they had a hell of a time." June laughed.

"Is he in the same room?" Simon paused with his hand on the doorknob.

"The dayroom, yes. You remember how to get there?"

"Yes. Thanks. Through the French doors and straight ahead to the end." Simon paused in the doorway. "Did he say what his sister's name was?"

"Yes." June nodded. "Dorothy."

Simon stepped into the cool quiet of the lobby and waved to the receptionist, who never missed a beat in her telephone conversation while pointing to the sign-in book. Simon wrote his name and the date and proceeded on his own to the dayroom, where he found Miles Kendall in the same chair close to the windows.

"Hi, Mr. Kendall," Simon said as he approached the chair.

Kendall turned and smiled. There was a life in his eyes that Simon hadn't seen in his previous visit.

"How are you today?"

"Quite well. And you?" Kendall appeared alert and tuned in to his surroundings.

"I was just speaking to June outside," Simon said as he pulled up a chair.

"June?"

"One of the aides."

"Ahhh, the cute little strawberry blonde?"

"Yes." Simon smiled. The old man may be forgetful, but he wasn't blind. "June was saying that you'd told her about a trip you took to Chicago with your sister."

Kendall nodded. "I met Dorothy in New York, and from there we took the train to Chicago. It was very pleasant; do you remember?"

"I wasn't there with you," Simon told him. "What year was that?"

"It was for Cousin Eileen's wedding. Lovely week in May we spent there."

Simon's heart fell. He couldn't even begin to guess at what year it might be in Miles Kendall's world.

Simon dug his hand into his pocket and pulled out a box of mints. He had started to hand them to Kendall when the old man said, "Dorothy wanted to stay an extra week, but I had to get back to Washington."

Simon's hand froze in midair and his heart tripped at the words.

"Flying was faster, but Dorothy wouldn't fly, so I took the train out and back with her," Kendall added.

"Why were you going to Washington?"

Bony fingers reached out and grabbed the box of mints. "Because I worked there, of course." He scrutinized the box, shook it, and started to bite into an end.

"Of course. I'd forgotten." Simon took the box and opened the bottom flap before handing it back to him. "When Graham was President, you worked in the White House."

"You do remember." Kendall popped a mint into his mouth and sucked on it loudly. "Remember when the bagpipers were there? They always had bagpipers around Christmas. That Christmas . . . remember the Christmas Ball?"

Simon nodded and slipped a hand into his pocket to turn on his recorder. He shouldn't, of course, record without permission, but since asking for permission might only serve to distract Kendall, Simon let it pass. After all, no one would ever know about the tape. Simon only intended to use it in place of the notes that he would normally take on paper, and who knew that even that might serve as a distraction to the old man? The last thing Simon wanted was to run the risk of stopping the flow of memories now that Kendall apparently had some.

"Wasn't she lovely that night?" Kendall stopped chewing for a long minute and looked out the window, as if watching something that only his eyes could see.

"Beautiful." Simon leaned forward hoping to catch every word.

"She wore that long dress of pale lavender. Matched her eyes. We danced and danced. . . ."

"She was your lady friend?"

"She danced like . . . well, light as a cloud. Everyone was watching us." Kendall began to slip into the past. Simon wasn't sure where it would take them, but he was happy to follow. "All the women, they all wanted to be her; you could tell by the way they looked at her. And all the men wished they were me. If they only knew . . ." He shook his head slowly; a sadness settled into the lines of his face.

"She was *who*, Mr. Kendall?"

"She could light up a room just by walking into it. And her laughter . . . just like those little silver bells on the tree." He cocked his head slightly to the side, as if listening. "She loved to dance. And everyone wanted to dance with her. Cut right in whenever they saw a chance. But not *him*. Not that night. *She* was watching him like a hawk that night."

"So all the other guys were lining up to dance with

your lady?" Simon wondered who *him* and *she* might have been. "That's some feeling, isn't it, when all your friends stare at your girl and wish she was with them?"

"Oh, not really my girl," Kendall said softly, the sadness deepening. "Not really. She never could see anyone but him."

"Your lady had her eyes on someone else?"

"Who could blame her? He was everything. *Had* everything . . ." The tired blue eyes drifted to the window and beyond once again. "He couldn't stop looking at her, couldn't take his eyes off her. And *she* knew; if I'd suspected it before, I was pretty certain then. 'This is dangerous,' I told him. 'Can't you see that she's watching every move you make?' Of course, he knew that I loved her, too. Maybe he thought I just wanted her for myself." He turned back to Simon and smiled a half smile that was etched with pain. "And of course, I did."

"You and a friend were in love with the same woman," Simon said softly.

Kendall nodded.

"And he was married? It was dangerous because he was married and his wife was there, too?" Simon was touched that, so many years later, Kendall still felt the loss of his old love.

Another nod.

"I'm sorry, I don't remember her name—"

"Blythe."

"Of course, Blythe. And she came to the party with you."

"She always went there with me. Everyone thought she was my girl, because she always came there with me. But she was his. She was always his. Only his."

"Remind me again who *he* was." His curiosity piqued, Simon leaned forward.

Just far enough for Kendall to drop a bomb in his lap.

"Graham," Kendall whispered. "She was always Graham's."

When his wits resurfaced, Simon asked, "Graham Hayward? The President of the United States, Graham Hayward?"

Kendall paused, his face softening just a bit, as if suddenly amused. "She was so young. Much too young for him. Much too young for me. And yet, we both . . ."

Kendall stopped, as if unable to speak the words.

"Loved her." *Mr. Morality, Graham Hayward?*

"Yes. We both loved her."

"And you took her out in public because he could not?" *Graham "High Road" Hayward?*

Kendall's eyes welled up.

"That must have been very hard for you, sir. To be with the woman you loved, knowing she loved someone else." These were the ramblings of a confused old man, weren't they?

"Every minute she was with me, she was only waiting for the time she would be with him."

Simon reached out a hand to touch Kendall's arm. "Mr. Kendall, are you saying that Graham Hayward had an affair while he was President?" He tried to keep the words from gasping out of his mouth.

Tears sped down Kendall's face, some falling onto his chest as he nodded.

"Graham Hayward had an affair?" Simon repeated, wondering if Kendall could possibly be telling the truth. And yet the pain on the man's face was so keen.

Even after the passage of so many years, it had a fresh, new look.

"Yes."

"With . . . ?" Simon had to hear Kendall say it. Say the name.

"Blythe. My Blythe."

"Are you sure of this? How can you be sure they actually had an affair?"

"Because I brought her to him."

Stunned, Simon sat back and felt the thunder roll through him. "You brought her to the party . . ." He swallowed hard, trying to imagine how it might have been.

"As my guest, yes. And we would stay, sometimes, stay the night at the White House. Until it became too dangerous. And only when *she* was out of town, of course." Kendall's voice had fallen to a whisper so low that Simon had to lean forward to hear him. "Blythe loved him, but she would never have dreamed of staying there while *she* was there. It just wouldn't have been . . . right."

The rest hung between them, unspoken.

"By '*she*' do you mean the First Lady?"

Kendall nodded.

"Was she aware of the affair?"

"There were times when she would look at me . . . at Blythe. At *him*. Nights when she never let him out of her sight. For a long time I wondered if she knew, or if she merely suspected. But there at the end, I believe that she knew."

"The end? How long did this go on?" Simon asked. "This affair. How long did it last?"

"Till she died."

"Until Blythe died? When? How did she die?"

"She left, remember? But she came back." Kendall's bottom lip began to quiver uncontrollably as tears began to stream down his face. "I told her not to come back. Begged her to stay away. If she'd stayed away, she wouldn't have died."

"Mr. Kendall, when did Blythe die? How did she die?"

"Hit-and-run, they said." Kendall turned to the window, his mumbled words coming in an incoherent rush between his sobs. ". . . a terrible thing. A terrible, terrible thing . . ."

A stunned Simon sat in the parking lot, keys in the ignition but the engine not yet turned on, trying to make sense of what he'd just heard.

If Miles Kendall was to be believed, Graham Hayward had had an affair while in the White House.

But could Kendall be believed?

On the one hand, Miles Kendall had, admittedly, a frail memory at best. On the other, he'd sure as hell sounded like he knew what he was talking about.

And yet hadn't Simon plowed through mountains of biographical material about the former President, written material, interviews and articles written by admirers and detractors alike? Nowhere had there been even the slightest hint of scandal. How then could such a story be true?

Could Miles Kendall have made up such a tale?

Yet there had been something in the man's face, something in his eyes, when he spoke of the woman. Blythe . . .

If it was true and Simon could prove it was true, he'd have one hell of a story.

He started the Mustang and drove slowly toward the exit, his head spinning with possibilities.

He wondered if there might have been something in one of the boxes he hadn't gotten to yet, then realized that there would be nothing of this story in any of the material he had. Hadn't all of his research material come from Philip Norton?

Dr. Philip Norton, the keeper of the Hayward flame.

What was the likelihood, Simon stopped to consider, that Norton had not known about Blythe?

Yeah, right, Simon snorted. How could he not have known?

Of course there would be no mention of the President's fling in the material provided to Simon. If Norton wanted a book that cast Hayward in the best possible light, the last thing he'd want would be for that book to air Hayward's dirty linen. Especially since it had always been believed that there *was* no dirty linen.

And if Norton was in fact in the market for such a book—a book that would perpetuate the myth of Hayward as saint—who better to entrust it to than a former student? Someone who knew and trusted him?

Someone who was writing a book of his own.

Someone who'd need a publisher for that book.

"Damn it!" Simon slapped at the steering wheel. "Damn!"

Hadn't his mother always said that if something sounds too good to be true, it probably is? Hadn't his little voice tried to warn him that things might have been just a little too easy? Hadn't he been willing to overlook the whisperings of that little voice because he wanted what Norton had offered?

Anger surged through Simon, followed by a wash of disappointment. Had Norton really believed that Simon would not do a little digging of his own, regardless of how much material with which he'd been provided? Or did Norton think that Simon would put his objectivity aside—or, worse, ignore the truth, if, in fact, he managed to stumble over it?

Did Norton really think he could manipulate him so easily?

Simon hated being manipulated.

He stepped on the gas and headed toward the bridge that would take him home, determined to move heaven and earth to find the truth about Graham Hayward. Whatever that truth might prove to be.

And when he did, Philip Norton would get his book, all right. It just may be more than he'd bargained for.

Still, through the night as Simon pored over box after box, it nagged at him. Somewhere there should be some hint of Hayward's fall from grace, and Simon hadn't found so much as a trace. Somewhere the woman's name should appear, yet so far he'd found no mention of a woman named Blythe.

At three in the morning, Simon sat on the sofa in his apartment, piles of articles at his feet. His search had come up dry at every turn. He hunted for the list of names he'd made, people he'd planned on interviewing. First thing in the morning, he'd start making calls. He'd make appointments to meet with those who sounded as if they had something to contribute. If there was something in Hayward's past that had been covered up, Simon would be the one to find it.

The first person Simon called was Adeline Anderson. Hadn't Norton himself said that if Addie Anderson didn't know about it, chances were it had never happened?

If there had been gossip, wouldn't she have heard it? Simon had come across several of her columns from the seventies and had found them to be full of who attended this party, who wore what to that dinner. Social stuff, nothing heavy. But that doesn't mean she didn't *know*. If there had been something to know.

How would one go about asking such a question?

Now, tell me, Ms. Anderson, were you aware of an affair between President Hayward and a mysterious woman named Blythe?

Simon was still wondering exactly how best to bring up Blythe's name even as he dialed the phone number of the long-retired reporter. He'd explained who he was to the gravelly voiced woman on the other end when she interrupted him.

"You're the one who caused that big stir at the *Press* a year or so back, aren't you?"

"Well, yes."

"Good for you. About time that someone put that pompous fool Walker in his place."

"Ahhh, thank you." Simon cleared his throat softly. "I think."

"I strongly believe that you had every right to expect your editor to respect your sources. Political pressure aside, Walker should have backed you up. He lost a tremendous amount of respect in the journalistic community by not doing so. Not that he cares, mind you. He's still the editor of the *Washington Press.*" She chuckled. "But I do admire that you stuck to principle, Mr. Keller."

"Thank you, Ms. Anderson. I appreciate that."

"Now tell me what an old retired reporter can do for you."

"Ms. Anderson, I'm working on a biography of the late President Graham Hayward, and I was looking into the social climate of the times. I've read many of your columns, by the way. You certainly seem to have known the scene in the capital back in the seventies."

"No one knew it better," she said confidently.

"That's what I've been told."

"May I ask by whom?"

"Philip Norton."

"Ah, Dr. Norton. How is he doing these days? So sad about his poor wife . . ."

"Yes, yes, it was certainly sad. And he seems to be doing well." Simon bit back bitter words. This wasn't the best of times for anyone to ask him about his old mentor. That was a wound that still throbbed.

"Is he publishing your book?"

"Yes."

"Then it's guaranteed to be a quality production. Good for you. That's quite a feather in the cap of a young man like yourself."

"Yes, well." Simon bit his tongue. That feather was threatening to choke him right now. "Thank you."

"So tell me what you'd like to know."

"To start, I thought perhaps you might be able to give me a feeling of who the players were."

"Who was in, who was out?"

"Exactly."

"Who was doing what to whom."

"Even better. And I wondered if you might remember—"

"Like it was yesterday." Adelaide Anderson chuckled. "It was a grand time to live in the capital. The Haywards loved to entertain. And they were such a lovely couple."

"Did you have the feeling that they were really as devoted to each other as all those old articles would lead one to believe?"

"Absolutely."

"Really?"

"Oh, yes. They just always seemed to be so in sync. And they had the best parties—always heavy on foreign dignitaries. Ambassadors and such. I heard it said on more than one occasion that President Hayward always felt that he was a little light when it came to foreign affairs, so he made it a point to get to know the diplomats. On any given night it would not surprise you to see half of Embassy Row walking into the White House. Along with the usual entertainment types and American lawmakers. And then, of course, there were the President's regulars."

"His regulars?"

"His cabinet. High-ranking military. The usual Washington A-list."

"I suppose over the years you got to know them all well."

"Everyone who was anyone."

"Did you know Miles Kendall?"

"Of course I knew Miles. Had a terrible crush on him when he first came to town. I don't mind admitting it now." Addie giggled and for a moment sounded more like a young girl of sixteen than a woman in her eighties. The moment passed quickly. "I hear he isn't doing well these days."

"He looks well enough, for a man of advanced years, but he is having some problems with his memory."

"You've seen him?"

"Yes. I was hoping to be able to cull some of his best memories for my book, but . . ." Simon left the thought dangling meaningfully.

"Terrible, terrible shame. Miles was quite the guy, back then." Addie's voice dropped just slightly. "Handsome, witty, oh, and a great dancer. Plus he was very close to the power. He and Hayward were best of friends, I'm sure you've heard."

"Sounds as if he was on that A-list you were talking about."

"Oh, at the very top. Miles was the town's most eligible bachelor. He was on everyone's list."

"Was he a ladies' man, back then?"

"Miles?" Adelaide paused to consider before answering. "Not really, though he did have lots of ladies more than willing to give him a tumble. Myself included, I daresay."

"Did he have a steady girl?"

"Oh, no, not really. Though for a time there was one girl . . . what was her name?"

Simon could almost see the old woman's brows knitting in a frown.

"Oh, you know who I mean." She tsk-tsked at her

failing memory. "Lovely girl. Stunning, really. Young, but quite sophisticated—that old Philadelphia Main Line breeding, you know. Miles was quite taken with her there for a time. Oh, what was her name?"

"Somewhere I saw the name Blythe . . ." Simon offered.

"Ah, of course. Blythe. There was a time when you almost never saw him without her on his arm."

"I can't seem to locate her last name in my notes—"

"It was Pierce. As in Pierce Tires."

"Oh, right. Pierce." Simon grabbed a piece of paper and printed the name in inch-high letters across the top sheet of his notebook. "BLYTHE PIERCE."

"Such a tragic loss that was, though."

"What was that?"

"Oh, she died so terribly. Hit-and-run, right there on Connecticut Avenue. Bastard who ran her down never bothered to stop, just left her lying there in the street."

"And they never found the driver of the car?"

"Never so much as a clue. The police thought it may have been someone from out of town, just passing through the city."

"Wasn't there an investigation?"

"Oh, of course there was. Especially with her father being who he was—"

"Who was her father?"

"Foster Pierce. He was Ambassador to Belgium at the time. I believe that Blythe's first trip to the White House was on the arm of her father. That's how she met Miles, through her father."

"Really?"

"Really. Word was that after the police investigation

came up with nothing, Foster Pierce brought in his own private investigator, but as far as I know, he might as well not have bothered. They never did find the car or the driver. I heard the case just went cold after that."

"Where did the accident happen?"

"Out in front of Blythe's apartment building. It was late; it was dark; she must have just come home from something or other."

"Were there any witnesses?"

"None that I'd heard of. Of course, it was so late—two or so in the morning, as I recall. We were all hoping someone would have seen something, you know, but I never heard if anyone stepped forward."

Simon paused, knowing he needed to get as much information about Blythe in as short a time as possible, before Addie Anderson changed the subject and went on to something else. "Ms. Anderson, what did Blythe Pierce do, do you remember?"

"What do you mean, what did she *do*?"

"Did she have a job? Did she work?"

"I don't recall that Blythe had a paying job, though I do think she was involved in some type of volunteer work. I think I would have heard if she worked for the government, but of course, being an heiress, perhaps she didn't have to work at all. And poor Miles, he just wasn't the same after that." Adelaide sighed. "And truthfully, looking back, it seems that a lot of things weren't the same after that accident."

"What do you mean?"

"Oh, I guess because Miles was in mourning—anyone who'd ever seen him with Blythe knew that he was so much in love with her—well, it just seemed that even the parties at the White House weren't as lively for a time. Of course, I always thought that the President did his best to help his friend get through that terrible time."

"In what way?"

"Oh, after Blythe it seems they spent a lot of time together, just the two of them, Miles and the President. In times of such sorrow, you do most appreciate your oldest, your closest friends, don't you think? So I would imagine that the President must have been a great comfort to Miles. It must have been hard for him, to have lost the woman he loved."

But which man had been in the greater need of comfort? And if it was true that both men had loved this same woman, which man had the greater need to grieve behind closed doors?

Simon sat staring out the window for a long time after thanking Adelaide Anderson for her time and promising to send her an autographed copy of his book.

Who, beside Miles Kendall, had known about the President's affair with Blythe Pierce?

Assuming of course that it was true. After all, all he had really managed to confirm was that Blythe Pierce had been a frequent visitor to the White House as Kendall's guest. What, really, could he prove beyond that?

How to prove something thirty years after the fact?

Simon tapped his pen impatiently on the tabletop, pondering the tragic demise of the object of the affections of both men. How peculiar that this same woman had been the victim of a random crime. A crime that had never been solved.

How, he wondered, could that be . . . ?

And how could he uncover the truth when two of the key players were dead and the third was senile?

Simon glanced toward the door just as a tall woman with casually coiffed salt-and-pepper hair entered the bar and slid off her large black-and-white zebra-print sunglasses. Her eyes scanned the room before coming to rest on Simon. The corners of her mouth eased into a smile. She walked toward him in a long-legged stride that could have been described as youthful if not for the fact that she favored her left leg and was clearly in her late fifties.

"Hello, Simon Keller," she said as she approached his table.

"Hello, Madeline Shaw." Simon stood and took both of her hands in his. "You're looking good, as always."

"As are you, pup." Madeline Shaw, a longtime detective in the District, pulled out her own chair and seated herself solidly upon it. She nodded to the waiter who hovered nearby with a menu, and reached out her hand to take it.

"How've you been?" Simon studied the face of the woman he'd admired for almost a decade.

"I've been better. They've still got me working a desk." She raised an eyebrow. "Need I tell you how annoying that is?"

"I can only begin to imagine." Simon grinned. Once upon a time, Detective Shaw had been hell on wheels. It had taken a bullet to her left thigh to slow her down. "You feeling all right, though, other than the fact that you're bored?"

"I'd feel a hell of a lot better if I could get back out on the street, but I know that won't happen. My inability to run like a deer—even a three-legged one—has hampered my forward motion more than a bit. I'm resigned to the fact that I'll be on the desk for as long as I'm on the job."

"How much longer will that be?"

Madeline shrugged. "I can retire in eight months."

"Will you?"

"Who knows?"

The waiter returned and took their orders, then disappeared, tucking the menus under his arm.

"What are you up to these days?"

"As of the first of the month, I've been living in Arlington and working on a book." Simon leaned back as the waiter set a frosted mug of beer in front of him.

"Based on that infamous case of yours, no doubt."

"Actually, I've had to put that one aside for a time. Right now I'm working on a biography of Graham Hayward."

"The congressman?"

"The late president."

"Why?"

"Because I need to pay the bills."

"Who's behind that?"

"Philip Norton."

"Norton's back?" She appeared surprised. "I thought he moved across the pond after his wife died."

"He traveled around for a while. I think he's only recently back in the States within the past six months or so."

"Tough about his wife." Madeline sipped at her iced tea. "Did they ever find out why . . . ?"

Simon shook his head. "I haven't heard any explanation."

"Like I said, tough. Tough on everyone involved." Shaw tapped her fingers on the tabletop. "Her daughter has popped up on a few cases we've had come through."

"What do you mean?"

"She's a compositor, did you know? Freelances for various law enforcement agencies."

"She any good?"

"A lot of people think she's one of the best. The Feds use her, too. We used her to draw the composite sketch of the kid who took a shotgun to a commuter train last summer."

She paused while the waiter served their sandwiches.

"I heard the congressman may be making a run for the White House in two years."

"So they tell me." With his fork Simon moved a pile of French fries to the side of his plate to make room for a small mountain of catsup.

"Guess now's a good time to remind everyone just how fine a President his daddy was."

"You always were too smart for your own good, you know that?"

"Been hearing that all my life." She grinned. "But you have to admit that it's pretty interesting."

"What is?"

"Well, as I recall, you preferred the stories you had to dig for. I wouldn't have thought a book like this would interest you."

"Under ordinary circumstances, it wouldn't," Simon said frankly. "But I'll make enough money on this book to keep my head above water for a good long time. Certainly long enough for me to finish that book you brought up earlier."

"So how can the DCPD help you?"

"I need a copy of an accident report. A hit-and-run."

"Simon, you didn't have to buy me lunch to get a copy of an accident report." The detective looked puzzled.

"I'm happy to see you again." He grinned. "And besides, it's a pretty old report."

"How old?"

"Thirty years give or take."

"Thirty years?" She laughed. "You *are* kidding, right?"

"I'm afraid not."

"Why would you want a thirty-year-old accident report?"

"I'm just curious about something, that's all."

"Curious," she repeated skeptically.

"Yes."

Madeline sighed and took a small notebook from her shoulder bag. "What's the name of the victim and the date of the accident?"

"The name is Blythe Pierce. And the date . . . damn, I don't know the date." He frowned. "Sometime in November or December of 1971." He tried to recall the story Miles Kendall had told him. Hadn't there been something about a Christmas Ball? "Probably December of '71."

"*Probably,* he says," she muttered. "Are you going to tell me why you're looking into this?"

Simon hesitated. Before he could respond, she said, "Never mind. If you have to take that long to think about it, it's clearly something you don't want to talk about, so forget that I asked. And of course I'll look for the report as soon as I get back this afternoon. Give me a number where I can reach you, and I'll give you a call as soon as I can get my hands on it. It may take a few days, though. Is that okay?"

"That's fine. A few days would be fine."

It had taken Madeline Shaw less than twenty-four hours to find the report that Simon had been seeking.

"Do you have a fax?" the detective asked when Simon answered the phone.

"Yes, yes, let me give it to you." Simon gave her the number. "I take it your search was successful."

"Well, I came up with a report. Such as it is. . . ."

"What does that mean?"

"It means that I have a report, but it doesn't appear to be complete."

"Why not?"

"There's an indication that the report was six pages long."

Simon could hear the pages rustling in the background.

"But . . ." he urged her to go on.

"But there are only two in the file. Now that I look a little closer"—she paused as she shuffled through the file—"it looks like . . . well, like some things that should be in the file aren't."

More paper crinkled. Then Madeline said softly, as if to herself, "Odd that this file was closed so soon after the accident. . . ."

"Any reason why?"

"You'd have to speak with the investigating officer."

"I'd love to. Got a name?"

"Looks like . . . something . . . Hughes."

"Any idea of who that is?"

"Well, I knew several Hugheses over the years. If you

hold on, I'll run the badge number through the computer."

Simon had started to wonder if the detective had forgotten that she'd placed him on hold by the time she came back on the line.

"Your Hughes was Kevin," she told Simon. Before he could ask, she added, "He retired about six or seven years ago. He was a good man. We worked together for a while."

"Any idea of where I could find him?"

"You want a lot for that lunch, buddy," Madeline said good-naturedly. "I may have to call you back with that."

"I'd really appreciate it, Madeline. Thanks."

"Don't mention it. I hope you find what you're looking for. Must be something hot. Maybe someday you'll even tell me what this was all about."

"Maybe," he said as the first page began to come through the fax. "Maybe someday . . ."

Simon found Kevin Hughes alive and well and living in Trenton, New Jersey, where he offered his services as an expert witness in the area of police procedures to insurance companies obligated to defend officers who had been sued for civil rights violations of one sort or another.

At the time Simon called, Hughes was on his way to a trial in Connecticut but offered to look at the report that bore his name. All Simon had to do was fax it to him. Simon did, blessing the marvels of modern technology.

Hughes called him back right away.

"I remember this accident. I can't believe you have this report. I remember this accident," Hughes repeated somewhat excitedly. "It was actually one of the first accidents I investigated after joining the force. Damn. I can't believe you're calling about this accident. Madeline didn't tell me it was *this* accident. . . ."

"Was there something special about this accident?" There was something in the former police officer's voice that set Simon's nerves humming. "Other than the fact that it was one of the first you investigated?"

"How 'bout the fact that she was hit twice?"

"Hit twice?" Simon sat up straight in his chair. "You mean she was hit by two different cars?"

"Nah, I mean she was run over twice by the same car."

"But that would mean that the car . . ." Simon said slowly.

"Yeah. Backed up and ran over her a second time."

Simon sucked in a sharp breath. "I'm looking at the police report. It doesn't say anything like that."

"No shit."

"Did you write it up that way? To reflect that she'd been run over twice?"

"Yes. It was all in my report. Two sets of tire marks on the woman. And it was on the coroner's report as well."

"Your report now consists of two pages. And the coroner's report is missing from the file."

"Surprise, surprise," Hughes murmured.

"Any idea of who would have removed those reports?"

"Honestly, no. I haven't a clue. I was a rookie. I knew better than to ask."

"And you never told anyone?"

"Some of the other guys knew about it. And right

after the accident there was a private detective asking some questions, but I wasn't allowed to speak with him. Seems the victim's father was some big shot in D.C. But I don't think even he ever got the full report. So if you mean did I speak with anyone outside the force, no. The only reason I'm talking to you now is because Detective Shaw asked me to give you whatever you wanted. She and I go back. If she trusts you, that's enough for me."

"Didn't it bother you? That your report was changed?"

"Hell, yes, it bothered me. But the order to purge that file would have come from someone way over my head."

"Did you ask who?"

"No. Like I said, I was a rookie. But it must have been someone really high up." Hughes coughed away from the phone, then said, "I mean, you have to be way up there toward the top of the food chain to cover up a murder."

"Murder . . ." Simon repeated as the full implication of what Hughes had told him sank in.

"What would you call it?" Hughes coughed again. "Whoever hit her sure enough wanted that woman dead."

Chapter Seven

The phone seemed to ring and ring forever before it was answered with a curt, "Yes?"

"Your friend, ah, he had company. I thought you might want to know."

"Of course I want to know." A brief pause, then, "Who?"

"I wrote down the name. . . . It was in the book." He held the mouthpiece closer to his face. "Simon Keller."

"Simon Keller." The name was repeated softly.

"Yeah, Simon Keller."

"When was he there?"

"Um, let's see; I wrote that down, too." He turned over the piece of paper. "He was here last Tuesday, then again on Wednesday. . . ."

A sharp intake of breath, then, "He's been there twice?"

"Ah, well, yes. . . ."

"Why am I just hearing about this?"

"Well, you see—"

"What do you think I'm paying you for?"

"I didn't know—"

"You're *supposed* to know. I *pay* you to know!"

"I'm sorry. But—"

"No *buts*," the voice hissed, a snake shimmying through the phone line.

"Look, see, I was off on—"

"Be quiet. Let me think."

Silence.

Finally, "How long did he stay?"

"I don't know." He scratched his head.

"Then go back, look at the log, and call me back." Forced patience, as one might speak to a child. "Write down dates and times. Times in, times out. Do you think you can handle that?"

"Okay. My break is over now, but I'll check when I—hello? Hello?"

The order having been issued, the line had gone dead.

Sighing, the orderly hung up the pay phone and waited a second or two, routinely checking the coin return to see if there was spare change to be found. Then he stubbed out his cigarette and went through the locker-room door and back to work, determined to get the information exactly as it was requested. After all, side gigs like this didn't come along every day, and he figured out that if he could just keep it going for another five months, he'd be able to buy that hot Camaro he saw in the used car lot his bus took him past every day on his way to work.

There were so many old men in this place, he was thinking as he walked down the deserted hallway, why that one old man should matter so much was beyond him. There were other old guys in here who were much more interesting. Like old Mr. DiGiorgio, whose sons and grandsons dressed in black and who all came down once a month from New York in a limousine carrying a hamper filled with pasta and wine. Now Mr. DiGiorgio, *he* had been somebody. *He* had some stories to tell. But old Mr. Kendall, he just sat there, staring out the window.

The orderly paused in front of Kendall's doorway, then pushed it open only far enough for his head to poke through. The old man wheezed in his sleep but, other than that, slept like a baby.

"*Just in case I'm asked if the old SOB talked in his sleep, I can honestly answer no,*" the orderly muttered, still not understanding the importance of his mission but knowing that carrying it out would mean the difference between *wheels* and *no wheels*. He closed the door quietly, then headed toward the lobby, where the visitors' sign-in logs were kept.

This time, when he called back he'd have the information. There'd be no reason to ask him again—in that mean, snotty tone of voice—if he knew what he was being paid to do. He knew. And he'd deliver.

Chapter Eight

The home of Foster Worthington Pierce had been ridiculously easy to find once Simon knew where to look. All he'd needed was a computer and a quick stop or two on the Internet to find it. Wild Springs, Malvern, Pennsylvania.

Simon packed a bag and headed north. His interview with Celeste Hayward was scheduled for the following day, and he figured he could as easily make the flight to Rhode Island from Philadelphia as he could from D.C. or Baltimore. The Philadelphia suburbs were little more than two hours away. He wasn't quite sure what he hoped to find, but he knew he wouldn't be content until he stood on the steps of the Pierce home and rang the doorbell. What questions he would ask once someone opened that door, well, he'd think about that on the drive up. All he knew was that he had to go.

Wild Springs would have been described by the tony magazines as a gentleman's farm. There were vast fenced fields where beautiful horses stood in the chill of the afternoon and watched Simon's old car pass on its way to the rambling fieldstone farmhouse at the end of the meandering lane.

Definitely horse country. Simon nodded to himself as

he got out of the car and looked around at the fields where jumps had been placed. A large barn stood off to the right, and several smaller barns and a carriage house were built around an outside riding ring. There were several other outbuildings, and what appeared to be a walled garden directly behind the house. A woods formed a natural border to Simon's left, and all in all, the property was pristinely manicured. Even the pastures appeared beautifully maintained.

Mr. Pierce obviously didn't mind spending a bit on upkeep, Simon noted as he walked to the front of the house and up the three steps to the door, which was painted red and had a knocker in the shape of a horse's head.

"Yes?" A white-haired woman wearing slacks, a sweater, and an air of suspicion answered the door.

"My name is Simon Keller. I was wondering if I might speak with Mr. Pierce."

"I'm sorry, but Mr. Pierce is deceased."

"Oh . . ."

As Simon digested this news, a voice from inside called, "Who is it, Mrs. Brady?"

"Someone asking to see your father."

Through the open door Simon could see a figure approaching in a wheelchair.

"Did you ask the nature of his business?"

"I was just about to, Miss Pierce." The housekeeper turned back to Simon.

"I'm a writer. I was hoping to speak with him about—"

"A writer, are you?" The wheelchair drew close enough for Simon to see the middle-aged woman seated in it.

"Yes."

"What is it that you write?" The woman stopped the chair near the open door. At close range, she looked a bit younger than Simon had originally suspected, closer to mid-forties than fifties, the hair more blond than gray, her legs motionless but her eyes dancing with curiosity.

"Actually, I'm writing a book about President Graham Hayward. In going through some of the old White House social records from the day, I found that the name Blythe Pierce came up several times. Enough times that I became curious about her. I started following a trail and it led here." Simon wasn't sure where he'd go from there, but it was a start.

"Blythe." The woman in the chair seemed to smile automatically as she spoke the name aloud. "My God, no one's asked about my sister in . . . well, it's certainly been some time. I'm Betsy Pierce." The woman extended a hand to Simon. "You are again . . . ?"

"Simon Keller." Simon leaned forward to take the hand, which was surprisingly strong.

"And you're writing a book about President Hayward and you want to know about Blythe." Betsy Pierce recited the information slowly, as if trying to piece it together. "Exactly what sort of records were you looking at, where Blythe's name might have appeared?"

"I found her name on a number of old White House guest lists. She apparently attended quite a few dinners and other social gatherings there."

"Do come in, Mr. Keller, and tell me what else you found."

"Miss Pierce . . ." Mrs. Brady, who appeared to be

the housekeeper, raised an eyebrow in what Simon interpreted as a warning.

"Oh, it's all right, Mrs. Brady. We'll sit right here in the front parlor where you can watch his every move. And if it makes you feel better, you can even have that burly new groom come up and brandish about that shotgun he uses to scare the groundhogs with." Betsy Pierce turned her chair to the right and wheeled it through a pair of thick white columns, waving for Simon to follow.

Simon held up his hands as he passed the housekeeper as if to show that his intentions were strictly on the up-and-up.

"I haven't talked about Blythe in so long," Betsy said. "She's been gone for . . . well, it seems a lifetime. Could it really be thirty years? And my father's been gone for nearly twenty-five years. No one seems to remember her except for me."

"Your father's still listed in the phone book," Simon noted.

"I just never bothered to have it changed."

"I hope my visit isn't upsetting to you."

"No, no, not at all. Now sit there on the sofa and tell me what it is you wanted to know about Blythe."

Simon sat as directed and hesitated. How to begin?

"Well," he chose his words carefully, "for my book, I've been gathering some personal reminiscences about Hayward. In doing so, I've been taking a look at some of the players he was close to, such as his Chief of Staff, Miles Kendall. Your sister's name came up in connection with Kendall's on a number of occasions. It appears they may have been an item, as they say."

"I'm afraid I'd know nothing about that." Betsy folded her arms across her chest. "Blythe always seemed to play her cards close to her vest."

"What do you mean?"

"She was never particularly chatty about her social life. At least, not with me. Then again, she was ten years older than I. Back in the days when she lived in Washington, I was . . . let's see, she was in her mid-twenties when she first moved there, so I would still have been in high school. We weren't particularly close in the way that some sisters might be, mostly, you see, because of the age difference."

"So you wouldn't have known what her life was like back then? Where she lived, who she dated, who her friends were?" Simon asked casually.

"Well, I do know where she lived. I visited her a few times during school breaks. She lived in a lovely apartment over in the Woodley Park section." Betsy's voice dropped. "I just loved going to see her in those days. It was one of the few times that she and I really connected. Blythe would just drop everything when I came to visit, and we'd go to all of the tourist places and wonderful restaurants. If the weather was nice, we'd walk through Rock Creek Park in the morning." Betsy noted Simon's raised eyebrows, then smiled and added, "I haven't always been in a wheelchair, Mr. Keller. I cracked my spine in a riding accident some years ago. But before that, I was very active."

"I'm sorry; I didn't mean to—"

Betsy dismissed his apology with a wave. "Please, don't. Frankly, it's been a while since I thought about how good it feels to walk. I'm not distressed by the memory. I rather enjoy it."

"Was your sister attending school in D.C.? Or did she have friends there?"

"No, she'd graduated from college by then. I don't know of any friends who lived there. Why do you ask?"

"I was curious about why she moved there in the first place. Did she have a job, perhaps?"

"I recall that she volunteered somewhere, but Blythe never had a job. She didn't need the money, frankly. And as for why she moved to Washington, as I recall, she first visited with Dad for some embassy function or other. She was fascinated with all there was to do, socially, that is. She went back several times, I believe, before leasing her apartment." Betsy smiled. "Blythe loved the nightlife. The pastoral life bored her to death. I, on the other hand, could never live anywhere but here."

"Did you ever meet any of her friends? Any of the men she dated?"

Betsy shook her head. "No. As I said, when I visited with her she devoted all of her attention to showing her little sister a good time. She always planned things that she and I could do together, and since we didn't see each other often in those days, she never invited anyone else to join us. Actually, the only friend of Blythe's that I ever really knew was her college roommate. She and Blythe had remained very close. If Blythe was dating someone while she was in D.C.—even someone important in the government such as Mr. Kendall, as you have intimated—she never mentioned it to me. Though it certainly wouldn't come as a surprise if she had been. Dating someone important, that is."

"Why is that?"

"Blythe was a magnet. She couldn't walk down the street without men falling at her feet." Betsy laughed good-naturedly and rolled her chair to the piano that stood at one end of the handsome room. She lifted a framed photograph and returned to where Simon sat. "This was the last picture we had of Blythe. She was twenty-seven or so at the time."

She handed the photo to Simon, who tilted it toward the light. The woman in the photograph was every bit as stunning as Adelaide Anderson had described. Rich dark hair framed a face to which Mother Nature had been very kind. A pert turned-up nose, generous mouth, large round eyes of the deepest lavender-blue fringed with thick black lashes. A megawatt smile that lit up those eyes with the very fire of life.

"She was beautiful," Simon said simply.

"That is an understatement. I've no doubt that she had plenty of dates and may certainly have had a boyfriend—or two, or three—while she lived there. I don't recall that she ever mentioned anyone special." She took the photograph that Simon handed back to her and placed it on the table between them. "Of what importance to your book might Blythe's love life be?"

"Not important, really. Her name just seemed to pop up a lot in connection with Kendall, as I told you, and since he was an important member of the Hayward administration, I thought I'd find out what I could about her. And when I realized that Blythe was from the Philadelphia area and I found the listing for your father in the phone book, I thought, well, Philadelphia's not so far from Virginia—why not just drive up there and see what I can see?" Simon flashed what he hoped would be his most endearing smile.

"Why not indeed?" Betsy Pierce appeared to study the photo of her sister for a long while.

"Miss Pierce, what do you know about your sister's death?"

Betsy appeared to jolt in her chair.

"I'm sorry; I probably should have led up to that more gently than I did." Simon grimaced at his gaffe.

Betsy cleared her throat as if formulating an answer. "I know that she was hit by a car. I know that my father had a lot of unanswered questions. He was very much disturbed that the police never found a suspect. He thought they gave up too easily. He even hired a private detective to look into it, but nothing ever came of that."

"Adelaide Anderson mentioned that."

"Who?"

"A reporter who covered the Washington scene back then. She remembered your sister. She mentioned how things changed after Blythe's death."

"What things?"

"How the social scene seemed to slow down. She thought perhaps it was because the President was busy comforting his friend."

"Comforting his friend," Betsy repeated slowly, her voice flat.

"Miles Kendall," Simon reminded her.

"I see." Betsy Pierce went very still, her hands folded in her lap.

"So . . . well, one thing just sort of led to another in my mind." Simon clasped his hands together and leaned his elbows on his knees. "I mean, here I was gathering information for this book about a former President, and I stumbled onto all sorts of other things." Simon took a breath, debating with himself for a long minute before adding, "Including an old, apparently unsolved murder."

Betsy looked up at him sharply.

"I recently had an opportunity to look at the police report regarding your sister's death. It was surprisingly brief. So I tracked down the police officer who was first on the scene."

"And he told you . . . ?"

There was no gentle way to say it.

"It appears that the vehicle that ran over your sister did so twice."

Simon watched her face, waiting for a reaction. When there was none, he said, "Your sister was deliberately run down, Miss Pierce. I wouldn't be at all surprised if your father knew it. I think he just couldn't prove it."

Betsy wheeled her chair to a window overlooking the pastures where her horses grazed in the afternoon sun. When finally she spoke, Betsy asked, "Are you going to try to prove it, Mr. Keller?"

"If I can." As soon as the words were out of Simon's mouth, he knew they were true.

"Why?" When she turned back to face Simon, her eyes were rimmed in red.

"Because someone has gotten away with murder for almost thirty years."

"I suppose you could get a nice book deal out of a story like that, couldn't you?" Betsy said. "What are you really looking for?"

"The truth." He looked directly into her eyes. "I'm only looking for the truth."

"That sounds awfully noble," she scoffed.

"You make that sound like a bad thing."

"And supposing you do find the truth, Mr. Keller. What will you do with it?"

"I don't know," Simon responded as honestly as he could. "Not knowing what that truth might be, I can't say where it would lead or what I might do."

Betsy wheeled herself back to the window and stared out for so long that Simon began to think she'd forgotten he was there.

Finally, she turned and asked, "Do you have any suspects in mind, Mr. Keller?"

"None. But I thought if I could find out who her friends were, who her lovers were . . ."

Betsy chewed on the inside of her bottom lip frantically, as if debating something within herself.

"She may have confided in Jude," she said with a certain deliberation.

"Jude?"

"Her roommate from college that I mentioned earlier."

"You wouldn't happen to know where I might find her?"

Betsy's gaze shifted from the image of her sister to Simon and back again, as if the internal debate continued. She held the photograph with both hands, her response so slow in coming that Simon thought perhaps she was ignoring the question.

"As a matter of fact, I do. Just the other day I got a copy of a letter that Everett sent to her, and it had her address on it."

"Who is Everett?"

"The family lawyer." Betsy returned the photo to its place atop the piano. "Jude was the sole beneficiary of my sister's estate. Everett Jackson was the executor. There is a trust that pays out annually, so of course he would know her whereabouts."

"Your sister named her college roommate the sole beneficiary of her estate?" Simon frowned and without thinking asked, "Not you?"

When he realized what he had said, Simon flushed deepest red from his scalp to his toes. "I am so sorry. I can't believe I said anything that crass. Of course, it's none of my business."

"You're certainly not the first person who commented on that very thing, but I assure you, I don't mind at all. My sister and I had equal shares of our mother's estate, and that was what went to Jude. As the only surviving child, I have inherited Wild Springs and my father's entire estate. Unfortunately, I have no children to pass it on to. . . ."

Betsy's eyes clouded again, then, just as quickly, cleared.

"I've never begrudged Jude the portion of Mother's estate that went to her," Betsy continued. "She's had to work very hard for everything, or so I understand. Worked her way through college, through graduate school. Blythe mentioned once that Jude had thousands of dollars in college loans to pay off."

Betsy paused again, then added, "Jude was a very good friend to Blythe. I thought it was wonderful that my sister chose to take care of her. Frankly, I didn't need the money. Jude did. I'm sure it has made her life much easier."

"That's generous of you."

"It's the truth. Oh, not that one couldn't always find a way to spend an extra six or seven mill, you know."

Simon choked.

"Oh, for heaven's sake. The money was Blythe's to do with as she pleased. I daresay she spent her share of it while she was alive. Blythe liked to travel, liked pretty clothes, and had quite the adventurous spirit." Betsy wheeled her chair to a bookcase and slid a fat leather album from a center shelf. She flipped through it for a moment, then turned and, holding it out to Simon, said, "This might give you a sense of what I mean about Blythe's spirit. Feel free to look through it while I locate that letter from Everett."

Betsy handed over the album, then left the room, the wheels of her chair turning silently on the thick Oriental carpet. Simon watched her disappear around the corner into the hallway, then opened the leather-bound book to find page after page chronicling Blythe's travels. In front of the pyramids in Egypt, a gold-domed temple in Jerusalem, an overgrown path in some jungle region, on the steps of a Mayan ruin. Blythe shared that same easy smile with her sister, Simon noted, but there the similarity ended. Where Betsy exuded calm, Blythe appeared to be nothing less than energy incarnate. There was a vibrancy to her that even thirty-year-old photographs could not deny. When the vibrancy was combined with her natural beauty it was easy to see what had drawn both Hayward and Kendall to her.

A loose snapshot sat between the fourth and fifth pages. Blythe in a garden, one arm over the shoulders of a much older man. Turning it over, Simon read: "*Father and Blythe at a reception for the French Ambassador*."

The camera's focus was on Blythe, her features clear and flawless. With barely a thought, Simon slipped the photograph into his pocket and closed the album, then walked to the window and gazed out.

The sun was low in the March sky, the leafless trees stark against the dense gray clouds. He watched a young horse frolic in the chill wind that blew across the pasture and made the grasses bend, and wondered about Blythe Pierce, who had come from such a beginning and had met such an untimely and mysterious end.

And wondered who it had been who'd helped her to that end.

"It turned into a nice day after all, didn't it?" Betsy had stopped in the doorway.

"Yes. It was good to see the sun again, however briefly." Simon turned toward her. "I was just watching one of your horses out there, running with the breeze."

"Ah, Magnolia. My little filly. She's going to be a great jumper someday. Mark my words."

"She looks quite lively."

"She's got heart, that one. Now"—she offered him a slip of paper—"here's Jude's address."

"I appreciate this." Simon crossed the carpet and took the folded sheet of paper, opening it long enough to note that Jude's last name was McDermott and that she lived in a small town on Maryland's Eastern Shore about forty miles from Simon's old apartment in McCreedy. "I appreciate your help."

"Don't mention it. I'm interested in seeing what you come up with myself." She smiled then, and in her smile Simon could see a touch of that same liveliness he'd seen in the photographs of her sister. "After all these years, the thought of someone being held accountable for Blythe's death holds great appeal. Not that I think you will be able to find out what happened, mind you. Though knowing that you might try . . ." Betsy cleared her throat again. "I loved my sister very much, Mr. Keller. I can't even begin to tell you how much it would mean to those she left behind to have the truth."

"Your father's investigator must have made a report of his findings."

"He well may have, though I don't recall having seen it. I did go through some of my father's papers after his death, but I admit there are files that I never got into."

"Perhaps if you might take time to look—"

"I'll do that. Perhaps there is something I've overlooked." Her gaze was steady now and her eyes filled with purpose.

What a shame, Simon thought, *for so much spirit to be so confined.*

"Now, if you don't mind coming out through the back, there's a ramp there. I can accompany you to your car." She gestured to him.

Simon followed Betsy to the end of the long hall and through a door to the left that led into a morning room, from which French doors opened onto a deck where a ramp sloped down to a path of smooth stone.

"That's my boy, Moon Dancer, there in that first pasture. Isn't he magnificent?" Betsy's eyes blazed with pride.

"He's beautiful," Simon said of the sleek chestnut horse that ran along the inside of the fence.

"Tops in his field, three years running." Betsy grinned. "And a terrible show-off."

"He looks as if he'd be a handful," Simon, who knew nothing about horses, noted as the chestnut took off across the pasture.

"He is that." Betsy laughed, watching the brown blur race with the wind. "Do you ride, Mr. Keller?"

"I haven't in years. Not since I left Iowa."

"I miss it terribly. It's the only thing I really do miss," Betsy said wistfully. "Oh, I can still sit atop a horse and ride in a somewhat limited fashion, but it's the jumping I miss. This is hunt country, you know."

"And has to be some of the prettiest country I've ever seen." Simon smiled, then, nodding to the beds where bare-caned rosebushes and mounds of newly green leaves broke through the still-cool soil, added, "I'll bet your gardens are beautiful in the summer."

"Oh, the gardens were Dad's," Betsy told him as they followed the drive around to the front of the house. "My grandfather was an amateur horticulturist. He planted up these beds, and after he died, my dad kept them up with the help of a gardener. The good news is that Dad's gardener has stayed on with me, or it would look like a jungle out there. The bad news is that the gardener has terrible arthritis and can only do a little bit at a time. I never did develop a taste for growing things, lacked both the touch and the inclination. Blythe had both, though. She spent hours out there, working alongside Granddad. . . ."

She paused, as if remembering, then added, "Some of those roses are fifty years old. The peonies, which are just starting to shoot up now, are even older. And there are specimens of several rare perennials. You should plan to stop back in June. You'll be able to see for yourself just how beautiful they are."

"Perhaps I'll do that." Simon stopped several yards from his car.

"I'll look forward to it." Betsy's eyes narrowed suddenly, as if sizing him up; then, just as quickly, her smile returned.

"Thank you again for your time. You've been more helpful than I can say."

"If you catch up with Jude, please give her my best." Betsy's smile was still in place but now appeared to be touched with a hint of nostalgia. "Tell her . . . tell her that the door is always open."

"I'll be sure to do that."

"Might I ask a favor?"

"Of course."

"Perhaps if you could be in touch. If you learn something." Betsy's voice faltered ever so slightly. "Whatever you find, it may be the last . . . the last I have of Blythe."

"Certainly," Simon promised as he opened the door of the Mustang and slid behind the wheel. "And you'll let me know if you find that report from the investigator."

"I will. I have your card right here in my pocket."

Simon backed up the car and turned around, then waved as he passed by the old stone farmhouse and the woman who sat in the stark chair on the gray stone.

"Good-bye, Mr. Keller," she said softly as she watched the red car grow smaller as it traveled back down the lane.

Still she sat, long after the car had disappeared.

When the day grew colder, she turned her chair back to the house, wondering if she'd have cause to regret the events she may well have just set in motion.

She retraced her route and returned to the warmth of the room where she had visited with Simon. Lifting the album, she turned the pages, then smiled to find that the loose photograph she'd left there was missing.

Somehow, she'd known he wouldn't be able to resist.

Betsy returned the album to the shelf, then wheeled herself to the piano, where she idly picked out the notes of a song for which she could no longer recall the name, trying to ignore the prickling of her conscience.

For one thing, she hadn't been exactly honest with Simon Keller.

Over the years, there had indeed been inquiries about her sister, mostly about her sister's relationship with Miles Kendall. Of all of them, Simon had been the only one who'd cared more about how Blythe had died than how she had lived.

But was that reason enough to trust him with so much?

Only time would tell.

Besides, if not Simon Keller, she rationalized, eventually someone else would be probing. Sooner or later, someone might even find the truth. Perhaps Simon Keller might be that someone.

Betsy shivered with the anticipation of what that truth might bring to her door.

After all these years, wasn't it time?

Chapter Nine

Under any other circumstances, Simon would have considered himself lucky to be allowed the privilege of interviewing Celeste Dillon Hayward, former First Lady and widow of Graham T. Hayward. But these were not ordinary circumstances. For one thing, the questions he most wanted to ask outright were ones he simply could not. *(Mrs. Hayward, is there any truth to the story that your husband had an affair with a woman named Blythe Pierce?)* For another, he was really anxious to make that trip back to Maryland to pay a call on Jude McDermott and see just what she knew about her old roommate's love life.

First things first. . . .

Simon sat on the edge of the white damask love seat and did his best to focus totally on his hostess. She'd been christened Lady Celeste by her detractors for her outwardly cool and collected manner, those qualities that her defenders had always maintained were due to her natural shyness. Now, already three hours into his interview, Simon was still wondering which assessment was closer to the truth. So far, she'd discussed watching her husband agonize over a crisis in the health care system, the deaths of her parents, and state trips abroad with her husband, all with the same level detachment. Simon knew he'd barely scratched the surface.

"Of all the people you met while living in the White House, whose face would you see if you closed your eyes right now?" Simon asked. "Who made the greatest impression on you?"

"Oh, my!" Celeste Hayward covered her mouth with a delicate hand and pretended to stifle a laugh before closing her eyes, thus proving that she was, after all, a good sport. "I suppose I should say my husband, shouldn't I?"

"If that's who you see." Simon smiled.

"Well, of course I do. But I suppose you mean who else." Mrs. Hayward tilted her head slightly and appeared to ponder the question. "The first person who comes to mind is Reverend Preston. He was our pastor for so many years, you know, and we had him at the White House for so many dinners and such. And then there was Mrs. Ellis, Kathryn Ellis, the wife of the British Prime Minister. A lovely woman. We became quite close friends. She passed away several years ago, you might recall. I still miss her." Mrs. Hayward's eyes were open now and she gazed pensively out the window. "And of course, there was Jeanine Bayard. Only the most talented singer of our time. She sang for us on several occasions. Magnificent voice, I'm sure you agree. But mostly, I remember the people I saw every day. David Park, the vice president. Philip Norton comes to mind. He and Graham were thick as thieves. And of course, there was Miles Kendall, my husband's Chief of Staff and closest friend." She smiled coyly and added, "After me, of course."

"Mr. Kendall and the late President had known each other for many years, if I recall correctly."

"Oh, yes, since grade school. They went to prep school together. College. Even went to law school together, so you could certainly say they were lifelong friends. Though unfortunately, Miles isn't well these days." She sighed deeply. "Such a shame. He was such a wonderful man. Such a wonderful friend to Graham." Mrs. Hayward's eyes filled with tears. "Alzheimer's, you know. We—the children and I—visited with him last fall on his birthday. He had no idea of who we were."

"Perhaps you might try visiting again. He appears to have good days and bad days."

"Excuse me?"

"There are some days when he doesn't remember who he is," Simon told her. "Then there are days when he seems very clearly to recall his days in the White House with your husband."

Simon watched his words land, then studied their effect.

Celeste Hayward went perfectly blank for one long moment before asking, "Then, you've . . . ?"

"Been to see him, yes." Simon nodded.

"Why . . . I had no idea . . ." She faltered for just a second. "I'd been under the impression that he had no recollection of anything at all. . . ."

"As I said, he seems to have his good days and his bad days."

"Isn't that something?" She still appeared flustered. "I'll have to tell Sarah and Gray. Perhaps we should plan to visit him again."

"Perhaps you should."

"Well then." She coughed lightly, one hand to her throat. "What other questions do you have there? I would expect you must be close to the end of your list by now."

"I am, Mrs. Hayward. Just a few more. Of all the memories you have of your husband's presidency, is there one moment that stands out in your mind, one that you treasure above the others?"

"Standing in the frigid wind, watching Graham place his hand on the Bible, as he was being sworn in for his first term." Celeste Hayward's gaze drifted back to the window, beyond which a cold wind blew.

She was the picture of a woman who, in her time, had been very much an Important Person. From her perfect pale blond hair to the tips of her manicured nails, Celeste Hayward bore the air of a woman of authority. Her casual attire—a dark gray wool skirt and a matching twin sweater set, modest pearl-and-gold earrings—set the tone for the interview: At Home with the Former First Lady. There was no question as to who was actually in charge of the interview. Simon may have been asking the questions, but Lady Celeste was definitely directing the flow. Even at seventy-three, she was a quiet though deliberate force.

"It was a wonderful day." Mrs. Hayward turned blue eyes on Simon and smiled. "Not so very unlike this one. Cold, windy, a hint of snow. But we were all there—the entire family—to share in Graham's greatest moment. Being sworn in as President of the United States of America." As she spoke, her chin jutted upward ever so slightly. "Both of his parents were still alive then, you know, and they were there. His brother,

Tommy, who lost his battle with lung cancer the following summer. And of course, our children were there as well. We were all so proud." Her eyes flickered just ever so slightly. "By the time Graham's second term came around, his father had been dead for almost a year, his brother for three. And both of the children were . . . well, they were no longer children. So very much had changed in those four years. . . ."

There seemed to be something else, something unspoken, but of course there would be. Simon tried not to read too much into it. After all, a woman like Celeste Hayward would have many memories of those days, and while she may be willing to share carefully selected memories, she wasn't about to bare her soul or share her secrets.

Celeste rose from her chair and walked to one of the wide windows, her hands on her hips, her back turned to Simon, who wished at that moment to see her expression.

"That first inauguration . . . Graham had lived for that moment. It was the high point of his life." She glanced over her shoulder with a smile for Simon. "And of mine, of course."

"You spent eight years in the White House as First Lady," Simon reminded her. "Surely there were many moments of personal triumph."

"I'm a very old-fashioned woman, Mr. Keller. I am not ashamed to say that I built my life around my husband and my children. My moments of personal triumph, as you say, were always centered around Graham or our son or daughter. Nothing matters more than family." Mrs. Hayward seemed to bristle slightly. "Nothing ever has."

"You and Mr. Hayward were married for . . ." Simon ran a searching eye over his notes.

"We were married for twenty-nine years, the year he died." The gracious smile had returned.

"Happy years?"

"Oh, my yes. Very happy. My husband was a wonderful man, Mr. Keller."

"Everything I've ever read about him tells me exactly that, Mrs. Hayward."

"Graham was a devoted husband, a wonderful father, and a truly great President. He deserves to be remembered as an ethical, compassionate leader. A true statesman. A man of high moral character." Her arms were crossed firmly over her chest as she faced him. "To Graham, being President was a sacred trust. The American people had elected him because they understood that he was a man who would always give his best and that they—the citizens of our country—would never feel betrayed by him. That while in office he would always maintain the highest standards, no matter the sacrifice. That was what was expected of him. That was what was expected of all of us. It was a promise Graham made every time he ran for office, whether as a young congressman here in Rhode Island forty years ago or later as president of the United States. Whatever else his failings might have been, Graham promised to never break that moral code. He never did, because he always believed that without his good name a man had nothing."

"What other failings might he have had, Mrs. Hayward?" Simon toyed with his pen.

"I beg your pardon?"

"You said, 'Whatever else his failings might have

been.' I don't recall anyone ever mentioning that your husband had any failings whatsoever."

Sensing that he was teasing her, Celeste Hayward laughed. "Well, you know, he had his weaknesses, as do we all. He had a scandalous addiction to Hershey bars. The kind with the almonds." The former First Lady sat back down and leaned closer to Simon as if to share a confidence. "And—I've never admitted this publicly—my husband could not abide cats."

Simon laughed appropriately. "I knew if I dug hard enough, I'd find that skeleton in the closet."

"And there you have it." Mrs. Hayward sat back in her chair and smiled graciously. "Is there anything else you need to know?"

Sensing dismissal, Simon closed his notebook and stood. "No, I think we're fine. For now, anyway. And we discussed earlier the list of questions that I would be faxing to you as a follow-up." Simon opened his briefcase and tucked the notebook in, then said with a snap of his fingers, "Oh, I almost forgot. I found some old photographs in one of the boxes that Dr. Norton sent over. I thought maybe you'd like to see them. Maybe you could even identify some of the people."

"I'd be delighted to see them, and of course if I recognize . . ." The former First Lady studied the first in the small stack of photos. "Yes, this is the former Speaker of the House, Andy Liston, and his wife, Marguerite. Lovely, lovely woman. She was from Madrid. And this one"—she moved on to the next—"hmmm, let's see. This is my husband, of course, with his brother, Tom; his wife, Alice; Miles Kendall; and Philip Norton, of course. This was at a Brown reunion, I believe. And this next one . . ."

Celeste Hayward's face froze.

"This was . . . oh, some Ambassador, I believe. I don't recall his name." Some dark emotion—a passionate fury—flashed momentarily across her face.

"And the young woman?" Simon asked even as Celeste buried the photo at the bottom of the pile, as if she could not put it aside quickly enough.

"His daughter—the Ambassador's—I believe." Her nostrils flared slightly. "I . . . I don't remember her at all."

She handed the photos back to him and stood in a single motion.

"Now, when will you be meeting with my son?" She took a few steps toward the doorway as if to show him the way out.

"I believe we're on for next Thursday morning." Simon tucked the photos back into the briefcase and snapped the lid, then followed her into the hallway.

"Have you met him before?" The gracious, composed, self-assured woman had already returned, her face once again composed and pleasant.

"I might have met him briefly years ago when I was covering a story at the House." Simon tugged on his overcoat, marveling at her control. "He wouldn't remember, of course. Do you see him often?"

"As often as possible." She nodded. "Gray has a home nearby, so when he and Jen are here in Rhode Island we spend lots of time together. And I do travel to Washington when the weather is kinder on old bones. I don't see Sarah quite as often as I'd like. She used to visit once every month for a weekend with her daughters, but now the girls are getting older, you know. They both have busy schedules of their own I'm afraid. Emily, the older girl, is almost twenty now, and in college. Sometimes it seems only yesterday that Sarah was the one in college. . . ." Her voice trailed off for the briefest of moments. "But that's life, isn't it? Time has such a way of flying right past us when we're not looking."

"Mrs. Hayward, I can't thank you enough for fitting me in. . . ." Simon stood at the front door, preparing to open it.

"Mr. Keller, I love to talk about my family. My husband, in particular." She leaned past him to open the door, then settled back against the wood frame after Simon had stepped past her. "Those days in Washington . . . they seem so long ago." Here she laughed. "Well, yes, of course, they *were* so long ago. So many years since we left. There are some things you never forget."

"Ah, secrets, Mrs. Hayward?"

"Everyone has their secrets, Mr. Keller." She smiled as she closed the door.

Simon rehashed the interview as he drove to the Green Airport to catch his plane back to Philadelphia, where he'd left the Mustang. Mrs. Hayward had appeared to be exactly as she had been in the old television and documentary footage he'd watched over the weekend. Gracious, charming, a hint of humor, obviously well-bred. Obviously devoted to her children and to her late husband's memory. And, all in all, as had her daughter, Celeste had come off as one cool customer.

Especially when confronted with a picture of her husband's mistress. If Simon hadn't been studying Celeste's face carefully, he might have missed the way her eyes had narrowed with hatred. The way her nose had turned up as if in memory of an incredibly offensive odor.

Simon was convinced that the former First Lady had been well aware of her husband's affair with Blythe Pierce and that the years had done little to ease the rage that awareness had evoked.

Even now, almost thirty years later, for just the briefest of moments, Celeste Hayward had looked mad enough to kill.

Chapter Ten

Simon stood in the shelter of a small grove of trees that defined the perimeter of a tiny parking area adjacent to a playground and for a long moment studied the house across the street.

It was a tidy little place, a pristine white Cape Cod with dark green shutters, a small wreath of silk pansies on the front door, which was painted to match the shutters, and the number 218 in black wrought iron affixed to the siding. There was a small porch with two rocking chairs, and narrow wooden boxes under the front windows. Blue hydrangeas were painted on the mailbox that was attached to the wall just next to the front door. At the end of the driveway, a dark green Taurus station wagon—several years old—was parked in front of the one-car garage. The yard was defined by white picket that matched the fence that separated it from the neighbors'. All in all, the house looked homey and comfortable and fit right in with all the other houses on the street in this middle-class neighborhood.

Whatever Jude McDermott did with Blythe Pierce's money, Simon thought, *she sure didn't splurge on a big fancy house.*

Glancing back at the station wagon, he added, *Or on her wheels.*

Modest house, modest car. Simon wondered just what it was that the McDermott woman had spent her $6 or so million on.

"You looking for Jude?"

Simon paused, halfway up the sidewalk. The question came from the opposite side of the fence that separated one tidy house from the other.

"Yes," he replied.

"Won't be back till after five." An elderly woman toddled around from behind a forsythia that was in full bloom. "She's at work."

"Oh." Simon glanced back at the car in the driveway, wondering how the woman had gotten to work if her car was here. If, in fact, that was her car.

"Down to the library," the woman volunteered.

"Oh. Down in town there?" Simon pointed toward the commercial district he'd driven through that morning.

"That's right. Just a block off Main. You a friend?"

"A friend of a friend."

"Well, she's there till five. If you see her, tell her I brought Waylon over for a spell."

"Waylon?"

The woman gestured to a sleepy-eyed basset hound that lounged under a lilac that was just coming into bud.

"Waylon doesn't look too lively this morning," Simon observed.

"Don't let him fool you. He's quick as a whip. When he has a mind to be."

"Thanks for your help," Simon replied, smiling at the improbability—Waylon looked anything but quick—and nodding to the helpful neighbor.

Simon opted to walk the few blocks to the town square, which would allow him an opportunity to check out the neighborhood as well as the town.

Three streets down, a neat wooden sign bearing the painted likeness of a redbrick one-story building pointed east and bore an arrow upon which "LIBRARY" had been scripted. Amazing, Simon noted, how easy it is to find things in a small town.

The weather had turned surprisingly warm, and as he walked along Simon unzipped the leather jacket he had worn over a lightweight sweater. In the jacket pocket was an envelope in which he had placed the photograph he'd lifted from Betsy Pierce's photo album. After today, after he'd chatted with Jude McDermott, he'd pop the picture into the mail and send it back to Betsy with an apology. He'd impulsively pocketed it thinking perhaps Jude might be more inclined to speak with him if he had something he could show to her that would prove he'd been to Betsy's home.

And it had been of enormous value to him yesterday when he'd met with Mrs. Hayward. . . .

The real truth was that he'd hate to part with the picture. There was something about Blythe's face that drew him, again and again. The more he looked at it, the more he began to understand why a man would consider risking everything if only such a woman loved him.

Simon briefly considered what Philip Norton would say when he learned that Simon had expanded his investigation to include the death of Hayward's secret mistress.

He'd deal with that soon enough.

Right now, there were so many pieces of the puzzle still missing. Who else—beside Kendall, Norton, and Celeste Hayward—had known about the President's affair? And why such secrecy, even now? Would this one indiscretion—assuming of course that there had been only this one—have been such a blight on the President's reputation? Though the moral climate of the seventies was certainly not as open as was current, certainly other Presidents—before and after Hayward—had had affairs.

Maybe Blythe's death had nothing to do with her affair with Hayward.

Right. And maybe that car had backed over Blythe by accident.

Maybe, maybe, maybe . . .

The word pounded into his head with every step he took.

The Henderson Public Library was a one-story redbrick Federal-style building with white pillars and shutters that sat on a small rise overlooking a pretty lake. To the right of the building, a fence had been erected to enclose the entirety of the wide slope that led down to the water. The gate was open, and Simon peered in as he passed by.

Beyond the gate, a path of interlocking cobbled stones led down the slope into a garden that was clearly under construction. From the center rose a gazebo, freshly painted if one were to believe the sign that hung from the door. Newly planted flower beds encircled the gazebo, and paths led out like spokes from a wheel. Simon wandered along several of the paths to find that each led to a different patio-type clearing wherein seating had been arranged in a variety of groupings, some containing several benches, others but a solitary chair. Trees had been strategically planted to provide shade to the seating areas, and here and there, throughout the garden, birdhouses sat atop wooden posts. Numerous potted plants appeared to have been set down and left to one side of one path, and several large bags of mulch lay in a heap on the ground. Simon stepped around them and headed back toward the gate just as it swung open.

A young woman struggled with a squeaky wheelbarrow that was piled high with plastic bags that Simon assumed contained more mulch. Simon hurried to the gate to hold it aside for her.

"Here. I'll get that," he said.

"Thanks." The woman pushed the unwieldy load onto the cobbled path.

Simon might have just nodded a friendly, "You're welcome," and continued on to the library that had been his destination. But just at that moment she glanced back over her shoulder and flashed a smile that went all the way to his heart.

There was something about that smile. . . .

When the buzzing in his head began to subside, he followed her halfway down the path, drawn as if on a towline, and asked, "Can I give you a hand?"

She brought the wheelbarrow to a stop in front of the gazebo. "Thanks, but I think I can manage from here." And she rewarded him for his trouble with one more smile.

Simon stood rooted to the spot and took her in.

She was tall and willow slender and wore dusty jeans and a dustier T-shirt, large, round tortoiseshell sunglasses that hid far too much of her face. Her hair was tucked up under a baseball cap, all but one brave dark strand that hung down the side of her face.

With seemingly little effort, she lifted the top bag of mulch and tossed it onto the ground.

"That bag weighs, what, forty pounds?" Simon asked.

"Fifty," she replied as she hoisted another and tossed it to land next to the first.

"You must work out on a pretty regular basis."

"Every day." She grinned and grabbed another bag.

"You lift?" Simon was obviously impressed.

"Constantly." The woman appeared infinitely amused by the question.

"You must spend a lot of time at the gym," Simon observed.

She straightened up, still grinning, and told him, "Gyms are for desk jockeys."

Simon laughed. "I get it. You're the gardener here."

"If you stay in school long enough, they let you call yourself a landscape architect."

"This all looks new." Simon gestured around him.

"It is new. Brand spanking new, every bit of it." She grabbed hold of another bag and lugged it a few feet away before dropping it onto the ground.

"You do all this work yourself?"

"I'm good, but I'm not that good. I had lots of help." She stopped at the back of the wheelbarrow and appeared to be looking him over. "This was a community effort. I did the design, furnished most of the plantings, but just about everyone in town had a part in its creation in one way or another. The gazebo, for example." She stepped back as if to admire the structure. "It was designed by a local contractor, but it was built by the carpentry students at the high school."

She pointed to the stone walks on which they stood. "The stones were donated by a builders supply company and the paths were laid by volunteers."

"I see what you mean by community effort."

"Right down to the bake sales and the flea markets that helped pay for the fencing and the lumber. The people in this town did everything to raise money but put on a show in the barn. When it comes to fund-raising for a good cause, never underestimate small-town USA."

"What's the cause?"

"The garden was intended to celebrate cancer survivors. A place to come and find a few minutes of peace, of inspiration. A place for contemplation. We've planned it as a place where families can gather quietly together."

"Ah, hence the separate rooms." Simon nodded and knew there had been no "we" involved in the planning. He'd have bet his Mustang that she'd designed the entire garden—maybe even proposed the idea—herself.

"Exactly. I—we—thought that there should be places that offered privacy, a little serenity. Often badly needed while doing battle with the disease."

"Sounds as if you've been close to the action."

"My mother is a survivor. It will be five years in May."

"You did this for her." It wasn't a question.

"Watching her struggle made the disease real to me for the first time. Before that, cancer was just an ugly word. My mother's illness certainly did bring me closer to it than I ever wanted to be." She spied a handprint of dirt on her jeans and attempted to brush it away. "But the garden . . . it's really a memorial for an old friend, a high school classmate. She grew up here, came back after college to teach. And she was quite an artist. Everyone in town knew her and liked her. Respected her. This was just a means of honoring her memory."

A teenaged boy appeared at the gate just as Simon was about to comment.

"Over here, Will." She stepped to the path and waved.

The boy, in no apparent hurry, lumbered toward the gazebo.

"You're late, William." The woman made a show of looking at her watch.

"I, um, got tied up at school," the boy mumbled.

"Ummmm, let me guess. The girls' softball team was playing today," she teased, and the boy's face reddened. "Okay, Mulch-boy, you start on that side of the gazebo; I'll take this side. We need to get this done before Saturday."

She pulled a penknife from her pocket and glanced back at Simon, saying, "This stuff is pretty pungent, if you're not used to it."

"I can take a hint." Simon stepped back good-naturedly. "Good luck with your garden. It's going to be beautiful."

"Thank you." She straightened up, both hands on her hips, as if studying him. "Come back and see it when it's done."

"Will I get a private tour?"

"Maybe. If you play your cards right." There was just a hint of tease in her voice.

"Then I just may have to do that." Simon paused at

the gate, reluctant to leave but knowing that he was overstaying his welcome. She had work to do, and he had work of a different sort to tend to. It was best that he get on with it.

"I'll see you around, then." She touched the brim of her baseball cap, flashed that smile again, then turned her attention to the business at hand.

"Count on it," Simon said under his breath, stealing one more backward glance at the woman before heading into the building and the business at hand.

Simon stepped into the cool of the library and wandered the main floor. Stacks of books reached almost to the ceiling, and he scanned the fiction shelves. All the familiar books were there and some he'd read long ago and all but forgotten. Life had held little time for fiction lately, he noted with some regret. These days, his reading consisted more of nonfiction in general and research material in particular. He picked up a copy of Steinbeck's *The Red Pony,* recalling the images the book had inspired when first he'd read it, so many years before.

"Did you want to take that out?" a heavyset woman with short dark hair stopped to ask.

"Ah, no, actually, I was looking for Jude McDermott."

"Oh, she's not here. Is there something I could help you with?"

"Actually, I was hoping to speak with her. I was under the impression she was working today." Peeved, Simon looked around the large room, as if he'd recognize the object of his search.

"Ms. McDermott was here this morning, but she left for a meeting around eleven."

"Will she be in tomorrow?"

"I think tomorrow she goes to Baltimore for a conference. She'll be back on Friday, though. Would you care to leave a message for her at the desk?"

"No, I think I'll just catch up with her at home. Thanks." Simon returned the book to the shelf and paused to look out the window onto the garden. The pretty young landscaper was nowhere in sight.

Simon left by the front door in time to see the lithe figure disappear into the cab of a dark green pickup truck with GARDEN GATES painted on the door. Mentally tucking away the name of the company for possible future reference, Simon watched her drive away, kicking himself for not having asked her name.

On Saturday morning, Simon followed the same road back to Henderson and parked his car in the same spot across from the McDermott house. The green station wagon was in the same place it had been in earlier in the week.

He walked across the street and started up the path.

"You here to see Jude again?" the old woman next door called from her front steps.

"I haven't caught up with her yet." Simon called back as if to an old friend.

"Well, you won't find her here now, either." The woman took the steps gingerly. "She's down at the cancer garden."

"The garden by the library?"

"Right. The one they made for that artist who died last year. You know the one I mean. Did all those pictures of naked ladies on the beach. You know who I mean," the woman insisted. "But you want to hurry, if you're going to make the dedication. It starts at one."

"Aren't you going?" Simon asked, his spirits picking up at the possibility of seeing the pretty dark-haired gardener again.

"Nah. My arthritis is acting up. I'm goin' back inside. This weather is bad for my hip." The woman turned and shuffled back to the house with a wave. "I'll see ya later."

"See ya!" Simon called back to her, a grin on his face.

Simon's step was lively as he headed toward the library, again on foot. *This time I'll introduce myself. I'll ask her name. . . .*

He blended in with the gathering crowd that gravitated toward the library, then passed through the gate, his eyes searching, searching . . .

And found her.

Her face was still obscured by the oversize dark glasses, but her hair hung down past her shoulders in glossy black ringlets. She wore a dress of soft green that followed the curves of her body gently and swung loosely around her calves, and she stood with her hands on her hips, speaking with an eager young man who scribbled down every word she said in a spiral notebook. Amused by the antics of the apparent cub reporter, Simon stepped closer.

". . . and was really going for a space where visitors might find comfort and inspiration. I wanted to create a serene environment where groups or individuals might experience a sense of peace, which is so necessary for a cancer patient." The woman leaned forward slightly as if to better hear the reporter's next question, which Simon couldn't quite hear.

"Well, of course I had planned this as a memorial for

Laura Bannock, who as you know lost her struggle last summer. . . ."

She had taken the young reporter's arm and steered him in the direction of all the things she most wanted him to see, though any fool could tell the poor man was mesmerized by her.

Not that I blame the guy. Simon smiled and watched as she wrapped the young man around her little finger.

"Now, there will be a fountain in the center of the oval and, eventually, a stone bench nearby. We're still soliciting donations; do you think you might be able to fit that into your article somehow?"

Oh, I'd bet the rent on it. Simon chuckled to himself and walked down a grassy slope to the lake, leaving her to her business. For the moment.

There were several small rowboats tied to a narrow wooden dock, but no one seemed interested in taking them out onto the lake. Several wood ducks swam noisily through the reeds that grew at the water's edge, and a small flock of sparrows chirped from a nearby hedge. All in all, it was peaceful enough, certainly, Simon thought as he strolled along, a fitting-enough setting for the memorial to a woman who apparently had been well regarded in the community.

Simon looked back to see that the crowd had started to surround the small gazebo that stood at the farthest edge of the garden. He wandered back up the slope, arriving just as the dark-haired woman began to address the crowd.

"We thank you all for coming. It gives me so much pleasure to see the community so well represented. As a longtime friend of Laura Bannock's, I mourn her, as so many of you do. But I'm so pleased with the manner in which her family chose to celebrate her life. I am so honored to have been asked to design her memorial. This little park, this garden, is a place where we'll all be welcome to take a moment from our day-to-day and just relax and reflect." She held up a pair of scissors with exaggerated blades. "Mrs. Bannock, I think you should cut the ribbon on the gazebo and officially open the garden."

A thin woman with spare features wearing a wide-brimmed hat and a dark blue pantsuit stepped up and accepted the scissors. "I think we should all thank Dina for the lovely garden she designed for us." Mrs. Bannock tucked the scissors under her left arm and led the applause. "You should all know that Dina did all this work for free and donated the plants, too."

Dina. The name rang in Simon's ears. *Her name is Dina.*

More applause.

"She and Polly Valentine, there—Polly, we all thank you and welcome you to the community—and, of course, Jude . . ."

At the sound of the name Simon's head snapped up.

"And the students in the horticulture class from the local high school, who helped plant all of the trees."

The applause spread around him. Simon craned his neck to see if he could tell who was who, but there were too many people gathered around the gazebo. Finally, he tapped the shoulder of a man several feet in front of him and asked, "I'm sorry, I missed the names of the people Mrs. Bannock just thanked. Did you happen to . . ."

Without turning, the man said, "The high school kids who planted the trees."

"Before that. The women she named by *name*."

"Oh, Dina there, in the sunglasses, she designed the garden, and Polly Valentine, she works for Dina. . . ."

"And Jude is . . . ?"

"Oh, she's the little blonde with the short hair there in the white jacket. Jude McDermott. She's our librarian. Right next to her daughter."

"Her daughter?"

"Dina. Dina is Jude's daughter."

The words shot through Simon like a heavy charge of electricity.

He stepped forward just close enough to see Dina flash a wide smile for the local press.

There was something about that smile. . . .

Drawn to her, Simon stepped closer.

And then she took off her sunglasses, and Simon's heart stopped in his chest.

Simon knew that face.

His hand found its way to the inside pocket of his sport jacket, sought the photograph he had tucked away. He slid it from the envelope and held it up, checked to see if his memory was playing tricks on him. But no, the face in the photo was just as he had remembered it.

There was no mistaking what he saw before him but no explanation for it, either.

Dina McDermott was a dead ringer for Blythe Pierce. Right down to her megawatt smile.

Simon sat in his car, across the street and a safe distance from the McDermott house, and tried to make sense of what he'd seen and what he knew.

He'd seen a young woman who looked exactly like a woman who'd been dead for almost thirty years.

Unless her mother, Jude McDermott, was a close relative of the deceased, how could this be?

But if Jude was related to the Pierces, wouldn't Betsy Pierce, who seemed to be so open and forthcoming, have referred to Jude as such, instead of merely as her sister's college roommate?

The only logical explanation was even too farfetched for Simon to consider.

The front door of the McDermott house opened, and the tall, graceful young woman stepped out, accompanied by the basset hound. The pair set out on a walk that brought them past Simon's car on the opposite side of the street. He decided to take the direct approach, but by the time he got out of the car Dina and the dog had stopped to speak with a neighbor and hadn't seemed to notice him at all. Simon leaned against the car, considering his options.

He could follow her and try to engage her in conversation. Or he could walk across the street and ring the doorbell. Daughter was oh, so appealing, but it was Mom he was here to see. And besides, sooner or later Dina would finish walking the dog and return.

Following his head rather than his heart, Simon crossed the street and walked up to the front door. Inside his busy brain there were countless questions crashing into one another with far too many intriguing possibilities. Only Jude McDermott could separate fact from fiction. Whether or not she would do so remained to be seen.

He was still working on his opening line when the

door opened and he stood face-to-face with the woman he'd come to see.

"Mrs. McDermott, my name is Simon Keller. I'm a writer, working on a new book about former President Graham Hayward, and I was hoping for a few minutes of your time."

"I . . . I never met the man. I'm afraid there's nothing I could tell you." Jude McDermott's pretty face faded to chalk white in a heartbeat as she froze in the doorway.

Interesting reaction.

"I understand you had a mutual friend."

"You've been given bad information." She recovered, stepped back, and attempted to close the door.

Simon's foot, wedged into the narrow opening, stopped her.

"Please go away, Mr. . . . whatever you said your name was. I know nothing about Graham Hayward." She pushed against the door, but Simon would not budge.

"Betsy Pierce told me otherwise," he said softly.

The words hit the woman much like a quick blow to the abdomen. She all but doubled over with the force. Her eyes were wide with what could only be described as terror.

"What exactly did Betsy tell you?"

"She said that you and her sister, Blythe, were best friends. That you might have known who Blythe's friends were, who she dated, while she lived in Washington."

"I never visited Blythe in Washington." Jude raised a hand to her forehead, as if confused. "What is the purpose of this?"

"I'm sorry, I suppose I wasn't very clear." Simon gave her his gentlest smile, hoping to put her at ease, though fearing he was already too late. "I'm writing a biography of the late President. In doing some research, I've come across some old White House social records. I thought it might be interesting to include in my book something about some of the people who were frequent guests at the White House during the Hayward administration. Blythe Pierce's name occurred frequently. I thought I'd find out a little about her, along with some others, as little anecdotes for the book."

"Oh. . . ." Still leery, still flustered, Jude appeared to be trying to decide on her best course of action.

"Look, I've upset you. I sure didn't mean to. I know that you and Blythe were friends, so I can understand how someone showing up on your doorstep asking about her so long after her death could be upsetting. Would another time be more convenient?"

"No, no. . . ."

"Because if you'd rather I came back, that would be fine. I just had a few questions I wanted to ask about her."

"Ask them now. I'll see if I can answer them," Jude responded at length, not moving from her place at the door.

"I was wondering what you knew about her relationship with Miles Kendall."

"I think I may have met him once. I understand he had a thing for Blythe."

"Where did you meet him?"

"What?"

"You said you never visited Blythe in Washington, but that you'd met Kendall once." Simon shoved his hands in his pants pockets and tried not to look threatening. He wished he'd brought his little tape recorder with him. "I was just curious where you met him."

"I . . . don't remember." Jude averted her eyes.

"You've met so many important people in your life that you don't recall where you met a White House Chief of Staff who was in love with your best friend?"

"I don't think I want to talk to you after all, Mr. . . ." She waved an impatient hand. "Blythe has been dead for almost thirty years. Let's permit her to rest in peace, shall we?"

"Do you suppose that the victim of an unsolved murder can ever rest in peace, Mrs. McDermott?"

"I suppose hit-and-run constitutes murder," she countered.

"It does when the victim was run over twice by the same vehicle."

"Who told you that?" Her eyes bore into him.

Jude's focus on Simon had been so complete that she'd neglected to notice that Dina was heading up the walk with the dog until they were a mere ten feet away. Simon sensed the sudden alarm—the *panic*—in Jude's eyes and turned.

"Hey, you did come back." Dina smiled up at him, clearly pleased. "I thought that was you at the park. I looked for you after we finished with the photos, but you'd gone. Then I wasn't sure that you'd been there at all."

"You appeared to be busy with all your admirers. I didn't want to be in your way." The buzzing was back. It filled his head and clouded his vision.

"You wouldn't have been in the way." Dina turned to

her mother. "Mom, shame on you, holding court on the front porch. What will the neighbors say?"

The gentle beauty of her face took his breath away. He tried really hard to come up with something clever to say but could not.

Jude, too, appeared to have been struck dumb.

"What's up, you two?" Dina's eyes narrowed. "Mom, is something wrong?"

"No, no, sweetheart. I was just chatting with Mr. . . ."

"Keller. Simon Keller." He reached a hand to Dina instinctively, grasped her smaller hand with his own.

"I'm Dina McDermott."

Of Blythe Pierce, Miles Kendall had said, she could light up a room just by walking into it. The same could be said of the young woman who stood before Simon at that moment.

She dazzled the eye. It was as simple as that.

"It's good to put a name with the face." Dina unhooked the leash from the dog's collar, and the dog immediately climbed the steps to sniff at Simon's leg. "I didn't know you knew my mom."

"Actually, I'm writing a book and happened to come across the name of someone who, it turns out, was an old friend of your mother's."

"What's the book about?"

"Former President Hayward."

"Mom, you had a friend who knew a President? You've been holding out on me! Who was this friend?"

"Her name was Blythe Pierce," Jude said tersely.

"What was her relationship with the former President?" Dina asked as she stepped past Simon to enter the house. A soft wake of fragrance trailed behind her, just enough to tease Simon's senses and send a wave of tension running through him.

"She had no relationship with him." Jude's response came just a few beats too quickly. "She dated his Chief of Staff for a time, that's all."

"She apparently attended a lot of events at the White House with Hayward's Chief of Staff," Simon added, sensing Jude's unease. "Her name came up on a lot of White House records—dinner parties, dances, special events—and I just became a bit curious about her."

"Wow, I'll bet she has some stories to tell." Dina raised an eyebrow. "Mom, are you going to make Mr. Keller conduct his entire interview on the front porch?"

"Well, I thought he was almost—"

"Simon." He looked past the mother to the daughter. "Please call me Simon."

"Simon, can I offer you an iced tea, since my mother appears to have forgotten her manners?"

"That would be very nice." Simon smiled. "Thank you."

"Mom, you take Simon into the living room and I'll get his drink. What can I get for you?"

"Nothing," Jude replied roughly.

The younger woman held the door open for Simon while the older woman stood as if rooted to her spot.

"Mom, are you all right?" Dina asked.

"Yes, yes. I'm fine. I have a bit of a headache. . . ."

"Then I won't take much more of your time," Simon promised.

"I'll bring you some aspirin," Dina told her, then to

Simon said, "Please. Sit and chat with my mother. I'll be right back."

Simon stood in the doorway of the living room, waiting for Jude to react.

Finally, he reached out to take her arm. "Mrs. McDermott, would you like to sit down?"

"I'd really like you to leave," she whispered, shaking off his hand.

"I promise I won't stay long. There are just a few questions I need to ask." Simon went to the sofa and sat down. The basset followed. Simon dropped a hand down to rub behind the dog's ears, and the dog fell at his feet, contented and unaware of his mistress's inner turmoil.

The phone rang and was answered somewhere in the house on the second ring. A minute later, Dina came into the living room carrying a tray with two glasses and set it on the table that stood between her mother's chair and the sofa. She offered Simon his glass, then handed her mother a glass of water.

"Here, Mom, here's some aspirin." Dina dropped two white tablets in the palm of her mother's hand. "That was Polly on the phone. She's locked herself out of the greenhouse. I'm going to have to run."

Simon started to stand up, his good manners inbred.

"No, please, stay seated," Dina said, then turned to her mother. "I'll call you later. I want to hear all about this mysterious friend of yours."

"I'm sorry you have to leave." Simon found himself standing anyway.

"I'm sorry, too." She looked as if she meant it. "Make sure we know when your book comes out, so Mom can get lots of copies for the library. I'll definitely want to read it. Maybe I could get an autographed copy."

"I'll be happy to personally bring you one."

"Can I count on that?" She smiled, and her eyes held him spellbound.

"You betcha."

She turned and disappeared through the front door before Simon could react.

"She's beautiful, Mrs. McDermott," Simon said softly.

"Leave her alone," Jude growled, obviously not pleased by the interplay between her daughter and her visitor.

"I was asking about Blythe," Simon reminded her.

"What is it you want to know?" she asked coolly.

"I want to know about her relationship with President Hayward."

"I don't know what you're talking about."

"I think you do. I think you know everything about it."

The silence between them stretched wide before being filled by the sound of the dog scratching behind his ear and a clock on the mantel ticking.

"I think I would like you to leave." Jude stood up, her back ramrod straight, her face grimly resolved.

"Mrs. McDermott, I found you. Very easily, I might add, once I knew who to look for." Simon remained seated. "How long before someone else finds you, too?"

"I can't imagine what Betsy was thinking." Jude's eyes filled with tears.

"I've been asking myself the same thing." Simon removed the envelope from his pocket and took out the photograph of Blythe that he'd taken from the Pierce home, then placed it on the table between them.

Jude turned from it as if she could not bear to look upon the face. "Please leave, Mr. Keller."

"Mrs. McDermott, how do you explain the fact that your 'daughter' looks like a clone of your best friend? Your friend who has been dead for almost thirty years. And your daughter is how old?"

Jude went to the front door and opened it. "Please leave now."

Simon stood and leaned over to pick up the photograph but made no move to the door.

"What is it that you want from me?" Her eyes pleaded in a way that words could not, her fear strong enough that it reached toward Simon from across the room. "Are you blackmailing me?"

"No, no, of course not," he tried to reassure her. "I just want the truth, Mrs. McDermott. I'm only looking for the truth."

She merely shook her head and gestured for him to leave.

"Does she know?" Simon asked. He took a card bearing his name and phone number and placed it on a table near the door.

Jude turned her head away.

"Please . . ." Jude pleaded as she opened the door.

"Does she know that her birth mother died when she was just a baby?" Simon whispered, sympathy welling in him for the woman in spite of his compulsion to search out the story. "That she was deliberately run down on a city street and that the police made little more than a cursory effort to find the car that killed her?"

Jude stood silent.

"Or that her father was a former President of the United States?" The random, impossible thought that had been lurking in the far recesses of his mind slid from his lips before he even had time to examine it.

The stricken look of sheer terror on Jude's face told Simon all he needed to know.

Simon stepped through the open door and paused on the top step. "Who does she think her father is, Mrs. McDermott?"

Jude reached out and with one hand slammed the door in his face.

Chapter Eleven

Simon watched Miles Kendall take bites out of the small chocolate-covered mint patty, one of several Simon had stopped to pick up on his way to St. Margaret's. When the chewing had ceased, Simon settled against the hard wooden back of the chair and studied the face of the old man before him. He seemed quite cheerful and alert. His eyes were clear and bright. It looked like he might have found Miles on a good day. He could only hope.

"Miles, can we talk about Blythe?" Simon asked. "Do you remember Blythe?"

Kendall nodded slowly. "She had lavender eyes."

"Yes, I know." Simon nodded and thought of Dina.

Simon's hand slipped into his pocket and switched on the recorder. "Miles, can we talk about Blythe's death? Do you remember when she died?"

Kendall stared straight ahead, and for a moment Simon thought he'd lost him.

Then the old man spoke, his voice barely a whisper: "She'd only been back for a few days. Less than a week."

"Where had she been, Miles? Do you remember?"

"Where her friend was."

"Who was her friend?"

"Jude. Blythe left the baby with her, and came back."

"Blythe left the baby with Jude?"

Miles nodded.

"How do you know about the baby, Miles?"

"I saw her." Kendall looked up, a tiny smile on his lips.

"You saw Blythe after she had the baby?"

"I saw the baby. She was just . . . perfect. Perfect, just like her mother. Dark straight hair, big round eyes. Just as beautiful as her mother. He wept when I told him about her."

"By 'he' who do you mean, Miles? Who wept when you told him that you saw Blythe's baby?" Supposition wasn't enough. Miles had to say the name.

"Graham."

"Was it Graham's baby, Miles?"

"Oh, yes. Graham's and Blythe's."

Bingo.

"And did Graham go to see the baby with you?" Simon willed his pulse to remain steady. There was much more ground to be covered. The story was far from complete.

"No, no, he couldn't do that. That's why I went. To make sure she was all right. That everything was all right."

"And was everything all right?"

"As long as she stayed there, it was. But as soon as she came back . . ." Kendall's eyes closed tightly and his hands began to shake. "She wasn't supposed to come back. I never counted on her ever coming back. I never thought she would be in such danger. . . ."

"What happened when she came back? Who was the danger, Miles?"

"She begged me to bring her to the party. I didn't

want to do it. I didn't want her there. It was not a good idea. I told her, 'Blythe, you don't understand how it is now.' But she was insistent. She promised she would never ask me again. 'Just this one last time, and then I'm leaving and I won't be back,' she said. 'Just this one last time.' "

Miles was openly weeping. "He talked about getting a divorce, about divorcing Celeste and marrying Blythe. About not running for a second term—"

"What?!" Simon exclaimed. "What did you say?"

"—but she wanted him to. Thought it was his duty. She could take care of the baby, raise her, until he was finished. He was too good a President, she said. The country needed him. But then he would marry her."

"Graham Hayward considered *not running for a second term*?" Simon whispered the words aloud, incredulous. This sure hadn't shown up in any of the material provided by Philip Norton.

Simon wondered if Norton knew. . . .

"She had orchids in her hair that night." Miles was rambling now. "And she wore her lavender gown."

Oblivious to his tears, Miles shook his head slowly. "I took her home that night. It shouldn't have happened. I never thought anything like that would happen. It wasn't supposed to be like that. . . ."

"Miles, this is important." Simon leaned closer and lowered his voice. "Who else knew about the baby?"

"I didn't tell about the baby. Not ever," Miles protested. "I never told. . . ."

"Who else might have known? Who else would Hayward have confided in?" Simon wondered aloud. "Who else knew about Blythe? Who knew about the baby?"

But the veil was descending, and Miles Kendall began to slip back into a place where no one could follow.

"Just like that." Kendall turned slowly to the window, a look of bewilderment crossing his face. "Just like that, she was gone. It shouldn't have happened like that. It wasn't supposed to happen like that. . . ."

All the way back to Arlington, Simon tried to digest the dramatic information that Miles Kendall had shared, wondering how much the man's memory could be trusted.

If what Kendall had said was true, Graham Hayward might have served only one term, not two. He'd have left Celeste for Blythe. He'd have acknowledged his child.

Someone very obviously had not wanted any of that to happen. And Miles, Simon was beginning to realize, knew who that someone was.

Had Miles kept that secret all these years?

And who else, Simon wondered, had Graham told about the child he had had with his would-be bride, about his plans for a happily ever after that had nothing to do with the wife and children he already had?

The orderly took his time walking from the bus stop to the dirt path that led down to the parking lot. It wouldn't be long, he figured, before he had the keys to that sweet Camaro in his pocket, so every day now he scouted the lot for the primo parking spots. Not too close to the trees, lest a storm bring down a branch, but not too far out into the open, either. The hot sun could do a number on that excellent paint job.

He passed through the front door and into the lobby,

as usual, smiling at the new nurse's aide who worked the second shift, the redhead with the long legs and tight sweater under the jacket of her uniform. And as usual, she pretended not to notice him. Today it didn't bother him so much, though. He figured she'd be smiling back soon enough, once she got a look at what he'd be driving before the month was out.

He stopped to take a glance at the visitors' log, as he'd gotten into the habit of doing. There'd been no activity in a while, but since he was being paid to look—and since he didn't want to be reminded again that he was being paid to look—he looked. He almost missed it, because there'd been that one hundredth birthday party for Mr. Harris today and all of his children and grandchildren—all thirty-two of them—had shown up for the luncheon and signed in. But there it was, right after the last of the Harrises.

S. Keller to see Mr. Kendall. In at 1:25. Out at 3:00 on the nose.

He didn't bother to wait for his break but went directly to the locker room and dialed the number.

"Hello?"

"Your friend's visitor was back today."

"Keller?"

"Yes. He signed in around one-thirty, out at three."

"What kind of a day is our Mr. Kendall having?"

"I don't know. I figured you'd want to know right away, so I haven't seen him yet."

The pause was long and somber.

"Want me to go in and talk to him, then call you back?"

"No. I'll come see for myself. I'll be there around eight. You'll watch for me at the side door?"

"You got it."

"Have him in his room before I get there."

"Sure, fine. Okay," the orderly replied, even as the line went dead.

He whistled on his way back to the nurses' station to see what was happening on the floor that day, mentally jingling those car keys as he went.

The visitor was there, at the side door, at eight sharp. It was already dark, and the figure slid into the dim shadows of the dayroom like a wraith. Barely acknowledging the orderly, the visitor followed the short hallway to Kendall's room, nodding to the few sleepy residents who lingered here and there in the corridor, none of whom, by tomorrow morning, would recall that Miles Kendall had had a visitor this night.

"Don't get lost," the visitor told the orderly before closing Kendall's door. "I'll need you to let me out."

"I'll be around," the orderly promised, then went to make himself useful in the room across the hall.

Miles Kendall sat on the edge of his bed gazing out the window at the dark beyond. Somewhere out there, he was thinking, was a river. On warm nights like this, with the window open, he could smell it.

"Hello, Miles." The visitor sat on a nearby chair.

"Hello." Kendall nodded warily. His eyes flickered, narrowing with recognition.

"Do you remember me?"

Kendall stared for a long time but didn't respond.

"I hear you had company today."

"I did."

"What did you talk about?"

"I don't think I remember."

"Think harder."

"Ummm . . . I think . . . Washington." His chin went up a notch. "I worked at the White House."

"What did you do there?"

"I worked with the President."

"Yes, you did. He was your friend, once upon a time, wasn't he?" The visitor leaned forward. "And I guess being the President's friend, you know a lot of things, Miles. I'll bet you know a lot of secrets."

Miles continued to sit stiffly.

"Did you tell your company—Mr. Keller—any secrets today, Miles?"

"I don't remember," he answered, a bit too quickly perhaps.

"What did you talk about today with Mr. Keller?"

"He brought me mints. Flat mints with chocolate on them."

"That was very nice of him, Miles. Did you tell him secrets after he gave you your mints?"

"I don't remember."

"Did you tell him about Blythe, Miles?"

"Maybe we talked about Blythe," Kendall acknowledged, then leaned forward to ensure the impact of his words. "Maybe we talked about the baby."

"What baby?" The visitor's head snapped up.

"Blythe's baby." Kendall sat back, watching the effect of his words.

"Blythe's baby . . ." The visitor's eyes were wide, the voice almost a hiss. "Blythe's *baby*?"

Kendall nodded.

"Where? Where was the baby?"

"I don't remember."

"Was it your baby?"

"Of course not." He waited for the question to come, knowing that it would.

"Whose baby, old man? *Whose baby?*" The hand grasped Miles's arm tightly, but in spite of the pain, he smiled.

"Graham's baby, of course." He spoke the words knowing what their effect would be, wanting, after all these years, to watch, wanting to see the confusion, the disbelief. Wanting to see pain . . .

"Graham's baby . . ." This hitherto-unknown piece of the puzzle hit like a shot and shattered into a million pieces.

"A girl. A beautiful girl." He might have told how he'd held the child many times and wished with all his heart that the child had been his, how fiercely he'd fought against the envy that had, in the end, consumed him and coaxed him to do something for which he'd never forgiven himself, something he'd spent a lifetime trying to forget.

But tonight Miles Kendall was tired of fighting the past. Tonight was a night for regretting words he never should have spoken, secrets he never should have shared. Tonight the guilt he'd harbored for almost thirty years surfaced with startling energy and shook him to his soul. At the same time, it made him strong. Strong enough to mourn the woman he'd once loved, the friendship he'd betrayed.

Strong enough for vengeance.

"What do you know, old man?" Patience began to draw thin.

"I know you," he said with certainty.

"Do you now?" A wicked smile. "How unfortunate . . ."

"Yes. I know you."

"Why did you keep this to yourself all these years, old man? *Why didn't you tell me about this baby?*" Anger rippled along every nerve; rage built with every heartbeat.

"Because I knew what you'd do to her." He leaned forward, his voice sure. "I couldn't let you hurt her. I owed him that much."

A snort of derision. "You have an odd way of repaying your friends, old man. Now tell me, who else knows?"

"I'm not going to tell you." He spoke defiantly.

"Where is she?" The face loomed close, the voice a hiss. "Tell me where she is. I'm not going to ask you again, Miles."

Miles shook his head slowly. "No."

Standing now, the visitor reached into a deep pocket and removed a leather pouch from which a long needle was extracted with anxious hands. The tip was plunged brusquely into the folds of the old man's neck before he could protest. Miles winced at the force, but he did not blink.

For a very long moment, he stared into the blank eyes of his killer.

Waiting for me to die, Miles told himself. He tried to speak, but his mouth wouldn't work. Just as well, he thought. He'd waited long enough to atone for his sins. Now was as good a time as any. . . .

When his head fell forward, the visitor pushed a firm finger into the old man's chest to help direct his body backward onto the bed.

Content in the knowledge that the old man would not be telling anyone else about Blythe or her baby, the visitor stepped into the hallway and waited for the orderly.

"All done for tonight?" the orderly asked.

"Oh, yes. I'm quite finished."

"This way, then."

The orderly led the visitor through the quiet hallway to the back door he'd opened earlier. The visitor stepped through it, then turned to hand the orderly an unusually fat envelope.

Without either a word or a backward glance, the visitor stepped through the door and disappeared into the night.

Chapter Twelve

Simon stood on a rise overlooking the cemetery and watched the dignitaries gather near the open grave.

The news that Miles Kendall had died quietly in his sleep just hours after Simon himself had left St. Margaret's had given him a serious jolt. While a check with June at St. Margaret's assured him that Kendall had serious heart disease that could have taken him at any time, still Simon could not help but marvel at the timing. Had he waited even one more day to visit Kendall, he'd never have discovered that Graham had acknowledged that he was in fact the father of Blythe's child. Or how Graham had flirted with the possibility of redirecting his future to be with the woman he loved.

How close had Simon come to not hearing this story at all?

The near miss—the *coincidence*—had raised gooseflesh on Simon's arms and on the back of his neck. As a reporter, he'd found there were so few true coincidences in life. That nagging little voice inside kept suggesting that this may not be one of them.

It was time for a little chat with Philip Norton.

Simon started down the grassy slope, staying slightly

to the left to better position himself where he could observe without being observed. He couldn't hear much of what the young minister was saying, so far back behind the group, but had a pretty good view of the mourners. Simon had expected a smaller crowd and found himself pleased that so many people had remembered the old man. Several older members of Congress and a number of senior diplomats took up the first several rows of chairs. The Haywards, he noted, sat in the very front row with a man who appeared to be in his forties and who was accompanied by a woman of roughly the same age and three children somewhere between the ages of eight and sixteen. Kendall's nephew and his family, Simon assumed.

The graveside service had been succinct, and before Simon knew it the group in the front row had stepped forward to file past the grave, each dropping a single rose onto the coffin. The gesture was repeated by those in the subsequent rows until all had passed the grave and all the roses had been put in place.

The Hayward family—Celeste, Graham and his wife, Sarah and her husband—stopped to chat several times with this one or that while en route to their waiting limousine. Simon had felt no urge to step forward and speak to them or to otherwise make his presence known, though he wasn't exactly sure why, other than the feeling he had of being an outsider on that day. The only person he really wanted to speak with was somewhere in the small mix to his left, and Simon did not want to lose sight of him.

He caught up with Philip Norton just as the former professor neared his car.

"Philip!" Simon called to him.

The man turned at the sound of his name, then smiled when he saw Simon approaching.

"Simon! I wasn't aware that you were here. I didn't know that you knew Miles."

"I had several meetings with him."

"I see." Norton's eyes narrowed slightly. "I've been trying to get in touch with you for the past week. Haven't you been checking your answering machine?"

"I've been busy."

"So I've heard."

"Actually, I'd been to see Miles Kendall on more than one occasion." Simon stuck his hands in his pockets. "And that's what I wanted to talk to you about. If you have a few minutes. It's pretty important."

"Now?" Norton's hand held the car key and poised over the lock, ready to open the car.

"Right now."

"Would you like to go someplace and chat over lunch . . . ?"

"No, I'd just as soon do it here."

"Oh, certainly. Of course."

They walked back up the hill where a line of tall stone angels kept watch.

"I spent several hours with Miles Kendall on Monday afternoon," Simon told him.

"This past Monday?" Norton's eyebrows rose in surprise.

"Yes. Just hours before he died, I sat with him and we talked for quite some time. He was alert and in good spirits when I arrived, though I have to say that he seemed upset, almost depressed, when I left. And then, just a few short hours later, he was dead." Simon paused, then asked, "Some coincidence, eh?"

"You know how I feel about coincidences."

"Yes. And I agree. Especially after hearing what Kendall had remembered about his White House days."

"Which was . . . ?"

"He talked a lot about a woman he had been in love with years ago. A woman named Blythe Pierce." Simon glanced sideways from the corners of his eyes to see if Norton reacted in any way. He did not. "It wasn't the first time he'd mentioned her, by the way."

"And . . . ?" Norton gestured for Simon to get to the point.

"And he claims that Graham Hayward was in love with her as well." Simon stopped. He had to ask. The time for assumptions had passed. "Did you know this woman, Philip? Did you know Blythe Pierce?"

Norton's eyes flickered to Simon's face and away again, and Simon knew at that moment that regardless of what Norton might say, he had damned well known Blythe Pierce.

"Well," Norton laughed uneasily, "this is all certainly out of the blue."

"You knew her."

"Yes, I knew her." Norton nodded. "I think it's safe to say that back then everyone who was anyone in D.C. knew Blythe. She was young and lovely, but there were a lot of lovely young women in the capital in those days."

"What set her apart?"

"What set Blythe apart from all the others . . . ?" He seemed to consider the question. "It's hard to define. She came from a wealthy background—daughter of a diplomat, heiress to a fortune. She was accustomed to moving among the rich and powerful. The climate in the capital suited her. She was well educated. Best schools, all that. But again, D.C. was filled with such women. Blythe was just a little *more* than all the others—more intelligent, more poised, more intuitive, more knowledgeable, more fun, more beautiful. People sought her out. That combination of looks, good breeding, intelligence, and her genuine warmth drew people to her."

"Was the President one of those people?"

Norton visibly tensed.

"According to Kendall," Simon continued, not bothering to wait for a response, "not only was Hayward in love with her, he had a child with her and was seriously considering—"

"Miles Kendall was a rambling old man—"

"—seriously considering not running for a second term so that he could divorce his wife and marry Blythe." Simon spoke softly as if fearful that somehow his words would be carried on the wind and overheard, even though he and Norton appeared to be the last of the mourners.

"Someone believed it, Philip. I think someone believed it, and killed her because of it. But you know that, don't you? That the accident that killed Blythe was no accident? That the car that ran over Blythe did so twice?"

"Simon, do you have any idea of what you're . . ." Norton had visibly paled.

"Oh, but there's more. I found the child."

Norton turned slowly toward Simon, his eyes cautious. "What?" he asked, quiet disbelief spreading over his face like a shadow.

"I found Blythe Pierce's child."

The statement hung in the air between them.

"You found . . ."

"Blythe Pierce's child, yes," Simon repeated meaningfully. "And the interesting thing is, she doesn't know about Hayward. She doesn't even know about Blythe."

"Then for God's sake, Simon, leave it alone." There was desperation in Norton's grasp when his hand closed over Simon's arm.

"I can't leave it alone. Aside from the fact that this is the biggest story that I may ever uncover, think about the implications. Graham Hayward has been held up before the American people—and all subsequent Presidents—as an icon of morality. What hypocrisy—that a man who preached honesty yet had a young mistress and an illegitimate child is still being touted as the standard of morality for his time. And then let's talk about how Blythe died. Let's talk about the fact that the person who ran Blythe down has never been identified. That someone somehow managed to stop the investigation of the accident dead in the water. How do you suppose that happened? Now, let's not forget that this woman was the daughter of an Ambassador, yet even he didn't have the clout to keep that investigation going. So who do you suppose would have been powerful enough to have done that?"

When Norton attempted to step away, Simon grabbed his arm and held it. "That's the real story here, isn't it? That the murder of the President's young mistress—the mother of his illegitimate child—was covered up and that that cover-up came from the highest level of our government. That's the story, Philip."

"Simon, there is so much that you don't understand. . . ."

"Enlighten me."

"I can't do that."

"Then I have to believe that you had a part in covering up Blythe Pierce's death. And that makes me wonder if the person you were covering for was the President himself. An older man, a beautiful young woman—"

"Dear God, Simon, that's preposterous."

"—an affair, a child he might not have wanted. . ."

"Whatever else you believe, believe that Graham Hayward loved Blythe Pierce with all his heart."

"Believe it because you say it's true? Your credibility isn't quite what it used to be, Philip."

"Simon, you have no facts—nothing even to prove that this girl is in fact Hayward's daughter. No proof, even, of the affair. All you have are the ramblings of an old man whose memory came and went from one day to the next. And that man is no longer with us, Simon. So even if you decided to try to print this story of yours, without corroboration it's your word against history."

"Maybe no one would believe me." Simon shrugged. "But since every word that Kendall had to say about the matter is on tape—"

"What?!"

"—you might be able to discredit me, but you won't be able to argue that the story came from anyone other than Miles Kendall. And incidentally, Miles knew who killed Blythe. I'm utterly convinced of it."

Norton ran his fingers through his hair, as if frustrated. "Did he say who it was?"

"No. By the time I began to suspect that he knew, he had slipped away again, and I wasn't able to question him further. But someone knew I was there that day, knew that I'd spoken with Miles, and, I strongly suspect, killed him for what he might have told me. I've gone back to St. Margaret's, I've checked the visitors' log, but no one else signed in to see him on Monday other than me. As I said, some coincidence."

"Simon, destroy the tape, and walk away from the story."

"I can't do that."

"Please. You don't know what you're dealing with."

"I know exactly what I'm dealing with. I'm dealing with the biggest story of my career. A story you did your damnedest to hide."

"Simon, you don't understand. For the sake of the girl, leave it alone." Norton backed away from Simon.

"You tried to manipulate me, Philip. If I hadn't been so flattered that you'd be interested in my own book, I might have given more thought to the reason that you sought out me for this job." Simon kept his voice level, in spite of his bitterness. "You never expected me to do much more than scratch the surface, did you? You figured I'd rush through this book to get to the carrot you were dangling in front of me. Your promise to publish *Lethal Deceptions* after the Hayward book was finished would have been incentive enough. Were you counting on me to simply use the materials you sent me for background, do a few cursory interviews, put the book together, hand it in, and get on with my own agenda?"

Norton appeared to want to speak, but no words came forth.

"I trusted you. I've respected and admired you for years. How could you have set me up like this?"

"Simon, I admit that I was not totally honest with you. I did not give you all the facts." Norton met Simon's eyes and sighed heavily. "But it is true that there was an interest in a new Hayward biography. I wanted to be the one to do the book—"

"So that you could handpick the biographer and could control the content."

"Yes. No. You simply do not understand the situation."

"I think I understand plenty. I'll be writing the book, Philip, but it isn't going to be the one you were expecting."

"Simon, don't do this. People will be caught up in this who don't deserve what will inevitably happen if this is made public."

"This is the biggest story that will ever come my way. I can't think of one good reason to turn my back on it. Even if you refuse to publish it, I'm betting that someone else will."

"I admit that I wanted you—specifically you—to write this book. Yes, I thought you'd do a good job; you're a good writer—"

"Don't flatter me now."

"—but yes, there was more to the motive, though not exactly what you think." Norton suddenly looked weary. "I did think there was a chance—a small chance—that someone might stumble onto the story about Blythe. A smaller chance still that Blythe's daughter might be discovered. I believed, however, that if you were the one to find her, you'd come to me with the information."

"So that you could talk me out of using the story and Saint Graham's secret would be safe."

"No, not to protect his reputation." Norton shook his head slowly. "To protect the *girl*. Simon, there's so much more that you don't know."

"Well, don't worry. I'll find out what that *more* is."

"Have you stopped to think what *good* it would do to make this public? Have you thought about the people involved and what might happen to them? You've already said that the girl has no idea of who she is. Think about the girl, Simon. Think about what could happen to her."

"I have thought about the girl. And the girl has a name, Philip. It's Dina. And she's a grown woman." For a split second Simon felt protective of her, before he realized that the one she needed protection against could well be him. He pushed the thought aside. "Don't you think she deserves to know who she is?"

"It's much more complicated than merely a matter of who she is."

Norton turned abruptly and headed back down the hill, turning once to look back at Simon and say, "I wanted you to be the one to do the book because I believed that should your efforts lead to the girl, you would have the maturity, the wisdom, to understand that sometimes something is more important than the story and your personal gain. I can see I overestimated you."

"You haven't given me a good-enough reason to let it go, Philip. Unless you can tell me who killed Blythe . . ." Simon waited for Norton's response.

"I can't tell you what I don't know."

"Well then. I'll do my job, and you'll continue to do yours." Simon ignored the stab of regret he felt at that moment. He'd admired this man, cared about him. Trusted him. "And for the record, you were the one who taught me that nothing—ever—was more important than the story."

"Perhaps I was mistaken."

Simon stood on the crest of the hill and watched Norton disappear behind a small grove of trees. He felt none of the satisfaction he'd thought he'd feel once he confronted Norton. He'd expected the man to admit to having attempted to manipulate Simon once the facts had been thrown in his face, but he hadn't expected Norton to appear offended by Simon's accusations. And Norton had definitely appeared offended. Offended and a bit frustrated—and worried.

The wind kicked up again, sending chilled fingers to prod through Simon's jacket, but he was rooted to the spot where he stood and tried to sort through it all. It was so unlike Philip Norton to hide the truth. Any truth.

It was one thing for Norton to be willing to overlook the fact that the sainted Hayward had in fact been a philandering husband who had left his mistress with a child, but there was still the fact that Blythe's death had been swept under someone's carpet for almost thirty years. Did Norton know whose? Or was it Norton's own?

Whom was he protecting?

What good would it do for the story to break, Norton had asked. What would be the effect on the people most closely involved in this?

What, Simon had to wonder, was really at stake here?

Think about the girl . . .

Norton's words echoed in Simon's ears throughout the night. Simon turned over yet again, punched his fist into his pillow, and pulled up the light blanket.

As if Simon hadn't been thinking about the girl, ever since he'd first seen her pushing an overloaded wheelbarrow through the gate at the garden she'd planned in memory of her friend. Even before she removed her glasses and he'd seen her face—before he had any idea of who she was—he'd been drawn to her.

Think about the girl . . .

Simon fell asleep doing just that.

And awoke sometime later, covered with sweat, the sheets twisted in his hands and a hole the size of Delaware in his gut. For a moment he felt disoriented, adrift, as one sometimes does when awakened from a nightmare, unsure of which world is illusion and which is reality.

He sat back against the headboard, his heart still pounding, and closed his eyes. It had been so real. . . .

It was dark and the woman was crossing the street, calling his name. There was a street lamp, but the light was too dim to see her face. Then the car came, traveling faster, faster. The woman had her back to the car, her hands cupped at her mouth, calling to him. As the car slammed into her body and drove it forward, she screamed his name.

Simon!

The sound of it had jolted him from his sleep.

He pushed the sheet aside and stood, walked to the

window, where he raised the sash to let the cold night air wash over his naked body. His breath still ragged, he leaned on the sill and stared out at the crescent moon, trying to convince himself that it was only because of his conversation that day with Norton that he'd had such a dream.

Think about what could happen to her.

In the dream the woman had been caught in the headlights of the speeding car. He'd seen her face, eyes widened in terror, her hair a dark tangled halo, as she had turned to him, pleading for help. There was no question whose face he'd seen, whose screams still rang in his ears.

Think about the girl. . . .

I do. Simon gazed out onto the night.

All the time . . .

Chapter Thirteen

The figure stood at the edge of the cliff and looked down into the dark water far below. One agitated foot tapped on the rock as the most pressing problems—and the most prudent solutions—were considered.

A child. There'd been a child . . .

The words, still too impossible to be true, resounded over and over and over, like the taunt of a mean-spirited seven-year-old.

Push it away. Out of sight, out of mind.

Still, Kendall's words rang clear. . . .

Graham's baby . . .

A shake of the head, marveling that such a secret had been kept all these years!

But where was the child? Who was she? Who had raised her? Someone who knew her origin? Surely Graham Hayward would not have entrusted the safety of his child to someone who did not know exactly who that child was. There must have been a someone. . . .

This sent yet another surge of anger coursing through limbs already taut with emotion.

How could such a secret have been kept?

The answer was all too obvious. Someone had gone a long way to protect the child. Secrets, deceit, whatever it took, to protect the President's daughter.

A shout from the house carried on the breeze. The party was about to begin. A wave of the hand acknowledged the message.

"I'll be just a minute."

But first, breathe. Breathe the anger away. Leave it here; leave it all behind. . . .

One deep soothing breath followed another, and then another, on and on until some semblance of normalcy returned. Once the rage had passed, it was dismissed. It no longer mattered. On to something else . . .

A twinge of regret over Kendall's demise snaked into the subconscious, but only momentarily.

Miles should never have told Simon Keller about that one little indiscretion. Had he lived, who else might he have told? *What* else might he have told? No, the risk had been too great.

The bottom line remained:

Graham Hayward's good name must be preserved at any cost. Safeguarding the legacy was all that mattered. Well, that and protecting oneself, of course . . .

A crisp breeze blew in from the ocean. Far below, waves dashed onto rocks, sending white spray ten feet into the air. The scent of salt water soothed.

Now. Concentrate on the task at hand.

How to find the daughter?

How to find the person who had raised her?

Follow Simon Keller, of course.

Sooner or later, he would find them, if he hadn't already, sooner being better, of course. After all, Keller was a reporter and couldn't be trusted to keep a story like this quiet for long. Surely he'd want the glory, want to gloat at his cleverness in having found a story that had been buried for almost thirty years. . . .

Deciding how best to dispose of them—starting with the daughter and ending with the reporter—now that could present a challenge. But it was a challenge that could be met. After all, such challenges had been met successfully in the past, had they not?

Putting all in order soothed the spirit and restored a certain . . . balance.

Soon everything would be all right again, wouldn't it?

Once the daughter was found . . .

Chapter Fourteen

By ten o'clock on the following morning, Simon was in the Mustang headed to Henderson. If, in fact, there was a real danger to Dina, she needed to know the truth about who she really was. There was only one person who could tell her. He felt obligated to make Jude aware that someone may be out to harm her daughter. It would be up to Jude to decide just how much to tell Dina.

Simon pulled along the curb in front of the library and, ignoring the NO PARKING sign, hopped out and followed the path to the front door. He walked inside, scanned the two large rooms for Jude. Not finding her, he went straight to the desk.

"I was looking for Jude McDermott," he told the woman who had offered assistance.

"Jude called in sick this morning," she said in an exaggerated whisper apparently intended to remind Simon where he was.

Nodding his thanks, Simon left as quietly as he could. He reached the Mustang just as a Henderson police car slowed and the officer pointed to the sign that Simon had blatantly ignored.

"I was just leaving!" Simon called to him.

The officer nodded but waited until Simon had

pulled from the curb, then followed him for a block or two.

Within minutes, Simon had parked his car in the lot across from the McDermott home and was standing on the top step ringing the doorbell. Inside he could hear Waylon alternately barking and sniffing at the door, but there were no other sounds from within the house. Simon glanced at the driveway, where the Taurus wagon was parked close by the back gate. He rang the bell again, eliciting more of a response from Waylon, but still the door remained closed.

Wherever Jude was, she didn't appear to be sick at home.

Of course, she could be sick in bed, Simon told himself, remembering his last bout with the flu, which had kept him down for three whole days the winter before. Or she could be at the doctor's, but there was the matter of the car in the driveway.

Maybe Dina had taken her mother to the doctor's.

There was one way to find out.

Besides, Simon told himself as he got back into the car, after the dream he'd had the night before, he wanted—needed—to prove to himself that it had been nothing more than a dream. The rational part of Simon's brain reminded him that he'd never had psychic powers. But the part of his brain that still held the image of the beautiful woman who had turned to him in terror and screamed his name was apparently still not totally convinced. He wanted to believe that he was merely a victim of the power of suggestion, that Norton's intimation that Dina may be in some sort of danger had preyed on Simon's subconscious during the night and had manifested itself in his dream. That was the only logical explanation for the edgy, uneasy feeling that had lingered into the morning hours.

Sure. Made sense. Logical. Reasonable.

Still . . .

Simon stopped once to ask directions, then took the road out of town for the designated 2.5 miles. Past the old yellow farmhouse and the orchard to the sign.

GARDEN GATES.
D. MCDERMOTT, ASLA

This would be the place.

Simon slowed down, made the right turn into the narrow lot, and parked near the door of the small shop. He got out of the car, leaned on his door, and looked around. The shop windows were crowded with wreaths artistically adorned with dried flowers and sheer ribbons, terra-cotta flowerpots filled with daffodils, and baskets of primroses. Across from the shop and set back fifty feet or so to one side was an old carriage house with lace curtains in the windows and pots of pansies near the door. The drive that wound past him led to a greenhouse, next to which was parked the pickup he'd seen at the library. Simon was hesitating, wondering in which of the structures he'd find her, when the greenhouse door swung open and a young man wearing headphones and carrying a flat of purple flowers emerged. Simon recognized him as Dina's helper from the cancer garden. Mulch-boy, Dina'd called him. Simon hadn't caught his real name.

"Excuse me!" Simon called to him.

The boy, who was just about to drop the back flap on the pickup, turned.

"Can you tell me where I can find Dina?"

Mulch-boy pointed to the greenhouse and continued to move his head in time with the music as he slid the flat of flowers onto the truck bed.

Simon nodded his thanks, slammed the car door, and stepped out of the way as Dina's helper drove past him in the pickup. He walked back to the greenhouse and opened the door.

"Did you forget something, Will?" Dina's back was to him, and he stood for a moment admiring the view.

"Yes. I forgot to ask for your phone number."

She turned, a quizzical look on her face, a look that turned to surprise, then to pleasure when she saw Simon standing in the doorway.

"Oh. Simon." Dina said, and then did something that went straight to Simon's heart.

She blushed.

"Did I startle you?" Simon couldn't keep from smiling.

"No, no. I thought you were Will. . . . He just took some plants to a customer." She gestured toward the drive and the place where the pickup had been parked.

"Yes. Something purple." Simon stuck his hands in the pockets of his jacket to keep them from reaching out and smoothing back her hair.

"Heather."

"Did you grow it yourself?"

"Yes. It's a big seller this time of year."

"Is all of this yours?" He indicated the fields behind the greenhouse.

"Yes. All mine."

"Looks like quite a business."

"Thank you, it is."

"You built it yourself." It wasn't a question.

"Yes."

"You must be very proud."

"I am." Dina moved a tray of seedlings and brushed her open palms on her jeans to clean them off. "How's your book coming along?"

"It's doing well."

"Good. Are you almost finished?"

"Almost finished with the research, yes."

"It must be exciting, to write a book about a famous person."

"It's had its moments"—Simon nodded—"but maybe not as exciting as owning your own business."

"Well, that has its moments, too." She grinned.

The phone rang, and she excused herself to him before turning to answer it.

"Yes. . . . Ohmigosh, I forgot. Go ahead, Polly, leave. I'll be there in a few minutes. Take my car; the keys are under the seat. Have fun."

She turned to Simon and said, "I have to run up to the shop. My assistant's daughter is in a play at school, and if she doesn't leave right now she'll miss it."

"That's okay; you go on. I just stopped by to see if you're free on Saturday night," Simon heard himself say.

Taken off guard, Dina turned and looked up into his eyes. "What?"

"I wanted to know if you were free on Saturday night. I was thinking dinner." Simon pretended to frown. "Or is there a boyfriend I'll have to beat up first?"

"No boyfriend." She was smiling now.

"Hard to believe. What is wrong with the men around here?"

"Aren't you from around here?"

"No. I live in Arlington."

"Arlington, Virginia?" Her pretty mouth opened in surprise. "You'd drive all the way from Arlington, Virginia, just to have dinner?"

"To have dinner with you, yes, I would."

"Now I am flattered. But wait; you're not doing this just to pump me for information about my mother's friend, are you?" She made an X over her chest. "She hasn't told me a thing, honest."

Simon laughed. "Actually, I did stop by to see your mother this morning at the library, but they said she'd called in sick. When I stopped at the house, no one answered the door."

Dina frowned. "I spoke with her last night and she was fine. She must be having one of her migraines. I'll run over this afternoon and see how she is. Sometimes those headaches keep her flat on her back for a full day. Thanks for alerting me. I'll check up on her later. Was there something you'd like me to ask her? About her friend? I could have her give you a call."

Simon hesitated. It wasn't exactly the type of thing he wanted to discuss on the phone.

"Maybe she could just give me a call when she's feeling better." Simon reached into a pocket and pulled out a card, which he handed to Dina. "Maybe if she's free I can catch up with her on Saturday before I pick you up. And speaking of Saturday, would seven o'clock be too early for dinner?"

"Seven would be great."

"Where should I pick you up?"

She pointed to the carriage house.

"Convenient."

"Very."

"I know you're busy," he said as he took a step to the door. "I don't want to take up too much of your time."

"You can walk me to the shop." She walked around the opposite side of the table and opened the door, gestured for him to step through it.

Simon fell into step beside her, liking the way her long-legged stride matched his own. A station wagon pulled in the drive, and Dina waved.

"Hi, Mrs. Evans. Polly finished your wreath this morning. It's all ready for you—"

"I'll get out of your hair." Simon stopped by the front of the Mustang. "I'll see you on Saturday."

"I'm looking forward to it." She waved good-bye as she waited for her customer near the door to her shop, then turned to bless him with a smile.

He wondered what would happen to that smile when she found out what he knew.

You shouldn't have done that, Simon lectured himself sternly as he drove away. *Bad, bad, bad move.*

At best, going out with Dina—a central figure in an investigation—was a conflict of interest. At worst, she could well see it as nothing more than a ploy to use her— once she did find out the truth.

"I hadn't planned on asking her out," he said aloud, wondering why he felt he needed to defend himself to, well, to himself. "I just wanted to make sure she was okay."

Simon had to admit she'd looked fine. Better than fine. She was beautiful.

And she was obviously none the worse for having

endured Simon's dream the night before, he noted wryly. Apparently *he* had been the only one to suffer the ill effects of that.

He slipped a CD in the player he'd recently had installed in his vintage car. He was in the mood for some Jerry Lee Lewis. Pounding piano, hot fifties rock 'n' roll.

Breathless.

"That pretty well sums it up," he muttered.

That was pretty much the way Dina made him feel. Breathless. Mesmerized. Drawn to her, he'd found it impossible to look away when she was near. It wasn't just her beauty, or the warmth that radiated from her. He'd had a heightened awareness of everything—her, himself, sights and smells—just being in her company, just having her look up into his eyes when she spoke, just hearing her laugh.

Just feeling that twist in his gut when he looked at her.

And he'd learned something in the brief amount of time he had been with her, something that helped him to understand events that were thirty years old: when a woman like Dina looked at you the way she had looked at him, you felt like a million dollars. In that moment, he'd known exactly why Graham Hayward had been willing to give up everything he had—power, family, position—for the sake of a woman. Simon had never felt that surge before, that flash to his core that was part sexual attraction and part recognition of something within himself.

And *that* was why he had asked her out. Given the opportunity, he couldn't *not.* It was as simple as that. Not good reporting, maybe, but there it was.

Besides, if Norton was right and there was some

danger to her, shouldn't someone be keeping an eye on her?

It might as well be him.

From her bedroom window Jude had watched Simon drive away. Her focus on him had been so intent that she'd barely noticed the dark van parked at the far end of the trees or the figure that stood back near the picnic benches, sheltered in the shadow of the pines.

"You don't understand what you are asking of me," she argued into the phone.

"It's time. Way past time," the caller told her.

"I don't know what this will do to her." She bit her bottom lip to force back the tears. "She's never had any reason to doubt that she was my child. How can I tell her that she isn't?"

"I'm sorry, Jude," the voice softened. "You should have told her the truth long ago. You've had almost thirty years."

"I just couldn't bring myself to do it. Every time I tried, I just couldn't get the words out."

"I'm afraid you're going to have to find a way now. She needs to know. She can't protect herself if she doesn't know."

"Do you really think that she's in danger?"

"I think that she needs to know the truth so that she can be aware that someday—perhaps someday very soon—someone might be looking for her. God knows what will happen if she's found. . . ."

Jude wandered from room to room, the words ringing in her head.

God knows what will happen if she's found. . . .

And if Dina was found, Jude knew exactly who to thank for lighting the way to Henderson. If she could get her hands around Simon Keller's neck, she'd break it.

Waylon barked at the back door to go out, and Jude moved like a zombie to the kitchen. She unlatched the door and stepped out onto the porch, then curled up in the far corner of the porch swing. She'd never felt so alone or so empty. Not since the night that Miles Kendall had called to tell her that Blythe—her best friend, her dearest friend in the whole world—had been run down on a Washington street and had been killed instantly.

That night Jude had sought a dark haven, driving out to the desert and turning off the car lights, Blythe's baby girl asleep in the basket on the car seat behind her. Jude had gotten out of the car and walked just far enough from it so that her sobs would not awaken the infant and sat in the sand, her face in her arms, and wept until she was hoarse and exhausted.

Jude had stared up at the stars that night and relived every moment of the past year, from the afternoon she'd arrived back at her apartment to find Blythe sleeping on her sofa. Blythe had charmed the superintendent into letting her in, she told Jude with a grin. Blythe's sister, Betsy, always said that she'd never met anyone who was immune to Blythe's charm. Certainly Jude's super wasn't going to be the first.

"So. To what do I owe the honor?" Jude had asked over dinner—takeout from a fine restaurant that normally only did dine-in, but Blythe had worked her magic on the maître d' and had returned armed with brown bags from which wonderful aromas wafted.

"I needed a little vacation," Blythe said.

"The Riviera too crowded this month?"

Blythe grinned. "Yes. Actually, it is." Then, "Actually, I was thinking about staying for a bit."

"Here? In Phoenix? I thought you loved Washington."

"Oh, I do. I do love Washington," Blythe sighed. "There's simply no place like it in the world, Jude."

"Especially if one travels in such heady company."

"It's the heady company I need to distance myself from for a while."

Jude left her fork on the side of her plate. "Okay, out with it."

"I'm in love," Blythe had told her, her eyes glistening. "Absolutely, totally head-over-heels, once-in-a-lifetime in love."

"And I'm going to go out on a limb and guess that the lucky fella is equally smitten."

Blythe nodded. "I can barely believe it myself. But he is."

"What's not to believe? I've yet to meet the man who hasn't been grateful just for an opportunity to kiss your feet."

"This man is different." Blythe's expression was uncharacteristically solemn.

"Now, are we talking about the White House aide you mentioned?"

Blythe shook her head slowly.

"Someone else? Someone new?"

Blythe seemed to struggle for long moment.

"Actually . . . no." Blythe bit her bottom lip, then said, "I haven't exactly told you the truth about something."

Jude's eyebrows lifted. Not because her friend had kept something from her—everyone was entitled to their secrets—but because Blythe's eyes had gone so dark.

"The man I told you about on the phone—Miles Kendall—I haven't really been seeing him. I mean, yes, I've been going to parties and dinners and things with him, but not to be with him."

"I don't understand."

"I went with Miles so that I could see the man I'm really seeing, but I can't see him publicly, so . . ."

"So Miles is the 'beard,' as the saying goes?"

"Exactly."

"So, let me guess, the man you're in love with is married."

Blythe nodded slowly.

"Oh, sweetie, that usually doesn't work out very well."

"There's a little more to it, Jude," Blythe said softly.

"I was afraid there might be." Jude reached behind her for the tissue box and brought it to the table just as the first of Blythe's tears began to fall. "Go ahead, sweetie. Get it all out."

"He's not only married, but he's . . . he's . . ." Blythe struggled, the words caught in her throat.

"He's . . . what? Much older?"

Blythe nodded.

"Has kids?"

Another nod.

"This is not good, Blythe."

"You haven't heard the worst of it yet."

"What could be worse than an older married man who has children?"

"An older married man who has children and happens to be the President."

"The President of what?" Jude frowned.

"Of the United States."

It was a long moment before Jude could react.

When she did, it was to laugh. "Blythe, that's ridic . . ." Her laughter caught in her throat. Blythe's face was white and drawn, and it was obvious to Jude that her friend was not joking. "Graham Hayward?" Jude all but fell into her dinner plate. "You're having an affair with *Graham Hayward*?"

Blythe whispered, "Yes."

"Graham 'High Road' Hayward? Graham 'I'll never lie to the American people' Hayward?"

"Stop it, Jude. This is difficult enough."

Blythe covered her face with her napkin. "There's more."

"No. Don't tell me." Jude leaned all the way back in her chair.

"I'm due in late September." The whispered words were thin and formless and hung in the air between them.

"I can't believe this. How could . . . oh, hell, what's the difference now?" Jude muttered. "For heaven's sake, Blythe, what are you going to do?"

"I've been trying to work it all out." Blythe tried to smile. "Want to hear the short version?"

"Sure."

"I'd like to move out here with you, if you'll let me. We'll get a house. I'll go back to D.C. from time to time, until Graham is finished."

"Until he's finished what?"

"His term. He's thinking about maybe not running again, but of course no one knows that yet."

Jude's jaw dropped open. "He's not going to run for a second term?"

"He's only *thinking* about not running."

"Why?"

"Because he wants to leave his wife and marry me."

If the words had come from the mouth of any other woman, Jude would have laughed in her face. But this was Blythe Pierce speaking and if ever there was a woman for whom a man would be willing to give up his world, Jude suspected it might be Blythe.

"This hasn't been easy for either of us. Graham has been married for a very long time. His children mean the world to him. He absolutely dotes on his daughter. And the last thing I ever thought I'd do is have an affair with a married man. It sure wasn't something I was looking for. But there's this . . . connection between us. It's stronger than anything I could have imagined. I never intended for any of this to happen, Jude, I swear. But it did, and I have to deal with the consequences. Graham doesn't want me to deal with it alone, that's why I think he's talking about leaving his wife and the office, but I think that's guilt speaking. Frankly, I don't want that to happen."

"What *do* you want to happen?"

"I told Graham that I thought he should go for the second term, follow through the commitment he's made, and then we'll see how things are after he leaves office and is out of the public eye. I think it would be best for everyone, especially for his wife and children. By then, both of his kids will be out of college."

"You know that he's a shoo-in for a second term.

Hayward's the most popular President we've had in years."

"I do know that. He knows that." Blythe smiled wryly. "And we both know they'll never let him *not* run."

"Christ, just like Prince Edward and Wallis what's-her-name Simpson," Jude muttered. "Giving up the throne for the woman he loves . . ."

"Except the Prince wasn't already married with a family and wasn't the leader of the free world."

"This is too much." Jude pushed away from the table. "This sort of thing is way, way out of my league."

Jude stood up and began to pace. "I never moved in your world, Blythe, and God knows I don't understand it. You grew up on an estate where diplomats and other important people came and went all the time. I grew up in a rented house in a small town with a mother who waited tables and a father who pumped gas. I don't even know how to react to something like this."

Blythe reached out and took Jude's hand. "Getting you as a roommate was the best thing that ever happened to me. You're the best friend I ever had. If you don't want to be involved in this, if it makes you too uncomfortable, it's okay. I'll understand." She tried to make a little joke: "Hell, I'm not so sure I want to be involved. But I can't walk away from it. You can. I'll love you anyway. Always. I promise, Jude. No matter what."

"If you're asking me if I'm going to turn you away—"

"Not asking you if you're going to." Blythe's smile was slow and sad. "Just making sure you know that you can. No hard feelings. Ever. I wouldn't think any less of you. I know that I'm asking a lot of our friendship."

"Whatever I can do, whatever you need me to

do . . ." Jude swallowed back the lump in her throat. "Tell me what you want."

"I want to lease a house out here, under your name. I want you to live there with me."

"What else?"

"Nothing." Blythe looked away, then back again. "Just that you'll take care of the baby for me if . . . well, if anything ever happened to me."

"What do you think is going to happen to you?"

"Nothing. I'm sure nothing." Blythe began to cry. "I just feel scared, Jude. For me and for my baby and for Graham, if anyone should find out about this."

"Then we'll just have to make sure that no one finds out." Jude massaged Blythe's shoulders. "Who else knows?"

"Just one or two friends of Graham's, as far as I know."

"Obviously people he trusts?"

"With his life."

"And you can trust me with yours. And with the baby's."

Jude continued to knead the muscles in Blythe's neck. "What are you going to tell your family?"

"I don't know." Blythe shook her head and wiped at her eyes. "My father's retiring as Ambassador at the end of next year. It wouldn't be good for him, certainly, for this to become public while he's still serving."

"And Betsy?"

"I trust her. She'll always do what's right."

"You're going to tell her who the father is?"

"I haven't decided yet. Sometimes the truth can be a burden, you know?" She wiped her eyes and turned to look up at Jude. "I have everything else planned, though."

"Okay, then, let's hear it." Jude sat back down in her seat, her head reeling.

"As I said, the first thing I'm going to do is find a house. I need something that is somewhat secluded, in the event that Graham can find a way to visit. I don't know that that will be possible, frankly, what with the Secret Service and all, but I want him to have that option." Blythe took a deep breath. "Then, I'm going back east for a week or so. I need to talk to my lawyer."

"Why?"

"Because I want to make certain that if anything does happen to me, my baby is taken care of. I inherited a small estate from my mother."

Jude smiled to herself, wondering just what constituted a small estate in Blythe's world.

"And I want to name you as guardian."

"Of course, sure."

"I want to set this up so that if something happens to me, you'll raise my baby. You'll have full access to the money for housing, schooling, clothing, trips, whatever you want to spend it on. Whatever's left the baby will inherit on your death."

"Blythe, I think it's always wise to look ahead, but . . . well, you just look so serious. What do you think will happen?"

"I don't know, to tell you the truth." Blythe's lavender eyes clouded over. "I just want to know in my heart that if for any reason I can't be around you'll raise him or her as your own."

"Of course I would."

"You promise, Jude?"

"You have my word."

The next few months had passed in a surrealistic blur. Blythe had found a house and leased it under Jude's name. There had been Lamaze classes and late-night phone calls from Washington. Days when Jude returned from her classes and found Blythe floating in the pool on a raft, slick with oil and complaining about the heat. There were shopping trips where baby furniture was purchased and tiny garments oohed and ahhed over. Since Blythe's only contacts were with other participants in Lamaze, there was no baby shower, a fact that Betsy—once the shock of her sister's predicament passed—had lamented. She'd flown in two weeks before the baby was due, lugging beautifully wrapped packages from Philadelphia's best stores and delighting Blythe by arranging for a catered lunch for the three of them so that Blythe could be showered with gifts as tradition dictated.

Jude had had no illusions about how difficult that time had been for Blythe, who, in spite of the situation, had never complained. After Dina's birth, Jude and Blythe had celebrated with champagne and performed their own private christening, with Miles Kendall arriving to serve as godfather and Jude serving as godmother. All had gone so well. All had been so right. Dina was a darling baby and a joy.

Things should have just kept right on going as they had been.

Then Blythe went back to Washington to see Graham.

And in the blink of an eye, everything changed.

It had happened so fast that even now, years later, Jude wondered how such a thing could have been true.

There had been the call from Blythe, telling Jude how fine everything was. How happy she and Graham were just to see each other again.

Graham's plans had changed, however. In spite of his protestations to the contrary, he'd been talked into running for that second term. Blythe hadn't sounded at all surprised, nor was she upset with his decision.

"I knew they'd never let him quit. But I think it made him feel noble to tell me that he'd give it all up for me and for Dina. I don't mind. We'll have the rest of our lives to spend together," she'd told Jude.

Then, two nights later, the second call. The one from Miles, who had had such trouble getting the words out.

It had been incomprehensible.

And Blythe's death made no more sense to Jude now than it had thirty years earlier. . . .

Waylon moved closer and sat on Jude's feet as he had a habit of doing. Absently Jude petted the dog and wondered where all this would end.

How could she now tell Dina that which she'd hidden from her all these years?

Oh, Jude had always known she should tell her—had to tell her someday. And she'd meant to do that. Someday.

Of course, Dina had to know the truth. Deserved to know the truth. There had just never been a right time, a right way, to tell her.

It had all happened so fast. . . .

After Blythe's death, there had been that hasty visit from Miles, offering a new birth certificate naming Jude as Dina's birth mother, in order to protect the baby from anyone who might have gotten wind of Blythe's relationship with Graham. No one, Miles had cautioned Jude, *no one* must ever know of Dina's true identity.

At the time it had seemed like a good idea, and it had been nothing for Miles to secure such a document. The only discussion concerned who to name as the father. Miles had offered to supply a phony identity, but Jude felt the baby deserved a real flesh-and-blood father, even one she would never know.

Jude had known just the man to call on.

Frank McDermott had been Jude's friend since grade school. At one point they'd been high school sweethearts, but always more than that. Together they'd spent long summer nights sitting on Jude's back porch talking about what they would do after graduation. With a combination of scholarships and loans Jude would be realizing a dream and heading east to attend college. Frank had just gotten his draft notice—a gloomy prospect in those days when young American boys were being loaded onto planes and flown into a jungle a half a world away. On those nights when the world was so full of possibilities, neither of them could have imagined that Frank would spend the next few hellish years in a cage as a prisoner of war and that the injuries he received there would end his life before he reached the age of thirty.

So when Jude came to Frank with a story about how she'd gotten pregnant by one of her professors—the only story she could come up with—and said that she needed a name to place on the child's birth certificate, Frank had gladly offered the use of his. As he knew that death was close, the thought of leaving behind a child that bore his name, even though he hadn't fathered her himself, had brought Frank a great deal of peace. The navy chaplain had performed a simple ceremony right there in Frank's hospital room, and in the blink of an eye Jude Bradley had become Jude McDermott. She brought the baby to the hospital for Frank to see, and the photos she had taken during that visit were framed and still stood in a place of honor on the table in Jude's front hallway.

How could Jude now tell Dina that the brave young man who so proudly held her in those pictures had been only a kindhearted friend from the past? That the daddy a very young Dina had talked to in heaven when, as a child, she finished her evening prayers had been no more related to her than any one of their neighbors?

Wasn't it Shakespeare who had said something about lies being tangled webs? And once you were in the web, Jude knew, struggling only made the threads pull tighter.

Well, she sighed, there was no point in struggling at this late date. She could no longer avoid the inevitable. Now all she had to do was figure out how—and when—to tell Dina the truth.

Chapter Fifteen

"Mom?" Dina called from the front door. "Are you here?"

"Out back, Dina."

"I brought you some soup," Dina announced as she tucked the container into the refrigerator. "Chicken soup."

"What's the occasion?" Jude came inside.

"Well, I thought with you being sick, you could use a little something. I won't even try to pass it off as homemade, though. I picked it up at Elena's on my way through town."

"Oh, I see. You called me at the library and Mary told you that I had called in sick." Jude nodded her head.

"No, Simon Keller told me."

Jude froze. "Where did you see Simon Keller?"

"He came to see me today." Dina grinned, the words fairly bubbling out. It was clear that she was more than a little pleased.

"Why?" Jude asked sharply.

"Why?" Dina's eyes widened. "A great-looking man comes to see me, and my mother asks *why*? Thanks a lot, Mom."

Jude still stood in the same spot inside the kitchen door.

"He came to ask me out to dinner on—" Dina stopped to study her mother's stricken face. "Mom, are you all right?"

"Dina, don't go out with him," Jude said softly.

"What's wrong with him?" Dina then asked, "What's wrong with you?"

"Nothing," Jude brushed her aside. "I guess I'm just thinking you don't really know him. You know how I've always warned you about strangers."

"And when I was nine and ten years old I needed to be warned. I'm almost thirty now. Do you think I still need you to remind me to be selective? To be careful? To not talk to strangers?"

Dina's fisted hands rested on her hips.

"I'm sorry, Dina. . . ." Jude's hand rose to her face. And suddenly Simon Keller was the least of her problems.

How do I tell her? She'll turn from me, and never turn back. How could she ever forgive me for lying to her all these years? Why didn't I tell her sooner?

Waylon whined at the front door. Jude turned her back on Dina and gathered the dog's leash from the back door.

"I'll take him, Mom," Dina said softly. "You obviously don't feel well."

"I can—" Jude protested.

"So can I. Go curl up on the sofa with that book you started reading over the weekend. We'll only be a few minutes."

Dina snapped the leash on the basset's collar and opened the door. "We'll be right back."

Jude watched from the living room window as Waylon stopped to sniff an early dandelion, and tried to screw up her courage to tell Dina everything she'd spent a lifetime keeping secret. Telling Dina the truth was going to change everything—the last thing Jude wanted at this stage of her life. There were plenty of other things that could happen to you once you hit your mid-fifties. Arthritis. Osteoporosis. Sagging jawlines and drooping body parts. You name it, the middle-aged woman was going to have to deal with it, in one form or another, sooner or later. Of course, the market was flooded with remedies, the health food stores stocked with herbal treatments, for many of the woes of aging. But there was no cure—natural or otherwise—for losing the love and trust of your child.

"Damn Simon Keller anyway," Jude grumbled, "for bringing this to my doorstep."

What difference would it make if she kept her secret for a little longer? What was the worst thing that could happen?

Most of the houses in the neighborhood were closed and dark. As she wandered toward the end of the block with the basset, Dina took note of the fact that there seemed to be more and more FOR SALE signs on the street these days as the older residents moved in with their kids or into retirement homes. Of course, a nice neighborhood like this, with the lovely park across the street, had been popular with young families for years. . . .

Though it is sad to see some of the older folks leave, Dina thought as she paused in front of the Petersons' house at the end of the block. No surprise, of course, everyone had been expecting it, since old Mr. Peterson died last year. Too big a house for one person, the widow had said when she announced her plan to move to Ocean Pines to live with her sister. The house would be snapped up in no time, Dina reflected as she stood on the corner. Needs work but has that great yard, and Mr. Peterson always did keep up with the mechanics.

Dina crossed the street and looked back to the Peterson property as Waylon sniffed the calling cards left behind by the other neighborhood dogs. In the light from the street lamp she could see the thick frame of the grape arbor that surrounded the rear portion of the corner property. Jude had recalled only days before that the spring Mr. Peterson had planted the first of his grapevines was the year that Jude had moved to Henderson to take the job as librarian. Dina had been a shy toddler with dark ringlets, Jude had told her, and it seemed like only yesterday that both Dina and the grapevines had stood on spindly legs. . . .

Tugging on the leash, Dina followed Waylon along the edge of the park, then started back across the street again, lost in thought and oblivious to the dark van that crept from the shadows of the parking lot, its lights off. It gained speed as it stealthily approached, so Dina failed to see the vehicle until it was almost upon her. Leaping for the sidewalk, jerking on Waylon's chain to pull him along with her, Dina found herself scrambling onto the Turners' lawn as—incredibly—the van jumped the curb and appeared to almost be following her before heading back to the street and disappearing around the corner.

Terrified, heart pumping way too fast, Dina crouched behind the Turners' hedge and tried to catch her breath, a hand over her mouth to keep from crying out. Clinging to a confused Waylon and trembling all over, she remained in the shelter of the boxwood till the gasping stopped. But as she sought to stand, she heard the hum of an engine idling nearby. On her hands and knees, a tight grip on Waylon lest he slip through the hedge and into view, Dina crawled to the end of the hedge to peer out at the street.

The minivan lurked several houses down from where Dina and Waylon hid. It must have gone around the block and circled back, she thought as she watched its slow but steady prowl. Holding tightly to the dog's leash, Dina leaned forward hoping to catch a glimpse of the license plate as the vehicle passed, but something—mud perhaps?—smeared the plate. Nor could she get a good look at the driver, whose face was hidden in the dark and further obscured by a hat pulled low over the forehead.

The van made one more reconnaissance, then finally turned right at the stop sign as if heading for town. A long ten minutes later, convinced that the van was not coming back, Dina emerged from the hedge and ran past the six houses to her mother's. Rushing through the front door, she slammed it behind her and leaned back against it, blood swirling in her ears. Snapping off the hall light to cast the foyer in darkness, still shaking, she attempted to gather her wits.

"Dina, my God . . ." Jude flew in from the living room.

Dina ran into the kitchen, removed the cordless phone from its handset, and dialed the number for the local police.

"Someone tried to run me down," Dina panted, pointing to the darkened street. "Can you believe it? Someone deliberately tried to hit me!"

For the first time in Jude McDermott's life, she fainted.

Tom Burton, who'd been on the Henderson police force for nearly as long as Jude had been the town's librarian, pulled into the driveway even before her pulse had had a chance to return to normal. Dina unlocked the door and stood on the porch while he walked across the lawn.

"Dispatcher said you had a car accident, Dina?" Tom asked quietly.

"No, not an accident. Someone tried to run me down."

"*Tried* to run you down?" The officer frowned.

"A van—a minivan—came out of nowhere and tried to run me over when I was out walking Waylon."

"When you say 'came out of nowhere' "—he removed his hat and ran his hand through graying hair—"what exactly do you mean?"

"I mean that I never saw it until it was almost on top of me. It came down the street with its lights off and waited until I got midway across, then accelerated, and tried to hit me."

"Maybe the driver was distracted and he didn't see you." Tom was still frowning.

"It chased me up onto the damned sidewalk. It was not a matter of driver error. That van followed me, then came back around, not once but twice. It was like a shark circling the block."

"Maybe the driver wanted to see if he'd hit you. Maybe he was coming back to see if you needed help."

"He was coming back to see if he could finish me off." Dina's patience was nearing exhaustion.

"Tom?" Jude called from the doorway.

"You see this, Jude?" Tom asked.

"No. I was in the house. But if Dina said the van deliberately tried to hit her, you can believe that it did."

"Dina, why would anyone want to hurt you? You haven't an enemy in this world."

"Apparently I've got at least one."

The words chilled Jude to her soul, even as Dina spoke them aloud.

"Look, I'll make a report, and I'll talk to the other guys on duty tonight to see if anyone saw a . . . you didn't happen to notice the color, did you? Or the make?"

"No, it was too dark. The only streetlight is around the corner by Peterson's. The middle of the block isn't well lit. It happened so quickly, and I'm afraid I was daydreaming and not paying attention. I didn't notice the van until the last minute. But hell"—Dina stood with her hands on her hips—"there's never any traffic out here after nine or nine-thirty at night."

"Get a look at the driver?"

She shook her head. "Only to see that he or she was wearing a hat, like a rain hat with a brim. That's all I could see."

"Not much to go on." He finished making his notes, then stuck his pen back into his notebook. "Doesn't make much sense—"

"That van jumped the curb right there in front of the Turners' house." Dina was starting to lose her temper. "Come on. I'll show you."

Dina led the police officer, her mother, and the dog down the street.

"There. Look right there." Dina pointed to the ground. "You can see the tire marks right there on the sidewalk."

"Hmmmph." Tom dropped down onto one knee and with his flashlight followed the dark tracks. "Looks like it came right on up here, then backed up off the curb."

"That's what I've been telling you. Someone tried to run me over."

"And no thoughts on who? Or why?"

"No."

Jude shivered as the night breeze picked up, heralding a storm.

"I'll stop back in the morning and take some pictures of the tracks, just for the record." Tom straightened up. "And like I said, I'll ask around and see if anyone saw an unfamiliar van around town tonight. But you know how it is with those minivans: half the young families in Henderson have 'em. Hell, my son just bought one for his wife to drive the kids around in . . ." Tom said as the small group started back toward Jude's house.

He paused at the foot of Jude's walk, then asked, "How 'bout if I check out the backyard before I leave? Just to make sure . . ."

"I'd appreciate that, Tom." Jude nodded and stood in the halo of the porch light until he came back around.

"No sign of anything, but I'll be by on and off for the rest of the night to keep an eye on things for you so that you can sleep in peace." He tucked his flashlight under his arm. "And I'll let the next shift know to do the same. Dina, I'll have someone out by your place for the rest of the night."

"We appreciate that. Thank you."

"If you think of anything—anyone with any reason to want to scare you—give us a call."

"I sure will. Thanks again for coming out."

The car left, and Jude, weary with the knowledge that the moment of truth had come, led her daughter by the hand into the living room. There was no question in Jude's mind that the driver of the van was somehow connected to the past. Why, after all these years?

"Simon Keller," Jude muttered. "Someone must have followed Simon Keller. He was here earlier today . . . and dear God, there had been a van across the street, by the park. . . ."

"Mom, what are you talking about? What has this to do with Simon?"

"Dina, there's something we need to talk about. . . ."

Dina's heart began to thump. The only time she had ever heard that touch of uncertainty in her mother's voice was the day that Jude had called to tell her that she had cancer. Her own earlier near miss was shoved into the back of her mind, for the time forgotten.

Please, God, not again.

"Oh, hell, there's no easy way to do this. Dina, there's something I need to tell you. Something we need to talk about. I know that I should have said something long before this, but—"

"It's back, isn't it?" Dina's eyes welled with tears.

"What?" Jude asked.

"The cancer. It's come back."

"Oh, no, no, sweetheart. I'm fine."

"You are?" Dina lowered her face to her hands and burst into tears.

"Oh, Dina, I'm sorry. There's just no easy way to do this. It never occurred to me that you'd think I was sick again." Jude sat next to Dina on the steps and wrapped her in her arms, just as she had so many times over the years when something or other threatened to break her daughter's heart. *Oh, if things could only be so uncomplicated again . . .*

"I'm not sick, sweetheart." Jude rocked her just slightly, savoring the feeling and wondering if she and her daughter could ever again be as close as they were at that moment. "I'm afraid it's nothing quite that simple."

"Simple?" Dina's jaw all but dropped. "Simple? I'd hardly call what we went through a few years ago simple."

"Well, once you hear what I have to say, you may wish that that had been the news."

"Mom, are you crazy?" Dina was horrified. "There's nothing—nothing—you could say that could be worse than that."

"Save your judgment till you've heard me out." Jude paused, praying for some last-minute divine inspiration. When none was forthcoming, she took Dina's hands in her own and asked, "Do you remember when Simon stopped by here a few weeks ago?"

"Yes, of course."

"Do you remember why he said he'd come here?"

"To ask you about an old friend of yours from college. Did you ever find out why he wanted to know about her?"

"Oh, I knew what he wanted to know and I knew why. But at the time, I just didn't know how much he knew."

"Mom, you're not making any sense."

"You were right when you said that anyone would have expected Blythe and me to stay close after having roomed together for three years. We had."

"So what was he looking for? What had she done? What was the big secret?"

"She . . ." Jude swallowed hard. *Here we go. . . .* "Blythe had an affair with Graham Hayward. President Graham Hayward."

"Holy shit!" Dina's eyes widened. "Your friend was sleeping with the President? Wow, Mom, you must have run with a racy crowd back then."

"Not at all. Blythe's relationship with Graham was not a casual fling. Oh, maybe it started out as merely a flirtation between a powerful man and a beautiful young woman, I don't know. I didn't know how it started." Jude looked skyward. So much more to say, and she didn't want to continue. . . . "Blythe said that they were soul mates. That they were deeply in love."

"And that's what Simon wanted to talk to you about? About your friend's affair with the President?"

"Yes."

"Couldn't he have found that in newspapers or magazines from the seventies?"

"Back then, things weren't as openly discussed. Actually, no one knew about their affair. The ironic thing is that he—Graham—had this reputation for being so moral. A great family man—"

"And no one who knew about it spilled?" Dina nodded. "Impressive that he was able to keep the lid on it. But I don't know what all this has to do with you and why you're so upset about it."

"Well, the piece of the story that Simon Keller

hadn't known about when he first came here was that Blythe had had a child by Hayward." Jude's eyes began to well with tears, but she forced her voice to remain steady. "A baby girl. A few months later, Blythe died. . . ."

"I'm sorry about your friend, Mom." Dina patted her mother's shoulder. "What happened to the baby?"

Jude took one last long, deep breath.

"I raised her as my daughter."

Dina's head tilted slightly to one side, as if she was trying to understand. "I'm not following this. I'm confused—"

"You were that baby, Dina."

"Mom, that's crazy."

"It's the truth."

"No, it isn't." Dina shook her head. "No, it's not."

"Sweetheart, I'm so sorry."

"No. No, this can't be true." Dina pushed Jude away and stood on trembling legs.

"I know I should have told you a long time ago. But I promised her and then—"

"No. I don't believe this." Dina began to pace. "How could this be? I don't understand."

"Dina, please sit down and let me explain. . . ." Jude reached for Dina's hands and found them suddenly cold. She began to rub them the way she had when Dina was little and had just come in from playing in the snow.

"Explain?" Dina pulled her hands away and appeared blank for a long moment. "How can you explain that I'm not your child? *I'm not your child?*"

"I think you need to hear the entire story."

"There's more?" Rage began to replace the confusion

in Dina's eyes. "You've been lying to me all my life. Isn't that enough?"

"It wasn't because I wanted to—"

"How could you have lied to me *all of my life?*" Dina was shaking from head to toe. "How could you not be my mother?"

"Dina . . ." Jude whispered, feeling more helpless than she ever had.

"Who are you?" Dina cried. "Who are you if you're not my mother?"

"Dina, please, if you'll calm down and listen—"

"Calm down? You tell me that everything I ever thought I knew about you—everything I knew about myself—is a lie, that my whole life, my whole existence, is a lie, and you think I should calm down?"

Dina's breath began to come in sharp, shallow spurts, and tears ran down her face. "Why didn't you tell me this before?"

"Because after Blythe died, your father made me swear not to."

"Why would he do that?"

"Because he was afraid for you. Afraid that someone would want to harm you if the truth came out."

"Why?"

"Because Blythe's death had not been an accident. You were only a few months old when she died." Jude knew she was leaving out a lot but figured this was probably not the time to go into detail.

"Why are you telling me now?"

"Because after what happened tonight . . . I just can't believe that it's coincidence. And I can't justify risking another 'accident.' I've already put you at risk by not telling you sooner."

"You don't think it was Simon, do you?"

"No . . . I don't know what I think. I don't know who to trust or who to turn to." Jude rose, wringing her hands. "I can understand how shocked you are, how hurt you are, and I'm more sorry than I can ever say. Yes, I've lied to you all your life. I won't blame you if you hate me, if you leave and never come back. But through the years, I've done the best that I could to keep you safe. Even now, nothing is more important to me than your safety."

"Will you tell me everything?" Dina studied the face of the woman who stood before her.

Jude nodded, her sad eyes never leaving her daughter's face. "I met Blythe my freshman year in college. We had one or two classes together and lived on the same floor in the same dorm, but that's all we had in common. She was beautiful and rich and everyone admired her. I was poor and only managed to get to college with heavy financial aid. Somehow we became friends—no one was more surprised than I was when she asked me to room with her sophomore year. Our personalities just seemed to complement each other, and over the years, we became the best of friends. That friendship lasted until the day she died."

Jude swallowed hard. All else aside, it was still sometimes difficult to speak of Blythe.

"Anyway, after college, I went right to Arizona to attend graduate school. Blythe went to Europe for six months, then decided to live in D.C. Her father was Ambassador to Belgium and kept an apartment there."

"How did she meet President Hayward?"

"She first met him at a reception that she attended with her father. Their paths crossed several times after that, when she'd been invited to attend a dinner in honor of a Belgian artist after her father had returned to Brussels. After that, I'm not really certain how the relationship progressed. I do know that over the following year or so Blythe attended a lot of White House functions as the date of the President's best friend. A man named Miles Kendall."

"That name is familiar." Dina frowned.

"He's been in the news. He died recently." Jude rubbed her temples. "Simon Keller had met with Miles while beginning the research for his book on Hayward. Miles was suffering from Alzheimer's. He apparently told Simon about the affair."

"And told him that Blythe had had Graham's child?"

Jude shook her head, "I'm not certain that he hadn't figured that out for himself."

"How?"

"He'd paid a visit to Blythe's sister, who'd apparently shown him photos of Blythe. When he came here seeking information about Blythe's affair with Hayward, I don't think he had any idea that there had been a child."

"Then how did he know?"

"I think he knew as soon as he saw you that you were Blythe's child. You look so much like your mother, Dina."

Dina winced at the reference.

"I'm sorry, honey, but anyone who knew Blythe would know whose daughter you really are."

"Then how did you think you could hide it?"

"Here, in this small town, the chances of running into anyone who had known Blythe Pierce were pretty remote."

"That's why you didn't want me to go to school so close to D.C.," Dina said.

Jude nodded.

"How did Simon find you?"

"Blythe's sister told him where I was."

"Does she know about me?"

"Yes."

"Then why would she tell him where to find you?"

"I don't know. I've been trying to figure that out myself."

"Have you asked her?"

"No. It's been a while since we've been in touch. We had a disagreement some years ago."

"Why?"

"Because Betsy wanted . . . to be a bigger part of your life than I felt she should be. She wanted you to know your Pierce relatives, but I resisted. I said that I was afraid that the situation would be too confusing to you as a child. You'd wonder what your connection was to Betsy. But looking back, I think the real reason was that I was selfish and shortsighted and utterly wrong. I knew that eventually I'd have to tell you everything, but I just kept putting it off and putting it off. . . ." Jude spread her hands helplessly before her. "I've always thought of you as mine, Dina. I can't help it. I know that someone else gave birth to you, but I've always felt in my heart that you were mine. I'm sorry. I know it's not a good-enough reason to have kept you from your . . . blood relatives . . . all these years. But I loved you so much, wanted so much for it to be true—"

"I can't hear any more." Dina clapped her hands over her ears. "I just can't hear any more of this."

"Dina . . ." Jude rose to follow her.

"Don't." Dina held up a hand as if to keep Jude away. "I need to go. I need to get out of here."

Dina fled through the gate that stood between the garage and the house.

"Dina . . ." Jude called from the gate.

Dina was halfway down the driveway when she stopped and looked back to ask, "Did she name me, or did you?"

Jude leaned against the gate and held on to it for support.

"She did," Jude whispered. "It was her grandmother's name."

Dina turned and ran, trying to escape from words she could no longer bear to hear and a reality she could not comprehend.

A tearful Jude let her go, knowing that all she could do was pray that once the shock had passed Dina would forgive her. And that someday maybe she'd be back.

Not true, not true, not true, not true, not true . . .

The words echoed over and over and over in Dina's head, like a bell that would not stop ringing.

She parked her car in front of the carriage house, though she barely recalled having driven home, and simply sat there, staring blankly out the window, trying to make sense of what had happened. The hollow area inside her had spread until she felt empty, as if everything had been removed and the void where her organs had once rested had been filled with a terrible chill.

From an open window somewhere she heard a phone ring several times. With no sense of urgency, she opened the car door, slid out, and walked woodenly into her house. She sat on the edge of a small side chair in her living room and looked out the window with eyes that saw nothing beyond the frame.

How can you not know that your *mother* isn't really your mother? And this man who had been her father . . .

A former President of the United States.

How absurd. Who could believe such a thing?

Dina picked up the photo of Frank McDermott that stood on a nearby table, the same photo that was prominently displayed in Jude's home. "Who did you think I was? Did you know the truth?"

A million questions gathered, ebbed and flowed, until Dina's head began to pound. There was no escape from the incessant buzz between her ears. She went upstairs and lay across her bed, hugging her pillow.

There was a family she had never met, had never even heard of until this day. Blythe had had a sister, Jude had said.

I have an aunt.

Are there grandparents, then, too? Cousins?

Did Hayward have other children? There was a son, wasn't there? A congressman or senator, something . . . Dina thought she recalled hearing something about him. Were there other offspring?

Do they know about me?

Blythe's sister knows about me. . . .

From some place deep inside the barest remnant of a long-forgotten image emerged. Dina closed her eyes and was, for the briefest of moments, enveloped by scent. Gardenia, she recognized it now, though she was certain that at the time she did not know its name or the name of the woman who wore it. That she had been tall and blond and had kind eyes Dina remembered, even as she remembered the touch of the softest fabric against her cheek when the woman knelt to embrace her.

Her fairy godmother. That's how Dina had come to think of the woman who always arrived laden with a mountain of beautifully wrapped presents. Always on birthdays, always on Christmas, sometimes just because. Dina tried to remember the woman's voice, but it was too far lost in time. The visits had stopped the year she turned five. She'd never gotten a clear explanation of why, and though the woman had appeared in her dreams for several years thereafter, over time the memory had faded.

Had that been Blythe's sister?

Dina went into her closet and reached for the half-forgotten wooden box that she kept on the shelf, the box in which she kept odd pieces from her childhood. She sat in the middle of the bed and opened it, searching through the treasured contents for that one item she sought.

The gold ring—a high school ring, Dina had realized as she grew older—the initials *BDP* engraved inside, the name of the school, "*The Shipley School 1964*," in script across the front. The ring that her fairy godmother had tucked into her hand that last time she visited. The ring that Dina had instinctively kept from Jude for years. When she'd finally asked about it, Jude's jaw had set squarely and she'd told Dina it had belonged to a cousin of hers. For reasons that Dina couldn't have explained, she hadn't believed her mother.

Dina slipped the ring on her finger.

Blythe's high school ring.

Dina held it up to her face. Where, she wondered, was the Shipley School? Had Blythe been smart? Popular? Athletic? What had she cared about when she was a student there? How had she gone from that place to falling in love with a President and bearing his child?

Mom—*Jude*—would know. Jude knew it all. Had known it all.

Suddenly the room seemed too small to contain Dina's anger. Her spirit agitated and her heart restless, she wandered outside into the dark fields. Across the rows where the winter's freezing and warming of the soil had caused the earth to heave, Dina walked, kicking a clump of dirt here and there, her thoughts a jumble. She sat down under a lone willow tree at the edge of the lake that formed the far boundary of her property. All was still, all quiet, a stark contrast to the rage that came and went inside her. She leaned back against the tree and cried, the sobs cracking the silence of the night like crisp claps of thunder that sent several small creatures that rustled in the grasses nearby to seek other shelter.

Perhaps if she cried enough her tears would flush away the anger, wash away the pain.

A flashback to the conversation with her mother and the way Jude had shaken. Fear, Dina now knew. It had been fear that had caused Jude to tremble.

"I'm afraid, too, Mom," she whispered aloud. "If I'm not your child, if I'm not Dina McDermott, who in the name of God am I?"

The sun had barely broken through the early-morning haze when Waylon nudged Jude and whined to be let out.

"Waylon, go away. It's too early," Jude, who'd lain awake all night, muttered, and turned over, still hoping that sleep might come, if only for an hour.

Waylon stood up on his short hind legs, leaned against the side of the bed, and whined a little louder.

"Oh, for pity's sake." Jude tossed the thin blanket aside. "All right. Let's go."

In bare feet and green-and-white striped pajamas, Jude padded down the steps, following the eager hound, who seemed especially lively for so early in the morning. Jude unlocked the door and pushed it open for Waylon to go out, then stood, frozen on the spot, as the dog bounced upon the figure seated on the top step.

Without turning around, Dina asked in a hoarse voice, "Do you remember when I was eight or nine and wanted to play softball with the girls club and they wouldn't let a kid sign up unless at least one parent agreed to volunteer for something? When they called and asked you to be assistant coach, you said sure, even though you knew nothing about the game, because you were afraid they wouldn't let me play if you said no. The next day, you came home from the library with your arms filled with books on baseball, stacked so high you could barely carry them all."

Dina paused momentarily, then added, "I didn't have the heart to tell you that softball and baseball weren't exactly the same thing."

"I wondered why they moved me from coaching to selling water ice at the snack bar after the second game," Jude said softly.

"Remember when I was ten and I nominated you for the Father of the Year Award?" Dina could barely get the words out.

"I remember," Jude whispered, the pride she'd felt in that long-ago moment pinching her heart. *Oh, yes, baby, I remember. . . .*

"I want to go back to who I was yesterday at just this time," Dina said. "I want to be Dina McDermott again."

"You are—"

"No, I'm not. I don't even know what my name really is. Is it Pierce? Is it Hayward?"

"Legally—"

"*Legally* doesn't mean a damned thing to me right now. If you're talking about what's on my birth certificate, that's just a piece of paper. What does that have to do with who I am?" Dina's voice was husky from lack of sleep and a fair amount of sobbing.

"Dina, if you want to change your name . . ."

Dina turned around and looked up to meet Jude's eyes, and Jude recognized the anger, the unbearable hurt, and what was left of her heart shattered.

"Tell me what you want, Dina."

"*I want you to be my mother.*" The words ripped from her throat.

"In my heart, you are—have always been, will always be—my daughter. What I did was so wrong, and nothing I can say will make it less wrong. The lie remains. But that I have loved you with all my heart since the moment of your birth, that is the truth. The purest truth."

Nodding very slowly, Dina said softly, "I know."

"Honey, if I could change this, if I could take the hurt away from you, I would."

"I know that, too."

"I don't know what to do for you," Jude said sadly. "I feel so helpless. I would do anything if I could just go back in time and undo what I've done."

Jude sat down, then somewhat tentatively put her arm around Dina's shoulders. When Dina did not push her away, Jude rested Dina's head on her shoulder, as she had done so many times in the past when her daughter was hurting.

"I've never felt this kind of anger before. It's frightening me, it's so enormous. It's overshadowing everything else right now. But at the same time, I know that I can't not love you, Mom. Whatever else is true, I can't not think of you as my *mother.*"

"Thank you, darling." Jude stroked Dina's hair, filled with gratitude for this unexpected gift. It was more than she'd ever dared hope for.

Together they sat, wrapped in the morning. There would be time to talk more later, time for more questions and more answers, for the airing of more anger and the shedding of more tears.

But right now, the bit of warmth they drew from the silence and their mutual pain brought some momentary comfort, some little bit of strength, and that would have to suffice.

A third of a box of tissues later, Dina said, "Last night you said that Blythe's death was not an accident. How did she die?"

"It was a hit-and-run on a dark street."

"Like last night?"

"Very much like last night."

"How do you know it wasn't an accident?"

"There was evidence to suggest that she was run over not once, but twice." Jude swallowed hard. "By the same car."

"Mom, that's horrible! Did they ever find the person who ran her over?"

"No."

"You don't think that the same person . . . ?"

"I don't know what to think at this point." Jude shook her head. "Maybe it's the same person; maybe the person who drove the car that killed Blythe was working with someone else. I don't know what to think anymore."

"You don't think that Simon had anything to do with this, do you?" Dina asked.

"Someone could have followed him. Maybe someone is afraid that the story will get out after all these years."

"But after all these years, why would it matter?"

"I can think of a number of reasons why it would matter. I imagine Hayward's family would not want this to be made public. Especially if, as they say, Graham's son—he's a congressman from Rhode Island—is thinking about running for the presidency."

"Do they know about me? The Haywards?"

"Mrs. Hayward may have known about Blythe. I don't know if the Hayward kids ever knew."

"How many children did he have?"

"Two. Graham Junior and a daughter. I don't recall her name at the moment."

"I guess it wouldn't help to tell the local police this story."

"How could I do that without telling them everything? And the truth being what it is, who'd believe me?" Jude picked a spent blossom from a pot of early pansies.

"We have to tell someone, Mom. I don't know about you, but I didn't take Conspiracy One-o-one. I don't know how to tell if I'm being followed and I wouldn't know what to do if someone jumped me from behind. I think we're out of our league, especially since we don't know who or what we're dealing with."

"Maybe you're right." Jude nodded. "But first we'd have to convince someone that this is all true."

"Simon Keller already knows it's true. And by now, he might even have an idea of who might be involved."

"I don't know how much I trust him."

"I trust him, Mom."

"Dina, for heaven's sake, the man is a reporter. He's writing a book—and we don't know at this point just what he plans to put into that book, do we?"

"If what you're telling me is true, Simon has known about this for several weeks. I haven't seen anything on the news. There's been no tabloid reporter at my front door. Simon didn't even tell me."

"I suspect that even some reporters have scruples. And besides, it isn't the sort of thing one brings up to someone one doesn't really know. That would be . . . tacky."

" 'Tacky' doesn't usually stop reporters from asking questions. I think he was being considerate of me."

"Because he's attracted to you," Jude said flatly.

"I hope so. I sincerely do, 'cause God knows I'm attracted to him. More than I've been attracted to anyone in a very long time. But I also think he *likes* me, Mom. Which is also a good thing." Dina tossed a ball at Waylon, who sniffed at it, then rolled on it. "Besides, I don't know who else we can turn to."

"There *is* someone else we should talk to. Would you

feel comfortable leaving town for a few days? Could you leave Polly in charge of your business till you get back?"

"Yes, but—"

"Good. Go home and make whatever arrangements you need to make with her. Pack for several days. We're taking a trip, you and I." Jude nodded decisively. "A long-overdue trip . . ."

Chapter Sixteen

Simon rang the doorbell of the home that Gray Hayward and his wife, Jen, had built three years earlier. It was the last of the family interviews and had been put off twice by the congressman's schedule. Simon had returned from Henderson the day before yesterday and found the message on his answering machine from Hayward's aide asking if the appointment could be moved to Thursday. Simon was happy to comply.

"Simon Keller." Gray Hayward himself opened the door and extended his hand. He was every bit as tall, dark, and handsome as his photos suggested. "Come on in. Have you had lunch? Jen is just making sandwiches. Did you have a good flight up?"

"Yes . . . fine. And no . . . that is, no lunch." Simon was taken aback by the welcome he received. He'd heard it said that President Hayward had been a man who could put anyone to ease in thirty seconds or less. It appeared that his son had come by the talent naturally.

"Right on back here to the den . . ." Gray led the way through a house that was bright and open and filled with green plants. "We'd hoped that the weather would warm up a bit so that we could show off our new patio, but the wind's picked up a bit too much. Great view though, wouldn't you say?"

"Wonderful." Simon nodded, trying to take it all in. The larger-than-life yet friendly young congressman. The house that looked like a sample for a designer who excelled at integrating heirloom antique furniture and primitive art with the large airy and open room. The breathtaking view of the Narragansett Bay. "The setting is awesome."

"Exactly what we thought the first time we drove out here. We stood right out there on that outcropping of rocks—come on; let me show you." Gray Hayward's enthusiasm was infectious, and within seconds Simon was standing next to his host at the top of a rocky point that overlooked the choppy bay.

"When the realtor brought us up here to look over a few plots of ground, he brought us here first. Didn't need to see any of the others. I knew this was it." Gray pointed out into the bay and said, "There's a small island out there. On a foggy morning, you'd swear the Sirens were singing. It's just magic."

"It must be hard for you to leave it behind all the time you spend in Washington," Simon noted.

"It is hard, but you know, Simon, I love my job. I love the people of Rhode Island. Love that they've put such trust in me."

Had anyone else made such a statement, Simon would have fought an urge to roll his eyes. But there was something about Hayward that was so earnest, something that made you believe that *he* believed every word he said. Another legacy from his father?

"And besides"—Gray continued to look out over the dark water—"I know that this place is always waiting for me. It's a great family home, but it'll make a great retirement home, too, when that day comes. Now, let's run on back to the kitchen and see what Jen has for us. I'm starving, myself. How 'bout you?"

"A sandwich would be great."

The sandwich *was* great—honey maple ham on pumpernickel with lettuce and tomato—served with a steaming bowl of New England clam chowder.

"I hope you like our local quahog chowder," Jen Hayward, a pretty strawberry blonde with a trim athletic build, told Simon as she set the tray down on the round wooden table in the den.

"It smells delicious."

"Well, enjoy it." The congressman's wife smiled and stretched out a hand to Simon. "I'm sorry I won't be able to stay and chat. Our son is in a play at school and I have to be there."

"I'm sorry, too." Simon pushed back his chair, preparing to stand.

"No, no, don't get up. I appreciate the gesture, though." She leaned over and kissed her husband on the cheek before bustling out of the room.

"You know, we could have rescheduled this interview so that you could have attended your son's play," Simon said.

"I went last night." Gray grinned. "Today is Jen's turn. We do try to attend as many of the children's activities as possible—preferably together—but when our schedules conflict we take turns."

"That's admirable, to be so involved with your children's lives."

Gray shrugged. "Family has always been a priority for

us. We figure the kids will be around long after I've left Congress."

"Or the White House."

"That, too, if it's in the cards." Gray's laugh was rich and easy.

"Your children are . . ."

"Twelve, nine, and seven."

"Wouldn't living in the White House be tough on children so young?"

"Living in the White House is tough on everyone."

"Any thoughts on having grown up there yourself?" Simon slipped his notebook out of his pocket.

"I didn't, really. I was already in college by the time my father was elected, so I was away from home by then. I think it may have been tougher on Sarah."

"In what way?"

"Sarah was the baby, and of course, being the only girl, she was the apple of Dad's eye. Before the election, she'd been accustomed to pretty much having her own way and a lot more of his time. It was hard for her to accept that she couldn't call all of the shots anymore."

"She mentioned that she was permitted to continue on at the boarding school she had been attending," Simon said, "so it seems that she didn't have to give up all that much."

"Oh, in reality, she gave up very little." Gray grinned again. "Sarah wasn't one to let much get in her way. When she wanted to come home, she came home. When she wanted to stay at school, she stayed at school. She pretty much had everyone wrapped around her fingers, including the Secret Service."

"You sound envious."

"I guess there were times back then when I was. The baby of the family always gets special treatment."

"Were you able to do any traveling with your parents while your father was President?"

"No, no. So many of their trips were during the school year, I couldn't take the time off."

"Ah, now from that should I assume that you were a more dedicated student than your sister?"

Graham tilted his head, as if poised to ask a question. When he did not, Simon said, "Your sister mentioned that she'd taken a year off from school—her senior year, I think she said—so that she could accompany your parents on several trips."

"Oh." Graham nodded slowly, his eyebrows rising slightly. "Of course. Her senior year. I'd forgotten about that. No, I never had the opportunity to travel with my parents."

"What are your favorite memories of those days?"

Gray put his sandwich down on the plate and appeared to be deep in thought. "I guess just being so proud of my dad. He was such a great man. A truly great man."

"And a great President?"

"Others will have to be the judge of that," Gray said softly. "I can only speak of what he was like as a father."

"How was he?"

"Loving. Interested. Always concerned, always caring. Never too busy to listen. Oh, at that precise moment when you wanted to talk he might have had someone else on the line, but he'd always find time. I can't remember a time when he brushed me off or made me feel that my problems were insignificant."

"It seems that he and your mother were very close."

"I think they were. I think they loved each other deeply."

Simon pretended to write longer than he really needed to, not daring to look up lest Gray sense that touch of doubt that had been nagging all day.

"Of course, we never really know what goes on between two people, do we?" Gray flashed that million-watt smile again, and Simon knew he didn't mean it. Of course, Gray believed that he did in fact know what was between his father and his mother. They loved each other. Were devoted to each other. Who could doubt it?

Gray nodded toward Simon's notebook as if in a hurry to conclude. "What else do you have there?"

"What was the defining moment of your father's tenure, for you, personally? The moment when you felt your father's power?"

"That's easy. Meeting Elvis. Without a doubt, nothing impressed me more than knowing that Elvis had come to the White House because my father had asked him to. I got to shake the hand of the King. I guess you were hoping for someone a bit more important in the grand scheme of things, but meeting Elvis was the really big moment for me." Gray laughed.

"Your family called the White House home for eight years. Did you have a sense of being part of history, back then?"

"Yes. Definitely." Gray's face sobered. "I felt that sense of greatness about my dad. I know I said it earlier and I know that everyone says it—that Graham Hayward was a great man—but he was. I always knew it.

And if you'd ever walked into the Oval Office when he was seated at that desk . . . well, you'd have known it, too. He had such an air about him."

"Power?" Simon suggested.

"Certainly that. But it went well beyond that. Because you knew that he would never abuse his power, that he'd always use it to do what was right." Gray Hayward looked Simon straight in the eyes and said, "My father really was as moral as everyone says he was. He always did what was right. Not in a self-righteous way. Just . . . *right.* He always stressed the importance of living up to your responsibilities, of being honest. Of earning your good name and working hard to keep it untarnished."

Hayward stood and walked to the window. Simon was grateful for the fact that he did not have to look the man in the eye at that particular moment, the late President's morality clearly being more of an issue to him than it was to his son.

"I was twenty-two the summer General Andrew Fielding was forced to resign. Remember the incident?" Gray smiled. "Of course you'd have been too young to have had a firsthand recollection, but you might have read about it."

"I did."

"Then you probably remember that General Fielding was a five-star general who'd earned his reputation in Vietnam. He was an exemplary soldier, from all accounts, and my father's most trusted military adviser. Unfortunately, in the years following the war he'd been part of a network that made a great deal of money supplying very young girls for the brothels in Thailand."

"I remember." Simon nodded.

"When the story surfaced, they wanted my dad to bury it. Wanted him to say that Fielding was retiring because his wife was ill. Let him retire from the public eye for a while before the story leaked out."

Gray blew out a long breath.

"My dad believed very strongly that the American people must always be able to believe that what their President told them was the truth. They might not always like it, but they always had to know that he would only tell them the truth. And he did. There are some in the military who never forgave him for that." Gray turned back to face Simon. "Whatever else history will say about my father, it will say that he never lied to the people."

"A novel approach to government."

"It's a legacy I hope to live up to."

"As President?"

"If it works out that way, yes, I would hope to follow in my father's footsteps. And *if* I'm lucky enough to follow him to the White House, I hope I can follow his example in the way he conducted himself there. But as a member of Congress I do try to live up to the standard he set." Gray walked back to the table and stood near his chair, as if debating whether or not he wanted to seat himself again. "Is that what you're looking for, for your book?"

"You've given me some great quotes, and I'm sure I'll use every one of them. My plan had been to focus the book's energy on reminiscences of your father as a man as much as a President. I've already compiled a number of personal remembrances that I think will make a great portrait of your father."

"Have you contacted Mrs. Williams at Dad's library?"

"Yes. She's been very helpful." Simon found it hard to meet the man's direct gaze. All that talk about honesty and never telling lies had made him a little antsy.

The rest of the afternoon was spent jotting down the congressman's recollections and impressions of his father's cabinet members, foreign dignitaries, and various crises, both foreign and domestic.

When Jen appeared in the doorway late in the afternoon to advise Gray of an important phone call, Simon took the hint and closed his notebook.

"Congressman, I can't thank you enough for the time you've given me this afternoon."

"Hey, it's I who should be thanking you. Philip feels that this book will introduce a whole new generation to my father."

"I'm doing my best." Simon picked up his briefcase and moved toward the door.

"As my dad always said, no one can ask more than that." Hayward followed Simon out into the hallway. "Now, we'll be looking for an advance copy, you know."

"Well, truthfully, I'm not sure when that will be available."

"Oh." Gray looked slightly disappointed. "I was hoping that the book could be out by the end of December, so that we'd have a shot at keeping the buzz going into the new year. Then just as it starts to die down—"

"Your candidacy will be announced." Simon paused at the front door.

"That was the plan."

"I'll do my best." Simon seriously doubted there would be a book by the end of the year but didn't feel it was his place to discuss that with the congressman. If Norton had led him to believe the book would be available by then, he'd let Norton break the news.

"You'll let me know if you need anything else, of course. From anyone." Graham Hayward stood in the doorway and nearly filled it. "I'll work on those questions you left for me and I'll fax my responses to you as soon as I can."

"That's great. Thank you. Thanks for your time."

Simon stood on the porch, adjusting his collar against the breeze. He'd been touched by the obvious pride and love that Gray Hayward had for his father and couldn't help but wonder how those feelings might change once the congressman discovered that he had a half sister.

Pausing as he reached the bottom step, Simon stopped to consider, for the first time, whether perhaps Graham already knew.

Chapter Seventeen

Betsy Pierce had parked her wheelchair at the front window and hadn't moved in over an hour. There was little traffic at this time of the day, and any car approaching from the east would have to crest that hill off to the right. Her eyes never left that point, despite the fact that it was only nine-thirty in the morning and Jude had said to expect them around eleven.

After having waited so long to see her niece again, Betsy would just have to wait a little longer.

She had barely been able to contain her joy when the call had come from Jude the night before. She'd finally told Dina everything, Jude had said, though it hadn't gone particularly well.

Well, of course it didn't go well! Betsy had wanted to shout. *You wait for thirty years to tell someone that she is not who she thinks she is, and chances are things aren't going to go well.*

But Betsy had shared none of her inner thoughts with Jude, choosing instead to offer sympathy for the situation and assure her that yes, of course she'd love to see Dina.

Simon Keller's name had not been mentioned.

It would appear, Betsy thought somewhat smugly as she focused on the black pickup truck that came over the hill, that her little gamble on Simon Keller had paid off quite nicely. He'd found Dina, and Dina was coming to Wild Springs, where she belonged. She was a Pierce and, as such, needed to know what would someday be hers. Betsy had no heir other than Dina and had long since made her will. She'd been hoping that Dina would discover her roots before such time as that will would be read. It would have been a hell of a way to find out who her real mother had been.

Betsy wondered if Simon had had as much success in figuring out what had really happened on that dark stretch of Connecticut Avenue so long ago.

But all in all, she'd realized a very large return for so small an investment.

"Miss Pierce?" Mrs. Brady stood in the doorway. "Can I bring you some breakfast now?"

"No, thank you."

"Some coffee, then, or tea?"

"Coffee, yes, that would be fine." Betsy turned and glanced back at the housekeeper, who had worked for the Pierce family for the past twenty years. These days Betsy had someone else come in to do most of the cleaning, leaving Mrs. Brady to act more as cook and personal assistant than housekeeper. Mrs. Brady, like Betsy, was no longer young.

"Did you find my note about lunch?"

"Yes. Lunch for three at half past twelve. On the back terrace."

"Do we have strawberries?" Betsy asked.

"No, but I can make a run out to the Wayne Farmers Market and see what's available, if you like."

"Thank you. I *would* like that." Betsy turned to her and said, "We'll be having company for another day or so. With any luck, they'll stay for more than one night. Mrs. Brady, did I tell you that my niece is coming?"

"Your niece . . . ?" Mrs. Brady frowned. As far as she knew, Miss Pierce had no niece. . . .

"Yes, my niece." Betsy turned back to the window. "So we really have to have strawberries for dessert."

"I'll see what I can find," Mrs. Brady assured her as she left the room, wondering about this sudden mention of a niece. She went straight to the kitchen and the nearest phone, where she intended on calling her husband and asking him what he knew about a niece. . . .

"Please do." Betsy smiled and leaned closer to the window, resting her elbows on the wide sill. "Blythe always loved strawberries. . . ."

The coffee sat untouched in the cup, and the chair had not moved from the window. It was ten minutes before eleven when the white Explorer came over the hill and slowed just before the next rise. Her heart pounding, Betsy wheeled herself to the front door and opened it, not bothering to wait to see if this was the car. She knew with all certainty that it was.

She watched as it drove slowly up the lane, watched as the driver parked on the circle in front of the house, watched as the trim young woman alighted and looked around as if trying to take it all in.

Betsy stared numbly.

My God, she looks just like Blythe. . . .

Jude got out from the passenger side of the car, but Betsy barely noticed her until the two women started up the walk. They both stopped, suddenly and in unison, when they saw Betsy in the doorway.

"Dina." Betsy forced herself to speak, forced down emotions that had been held in check for years.

"Hello," Dina said, not smiling.

"I wondered if you'd ever come," Betsy said, unable to take her eyes off Dina. The resemblance to Blythe was chilling. "All these years, I've prayed you would. . . ."

Dina froze where she stood, not knowing how to respond to the raw emotion in the woman's face and in her voice.

Finally, Betsy turned to Jude and said gently, "The years have been kind to you."

"Betsy, I had no idea," Jude stammered.

"Oh, the wheelchair?" Betsy glanced down at her still legs. "It has been a long time, hasn't it?"

"What . . . ?"

"Riding accident." Betsy turned to Dina and asked, "Do you ride?"

"Not really, no."

"Best not to take a jump before your mount does." Betsy smiled weakly, then wheeled herself back into the foyer. "I'm forgetting my manners. Please come in."

"Betsy, I'm sorry for giving such short notice," Jude was saying.

Dina stepped gingerly inside, as if she was almost afraid of what she'd find there. The foyer was wide and cool, the floors covered with vintage Oriental carpets and the walls covered with photographs. Oh so vague memories stirred within and swirled around her.

"Short notice?" Betsy paused in the doorway. "I've been waiting for twenty-five years, Jude."

"I've been here before," Dina whispered, as if not certain that it was true.

"Oh, a long time ago." Betsy nodded. "I can't believe you'd remember. I don't think you were more than four or five."

"I remember *her.*" Dina pointed to a painted portrait that hung over a handsome Eastlake-style table, a portrait of a young woman with a gentle face wearing a low-cut gown and a pearl choker trimmed in red stones.

"That's your . . ." Betsy paused, then looked at Jude for but a second before continuing. "Your great-great-great-grandmother. Eliza Donaldson Pierce. She was an outspoken critic of slavery before it was fashionable and a proponent of women's rights. It's said she gave her husband quite a proper run for his money."

And something else tugged at Dina's memory.

"Dogs barking . . ."

"We have always had a large kennel of hounds."

". . . and white birds in a cage."

"My mother raised doves. Her birds lived long after she did."

Emotions threatening to overcome her, Betsy turned the wheels in the direction of the sitting room. "Please, come in and sit."

Dina and Jude followed Betsy into the small room off the hall and sat side by side on a floral love seat.

"Dina, I have to say that I'm amazed that you remember so very much. You were only here a few times."

"I'm surprised myself. I've never consciously thought about being here."

"Has Jude told you how like your mother you are?" Betsy shook her head as if not quite believing the resemblance. She reached out to touch Dina's face, and as she leaned slightly forward, Dina said, "You came to see us, when I was little."

"Several times." Betsy nodded.

"I thought you were my fairy godmother."

"Ahhh, that's right," Betsy chuckled. "That's what you called me, then."

"Why did you stop coming?"

"Because we—Jude and I, that is—felt that as you got older, things would become much too confusing for you. How to explain to you who I was?" Betsy appeared to choose her words carefully. "We just didn't feel we could tell you the truth."

"Oh, I've already told her that you wanted to tell her everything years ago"—Jude turned to Betsy—"but I appreciate the attempt to cover for me. She already knows that keeping you from her was entirely my idea."

"Does she know that it was Graham's wish that in the event of his death or Blythe's, she not know who her parents were?"

"Yes." Dina nodded. "He shouldn't have made you promise. It was wrong to keep this from me."

"I agree, yes, but who's to say there wasn't some justification? After my sister died—the way she died—well, who knows what might have happened to you?" Betsy wheeled closer to the window, seeking the small patch of sun like a cat. "Your father became positively paranoid about you, saw danger behind every rock when it came to you. He trusted no one."

"If the danger's real, I suppose it's not really paranoia, is it?" Jude noted. "We're learning that the hard way, aren't we, Dina?"

"What are you talking about?" Betsy turned her chair to directly face Jude.

Dina told Betsy about the mystery van that attempted to run her over.

"My God, just like Blythe . . ." Betsy's face turned white, and her hands trembled.

"Yes. Just like Blythe. Dina, thank God, was quicker than she." A touch of bitterness rose in Jude's voice. "I believe we have you to thank for that, Betsy."

"What are you implying?"

"That you led Simon Keller to my door. All those years, I managed to keep her safe. And then Simon Keller showed up."

"Are you saying that you think Keller tried to run her over?"

"No. I'm saying that whoever was driving that van had followed him." Jude paused. "Yesterday morning, Simon came to my house. I was on a phone call, upstairs, and did not answer the door. Simon was parked in the lot at the park across the street. I watched him drive away. There was a van parked toward the back of the lot. It was late-model, dark green, just like the one that Dina described."

Jude's face flushed with anger. "Why did you tell Simon Keller where to find us?"

"Because it was time, Jude. I couldn't wait any longer for you to tell Dina on your own. I'm not going to live forever, and neither are you. She deserves to know who she is. She deserves to know who Blythe was. You weren't coming to me, weren't returning my phone calls, so I felt I had to take matters into my own hands. And I was weary of wondering about what really happened to my sister. Obviously, I never intended for a threat to be made on Dina, but it was *time*."

"But a journalist? You picked a journalist to tell? Do you know how lucky we are that this hasn't been all over the news?"

"Sooner or later, Jude, it would have come out. I've had reporters turn up on my doorstep every few years or so. They all ask about Blythe. About her relationship with Miles. About how many times she attended functions at the White House. It's all a matter of public record, Jude. Simon Keller isn't the only smart reporter out there. Sooner or later, someone would have put it together."

"But why him?" Jude asked. "Why now?"

"Because he was the only one who cared about how Blythe died. And because if someone is going to be looking at this as a story, I'd rather they be looking for a murderer than a mistress."

Betsy looked from Jude to Dina and back again. "It might as well be Simon Keller."

"If you hadn't told him where to find me"—Jude stood up, her hands on her hips—"if he'd stayed out of this altogether, we wouldn't be having this conversation. We wouldn't even *be* here."

"Exactly." Betsy nodded coolly. "Don't you think that twenty-five years was long enough to wait? She's my only blood relative, Jude. I have a right to see her, to know her. And she has every right to know her mother's family. To see what will belong to her someday . . ."

Betsy waved one hand in a sweeping gesture. "She's all I have, Jude."

"She's all *I* have," Jude snapped back.

"Stop it, both of you." Dina threw up her hands.

"Don't blame this on Simon. You were the one who decided to keep everything a secret, Mom. Don't blame him because he discovered it or Betsy for pointing the way. Look, I know that your biggest concern all these years was to keep me safe and protect me from scandal. But Betsy has a right to see what kind of a woman her sister's child has grown up to be. And I can't blame her for wanting some closure to her sister's death. She has that right, Mom." Dina looked from one woman to the other. "Once this is over, you two can bicker until you're both hoarse. But right now, we have a problem. And since the sum total of our collective investigative skills is apparently zero, I think we should call Simon. Maybe he's uncovered some information that he'd be willing to share. Frankly, I don't think we have a choice."

Dina held her hands up in a you-make-the-call gesture. "Unless you have a better idea?"

"We could try hiring a private investigator," Jude suggested.

"My father did that as soon as he learned that the investigation had been locked down so quickly," Betsy told her. "The official word was that Blythe was run over by an unknown driver. My father tried on several occasions to have the case reopened, but he was blocked at every turn. He'd pulled every string and called in every favor, but he never learned a thing." Betsy's mouth twitched slightly. "He died within a few years of Blythe's death, very angry and very bitter that the government he'd served for so long had let him down. No, ladies, a private investigator isn't likely to be of much use to us."

Jude blew out a long, reluctant breath.

"Well, what is it they say about the devil you know?"

Jude stood up, her arms crossed over her chest. "Where's the phone?"

"There's one on the desk right there in the hall." Betsy pointed toward the door.

"Dina, would you like to do the honors?" Jude asked.

The first thing that Simon noticed when he returned from his trip to Rhode Island was that the light was blinking on the answering machine on the hall table.

"Simon, it's Dina. Dina McDermott. Could you please call me as soon as you get this message? I'm at Betsy Pierce's."

Betsy Pierce's?

"Whoa. What have I missed?"

Only the late hour—it was close to one in the morning—kept him from returning the call right there and then. But he called first thing in the morning. Betsy answered the phone, though the conversation did little to quell his curiosity.

"We need to speak with you as soon as possible."

"We?"

"Jude, Dina, and I. We realize it's short notice, but—"

"I can be there by noon."

"Aren't you going to ask why?"

"Nope. Whatever the reason, I'm sure it's a good one."

"Yes, it is." Betsy's voice was somber.

Less than three hours later, Simon was being welcomed into the old farmhouse and led into the sitting room where the three women who had summoned him sat.

"Nice of you to invite me to the reunion, ladies." He touched Dina's arm and said out of the corner of his mouth, "How did this come about?"

"It's a long story," she whispered.

"I'll bet it is—"

"Let's go out to the patio," Betsy suggested, moving toward the door. "It's really quite a lovely morning."

"Did you have a nice drive?" Dina asked Simon as they followed Betsy to the back of the house and to the double doors, where she stopped.

"Things pretty glum?" Simon asked softly, so that only Dina could hear.

"I'm trying to shake it; I really am." Dina looked up into his eyes, and Simon saw the vestiges of what must have been a sleepless night. "I'm trying my best to act normally, but it hasn't been easy, these past few days."

Dina's hands were shaking, and Simon took them in his own.

"It's all a little overwhelming, you see," she added before Simon could say a word.

"Are you two coming out?" Jude called from the patio.

"We're right here," Dina said as she stepped through the doors, a smile pinned to her face.

Betsy gestured to comfortable-looking chairs that surrounded a glass-topped table with a vast umbrella overhead. The patio overlooked a garden and pool area with the tennis courts beyond. Simon took a seat and waited expectantly for someone to begin.

"Tell him what happened two nights ago, Dina," Betsy instructed.

Dina did.

"My God, why didn't you call me?" Simon turned to her, his eyes dark with panic. "Are you all right?"

"Only frightened." She smiled weakly. "And I did call you. You weren't home."

"I was in Rhode Island interviewing Graham Junior. If you'd told me this on my answering machine, I'd have been here last night. Did you call the police?"

"Yes, of course. Of course, at the time I spoke with them, I had no idea there was a reason why the near miss could have been something other than an accident."

"After that, I knew I had to tell Dina everything," Jude said. "She can't very well protect herself if she doesn't know there's a danger."

"That must have been very hard for you."

Jude nodded curtly.

"So what are you going to do now?" Simon asked.

The three women glanced at one another.

"Actually, we don't have a plan. This isn't something one deals with every day, you know." Dina cleared her throat. "We don't know where to start or who to talk to. How do you even start to explain something like this to a stranger?"

"And after all, you already know the whole story. We thought the fewer who knew—about Blythe, about Dina—the better," Jude added. "And since you were already looking into the affair—"

"This isn't about the affair anymore," Simon said pointedly. "It's about the fact that someone has gotten away with murder for nearly thirty years."

"But how can you separate the affair from the murder?" Dina asked. "Does anyone really think that

Blythe would have been killed if she hadn't been having an affair with Hayward?"

"I've thought about that every day since the day my sister died." Betsy leaned forward.

"And I've tried not to think about it," Jude admitted, a catch in her voice. "I always believed that as long as no one knew about Blythe and Graham—about Dina—there was nothing that could be done about Blythe's death without putting Dina in danger. Now I see how shortsighted that was."

"Is there any reason to think that someone *other* than the person who killed Blythe is the same person, or perhaps working for or with the same person, who was driving the van that tried to run me over?" Dina asked.

"I don't think there's any question that there's a connection," Simon told her.

"We need to find out who that person is before someone else gets hurt," Jude offered, though everyone knew that what Jude really meant was *before Dina gets killed.*

"Simon, we thought that perhaps in researching your book you might have learned something that could help us to figure out who might have known about Dina's birth. Who might have a motive for wanting Dina . . . out of the picture. And what we might do to keep that from happening. It's not the sort of story you take to your local law enforcement agency."

"Or, in this case, even to your federal law enforcement agency. You don't know who's who and who they might be connected to." Simon pondered the situation.

Simon turned to Betsy. "Are you certain that your father's investigator never found anything? Have you seen all the reports that he may have received?"

"I started looking for the file, but I didn't find anything," Betsy told them. "There's always the chance that perhaps I missed something. We can take another look after lunch."

"Simon, you must have some ideas about who might know about Blythe. About me." Dina leaned back in her chair.

"I've been thinking about this for several weeks."

Mrs. Brady appeared at the top of the ramp that led down to the patio below and asked about lunch. Betsy nodded that now would be a good time.

"And what have you come up with?" Dina asked.

"Well, there's Philip Norton. My old journalism professor from Georgetown. He was Hayward's press secretary, and he had been close to Hayward while he was alive and has remained close to the Hayward family over the years. He's the one who proposed the book I'm writing. Norton knows about Blythe and about Dina. I'm still trying to figure out what else he might know."

"Philip was very close to the President," Jude said.

"You know him!"

"It's been a few years since I've seen him, though we've spoken on the phone from time to time, so yes, I know him. I can't believe he'd have harmed Blythe. Or been involved in anything that could hurt Dina." Jude shook her head slowly.

"Okay, so we know that this Philip Norton knows. Who else, Simon?" Dina prodded him.

"Mrs. Hayward, I believe, knew about Blythe, but I don't know that she necessarily knew about Dina. It's possible. If Hayward had in fact told his wife that he wanted a divorce, he might have told her about the child he'd fathered with Blythe. As for the Hayward kids, I have no way of knowing that they knew about either."

"So you're saying that maybe Norton or Mrs. Hayward could be the person we're looking for?"

"I don't think we should count anyone out at this point. But I think that we also have to realize that there could be any number of reasons why someone may have wanted Blythe dead. This many years later, it's unlikely that we're going to be able to figure out all of them."

"We'll start with looking for the investigator's report," Betsy decided. "And we'll do that right after we finish this excellent lunch Mrs. Brady is bringing us. . . ."

It took them until nearly four that afternoon, but the report that Foster Pierce had received from his investigator was finally found in an unmarked file.

"Doesn't appear that there's much in here. Police report regarding the accident itself . . ." Simon noted.

"May I see that?" Dina asked.

Simon handed it over and continued.

" . . . and reports from the investigating officer to the effect that, other than one witness, who may or may not have been drunk, a canvass of the neighborhood found no one who had heard or seen a thing. The case was closed within the week," Simon mumbled as he skimmed the typed pages. "This isn't the entire police report. I've already spoken with the investigating officer. He said his report was six pages long when he turned it in. The report in the file is only two."

"Someone removed four pages?" Dina's eyebrows knit together.

"Exactly. The officer told me that the report he'd made had been purged by someone in the department way higher than he was. And since he was a rookie at the time, he was afraid to make waves."

"So someone with a lot of clout had the investigation stopped," Dina said softly.

"Well, if you are assuming that someone from our short list was that person, wouldn't that eliminate the professor? How much pull could he have had?" Betsy asked.

"Depends on whose behalf he was acting," Simon said. "Don't forget that he was the President's press secretary and close friend. So the request to quash the investigation could have come from Hayward. Maybe he didn't want anyone looking too closely into Blythe's life. Or her death."

"It could just as easily have been Miles, or someone else, acting on Hayward's behalf," Betsy noted. "Or it could have been someone *purporting* to be acting on Hayward's behalf without Hayward knowing it."

"I can't quite see Graham dropping the whole thing and just letting Blythe's killer go without trying to find out who it was. I do believe that he loved Blythe deeply. I think he would have moved heaven and earth to find out who had deprived him of his happily ever after," Jude said softly.

"We don't know that he didn't." Simon sipped at the iced tea Mrs. Brady had brought in.

"But if he had found out who had killed her,

wouldn't he have done something about it?" Dina frowned. "I mean, he loved this woman and someone killed her, he finds out who it was . . . he was the *President*, for God's sake. It just doesn't make any sense that he wouldn't have done something about it."

"Maybe he didn't know who it was. Or maybe it was someone he couldn't have retaliated against," Simon pointed out.

"Who could have had that much power over him?" Dina turned to ask.

A clap of thunder made them all jump.

"Weather report's been forecasting a big storm this afternoon and evening," Mrs. Brady announced. "I was wondering if perhaps I could leave after dinner."

"Go now, before the rain starts, Mrs. Brady," Betsy told her. "As long as there's something to cook, between the four of us we should be able to figure things out."

"There's chicken in tarragon cream sauce all made up. It only has to be baked. And there's salad and a strawberry shortcake," the housekeeper noted. "And I have one of the back guest rooms made up for Mr. Keller, just in case."

"That was thoughtful of you, thank you. Perhaps we'll be able to keep Mr. Keller with us for a while." Betsy smiled. "Now go on home, Mrs. Brady, before the roads start to flood out. We'll see you in the morning."

"Thank you," she said, then smiled her good-byes to the guests.

"Okay, my money's on Celeste Hayward," Jude said after Mrs. Brady had departed.

"Or one of his kids," Betsy suggested.

"Or someone very high up who wanted to put an

end to Graham's thoughts of not running for that second term." Simon threw his thoughts into the mix.

"How old were the kids back then?" asked Dina.

"Graham would have been around nineteen or twenty, Sarah maybe fifteen or sixteen. She was at boarding school," Simon told them. "And Gray was at college." He frowned. "At least, I'm pretty sure that's what Miles said. I can check the tape."

"What tape?" Dina asked.

"Twice when I met with Miles I taped our conversation," Simon admitted. "He talked about the night that Blythe came back from Arizona after Dina was born. And about the night that she died—"

"Is that legal?" Betsy raised an eyebrow.

"I only did it for my own use, so that I wouldn't have to try to take notes. I was afraid that whipping out a pen and notepad would distract Miles. So I recorded what he said thinking that I could just concentrate on what he was saying. Then when I got back home, I typed up my impressions, recollections of his gestures, facial expressions, that sort of thing, so that I wouldn't forget anything."

"Where's the tape now?" Dina asked.

"It's at my town house, in Arlington. It didn't occur to me to bring it. I'll drive back tonight," Simon told them.

"Wait until the morning, until the storm has passed," Betsy said. "And in the meantime, we can speculate to our hearts' content over dinner. Right now, I suggest we move into the kitchen and start cooking."

Dina was sitting on the bottom step of the grand staircase, a Bloomingdale's bag at her feet, when Simon came downstairs early the next morning. She was dressed in jeans and a red turtleneck sweater, her hair pulled back from her pale face with combs on either side. A denim jacket sat neatly on her lap.

"I didn't want to miss you." Dina looked up through red-rimmed eyes as he descended the stairs. "I didn't want you to leave without me."

"Was I taking you with me?" Simon paused a few steps above her.

"Would you? I'd like very much to go."

"Why?"

"Because I need to get away from here for a bit. Just to clear my head. I'm afraid I'm getting a bit stir-crazy."

"Do Betsy and Jude know what you're doing?" He stepped around her.

"I left them a note. I told them we'd be back maybe by dinner. We will be back by dinner, don't you think?"

Simon studied her face, the dark circles under the lovely eyes, the tension around her mouth.

Well, of course she's tense, Simon reminded himself. *Over the course of the past seventy-two hours, she's found out that she isn't who she thought she was, her mother isn't her mother, her father was the President, and someone tried to kill her. Enough to wear down anyone.*

"We should be back by dinner. Though I doubt Jude will be happy to find out that you've taken off with me. I can't shake this feeling that she still looks at me as close kin to the Antichrist. And she may be worried if you disappear for a day."

"She knows how to get in touch with me." Dina held up her cell phone. "Besides, I have my bribe all prepared."

Dina held the shopping bag open. "Coffee and warm blueberry muffins. Mrs. Brady thought we should have a little breakfast to take along."

"We?"

"You will let me come, won't you? I really need some time away from both my mother and Betsy."

Simon reached for the bag.

"Does that mean you're going to take me along, or are you planning on making off with the muffins?"

"I'd never pass up an opportunity to spend a day with you." Simon opened the front door and held it aside. "You didn't need the bribe, but as long as you've gone to the trouble, we can't let Mrs. Brady's muffins go to waste."

A low gray mist hovered over the pastures. In another hour, it would be burned off by the rising sun, which was, at that moment, still easing its way into the morning. The air held a slight chill and a dense warm scent that wafted up from the barn.

Dina stepped past Simon, thinking that Blythe must have known such mornings in this place, once upon a time. The sense of connection was unexpectedly strong, and she tried to shake it off.

"So, what do you think of Betsy?" Simon asked to break the silence as they reached the main highway.

"I think she's a nice lady who's had a few bad cards dealt."

"She seems delighted to have you at the ancestral home."

"That would make one of us." Dina opened the bag and took out napkins and a muffin, which she passed to Simon.

Simon raised an eyebrow. "I was beginning to think you were all right with this."

"If by 'this' you mean all the lies I've been told over the past thirty years, no, I'm not *all right* with it." Dina took a second muffin from the bag and began to nibble.

"But surely you understand why—"

"On an intellectual level, of course I do. I know that everyone did what they did out of love for me. But at the same time, the fact remains that I've been lied to about the most fundamental facts of my life. Even finding Betsy has been a bit of a shock, when I'd been told I had no family except my mother. . . ." Dina's voice cracked with the layer of anger that lurked just below the surface. "I love my mother—Jude, that is. We've always been very close, and that's what has made this all so difficult for me. It's always been the two of us. You have no idea of what a wonderful parent she has been. Mother and father and best friend. Everything that's happened"—she waved her hand—"can't change the fact that she's been an extraordinary mother. But what has changed is that she's not really mine."

Simon drove in silence. They had reached I-95 just above Wilmington, Delaware, before Dina spoke again.

"Even the money that I thought I'd inherited from my father was really from Blythe. It was money that Blythe had left to Jude for me."

"Does it make a difference, which parent had provided for you?" Simon asked.

"It makes a difference because it was a lie, too." Dina sighed. "Emotionally, this whole thing is much more complicated than you could imagine. The depth of the anger I feel is so great that it frightens me, but, I've discovered, so is the love. The bond between us goes so much deeper than even I understood. Blythe Pierce may have given birth to me, but I don't know her. I know almost nothing about her. She doesn't seem real in my life. Jude raised me. She's the only family I've ever known. No matter how angry I may feel toward her, she's still my mother. There are a lot of issues we need to deal with, she and I, but all that will have to wait until this is over. Right now, I'm more concerned with trying to find the person who tried to kill me. And, if possible, who killed Blythe."

"That's very mature of you."

"Are you being sarcastic?" Dina opened the bag that sat between her feet. "Are you ready for coffee?"

"Yes to the coffee, no to the sarcasm. And I think it's very generous of you to put your own hurt aside right now, even more remarkable that you're willing to do so in conjunction with Betsy *and* Jude."

Dina passed Simon one of the travel mugs that Mrs. Brady had filled with coffee.

"Betsy's been kept in the background long enough." Dina leaned her head back against the seat and closed her eyes for a minute. "And besides, it's time they made up."

"You sense bad blood there?"

"Oh, you could say that."

She rested for another mile or so, then turned to Simon and said, "Interesting, don't you think, that they each look at the situation from the opposite side?"

"What do you mean?"

"I mean that all along Betsy's been concerned mainly about Blythe's murder and all along Jude's been worried more about the affair becoming public and about protecting me."

"And which are you focused on?"

"Both. I want to find out who killed Blythe. I want justice for her. And I want to keep my anonymity." Dina sipped at her coffee, then asked, "Do you have any idea of what my life would be like if the press found out that I was Graham Hayward's illegitimate child?"

Simon shifted uncomfortably. He *was* the press. At that moment, he didn't want to think about being the one who could well bring yet even more distress into her world.

"It may not be possible to do one without the other," he said softly.

"Why not?"

"If we find the person—or persons—responsible for Blythe's death, how can we can seek justice without the truth being made public?"

Dina turned her head and looked out the window at the passing scenery, her silence testimony that if she hadn't considered this win/lose possibility before, she was considering it now. In the sun's light the circles under her eyes grew darker, more noticeable. Simon wished there was something he could do, something he could say, that would ease the pain she must be going through. He wondered when she'd had her last full night of sleep, uninterrupted by heartache.

"How did you get involved in all this?" she asked.

"I'm writing a book about Hayward."

"I know that part." She glanced at him from the corners of her eyes. "Why Hayward?"

"Why Hayward indeed," Simon muttered. "It's a long story."

"It's a long-enough drive to Arlington, I would think."

"I was working on a book of my own when I was offered the opportunity to work on the Hayward project by Philip. It isn't the type of story I'm really interested in, but I needed the money and he threw in the additional incentive of a two-book contract, presumably to publish the book I've been working on."

"What's your book about?"

"It's about laundering money coming out of South America and the involvement of several highly placed U.S. officials."

"Sounds intriguing."

"I thought so."

"Apparently Dr. Norton thinks so, too."

"It was a carrot." Simon checked the rearview mirror, then sped around the slow-moving station wagon that was straddling the white line.

"What do you mean, a carrot?"

"He offered to publish my book so that I'd agree to the Hayward biography." Simon's eyes never strayed from the back end of the car in front of him. "He knew I'd have problems getting a publisher to buy my book and he wanted me specifically to write his book."

"Why, and why?"

"I've come to the conclusion that he wanted me to write the book because he thought he could steer me away from the whole Blythe/Hayward affair. And he knew I'd have a problem getting a publisher on my own because I'd already quit my job with the *Washington Press* because of the book."

"You quit your job over a story?" Her eyes narrowed.

"The legal department wanted me to name sources, and I couldn't do that. My editor wouldn't back me up. I didn't feel I had much of a choice."

Dina seemed to be digesting his words. "So you decided to write a book about it." Dina nodded. "Without naming your sources—"

"Right." Simon changed lanes again.

"That takes a lot of nerve."

Simon floored it and eased around the back of an 18-wheeler, muttering, "I hate 95."

"What?"

"I hate driving on I-95."

"So I guess when you were given the opportunity to work on this book, it must have seemed too good to be true."

"And obviously was."

"You think he was using you so that you wouldn't put anything in your book that he didn't want made public?"

"Yes."

"Maybe that's not necessarily a bad thing, when you consider the people who could be hurt." She bit her bottom lip and looked pensive.

"You sound like Norton. That's pretty much what he said."

"How astute of him." Dina settled back again, studied the scenery, then asked, "Do you drive through D.C. to get to Arlington?"

"No. We can, but we don't have to. Why?"

"I was just thinking. . . ."

"About . . ."

"About maybe seeing the place where Blythe lived."

"Do you know the address?"

"Yes, I have it written down. Betsy said that she lived on Connecticut Avenue not far from the zoo."

"Easy enough to find. We can take a little detour."

"Do you mind?"

"Not at all. Arlington's only across the bridge from the city. We have all afternoon."

"Thank you. Betsy said she had an apartment in a lovely old Art Deco–style building that's still standing. And someday—not today, but someday—I'd like to see the park where she and Betsy used to walk. Betsy said there was an old gristmill there called Pierce Mill that she and Blythe used to stop at. And I very much want to see Dumbarton Oaks."

"You've never been there?"

"Oh, yes, many times. They have the most wonderful gardens there." Dina sighed. "Glorious at every time of the year. They were designed by Beatrix Jones Farrand, who was one of the first women landscape designers in this country. She designed some of the ironwork gates and the garden sculptures."

"Sounds like she was a very creative lady."

"She's my idol. When I was in school at College Park, I used to come into the city every chance I got to visit the gardens there, which are still for the most part as Farrand planned them, though of course they belong to Harvard now. Their Center for Studies in Landscape Architecture offers wonderful workshops and lectures, many of which are open to the public. I had planned to attend a symposium there a few years ago but had to cancel."

"What was the topic?"

"Environmentalism in landscape architecture."

"Sounds very intellectual." Simon raised an eyebrow. "I always think of gardening as being a little more down-to-earth. No pun intended."

"There's room for both dimensions in every field, the

ideological as well as the practical." Dina smiled for perhaps the first time since their journey had begun. "I'm surprised you've never been, since it's right there in Georgetown."

"Well, I've been to the museum. When I was a junior, I took a course in pre-Columbian art and a visit to the Dumbarton gallery was a must. They have a world-class collection of both Byzantine and pre-Columbian art."

"Betsy told me last night that Blythe was a volunteer there while she lived in D.C."

"You're kidding."

"Isn't that incredible? I'd been there as a student, so many years later. We walked the same paths. . . ."

"That is a pretty incredible coincidence." Simon paused to reflect.

"I thought so. It appears we may have had more in common than I originally thought. And it's funny, too, that I spent all those years at College Park—I got my master's there as well as my bachelor's—just a few miles from D.C., and now I find that I have connections to the city I could never have imagined."

Simon changed lanes and eased past the Honda that had been sticking faithfully to the speed limit for the past several miles.

"Including a father who lived in the White House." She spoke the words so softly Simon wondered if she hadn't been talking to herself.

Simon thought of passing the tractor trailer in front of him, but his steering wheel began to shimmy when the speedometer pushed eighty. He eased off the gas and fell back into the inside lane.

"What?" Simon asked when he glanced over and found Dina gazing out the window.

"I haven't taken a day off in so long that I feel like I'm playing hooky."

"You must invest a lot of time in your business."

"Every waking moment, in one form or another," she admitted.

Dina paused as if something had just occurred to her. "Simon, do you think there's a possibility that the person who was after me might go to my farm to find me?"

"I guess anything is possible, but they'd have to know that you own your business and where it is—"

"Neither would be difficult to learn in a town like Henderson. All you have to do is stop at the first gas station and ask." Dina shifted in her seat. "And speaking of which, maybe I should call Polly and tell her to let me know if anyone . . . strange . . . comes around."

"That's probably not a bad idea."

Dina searched in her purse for her cell phone, then hit the speed dial button.

"Hi," she said, forcing an upbeat note. "What's going on? . . . . They called this morning? Can you just call them back and tell them I'll be in touch as soon as I get back. . . . Well, I'm not sure. . . . I'm taking a sort of minivacation. . . ."

She appeared to be inspecting her nails—which were short and rounded, without polish—while listening somewhat pensively.

"But there is one thing. . . . If there is someone—anyone—who acts the least bit odd or suspicious, call me right away. I can't go into it right now, but if anyone asks, just say I took a week off. . . . No, no, I'm fine, really. . . . No, I'm not in any trouble. It's just . . . complicated," Dina sighed. "I'll tell you everything when I get back, but for now, if you could just hold down the fort . . . thank you. I appreciate that. . . .

"I think we need to figure this whole thing out before someone gets hurt," Dina told Simon after she ended her phone conversation.

"That would be the plan."

"Any thoughts on how we're going to go about doing that?"

"No, but the day is young," he told her. "Maybe after listening to my tapes again one of us will have some inspiration. In the meantime, just sit back and relax for a while. Try closing your eyes. You look like you could use the rest."

Dina lapsed back into silence, her head back against the seat, her eyes closed as Simon had suggested. He turned the radio on low and searched for a station that had more music than static. Finding one, he settled back, got into the rhythm of the traffic headed for D.C., and left Dina alone with her thoughts until they arrived at the city limits.

"Looks as if the sky has finally cleared up." Dina opened her eyes and squinted as she looked out the window.

"It's been sunny for the past twenty miles or so." Simon glanced over and added, "We're only a few blocks away from the zoo."

"Are you sure you don't mind stopping?" Dina asked as she searched her pocket for the scrap of paper on which she'd jotted down the address of Blythe's old apartment building. "I guess I was hoping that if I went to the place where Blythe lived, I'd have a stronger sense of her."

"As long as you're all right with it. You know, of course, that that's where she . . ." Simon hesitated.

"Yes." Dina nodded solemnly. "Where she died. Yes, I'm sure. . . ."

Chapter Eighteen

Simon circled the block several times before finding a parking place on one of the adjacent side streets. From there he and Dina walked around the corner to Connecticut Avenue and stood in front of the building that matched the address that Betsy had given Dina the night before.

The white apartment building had been one of many erected in the capital back in the 1920s and '30s in the Art Deco style, with a limestone porte cochere, octagonal columns, zigzag decorative bands, and carved panels incorporated into its facade. By current standards it was fancy and fussy and just a little bit camp.

"Betsy said that Blythe had the second-floor apartment there on the right." Dina looked up at the windows. "She said that back in the day, this was quite the place to live."

Dina turned toward the street and stared. "It's hard to imagine someone running down a pedestrian here—then reversing the vehicle to run over their victim a second time—without anyone seeing the accident." Dina frowned. "It's such a busy street."

"Well, it was, what, almost two in the morning, and there was a witness, according to the police report,"

Simon reminded her. "Albeit a somewhat intoxicated one . . ."

"I'll bet if they had looked harder, they'd have found someone who was looking out a window. Look at all the apartment buildings on both sides of the street." She turned back to Simon and said, "I don't understand why the police weren't able to find a more credible witness to the accident. Maybe they could have gotten a better description of the vehicle."

"I don't know that they spent much time looking for one," he told her. "We've already figured out that the investigation was brought to a premature halt by someone who had enough pull to get such a thing done."

Dina looked from one building to another, noting the number of windows that faced Connecticut Avenue.

"I don't believe for a minute that no one saw the accident."

"I agree, but thirty years later, what are the odds of finding that someone?"

"Slim to none," Dina muttered. "Slim to none . . ."

She stood on the curb and watched the cars zoom by, taxis changing lanes and out-of-state vehicles moving faster than the posted speed limit. When the light at the corner changed, stopping traffic, she stepped into the street.

"She would have been right here," Dina said, looking back at Simon, her eyes clouded. "The police report said she was struck at a point fifty-four feet from the intersection. She would have been right about here. . . ."

Dina stared at the street, as if envisioning the scene.

"The police report said she had stepped into the street on this side, that she was crossing the street." She turned to Simon, her head tilted slightly. "Why would she be crossing the street—headed away from her apartment building—at two in the morning? Where would she have been going at that hour?"

"That's a question that probably could have been answered thirty years ago, had it been asked."

Dina took another few steps forward into the street as if counting her steps.

"Twelve feet from the curb." Dina looked back at Simon. "Right here. This is where she was struck. This is where Blythe died. . . ."

"Dina, for God's sake." Simon stepped into the street and pulled her back as the light changed and a car sped through the intersection. "Could we not have history repeat itself?"

Dina seemed oblivious to the danger. "Don't you just feel so sad here, knowing what happened to her?" Her voice trembled. "She had everything in the world to live for. A new baby, a man she adored who loved her deeply, even though the circumstances weren't the best. How must she have felt, when she realized that the car wasn't going to stop? How must she have felt, when she realized that just that quickly, she was losing it all . . ."

Simon put an arm around her shoulders and led her back to the car, their hips bumping occasionally as they walked. Simon opened the door for her, tucked her into her seat.

"Maybe we could come back again sometime, maybe visit Dumbarton Oaks," Simon said as he slid behind the wheel, pausing to study the tension in her face.

"That would be nice, Simon. Thank you."

Simon tucked a stray lock of her hair behind her ear. "It'll give me an excuse to spend another day with you."

He started the engine and checked the rearview mirror.

"Simon?" she said as he pulled from the parking spot.

"What?"

"You don't need an excuse." Her fingers touched his, entwined with them. "You're the only thing about this whole mess that I wouldn't change."

"Even though I brought this mess to your door?"

"You're not responsible for the truth being what it is. Just tell me that you didn't ask me out because of my connection to your book."

"I asked you out in spite of it," he said honestly, and raised her fingers to his lips. He wanted to thank her for her generosity of spirit, wanted to comfort her, wanted to find a way to ease the painful emotions that must be churning inside her. Wanted to forget for a while that he was still a reporter and that he'd probably never uncover a story bigger than this one . . .

And so he said nothing but simply took a right onto Connecticut Avenue and headed toward the bridge that would take them to Arlington, thinking that for him, too, Dina was the best part of the whole mess. Both lost in their own thoughts, neither spoke until they reached their destination.

"Your development is really pretty," Dina said as Simon drove through the faux Greek columns that stood at the entrance to the community of rented town houses that he temporarily called home.

"Thanks. It's relatively quiet, too. There seem to be more single, executive types and young couples than families. I've only seen a few little kids around." He made a left onto his street. "They have a nice recreation center—a pool and a very well equipped gym."

"Do you use it?"

"Nah." He shook his head. "Gyms are for desk jockeys."

Dina laughed, pleased that he had remembered the remark she made the first time they met.

"Nice landscaping," she noted as she got out of the car. "A nice balance of shrubs and perennials, just enough trees . . ."

The mood had turned just a little lighter, for which Simon was grateful, for Dina's sake. She'd dealt with the morning's ghosts as best she could. He was thinking about how much he admired her strength as he went to put the key in the front door.

And realized that it was already open.

Not by much and not enough that you'd notice it from the street, but the door did in fact stand open by mere inches.

"Uh-oh," he muttered.

He held out a hand to stop Dina from entering with him. Who knew who had been there, or why, or if they remained?

"Call nine-one-one on your cell phone. Tell them there's been a break-in," he said quietly.

"Are you serious? . . . Oh, my God, Simon, don't go in there."

He pushed the door aside far enough for them both to see inside, enough to know that someone had done far more than simply paid a visit. Tables and lamps were knocked over; cushions from the living room furniture were scattered about.

"Stay out here and call nine-one-one," he repeated as he stepped into the hall. "And wait out there for the police to arrive."

"Why is it safe for you to go in and not for me?" she asked as she dialed the number.

Ignoring her, Simon stepped inside, cautiously, one step at a time, though he was pretty sure that the person who'd broken in was long gone. There were no strange cars outside, and it wasn't likely that someone would break in during daylight hours. Most likely, he was thinking, this had occurred during the night. His neighbors on the one side rarely arrived home before midnight and didn't leave in the morning until after ten, and the town house on the other side had been vacant for two weeks.

The inside of the house was cool and silent. Simon paused in the hallway and listened for the sound of someone taking cover, but there was nothing to indicate that he was not alone in the house. He peered through the living room into the dining room. He'd been working on his laptop on the dining room table two nights ago, before he left for what he thought would be a day trip to the Pierce farm. It had never occurred to him to take the computer with him. But he could see from where he stood that it was gone.

"*Shit!*" he yelled to no one in particular. "Damn it!"

Dina ran through the door. "Simon . . . ?"

"My laptop is gone. Along with the disk that was in it." He met Dina's eyes from the next room. "The disk on which I'd kept a running set of notes . . ."

"Oh, no . . ."

The center drawer of the small sideboard stood partially open, its contents dumped unceremoniously onto the floor. Simon opened the drawer all the way and stuck in his hand. It came out empty.

"The tape is gone."

"Damn." Dina slumped back against the wall. "Now we have to worry about someone else knowing—"

"I don't think so," he told her, his eyes darkening with anger. "This was no random break-in, in spite of the fact that someone took pains to make it look like one. The person who broke in knew there was a tape and came for it."

"Who . . . ?"

Simon looked beyond her and waved to the first arriving officer. "Hi," he called out. "We're in here!"

"What are you going to tell them?" Dina whispered.

"That it was a random break-in, of course."

The list of missing items was short, and the list Simon gave to the police was even shorter. He reported the theft of the laptop. "I'm renting here, so I don't have a lot of personal items with me. There really wasn't anything else to steal."

"Except the television." The young officer wandered back into the living room. "I've been wanting one of these wide-screen jobs myself. Nice stereo. Nice VCR. Wonder why they only took the laptop?"

"Maybe that's all they could carry," Simon offered.

"You go upstairs?" the officer asked.

"Ah, no," Simon admitted.

"I'll just take a look and make sure no one's up there," the officer said as another patrol car pulled up out front, lights on but no siren. He waved to the newly arriving officer and waited until he'd reached the front door. "Looks like only a laptop, so far."

"You in the FBI?" the newly arrived officer asked Simon.

"No."

"CIA?"

"No. Why?"

"Just asking." The officer shrugged. "Usually the only times you see a job like this—the place tossed and nothing stolen but the computer—it's got something to do with the government."

He followed the first officer up the stairs. Within moments both officers were coming back down.

"Did you have another TV set upstairs?" the first one down asked.

"No, only the one in the living room."

"Would you come on up and take a look around and let us know if anything's missing?"

Simon did, but there was nothing out of place.

"Odd, you know, that they only tossed the first floor," the younger of the two officers noted.

"Maybe he got scared away. Maybe he heard my next-door neighbors come in last night."

"Maybe he found what he was looking for in the laptop," the second officer said as he took a notebook from his back pocket. "Now, let's start at the beginning. . . ."

From the beginning to the end took all of twenty-five minutes. There was not much to tell, Simon explained. He'd gone out the previous morning and returned this afternoon to find his house broken into and his laptop stolen.

"Call us if you find that anything else is missing," the second officer said as he left, stealing one last appreciative glance at Dina before closing the door behind him.

"So. What now?" Dina asked when both patrol cars had departed.

"First, we check the jacket pocket," Simon muttered.

"Excuse me?" She frowned.

"I'll be right back," he said as he took the steps two at a time.

He was back in a flash, holding a tape in his hand. "All is not lost."

"I thought you said that the tape was stolen."

"They only found the copy. This is the original."

"But someone else has the other. Which means someone else now knows—"

"I suspect that this someone has known all along, so he didn't need the tape to tell him something he didn't already know." Simon slipped the tape into his pocket and took Dina by the hand. "This someone took the tape so that I wouldn't have any evidence of Kendall's statements."

"You think you know who took it?"

"Only one person knew about it." He locked the door behind them. "Dina, I think it's time you met Philip Norton. . . ."

The trip back to Georgetown was not the leisurely ride they'd taken earlier in the afternoon. This time around, Simon drove like a man possessed. In less than thirty minutes, Simon was on his way up the steps to Philip Norton's front door and ringing the doorbell.

"Simon, I wasn't expecting—" Norton stood in his doorway, his pipe suspended halfway to his lips, his eyes fixed on Dina, who, at that moment, was standing a foot behind Simon.

The smile froze on Norton's face. "Holy Mother . . ."

"Philip Norton, meet Dina McDermott," Simon said brusquely. "Dina, this is Dr. Philip Norton. He's an old friend of the family."

Norton simply stared at the young woman who stood on his front steps.

"My dear, you'll have to forgive me. You look so much like . . ." He stopped, glanced questioningly at Simon.

"Yes, she knows." Simon nodded.

"You look so much like your mother," Norton told Dina.

"I've been hearing a lot of that lately."

"I want the tape, Philip," Simon said angrily.

"The tape?"

"Please don't insult me. Just give it back to me, and we'll be on our way—"

"Are you referring to the tape you made of Miles—"

"You know exactly what tape I'm referring to. I want it back. The secret is out, Philip. She's standing right in front of you."

"I didn't steal your tape, Simon."

"No one else knew about it."

"Simon . . . Dina, come in. Please, don't let's stand in an open doorway discussing this; you never know who is walking by. . . ." Norton stepped back to permit them entrance, then closed the door behind him. "Now, come in and sit down and we'll—"

"This isn't a social call. All I want is the tape."

"Simon, I don't have your tape," Norton said calmly. "Which I'm assuming has been stolen—"

"You know that it has."

"You've told me what's on it. Why would I steal it?"

"So that I wouldn't have proof of the affair between Blythe and Hayward. So that no one could prove it . . ."

"To what end?" Norton looked mildly amused.

"Maybe so that the story won't come out and overshadow Graham Junior's candidacy."

"These days, a story about a presidential affair might be considered little more than a sex scandal, tabloid fodder. Besides, the proof of the affair is standing right next to you." Norton gestured in Dina's direction. "If in fact hard proof were needed, DNA is quite conclusive."

"Then why take the tape if not to cover up the fact of Dina's existence?"

"Simon, lately you've accused me of a lot of things. Now you're accusing me of breaking and entering. I would think your energy would best be spent trying to figure out who has your tape."

"Who did you tell about it?"

"No one. I swear, I've spoken to no one about it."

"Then why would someone break into my house?"

"What else was stolen?"

"My laptop."

"Were there disks in it?"

Simon nodded slowly. "Disks with notes . . ."

"Notes about . . . ?"

"Blythe. Dina. Hayward's desire to walk away from his family as well as his office . . ."

"And was the tape marked?"

"Oh, couldn't have been more clearly marked." Simon slumped back against the doorjamb. " 'Interview with Miles Kendall.' Think that was clear enough?"

"I swear to you that I have told no one about the tape, so that means that outside of this room, no one knew about it."

"You think someone broke into my house looking for something but not knowing what they would find?"

"I think it's quite reasonable to think that someone would believe that a reporter would keep notes if he was tracking an important story. I don't think someone *knew*. I think someone may have *suspected*. I'd bet my life that no one could have guessed that you'd have taped Miles Kendall's conversations, or what was on that tape." Norton grimaced. "And depending on who hears the tape, someone is going to get quite a surprise, I suspect, when they play it through."

Simon jammed his hands into his jacket pockets and stared at Norton. "Philip, several nights ago, someone tried to run Dina down. Someone driving a dark van that jumped the curb and literally chased her up onto a neighbor's lawn. Any thoughts on who that might have been?"

"Dear God . . ." Norton sat on the arm of the love seat just inside the door. Simon and Dina remained in the hall. "And you're all right?"

Dina nodded.

"I don't suppose you could describe the vehicle or the driver?"

"No."

"Who else knew about the affair between Blythe and Graham Hayward? Who else knew about me?" Dina asked.

"There were several Secret Service men who knew. They're gone now, however. I checked after Simon and I spoke the first time. The party chairman, Peter Stinson, knew about Blythe but not, I believe, about you. Frankly, I don't think anyone knew about you. Graham kept that secret very closely guarded. I don't think anyone knew other than Miles and myself."

"You must have been very close to him, for him to have trusted you with that," Dina said.

"We were close." Norton smiled gently. "It broke his heart when Blythe died. It absolutely broke him. He was never the same. He loved her very, very much."

"Who had known that he had been thinking about leaving office other than you and Miles?"

"Stinson knew. He wouldn't hear of it, of course. Out-and-out dismissed it. Said no one in their right mind would even consider something so stupid and refused to believe that Graham would do such a thing. Conrad Fritz, who was Graham's campaign manager both times, might have gotten wind of it. And the vice president might have known. Who knows who one of them might have told?"

"And you?" Simon asked. "Did you tell anyone?"

"No. I don't recall ever discussing it with anyone, other than Graham and Miles."

"Where would I find Stinson and Fritz?"

"Stinson's living in Green Lake, New Jersey. Just off the Delaware Bay. I have his number somewhere, but I'd have to look for it. I saw both of them recently at a party fund-raiser at Gray's place in Rhode Island. I didn't ask where Fritz was living, but I can try to find out for you."

Simon handed the pen to Dina. "Do you have anything to write your cell phone number on?"

Dina opened her purse and pulled out a small notebook and proceeded to write down the number. When she finished, she handed it to Norton, who placed it on the table without looking at it.

"Call when you find out where Fritz is. I'm going to pay a visit to each of them. I'd appreciate it if you didn't give them advance warning." Simon moved slightly toward the door.

For a moment, Norton appeared to be deep in thought.

"Philip?" Simon asked, to bring the man back.

"Oh, sorry. I was thinking how interesting it was that the same method was used to go after you as was used to kill your mother." Norton smiled apologetically. "Sorry. This must be a terrible trial for you."

Dina nodded.

"We're assuming that the same person was driving both vehicles, of course," Simon said. "The one that killed Blythe and the one that attempted to run down Dina. Maybe he—or she—feels comfortable with using the car as their weapon."

"Because they got away with it once before." Norton nodded his agreement as he took his pipe from his pocket and tapped it lightly against the palm of his hand.

"That and maybe because the car removes them from the victim a little. They don't have to see or touch the body; they don't have to be eye to eye with their victim."

"Who's watching out for Mrs. McDermott?" Norton asked.

"I am," Simon told him.

"Why not bring her here, and I can help you—"

"Not on your life." Simon shook his head.

"Why not?" Norton asked.

"Because I don't know if I trust you."

Simon stared at his old mentor for a very long minute.

"I'm sorry, Philip," Simon said as he closed the door behind them.

"You don't really think that Dr. Norton was driving the van, do you?" Dina asked Simon as they made their way through rush-hour traffic in search of the Beltway.

"No." Simon shook his head. "He's not a murderer. And I can't see him covering up for one, either."

"Then why don't you trust him?"

Simon paused, reflecting. "I don't know that I don't. Maybe I just have a bad taste in my mouth because I still think he tried to manipulate me."

"Do you think that one of these men, Stinson or Fritz, might have killed Blythe?"

"I don't know. If they thought that Graham was even remotely serious about leaving office because of Blythe, they might have had a motive to remove her from the picture. Think of what a big blow such an action would be to the party. It would be a big setback for a lot of people's agendas and would have a huge effect on elections for the next few years."

"I'm afraid I'm not politically astute enough to understand why."

"Because it would turn the tide, so to speak. Give the opposition the momentum going into not only the next presidential election but the House and the Senate contests as well. It would have been seen almost as a treasonous gesture by some, a selfish one at the very least. To throw away the power and prestige not only for himself but for his party and candidates for lesser offices as well. It's the type of thing that simply isn't done."

"And you really think Graham would have done this?"

"I don't think he would have been permitted to do such a thing, even if he'd really wanted to. But I do think that the fact that he even raised the possibility would have made a lot of people very, very nervous."

"But why would someone come after me now?"

"Well, maybe someone thinks it could sour Graham's chances at the presidency. That maybe the affair and the truth of your parentage might overshadow Graham's nomination. Or maybe it's personal. Maybe someone doesn't want anyone to know that Graham had had an affair."

"Do you think that one of these men—Stinson or Fritz or whomever—was involved in Blythe's death?"

"I don't know, but I'll be looking up Mr. Stinson tomorrow and we'll see what he has to say about the matter. If nothing else, crossing his name off only makes the list shorter. And besides, who knows what I might learn from him?"

Chapter Nineteen

"Well, you two certainly made a day of it." Jude stood in the open doorway, her hands on her hips, her expression peevish. "We've been worried about you."

"Sorry, Mom; I really didn't think we'd be this late. As I told you when I called, something came up that took a little more time than we'd expected, and then, on the way back, we were hungry and decided to stop for dinner—"

"And are you going to tell us just what it was that came up?" Jude frowned.

"Oh, for crying out loud, Jude, at least let them get into the house before you start grilling them!" Betsy called from somewhere behind the half-opened door. "And for the record, I wasn't worried. I figured that Simon would take good care of you."

"Thank you, Betsy." Dina gave Jude a perfunctory peck on the cheek as she winked at Betsy.

"Don't mention it." Betsy pushed the door closed after Simon came through it. "Now, I trust you have the tape?"

"I have a tape, yes." Simon took it from his pocket and held it up. "Unfortunately, someone else has one as well."

"Who someone else?" Betsy turned halfway around in her chair.

"Someone broke into Simon's house," Dina announced, "we think last night, while he was here, and stole his laptop along with a disk that held his notes. They also took the copy that he'd made of the tape."

The two older women fell silent, the ticking of the grandfather clock there in the hallway filling the void.

At last Jude said, "But that means that someone else . . ."

"Yes." Simon nodded grimly. "Someone else knows what Miles told me. I'm sorry, Jude. I never expected this to happen."

"Who knew about it?"

"The only person I told was Norton. And he swears he did not take it." Simon told Betsy and Jude about the stop at the professor's home. "He also claims not to have told anyone about it."

"Do you believe him?" Betsy asked.

"I think I do."

"What are we going to do now?" Jude looked from Simon to Dina and back again.

"First, we're going to sit down in the study and have a brandy," Betsy announced. "Then we're going to see if we can develop a game plan."

"While you pour"—Simon put a hand on the back of Betsy's chair—"I have a call to make. Do you mind if I use your phone?"

"Go right ahead. There's one on the desk in the hall," she offered.

"Were you able to find that number for your old

buddy Stinson?" Simon asked when the professor picked up.

"Impatient, aren't you?" Norton chuckled. "Yes. I have it right here. I was just about to call Dina's cell phone. Now, do you have a pen?"

"Just a minute." Simon searched his pockets for his pen, then walked into the sitting room and helped himself to a piece of paper from a pad that sat on Betsy's desk. "Go ahead with the number. . . ."

Simon wrote it down, then asked, "Do you have his street address?"

"No. But it's a small town, Simon. Stinson should be easy to find."

"And how about Fritz? Were you able to locate him?"

"Yes. He's in Virginia."

Simon wrote down the second number. "Thanks. I appreciate it."

Simon toyed with the idea of calling Stinson, then decided against it. Better to drop in unannounced than to give him time to prepare a story.

Simon folded the paper in half once, then once again, and stuck it in his shirt pocket. It was too late to leave tonight. He'd have to ask Betsy for the use of her guest room again tonight.

"So," he said as he walked back into the front room where the ladies sipped their brandy and waited for him to join them. "Shall we listen to the tape?"

By midnight, the tape had been played and replayed, its contents and the repercussions that might be expected from having the copy fall into the hands of some other unknown party discussed without conclusion.

Finally, at ten past twelve, Betsy turned her chair around and wheeled herself toward the door.

"I'm too old to stay up this late," she announced. "As are you, Jude. Let's call it a night."

"But . . ." Jude gestured to Dina and Simon.

"Exactly." Betsy grinned. "Come on, Jude. You can help me with my chairlift. It was acting up again this afternoon."

"Good night, Mom." Dina blew her mother a kiss. "Sweet dreams."

"Sweet dreams, honey," Jude said in reply. She paused for a moment, then nodded to Simon. "You, too."

"Thanks, Jude." Simon tried not to grin. Betsy's efforts to leave him and Dina alone had been so overt, and Jude had clearly not been partial to the idea.

"So. Here we are," he said as the sound of Jude and Betsy's voices—bickering over the merits of a current bestseller—faded down the hallway.

"Yup." Dina nodded. "Here we are." She sat next to him on the small love seat. "Thanks for taking me with you today."

"My pleasure."

"Any chance you'll let me go with you tomorrow, too?"

"To see Stinson?" Simon raised an eyebrow.

"Yes."

"Sorry." He shook his head. "I don't want him to see you. Chances are, he knew Blythe. I don't want him to make a connection that he doesn't already know about."

"Do you think he'd remember her?"

"Dina, if she looked as much like you as everyone says she did, he'd never forget her."

Simon reached out and touched the side of her face. Her hand found his and held it for a long moment.

"Simon, do you want to kiss me?" she asked.

"I've wanted to kiss you since the minute I saw you."

"Why don't you?"

"Why don't I kiss you?" He smiled and leaned toward her. "Why don't I do just that . . ."

He lowered his mouth to hers and brushed her lips with his, side to side, then tugged, ever so slightly, on her bottom lip with his. She slid her arms around his neck and pressed into him, inviting more, and he traced first her lips, then the inside of her mouth. She tasted of Betsy's fine brandy and a ripeness not found in a bottle.

"Makes me wonder what I was waiting for," he murmured as he kissed her again.

"I was beginning to wonder the same thing." She held on to his collar, keeping him close, angling her face against the back of the sofa.

"Well, I thought about it. A lot. But then I'd think about everything you've been through and I'd think, well, the last thing she needs right now is some guy hitting on her."

"I don't think of you as just 'some guy.' "

"How do you think of me?"

"As a very welcome addition to my life."

"I like the way that sounds." He nibbled on her bottom lip. "So you don't blame me for having started all this madness?"

"This madness started thirty years ago. Sooner or later, it was bound to catch up with us. Sooner might turn out to be better than later, in the long run." She leaned back against the sofa and looked up at him. "I wasn't kidding when I said that you were the best thing that came out of this mess. I'm glad I met you, Simon Keller."

"I'm glad I met you, too." He leaned over and turned off the light on the table next to them, the only light in the room. "Just in case Betsy's groom is prowling around outside with his shotgun," he told her as he pulled her closer and took her mouth again with his own.

Dina's pulse began to pound and sharp slivers of heat flooded through her. *This is what I've been waiting for, what I tried to describe to Mom. I've waited all my life for someone to take my breath away, for someone to kiss me and set the world on edge.*

And that was exactly how it felt. Like the world had been set on its edge and the center of gravity shifted. She was wondering how much further one could slide down this slope when Simon leaned back and traced the side of her face with his fingers.

"You look tired," he said softly.

"I *am* tired," Dina admitted.

"When was your last full night of sleep?"

"What day is it?"

"That's what I thought." His fingers kneaded at the knots in her shoulders. "Your muscles feel like poured concrete. Here, turn around. . . ."

He turned her body so that her back was facing him, worked his thumbs just above her shoulder blades.

"Oh, my God," she gasped as he began to massage from the base of her neck to her shoulder blades.

"Just relax and let me see if we can scare away some of the tension. . . ."

"I'm beginning to feel like a rag doll," she said a few minutes later.

"That's good. That means it's working."

"Oh, it's working all right." Dina smiled to herself. *It's working just fine. . . .*

"Why don't you go on up and try to get some sleep?" he said after he'd reduced all of her muscular structure to jelly.

"I don't think I can move," she murmured sleepily.

"Then I'll carry you." He started to rise.

"That won't be neces—" Dina giggled as he lifted her from the sofa in one smooth motion. "Really, Simon, I can—"

"Too late." He chuckled and made his way to the stairwell.

"No, seriously, you can just put me down now." Dina stifled a laugh.

"Not till I have you safely to your door."

"That would be it, on the left," she pointed out when they reached the top of the steps. "Thank you for the lift."

"My pleasure." He leaned down to nuzzle the side of her face. "I'll see you when I get back from Stinson's."

"Simon."

"Ummmm?"

"I'm trying really hard to sort things out—about myself, I mean—but it may take a while." She looked up at him with eyes that darkened with all the swirling emotions of the past weeks. "It's hard to reach beyond yourself to someone else when your entire life is shifting right before your eyes. Hard to open up to someone—even though you may want to—when you're not really certain who you are."

"I understand." He settled his arm around her neck

and stroked her hair. "I'm in no hurry. I'll be here waiting when you do."

No matter how long it takes, Simon silently promised as he held her for just one more moment. Some things were well worth waiting for.

For the second morning in a row, Simon crept down the steps early, taking pains to avoid those steps he'd already identified as creakers. This morning, however, there was no Dina waiting on the bottom step, no thermos of coffee or fresh muffins.

He sat with the engine running while he located Green Lake on the New Jersey map that was in his glove box. Not too far if he took the Commodore Barry Bridge and then picked up Route 322. From there, he could take one of several roads. He'd stop someplace once he crossed the bridge to ask which might be fastest. Then of course, there'd be the matter of finding Stinson.

Green Lake, New Jersey, being what it was, however, with its population of roughly one thousand souls, finding Stinson had been relatively easy. Simon had stopped at the Green Lake Country Store, part of which served as the local post office, as he discovered when several folks walked up to a large open window and walked away sifting through the bundle of mail they'd been handed.

"Excuse me," Simon said to the gentleman behind the window. "I'm looking for Peter Stinson. I was told he had a home in the area. Could you tell me where I might find him?"

"You might ask in the store," the man told him. "Post office can't really give out addresses."

Simon went inside and repeated his question to the person behind the counter.

"You a friend of his?"

"We have a mutual friend."

"Heard he used to be something in Washington."

"Long time ago." Simon nodded.

"He and his wife bought the 1745 Isaac Martin House about eighteen months ago. They just finished renovating it. Sure looks good," said a fellow who sat sipping his morning coffee at a round table along with two other gents.

"Rebuilt the garage and everything." One of his companions nodded. "He's been real active with the local birders."

"I heard him tell Angus Simpson that he saw a Henslow's sparrow down near the marsh," a woman reading a newspaper commented without looking up from the page.

"That right?" The coffee drinker turned in his seat. "Which side of the marsh?"

"Would you happen to know the address?" Simon asked, trying not to appear impatient among the locals, who clearly were in no hurry.

"It's the 1745 Isaac Martin House," the first man responded.

"But what's the address?"

"That is the address," the man behind the counter told him. "All of the homes in Green Lake have historical designations, the whole village being on the National Register of Historic Districts. We just refer to the buildings by their names."

"How do you know which house is which?" Simon asked. "How do you tell them apart?"

"The houses all have signs on them," someone said.

"You want the 1745 Isaac Martin House, you want to go straight out here to the left, out toward the river. It'll be on the left side of the road; the siding's painted yellow and it has a big front porch," the woman with the newspaper told Simon.

Simon thanked them for their help, then paused on his way out to purchase a cup of the fragrant coffee and a copy of the local paper.

As promised, the 1745 Isaac Martin House, not three minutes from the country store, was clearly marked with a sign that hung next to the front door. Two rocking chairs graced the front porch. On one of them, a woman sat taking in the morning, a thick book in her hands and a fat cat on her lap.

"Good morning!" Simon called to her as he got out of his car. "I was looking for Mr. Stinson."

"You missed him by an hour." The woman smiled and slid an errant strand of pure white hair back behind her ear. "Are you from the birding magazine?"

"No, actually, I'm a friend of an old friend of his. Are you Mrs. Stinson?"

"Yes."

"I'm working along with Dr. Philip Norton on a book about former President Hayward. He suggested I look up your husband, since Mr. Stinson was the party chairman when Hayward ran for office both times. We thought maybe your husband might have some remembrances or some little anecdotes to share about the former President."

"Oh, my, I'm sure he'd like to be included in that."

Mrs. Stinson smiled. "He's just down to the marsh, straight on through that path. . . ." She pointed across the street. "But for heaven's sake, go quietly. He's been watching a pair of yellow-throated warblers build a nest down there for the past week, and there will be hell to pay if they're scared off."

"He'll never hear me coming." Simon held a finger up to his lips.

"Well, try not to give him a heart attack, either." The woman grinned.

"I'll do my best to strike a balance," Simon told her as he headed off in the direction Mrs. Stinson had indicated.

Simon trod softly on the path that cut through the tall grass, trying to avoid that bull-in-the-china-shop approach that would undoubtedly alienate Stinson before Simon could get within ten feet.

He smelled the marsh before he saw it. The salty scent borne on a spring breeze engulfed him. A midwesterner, Simon never quite became accustomed to the smell of the coastal wetlands, salt marshes and mud flats, brackish water and animal matter left too long in the sun.

Up ahead, a man stood motionless at the edge of the marsh, field glasses held to his face. Simon tried to make just enough noise to alert the man that someone approached without being loud enough to scare away whatever it was he was looking at through his binoculars.

"Green heron," the man whispered as Simon drew near. "I think they're building a nest there in that stand of reeds."

Simon leaned forward to take a look but saw nothing moving.

The man offered his glasses to Simon, telling him, "Look to the right of that one low branch."

"I see them." Simon nodded. He watched for a moment, then handed the field glasses back. "Thanks."

"You're welcome." The man gave Simon the once-over.

"Are you Peter Stinson?" Not certain of proper birding protocol, Simon kept his voice low.

"Yes. You are . . . ?"

"Simon Keller. I'm working on a book about Graham Hayward, and Philip Norton suggested that I—"

"Saw him not too long ago. He mentioned something about a book, but we didn't get much chance to chat." Stinson raised the binoculars to his eyes once again and seemed to be distracted by something that stirred in a clump of tall grasses. "What did you want to know?"

"Well, I know that you were the party chairman while Hayward was in office, and since this book is intended to contain a selection of personal recollections about President Hayward, I wanted to see if you had something to contribute."

"My recollections of Hayward, you say?"

Simon nodded.

"Graham Hayward was a horse's ass," Stinson pronounced as he pointed skyward. "Looks like a black-headed gull, right there. I'll be darned."

"Ummm . . ." Simon glanced up. To a boy from Iowa, a seagull was a seagull. "Would you care to elaborate on that?"

"He was a do-as-I-say-not-as-I-do sort of fellow."

"Everything I've read about him leads me to believe that he was a totally honest, moral, upright—"

"Oh, please," Stinson muttered under his breath. "You ever see a yellow-winged warbler?"

"Ah, no, I haven't."

"Look on the low-hanging branch of that dead tree straight ahead."

"Ah, yes, I see them. . . . Now about President Hayward . . ." Simon held on to the glasses, hoping to prevent Stinson's attention from wandering again. "Are you implying that he wasn't as moral as he—"

"Ask Norton. He knew."

"Knew about what?"

"About Hayward's girlfriend."

Simon feigned shock. "Hayward had a girlfriend?" he whispered.

"Yup. Young one. Beautiful girl, but young. Never a word slipped out about that, gotta hand it to Hayward's people there. Guess you're not going to slip it into your book, either, not with Norton involved."

"Why would you say that?"

"He'd never let that get out. He's like the keeper of the flame. Anyway, it's no secret that Graham's boy will be running in the next election. No way they're going to let that cat out of the bag. Why muddy the waters?"

"Then why did you tell me?" Simon passed the binoculars back.

"What's the difference?" He shrugged "You're working with Norton, so he must trust you. He won't let you use it anyway, but you probably already know that."

"So that's the only scandal about Hayward, that he had a girlfriend?"

"Isn't that enough?" Stinson snorted. "Can't tell you how pissed off I was when I heard about that. All those years of being Mr. Morality, making it hard on the rest of us to live up to his code, and here he was, doing just what everyone else wanted to do and was afraid to for fear he'd find out and give 'em hell."

Stinson shook his head. "Hayward was a damned hypocrite."

"How did you learn about her, the girlfriend?"

Stinson watched a flock of birds take flight from the opposite side of the marsh. "From David Park."

"The vice president."

"Yes. He was quite excited about the prospect of moving up the . . ." He stopped mid-sentence.

". . . the ladder?" Simon finished it for him. "Why would Hayward having a girlfriend make Park think he'd be moving up? Infidelity has never been an impeachable offense."

"Hayward was in no danger of being impeached. But at one time he did make some ridiculous rumblings about not running for a second term."

"Why would he do that?"

"Because for one brief shining moment Hayward thought that he might walk away from it all."

"From his office."

"Yeah. Because of the girl."

"But of course he didn't do that."

"Nah. It was a stupid whim on the part of a stupid man. He never would have been permitted to do it."

"Who talked him out of it?"

"I did. Me and Kendall, actually. But as it turned out, he wouldn't have gone through with it anyway."

"Why's that?"

"The girl died."

"Just like that?"

"Yes. How's that for a coincidence? Hit-and-run, they said, but who really knows about these things?"

"Did you know, Mr. Stinson?"

"No, no. But I did wonder about it; I sure did. Just seemed awfully convenient, and they never did find the driver of the car. Another bit of convenience, if you ask me. Officially, no one heard or saw a thing, even though this accident happened on one of the busiest thoroughfares in the city. Now, granted, it was the middle of the night, but still, you had to wonder, you know? It just never sat right." Stinson looked Simon straight in the eye and said, "I'd wanted to strangle Hayward with my bare hands when he started talking about how maybe he wouldn't run again. All the time and money that went into building his political career. Not to mention the potential fallout in the Congress. But killing the girl? I can't imagine anyone who would have gone to such lengths. And Hayward ended up staying in office, but between you and me, he never was the same."

"In what way?"

"He lost his fight. The girl died, and he just sort of dried up. He died within a month of leaving office."

"Yes, I know."

Stinson raised the glasses to his eyes and scanned the heavens. "Guess it's safe to assume that that's one little anecdote that won't show up in your book, eh?"

"Stinson admitted that he knew about Blythe, admitted he knew about Hayward thinking about not running for a second term, admitted he was less than pleased with it. But he gave no indication that he knew anything at all about your birth, and I don't see him as having anything to do with Blythe's death. He just gave me the feeling that he was as perplexed by that as we are."

Simon stood in the narrow phone booth, the door closed over to keep out the sheets of rain that blew against the clear walls and streamed down the sides in thin rivers, mentally kicking himself for losing the battery charger for his cell phone in his move to Arlington. At the same time, he wished he could just magically transport himself back to Wild Springs, so that he could see Dina's face as clearly as he heard her voice. He'd found himself thinking an awful lot about that face today.

"So we can cross him off our list of possible mystery drivers. Besides, he was leading a midnight bird walk through the marshes every other night for the past two weeks and would have been giving his lecture on migrating birds of prey at the time you were jumping over hedges."

"You're sure?" Dina felt a tug of a disappointment.

She'd wanted Stinson to be the one to have been behind everything, had been hoping against hope that somehow Stinson would quickly and easily and, without further threat to anyone's well-being, be revealed as the culprit so that they could be done with the uncertainty. Not a very likely or realistic outcome, she knew, but still, she'd hoped for a bit of a miracle.

"Before I left town, I stopped back at the country store, which is sort of the newsstand, coffee shop, post office, social center of the town. The man behind the counter was on that walk."

"Sounds like a neat little town."

"I think you'd like it. Lots of old houses with lots of old gardens. They even had their own tea-burning incident back in the seventies." Simon paused, then added, "That would be the seventeen hundred seventies."

"It might be fun to visit."

"That trip will have to wait until I get back from Virginia Beach."

"What's in Virginia Beach?"

"Conrad Fritz. I'm going to be stopping in to see him first thing in the morning."

"You're not coming back up to Betsy's tonight then?"

"No. I'm going to head on down through Delaware and over the Bay Bridge Tunnel tonight, so that I can catch up with Fritz early."

"And then what?"

"I guess that'll depend on what Fritz has to say."

"Simon, you're going to be careful, right? You're not going to . . . well, do or say anything that's going to cause him to, well, to *do* anything to you, are you?"

"Not if I can help it. The object is to narrow down the list of possible players on the bad guys' side, not on our side."

"We being the good guys."

"Absolutely we are the good guys."

"Well, you be careful. You know what they say about good guys finishing last."

"Not this time, sweetheart," Simon tried to cheer her with his best Bogie. "Not this time . . ."

Chapter Twenty

Polly glanced up as the little bell over the door announced a customer. A small figure in a sunny yellow raincoat stood just inside the shop, shaking water from an umbrella, which was left by the door.

"Hi!" Polly called from the counter where she'd been wiring dried hydrangea to a wreath. "Can I help you with something?"

"Are you Ms. McDermott?" the woman said from the door.

"No, I'm not. Is there something I could help you with?"

"I was looking for Dina McDermott."

"I'm afraid she isn't here right now."

"I was hoping to discuss a garden renovation with her. I've heard she's quite talented." The potential customer smiled warmly.

"She's the best." Polly smiled back.

"So they tell me. My husband and I are looking at an old farm that's for sale a few miles from here, and I was wondering if the garden was worth restoring or if we should just scrap it and start over." Another smile. "I thought perhaps we should get an idea of what something like that might cost. The renovations on the house alone are going to be major, so we thought maybe we should look at the whole picture."

"Get an idea of what the whole project might cost." Polly nodded. "A smart thing to do."

"So I was hoping to maybe get together with her as soon as possible. Is she expected soon?"

"I'm not sure." Polly debated. This was the third inquiry about a potentially promising landscaping job since she'd spoken with Dina two days ago. Whatever was keeping her, Polly thought, it must be really important.

"Look, why not leave your name and phone number, and I'll make sure she gets the message."

"That would be fine. The last name is Dillon. Here, I'll write down the number for you. . . ."

Polly waited until the customer had left the shop before grabbing the phone and dialing Dina's cell phone but was forced to leave voice mail.

"Hi, Dina, sorry to disturb whatever it is that you're doing—hope it's something good, by the way, something involving a gorgeous man and lots of sunshine, but I promised myself I wouldn't pry. Anyway, I just thought you should know that we've had three customers asking about landscaping. One McMansion—a neighbor of the Pattersons whose property you did last fall—and two other potential garden jobs. The one garden is a Mrs. Fields—she and her husband just bought that house with the red siding on the left as you go out of town. And the other is a customer who stopped by to see about getting an estimate for a renovation on an old farm a few miles from here, forgot to ask which one. Anyway, she and her husband are trying to decide whether or not to make an offer on this property and wanted your input on what it would take to bring the grounds back. Their last name is Dillon. I'll give you the numbers. . . ."

At Wild Springs, the three women had fallen into a guarded routine, the company sometimes more uneasy than at others. Betsy may have been in a wheelchair, but she was anything but sedentary. The hours not spent in the riding barn—where, with the aid of another instructor, Betsy gave lessons three afternoons each week as well as Saturday mornings—there was tennis. Or ambling along the fields and woods around Wild Springs. And for Dina, there was the garden.

Dina had spent several hours during the first two days at Wild Springs inspecting the beds, absently pulling a weed here or there, mentally dividing this clump of overgrown daylilies or that clump of iris—acts that were, for Dina, as natural as breathing. Dina had told Betsy that dividing overgrown perennials was something akin to using the Heimlich maneuver on a choking man in a restaurant. And to Dina, it wasn't work. It was therapy of the purest kind. If nothing else, it was familiar and soothing, so necessary in this time of turmoil, when her life had been turned inside out. It offered her time to be alone, to reflect on all that had happened and all she had learned. It was the one constant in her life, and she welcomed every chance she could get to dig her hands into the dirt.

"Your Siberian iris should be divided," she'd announced at breakfast on the morning that Simon had left to visit Stinson.

"I'll put it on the list for the gardener. I'm not sure

when he'll be able to get to that. He's had some problems with his hip, you know. Arthritis," Betsy had told her as she spooned scrambled eggs onto her plate.

"Have you thought of possibly hiring someone else to come in?" Dina offered.

"Shhhhh," Betsy shushed her. "It's Mrs. Brady's husband, and he's been working here for years. I'd hate to have him think that the minute he can't work like he used to he will be replaced. Not good for his morale. He worked with my dad and my granddad. I simply couldn't just replace him."

"Would you mind if I just tidied things up a bit, then?" Dina asked.

"Now, I don't want you to feel obligated, Dina."

"Actually, I'd feel better if I was doing something. I'm not used to sitting around. I hate the feeling that I'm hiding out and wasting time that could be spent doing something useful. I'm getting a bit stir-crazy."

"I understand completely, my dear. After breakfast, I'll show you where the garden shed is and where the tools are kept. Feel free to do as much or as little as you like."

"Maybe it will make me feel less guilty about the time I'm spending away from my business. We're just gearing up for our busy season, and I know I need to be there."

"You did say you had reliable help, though—"

"The best. But still . . ."

"Well, you have been on the phone with Polly about twenty times since yesterday, Dina," Jude reminded her. "And wasn't that Mrs. Fisher you were speaking with this morning? It's not as if you've been neglecting things altogether."

"I know, but it's not the same."

"Of course it isn't the same, but it's going to have to do until Simon comes back with a suspect."

"Having a suspect won't mean a thing without a game plan," Betsy noted. "Unless, of course, someone confesses to having killed Blythe. I for one am not holding out any hopes for that happening."

"Well, obviously, but we can't formulate a game plan without knowing who—"

Dina shook her head and walked outside, leaving the two women to bicker to their hearts' content.

She'd only thought to separate a few choice plants that were overgrown, but before the morning had ended she'd weeded out three beds and made room for the new plants she'd divided from the old. Besides keeping her physically busy and giving her a respite from focusing on something other than all the changes in her life, she found in the gardens at Wild Springs an unexpected connection to the grandfather and great-grandfather she had never known.

And in the afternoon, after she'd cleaned up from the garden and Betsy had cleaned up from the barn, the three women gathered in the sitting room for tea as they had every afternoon since Jude and Dina had arrived and went through the photo albums that lined the bookshelves. It was during those times that Dina got her first glimpse of what it meant to be a Pierce and just how much underlying hostility had yet to be resolved between Jude and Betsy.

"Now, these pictures were all taken when my father was Ambassador to Belgium. Lovely photos of Mother there, this was right before she took ill. . . ." Betsy's face grew wistful. "We lived in Brussels for a time. It was lovely. Blythe and I attended a tiny school for the children of diplomats where only French was spoken. I had to learn the language very quickly. Blythe already had taken French, of course, at school here, but I couldn't speak a word. We only stayed there for a year. After Mother became ill, we came home. Father, of course, stayed on. . . ."

"And then she went to the Shipley School?" Dina held up her right hand, where Blythe's school ring sat on the middle finger.

"I noticed that you were wearing that." Betsy smiled. She hadn't wanted to comment on the ring, thinking that if Dina wanted to ask, she would. "Yes, we both enrolled at Shipley when we returned home. It's a bit of a drive—it's in Bryn Mawr, some miles from here, you see—and it could be most unpleasant traveling in the winter. The school is still there, still thriving, though I understand it's co-ed now. Unimaginable back in my day, though I suppose it represents progress of a sort. . . ." Betsy sipped at her tea, which Mrs. Brady had served from the silver tea service. "Over the years, I sometimes wondered what you thought, when you looked at that ring. Assuming, that is, that you kept it."

"I never knew who '*BDP*' was, but for a long time something told me not to show the ring to you." Dina glanced up at Jude. "When I finally got up the nerve to ask about it, you said it belonged to a cousin of yours."

"Is that what you told her, Jude?" A frown creased Betsy's forehead.

"Well, you could have told me that you'd given it to her; it caught me completely off guard when she came downstairs one night with that ring on her hand and asked me who it had belonged to." Jude's voice rose in remembered anger. "It was the first thing that came out of my mouth. What did you expect me to say?"

"You could have tried the truth."

"It didn't seem like the appropriate time."

"It obviously never was the appropriate time," Betsy grumbled.

"I didn't care for the fact that you went behind my back."

"Well, I didn't see where you were doing anything to keep her mother's memory alive."

"*I* was her mother," Jude said emphatically. "I still am."

"Mom, Betsy, please. Could we please not do this?" Dina pleaded, the color draining from her face.

"Dina's right. Now's not the time for us to be arguing," Betsy said.

"You started this years ago when you insisted on slipping Dina little things that had belonged to Blythe and not telling me you were doing it," Jude snapped.

"I wanted her to know where she came from. I suspected—rightly so—that you would do whatever you could to keep her from us."

"I did what I felt was best for Dina. . . ."

"Which obviously wasn't or we wouldn't all be here now, would we?"

"Let me know when you've finished beating each other up." Dina rose. "I'm not going to sit and listen to this again. You have issues to resolve, resolve them. You're adults. Please start acting like it. I'll be outside. . . ."

For the second time that day, Dina retreated back outside, leaving the two women to air their grievances—

sometimes loudly, as their voices drifted through an open window.

Jude, mild-mannered, soft-spoken Jude, could really rip when she wanted to, Dina thought as she pruned a shrub. *And maybe it's good for her, maybe it's good for both of them, to finally get out so many years of words unspoken. It must have been so hard for Mom, harder still in some ways for Betsy, this silence between them all this time. Maybe it's time for them to deal with each other, once and for all and however loudly they choose; then maybe they can move on.*

Maybe they could even be friends. . . .

And maybe, Dina thought wryly, *the deaf would hear and the blind would see. . . .*

This was all wrong. All wrong.

Where was Jude McDermott? Where was the girl?

Too clever to return to Henderson in the van, the driver had borrowed wheels that were newer—and, most important, unrecognizable, should Jude arrive home and notice a strange car in the parking lot. Though that might be difficult, parked as it was, for the second night in a row, behind a veil of shrubs. The car was too low to the ground to give a clear overview of the surroundings, that sense of omnipresence one got from driving a vehicle that sat so high up over the road, but at the same time it was low enough to conceal behind foliage, and there was something to be said for that. And after all, tonight was merely surveillance of sorts. The next move could not be plotted without knowing where the quarry was.

Church bells from a tower somewhere close to town

rang ten times, their solid clanging punctuating the quiet night like exclamation points.

The driver sighed. Where was this woman?

Perhaps she'd been scared away.

If that was the case, where might she go?

Impatient fingers tapped a nervous tune on the steering wheel. Where might a woman like Jude McDermott go to hide if she thought there was danger?

And surely she must know that there is; she has to know that the near miss was no accident. . . .

Ten-twenty P.M., but still no sign of life.

Perhaps she was with the girl. Jude had been intended to be the original target—after all, *she* was the one with the information—but the girl had given an opportunity not to be missed.

The point was to eliminate anyone who knew.

Simon Keller knew, but perhaps he could still be of some limited use.

Jude definitely knew. The tape had revealed this, along with Jude's name.

Perhaps through targeting the daughter the mother would be made careless.

And careless prey, as everyone knows, is so much easier to catch. . . .

Chapter Twenty-One

On her way into breakfast early the next morning, Dina found her cell phone where she'd left it the previous day, atop the table in the front hall. "ONE MISSED CALL," the readout announced. She scrolled down for the number as she came into the dining room. She listened to Polly's message with a smile on her face.

"You look pleased," Betsy noted as she joined Dina in the dining room.

"I *am* pleased." Dina grinned. "I just got a message from Polly. I have three potential customers waiting to hear from me. One new property and two renovations. My favorite kind of work."

"I noticed how much happier you are after you've been out puttering around in the gardens." Betsy poured a cup of coffee for Dina, then one for herself. "Though frankly, with things so out of hand and overgrown, it's hard to imagine anyone enjoying the work."

"Oh, this is nothing." Dina waved a hand toward the back of the house and the garden area beyond. "These beds have been tended over the years. Some of the places I've worked on haven't been weeded in fifty, seventy years, or better."

"How do you know what to do first?"

"Well, first you get down on your hands and knees and try to see what's lurking beneath the overgrowth." Dina grinned. "Some plants can survive forever with the smallest amount of maintenance. Peonies can last for decades, as can roses, and some of the self-seeders, hollyhocks and such, can just keep on regenerating. On several occasions, I've found wonderful old varieties of plants in gardens I've restored, plants that I couldn't even buy seeds for because they're so rare. You never know when that will happen, and it certainly makes the work more interesting for me. I'm going to call these people as soon as breakfast is over."

"Call what people?" Jude asked as she entered the room.

"Polly left a voice mail message for me that a couple of potential customers called or stopped in over the past few days. Two are possible renovations on old properties."

"Oh, what properties? Someplace we know?" Jude helped herself to scrambled eggs from a covered dish that Mrs. Brady had placed on the sideboard earlier.

"One is that red house on the way out of town. Polly didn't know where the other was. But there are several places around Henderson that are for sale right now. It could be any one of them. There's the Otis place, and the Franklin farm. . . ." Dina paused to think. "Then there's that place out on Keansey Road. . . ."

"Well, hopefully, the prospective owners won't mind waiting until you can meet with them," Jude said.

"Wait for what?" Dina frowned.

"Until we know it's safe for you to go back to Henderson."

"I won't go into town. I'll just take care of my business and come back here."

"Maybe you should run this past Simon," Betsy suggested.

"Simon has his own agenda right now. If these people are serious about this property, making them wait is unfair. They could end up losing it to another buyer. Besides, I can't afford to pass up prospective clients."

"I don't see the harm in it, Jude," Betsy said from her seat at the head of the table.

"There probably isn't any," Jude conceded. "As long as no one knows that you're going."

"No one will know. I won't even tell Polly," Dina promised, feeling energized. "I'll call the numbers she gave me after breakfast and see what their schedules are."

"If you can put it off till next week, it might be better. Maybe all this will be over by then."

"Or the customers might have found another landscaper by then. It's been a while since I had a total renovation job. It's not only fun; it's a great moneymaker. Garden Gates needs a few jobs like this to keep solidly in the black. And frankly, it will be wonderful to have just a little touch of normalcy back in my life again."

"Well, Jude, the morning's slipping away. If we're going to make that trip to the farmers market, I think we need to get going." Betsy smiled at Dina and added, "We have a little cabin fever ourselves. I'm thinking that a drive down into Wayne might do us both some good. Want to come along?"

"No, I think I want to try to get in touch with Mrs. Fields and with the Dillons. Maybe the property they're looking at is one that I already know. But you two have fun. . . ."

"I just need to run upstairs and get my jacket," Jude said.

"Take mine," Dina offered. "It's right there on the chair by the back door."

Dina smiled at both women, who seemed to be slightly more cordial toward each other this morning.

Thank God for small favors, Dina mused fifteen minutes later as she watched Betsy's van disappear down the lane. *I've had about all of their picking at each other that I can take.*

Dina had had to leave voice mail for Mrs. Fields, but Mrs. Dillon answered the phone on its third ring. After the most perfunctory conversation, she gave Dina the address of the property that she and her husband were looking at.

"Is eleven this morning a good time?" Mrs. Dillon had asked.

Dina looked at the clock. It was ten past nine. "I think I can be there by then."

"Great. We'll see you there."

Next Dina called Simon, but she had to leave a message for him as well: "I have a hot job prospect lined up—a garden restoration down around Henderson. Right now, it's just a look-see, but it's just the kind of work I love best. Anyway, I'll be meeting my would-be client—pray that dear Mrs. Dillon loves whatever plan I come up with—and will be going right back to Betsy's, I promise. Hope to see you soon." She paused, then added, "I think I miss you, Simon."

It wasn't until Dina had gathered her purse and her sunglasses and was telling Mrs. Brady where she was going that she realized that her car keys were in her jacket pocket and her jacket had left the house with Jude.

". . . but I should be back by . . . *damn*! I have no wheels."

"Miss?"

"My car keys are in the pocket of the jacket my mother is wearing."

"Perhaps you might take one of Miss Pierce's cars," Mrs. Brady suggested. "I drive them when I need to run errands, and she lets the grooms drive them all the time. I seriously doubt that she'd mind. She has the BMW—of course, that's specially equipped for her, though she doesn't really care to drive it—a pickup truck, and two Jeeps. Look there; there's one of the grooms. Looks like Eric. Ask him to get you the keys for one of the Jeeps."

"If you're sure Betsy won't mind . . ."

"Honey, she lets everyone else drive them; she won't mind if you borrow one."

"Eric!" Dina called out the back door as the groom crossed the drive toward the barn. "I wanted to use one of the Jeeps for a few hours. Mrs. Brady said you knew where the keys are."

"Sure." He waved her to the garage, and Dina met him there at the door, which he opened for her.

"You know how to drive stick?" he asked.

"I used to." Dina nodded.

"Take the tan one, then," Eric suggested as he removed a key from the rack inside the door. "It's the newest."

"Thanks."

"Owners and insurance cards are in the glove box. Want me to back 'er out for you?"

"No, I'm fine, thanks."

Dina hopped into the Jeep and took a moment to familiarize herself with the gears and the placement of the instruments. She'd never driven a Wrangler before, but they always looked like they'd be a fun drive.

And it was. Even on I-95 with the canvas sides open, the Jeep held the road pretty well. It was a quick and easy drive to Maryland.

The property she was looking for was off Good Hope Road and was actually a good eight miles from Henderson, but Dina knew the area well. There was a realtor's *FOR SALE* sign near the road, Mrs. Dillon had told her, but the property could only be reached by driving past the sign to a duck pond a quarter mile farther down the road. Once she reached the pond, there would be a dirt road. From there, she would drive about fifteen hundred feet, taking a right onto yet another dirt road. Once past a wooded area, she would see the old farmhouse and several outbuildings.

And it had all been exactly as her prospective customer had detailed, right down to the ducks on the pond. Dina drove the Jeep carefully over the deeply rutted road, thinking that the first thing the potential buyers should look into might be the cost of some macadam. There was dense brush and much undergrowth lining the lane, and she wondered just how long the property had been vacant.

"Yow!" she said aloud as the house came into view. "Talk about your handyman's special. . . ."

The weathered farmhouse with its boarded-up windows on the first floor sported a front porch that suffered from serious sag on one side. The top course of brick was missing from the chimney, and a cluster of lilac reached clear up to the second-story windows. Behind the house several outbuildings stood—though only barely—and pastures outlined with rusted barbed wire ran along the far side of the lane. A black convertible was parked near the barn, and Dina drove the Jeep around the house to park next to it.

At the edge of an overgrown field, two black-and-white kittens played tag in an abandoned truck tire. They ducked inside it to hide when Dina got out of the car.

"Hello?" she called as she pocketed the key.

Her voice drifted over the fallow fields.

"Hello?" she called again. "Mrs. Dillon?"

No answer.

Maybe they're up at the house, Dina thought, but both the front and the back doors were locked. *Perhaps in the barn . . . ?* But a look inside proved that it, too, was empty.

A large black cat with white markings crouched behind an ancient combine just outside the barn door.

"Here, kitty-kitty!" Dina called to it. The cat swished its tail but did not approach.

"Come here, kitty; I won't hurt you."

The cat rubbed up against the combine's broken wheel.

"You're not a very wild cat, are you?" Dina reached a hand out to the animal. "Are you a runaway? Or maybe did someone drop you off here?"

The cat sashayed out from behind the wheel and permitted Dina to scratch behind its ears.

"Are those your babies out there by the road?" Dina crooned. "Pretty babies. And you're a pretty baby, too, aren't you?"

The cat purred deeply and wound itself around Dina's knees.

The sound of a door creaking on one of the smaller of the outbuildings caught Dina's attention.

"Come on, kitty. Let's take a look."

Dina walked to the shed and pushed the door open.

"Mrs. Dillon . . . ?"

Dina stepped inside but only heard the *whoosh* seconds before the two-by-four crashed into her skull and sent the blackness to claim her.

Dina awoke facedown on a dirt floor, her arms secured behind her, her wrists bound by tightly knotted rope, and her head pounding unmercifully. It took several long moments before she could remember where she was and what had happened. She struggled to roll over and then lay looking around the small space in which she was confined. There was one dirty window with a broken pane of glass on the top, evidence that someone had used it for target practice with a BB gun. From somewhere outside a long light flashed against the wall. Headlights, she suspected.

Shelves lining the two longest sides of the room gave evidence that at one time the small shed had been used as a chicken coop. Thin layers of straw, ravaged over the years by rodents, lined the shelves, and a few forgotten kernels of corn lay nearby. The shed smelled of damp earth and rotted wood. From somewhere near the window something buzzed loudly, and under the far shelf something rustled in the straw.

Dina grimaced. She had absolutely no desire to know what that something might be.

She forced herself into a seated position and leaned back against the wall, considering her options.

"Shit," she muttered as she realized she had no options.

"Are you comfortable?" a voice whispered through the darkness.

Dina sat tensely. The headlights had flashed briefly through the window, but the footsteps had been so soft that she'd not heard them, even though she'd strained her ears, waiting. "Not especially."

"Good." The voice was deep and hoarse, raspy, low, as it had been on the phone.

"Let's see. Mrs. Dillon, right?"

"The name isn't Dillon."

"Well, I know I'm surprised."

"Are you getting acclimated to your accommodations?"

"Oh, sure." Dina glanced around at the dark, dusty room that contained her and fought back the panic.

"Of course, you don't have to stay here, you know."

"And you're just about to tell me what I have to do to get out, right?"

"All you have to do is tell me where to find Jude."

"Oh, of course. I tell you where to find Jude, and you untie me and unlock the door. Right after you slit my throat." Dina paused, willing her voice not to quiver with fear. "Or will you take me outside and lay me on the road so that you can drive over me a couple of times, since that seems to be your favorite MO."

"Maybe tomorrow after you've spent a night here you'll have something useful to tell me."

There was the sound of something like pellets scattering through the broken window, then bouncing along the floor.

"What was that?" Dina asked warily.

"Corn," the voice replied.

"Corn?" Dina frowned. Corn?

"To make sure you have lots of company tonight."

The footsteps hadn't yet passed the door when the first of Dina's company arrived. She heard the faint rustling grow louder.

"Oh, God, not mice . . . I hate mice. . . ." She shuddered.

She drew her feet up as close to her body as she could and shrank back against the wall and fought back the anxiety that was steadily building inside her.

"At least I hope they're only mice. . . ."

Chapter Twenty-two

Simon tried to keep his eyes fixed on the road ahead and not on the enormous ship that was approaching the Chesapeake Bay Bridge-Tunnel on his right and hoped that he'd be on his way *out* of the tunnel before the ship was passing over it. As many times as he'd taken this route, he still felt a twinge of discomfort every time he slipped into one of the two tunnels when there was a large ship in the vicinity. He was always somewhat relieved to see the light at the end of that mile-long dip under the bay and happy when he reached the causeway or one of the bridges again. And happier still when he reached solid land, though he admitted that only to himself. How much more so at night, when, like now, the bridge seemed to disappear into the blackness and appeared to be little more than strings of Christmas lights strung over the bay.

Simon had stayed later than he'd planned in Virginia Beach, since he'd arrived at Conrad Fritz's home in the morning only to learn that the man had gone out at dawn on a charter boat and wasn't expected back until late in the day. Late in the day had turned out to be a little past 7:00 P.M. Simon had just about given up his watch when the new Buick pulled into the Fritz driveway and the object of his search stepped out.

Unfortunately, Fritz was no greater help than Stinson had been.

Fritz acknowledged that he'd known about Hayward's affair with Blythe. And yes, he had known about Hayward's stated desire to not run for a second term. But according to Fritz, *he'd* been the one to talk him out of that.

"I told him, 'Graham, you're a damn fool. That woman will still be there when you've done your duty. And then you can do whatever the hell you want with her and in another few years no one who matters will give a damn. But I can tell you right now that there's no way in hell we're going to let you ruin the careers of everyone who put you where you are. So you can take that stupid idea of yours and float it in the Potomac, because the only way you're leaving office before a second term is up will be in a pine box. And I can arrange that if I have to.'

"And I would have, by God, if it had come to that." Conrad Fritz had chewed on the end of his cigar, then tapped on it with pudgy fingers to knock off the ash. "Fortunately, for everyone's sake, it never came to that. Graham came to his senses and all was well. Course then the girl died in the meantime, which just goes to show you that you never make your life plans based on someone else, if you follow me."

"Did Graham change his mind before or after Blythe died, do you remember?"

"Yeah, Blythe. That was her name. What a looker she was, let me tell you. In all fairness, you almost couldn't blame the man. And I do remember, he changed his mind before she died. I remember because he told me that he'd talked to her about it. He said she agreed with me, that he should stay in office and run for a second term. Then she left town for a while—good while. I really thought the whole affair was over. But then, there she was with Kendall at one of those big Christmas parties at the White House. I figured Graham had just shuttled her out of town or something to keep the press from finding out about her. And as far as I know, they never did." Fritz paused and asked, "You're not going to put any of this in your book, right?"

"No. I'm not going to put it in my book."

"Good. Because with young Graham getting ready to announce his candidacy, it wouldn't look good. Even all these years later, it still wouldn't look good. Don't want to take the focus from the candidate, if you follow."

"I follow." Simon had nodded. "It's one story I won't be writing. . . ."

At least, I won't be writing it right now.

Simon sighed heavily. It was still a big story. Still an important story, maybe the biggest story he'd ever come across. All of his instincts as a journalist screamed that if he could solve the mystery surrounding Blythe's death, he'd have himself one hell of a story. Not just the righteous President and the heiress story, but the murder of the President's mistress. But right now, at this moment, Simon still wasn't sure what he was going to do about it.

Because in spite of all he knew of what a story like this could do for his career, there was one thing he hadn't planned on when he'd started tracking the story. He hadn't planned on Dina.

In the time they'd spent together, he'd become more and more drawn to her. Not just her beauty, though a man could bask in her glow for a lifetime. Not for the first time, Simon felt a twinge of envy for Graham Hayward, who'd been loved by such a woman. Simon wondered what it would take for Dina to love as deeply. It was something Simon longed to discover, and would, he vowed, as soon as this nightmare had come to an end for her.

And it was for her, Simon had come to realize, that he continued to pursue the truth. Not for the prize of fame that could await the one who told the story. But for Dina, because now the prize could well be Dina's life.

When, he wondered, had it become more about *Dina* and less about *Blythe?*

Simon would take on demons from hell to keep Dina safe. Now and always. The realization rattled him more than he'd have been willing to admit.

And the story? Well, that would have to be dealt with, sooner or later. But right now, Dina would be waiting for him at the end of this trip. That, more than anything, spurred him toward the truth. What he'd do with it, once he'd uncovered it, well, that remained to be seen. . . .

He stepped on the accelerator as he approached the Maryland/Virginia state lines, formulating his game plan. Since it was too late to pay a visit to the professor, he'd stop at the town house, get a few hours' sleep, a shower, and a change of clothes, then drive to Norton's house in the morning, tell him what he'd learned, what he suspected, and find out whether or not Norton had any thoughts on the subject.

To Simon's way of thinking, he'd pretty much eliminated any political motive for Blythe's death. Both

Stinson and Fritz, while having known about the affair, professed to have known that Hayward had made his decision to remain in office *before* Blythe died. Simon doubted that the fact that Hayward would have maintained his relationship with Blythe would have been a matter of concern to either man, and therefore it was not likely to have been an issue to anyone else from a political standpoint.

And so, Simon reasoned, perhaps they needed to start looking a little closer to home. Hayward's home. And if, as Simon had begun to consider, one of the Haywards was behind Blythe's death, he needed to narrow down that field quickly.

Dina's life could very well depend on it.

Dina leaned her head back against the wall and gazed out through a broken windowpane at a starless night and tried to settle herself enough to focus on a way out of the dark, dirty shed. Outside, night creatures went about their nocturnal business, made their night sounds. From someplace very close by Dina heard an owl screech and, a moment later, the cry of its prey. She pressed her back into the wall and bit her bottom lip to keep from crying out. She was pretty sure her captor was gone, but just in case she was lurking outside, Dina didn't want to give her the satisfaction of knowing just how frightened she was.

Whistling in the dark, Jude called it.

Dina puckered up her lips and tried to do just that, but her lips were trembling with fear and she couldn't do much more than hiss.

She'd used her feet to kick as much of the corn as she could reach into the far corner, and none too soon.

There were sounds of increasing activity from that direction, and as her eyes adjusted to the dark she became aware of more and more vague shadows moving in the corner—nothing distinct, for which she was grateful. As long as the shapes were merely shadows, she could try to convince herself that they were something other than what she knew they really were. Kittens, for example, climbing over one another in play, rather than hungry rodents seeking a meal.

Something bumped her foot, and she banged her heel on the floor. There was a mad scurrying, then silence for a moment; then the tentative rustle from the corner began again. Moments later something climbed over her calf, and she shuddered, repulsed.

"*Ugh!*" she cried out.

Dina pulled her legs up as close to her body as she could and prayed that nothing else would decide to climb on her. What she'd give for that Swiss Army knife that hung from her key chain. That same key chain upon which she'd clipped the keys to Betsy's Jeep before she carelessly tossed them into her purse—along with her cell phone—which she'd left on the front passenger seat.

Lot of good they do me now.

Jude had always insisted that you could get through anything so long as you kept your sense of humor, but it was becoming increasingly difficult.

Dina wondered if Jude had ever tested this theory by being locked in a small dirty space with little fresh air and lots of unfriendly, unpleasant furry creatures.

There was simply nothing funny about it.

There was another flurry of movement over near the corn and Dina poised to bang her heels, but the disruption stopped as suddenly as it started. She scootched into the corner to put as much distance between her body and the midnight snackers and rested her forehead against her knees—a most uncomfortable position, with her hands tied behind her back—and tried to convince herself that she was dreaming.

Maybe in the morning I'll wake up in my bed back in the carriage house and find that none of this is true. It will all have been a dream, like that old Dallas *episode. Jude will still be my mother and there will never have been anyone named Blythe Pierce.*

It occurred to Dina that she never did ask Betsy where Blythe was buried.

If I get out of here, I'm going to do that. I'm going to visit Blythe's grave. And someday, if I ever get the nerve, maybe I'll visit Graham's grave, too.

If I ever get out of here . . .

She glanced back at the sky and thought about Graham Hayward. If this were a fanciful tale, a fairy tale, she mused, then he'd see her down here, imprisoned in this sorry shed, and since he was her father, he'd send someone—something—to rescue her. But this was real, there was no magic, and no friendly ghost was likely to intervene.

"I'll put flowers on your grave if you lend me a hand here," she said aloud, knowing how silly it sounded.

I will put flowers on his grave—and hers, too—Dina silently vowed, *if I ever get out of here.*

I'll tell Jude how much I love her and that I've forgiven her for keeping the truth from me. And that even though it will not always be easy, we'll get through this as a family.

And that will include Betsy. I'll visit her often and make sure that there is always room in my life for her.

Oh, yes. One other thing.

I will kiss Simon Keller until he begs for mercy.

If I ever get out of here . . .

Morning had been a long time in coming.

Outside the shed, the first of the songbirds had started their chatter long before the new day had dawned. Dina watched the window, wondering what time it was and hoping the sun would arrive soon so she could get some sleep. Knowing she shared her space with so many unseen creatures in the dark had kept her awake. She hadn't wanted to open her eyes this morning and find that something small—or not so small—and furry had decided that some body part of hers would make a fine resting spot.

She'd kept herself awake all night by singing all of the Sheryl Crow songs she could remember from that last CD she'd bought. She'd gotten through "Am I Getting Through (Parts 1 and 2)" all the way to "Riverwide" before her throat started to bother her and she remembered that she hadn't had water since the previous afternoon and wasn't likely to be getting any in the near future. There was a bottle of water in her bag, she reminded herself, right there with the Swiss Army knife and her cell phone.

She sighed at the irony of it. She who had always been one to travel prepared for any emergency had brought along everything she needed—but all, sadly, was out of reach.

For the hundredth time Dina tried to figure out who had lured her here and prayed that Jude hadn't been found.

Jude McDermott, Dina shook her head, was such an

unlikely target for such intrigue. Small-town librarian. Volunteer for a number of organizations. Paid her taxes on time. Cleaned up after her dog on their walks around the neighborhood. A member in good standing in her church. The one who could always be counted on to come up with the best fund-raisers for the community's yearly literacy campaign. The one who always remembered Henderson's housebound by dropping off a new book by a favorite author or homemade soup.

And right now being hunted by some unknown someone because years ago she'd taken in her best friend's child and raised her as her own.

Tired and thirsty and weak, Dina fought back the recurring urge to panic. And panic, she reminded herself sternly, was the last thing she could afford. If she was to get out of here alive, she needed her wits about her.

Right. Like she had a plan.

Fighting despair, Dina bit the inside of her lip and stared up at the ceiling, through which she could see blue sky starting to emerge.

From time to time she called out through the window at the top of her lungs, but there was no one there to hear.

If she were home, she'd transplant today. Maybe she'd be having a cup of tea in the shop with Polly. They'd discuss what cut flowers were available from the wholesaler that week, and they'd have prices to quote to Gloria Wexler, who ran the bookshop in Henderson and who had stopped by last week to inquire about the possibility of Garden Gates doing the flowers for her daughter's wedding in October.

And there was Mother's Day coming up. Polly had mentioned to Dina just last week that she had sketched out her ideas for several unique arrangements to mark the holiday and had already taken an impressive number of orders.

"Damn it!" Dina banged her heels again, the only outlet she had for her anger and frustration.

How did the TV action heroes escape from those dark nasty places where the villains had locked them, hands tied behind their backs?

Oh, they always had something in their pockets that they managed to work out. Or they found a way to spin straw into gold, then use the gold to send an SOS through the window with the aid of the one ray of light in the room.

"Got the straw, got the open window, but no way to spin the straw into gold." Dina stared up through the broken window.

Broken window. Broken glass . . . Dina mentally slapped her forehead.

She began the tedious task of scootching herself along the floor carefully, mindful of how uncomfortable a bottom full of splinters could be, until she reached the opposite side of the small room. Turning herself around, she backed toward the wall, forcing her nearly numb fingers to search through the straw until they located a piece of glass.

"Too small," she muttered as her fingers rejected a sharp, smooth shard. "Let's see what else is in here. . . .

"Ow!" she exclaimed as a sliver poked into one side of her hand, forcing her to figure out a way to extract it before she could continue her search for a slice long enough to reach from her fingers to the rope that bound her wrists.

It took her well over an hour to find it.

"Thank you, thank you," she murmured, even as the blood from her fingers made the glass too slippery to maneuver. She tugged at the back of her T-shirt, tried to wipe away the blood so that the glass wouldn't slide from her hands.

Dina knew that, sooner or later, her captor would return. She wanted to be ready.

Chapter Twenty-three

Before setting out for Georgetown, Simon paused to listen, one last time, to the message Dina had left on his answering machine while he was in the shower, just to hear the way she said his name. He'd tried to call her back but had to settle for her cell phone's voice mail. While he wished she'd stay put for just a little longer, he'd have had to be deaf not to have caught the tinge of excitement in her voice at the prospect of a new project. Knowing how rough the past few weeks had been for her, he figured she was entitled to slip off for a few hours to do something she loved. And it wasn't as if she were going into Henderson proper, where she was likely to be seen. As long as she was careful—and he was certain she would be—she should be fine.

The ride to Norton's gave Simon time to go through his short list of suspects and motives. By the time he reached Norton's house, he'd gone over all of the most likely scenarios and he'd had an epiphany.

"Neither Stinson nor Fritz was involved in Blythe's murder or in the attempt to run down Dina," Simon told Norton as the older man opened the door to admit him. "They both treated the story as if it was old news, as if they hadn't given a thought to either Blythe or Graham in a very long time. But for someone this is very much a current event. I think that makes the motive to kill Blythe—and therefore Dina—personal, not political."

Simon sat at the round table in Norton's breakfast room, waiting for a reaction. It was a long time coming.

"Why come to me with this, Simon," Norton finally broke his silence, "since you've made it clear that you don't trust me?"

"Philip, I apologize for some of the things I said to you," Simon told him, not above eating crow when he was wrong. "I guess my nose was out of joint because of the book thing."

"Because you thought that I chose you for the project so that I could control what you wrote."

"Yes."

"Do you believe that my only concern was to prevent knowledge of Dina's existence from becoming public? That my goal was to protect her life, not her father's reputation? And that I thought that I could trust you to understand that, to respect that concern for this young woman's safety?"

"I do now. I'm sorry I doubted you. Sorry I offended you."

"Then I accept your apology."

"Good." Simon smiled wryly.

"Now, talk to me." Philip gestured for Simon to get on with it.

"Let's assume that I'm right about the motive being personal rather than political. I don't think that anyone would have taken Hayward's affair more personally than a member of his family. I was hoping you could help me narrow down the field to one."

"It wouldn't have been Gray. As I recall, he didn't return to Washington for Christmas break until the week following Blythe's death. I remember because he asked me on several occasions if I knew what was wrong with his father." Philip paused, as if remembering. "Of course, I said no."

"Then that leaves Sarah and Celeste."

Norton stood and began to pace, his unlit pipe in his hand, his gaze far away. Simon wondered where his thoughts had taken him.

"Any insights, Philip?" Simon said, hoping to bring Philip back.

"Go ahead." Norton nodded. "Let's walk through it."

"When I interviewed Celeste Hayward, I took along some of the photographs I found in a box of material that you sent to me. I slipped the picture of Blythe that I'd . . . *borrowed* . . . from Betsy Pierce into the stack. When Celeste saw that photo, her eyes went dark and deadly. There is no question in my mind that she knew full well that the woman in the photograph was her husband's young and very beautiful mistress."

"I can't see Celeste running a woman down in the middle of the night. I have no doubt that she wished Blythe dead a thousand times, but I can't believe for a minute that she'd have acted on it. It would have been beneath her." Philip paused to light his pipe. "Furthermore, the stakes would have been too high if she'd been caught."

"Could she have hired someone to do it for her?"

Norton shook his head. "Again, I think the stakes would have been too high. I doubt she'd have done something so reckless."

"But she'd never been in a situation like that before, had she? Supposing Graham told her about Blythe, about his plans to eventually divorce her and marry his young love. Wouldn't that have been enough to cause her to act in a manner that was uncharacteristic? Wouldn't that have been enough to make her snap?"

"Graham had told Celeste. I'm not certain what was or wasn't said about Dina, but certainly Celeste knew that Graham would eventually seek a divorce."

"One thing I've learned about Celeste Hayward over the past few weeks is that her position meant everything to her, Philip." Simon paused thoughtfully, then added, "Just as being the President's daughter meant everything to Sarah."

The two men locked eyes.

"How old was Sarah that year?" Simon asked.

"Fifteen or sixteen."

"Old enough to drive?"

"Miles taught her." Norton nodded slowly.

"Did she have access to a car while she was at school?"

"A classmate used to loan out her car to any one of the girls who'd put gas in it. Sarah was known to have slipped out now and then. It drove the Secret Service crazy. They complained to her father several times."

"How could she have gotten around them?"

"She'd pin her hair up or borrow a wig. Or have someone dress in her clothes and go to the library so that the agents would follow the wrong person. Or she'd slip out a window. There were several girls in the dorm who got a kick out of helping her fool the Secret Service. It was a game to them. And thirty years ago the agents gave their charges a lot more leeway than they might these days."

"There would have to have been some damage to

that car," Simon said thoughtfully. "And surely there would have been blood. How would she have explained that?"

"I imagine that she'd have taken the car to one of those self-wash places before returning it."

"Tough to do at that hour of the morning." Simon fought the urge to pace. "And surely the girl who'd loaned Sarah the car must have had to do some explaining to her parents about the damage to the car. But what are our chances of finding out who the owner was?"

"We do know who owned the car."

"We do?"

"Carolyn Decker."

"Julian's sister?" Simon's eyebrows rose with interest. "Sarah's sister-in-law?"

Philip nodded. "Sarah drove her car to the White House on several occasions, just to tweak the Secret Service. It was a Chevrolet station wagon that had belonged to Carolyn's grandmother."

"Can we get in touch with her? With Carolyn? Think she'd remember if Sarah ever returned the car with damage to the front end?"

"I do have her father's number somewhere—her mother died a few years back . . ." Philip muttered absently as he left the room, returning minutes later with a small green address book.

"We've pretty much agreed that deliberately running down a woman with a car is a reckless act," Simon noted as Philip thumbed through his address book. "How reckless was Sarah Hayward as a teenager?"

"Sarah was a very unstable young woman. I take it you're not aware that she'd been under treatment for mental illness for several years as a young girl? And, again, for a time, after her father's death, she was an in-patient in a mental hospital."

"What?! When was this?"

"Late high school—"

"Wait a minute. Sarah told me that she went to boarding school here in D.C."

"She did. But she had had a breakdown and had to take a year off from school."

"She told me she'd taken a year off to travel abroad with her parents."

"That was the official line, but no, she spent a year or so in a private school for disturbed children in Switzerland. Sarah was a very troubled girl, Simon."

"Why didn't you tell me this sooner?"

"Frankly, it never occurred to me that Sarah could have been behind this. Never."

"Sarah could have borrowed the car from her friend," Simon murmured. "But that means that she had to have known about Blythe. What are the chances that her father—or her mother—would have told her about her father's affair?"

"As disturbed as Sarah was, there is no way that either of her parents would have wanted her to know until she *had* to know." Norton shook his head adamantly. "She'd been pretty stable for most of her high school years, and Graham hoped that by the time his second term had expired Sarah would be out of school and her problems would be behind her."

"Then how would Sarah have even known about Blythe?"

"I don't know."

"Who had the accident investigation closed down?"

"As I recall, it was Miles who cautioned Graham about pursuing Blythe's killer, that any investigation involving Blythe would lead to Dina. His thinking was that if someone had wanted Blythe out of the way, they might next go after her daughter. Graham agreed—as much as he grieved and as hard as it was for him to let Blythe's killer get away with her murder—and gave the order to stop the investigation so that no one would know of Dina's existence. He just couldn't take the chance that something could happen to Dina."

"Miles . . ." Simon pondered aloud. "Miles, who mysteriously died of 'natural causes' within hours of telling me about Dina."

"Simon, what are you thinking?"

"When did Sarah leave for Switzerland?"

"Several weeks after Blythe's death, Sarah had an episode, the first she'd had in years. Her doctors felt she needed intensive treatment, which would not have been possible in this country if the press ever got on to the story. It was suggested that she be sent to this hospital in Switzerland. I remember how devastated Graham was when she left. He'd no sooner lost Blythe than he was losing Sarah as well. It was a very, very hard time for him."

"But he never suspected his daughter?"

"Of killing his mistress? No, no, Graham never would have believed that his Sarah would be capable of such an act. No." Norton shook his head. "Graham went to his grave not knowing who was responsible for Blythe's death."

"We have to confirm the dates with the school here in D.C. . . ." Simon rose.

"You'll never get into Beaumont's records. They'll be very protective of Sarah. As they should be."

"Then we'll speak with someone at the clinic in Switzerland—"

"You'll find no record of Sarah Hayward ever having been enrolled there."

"She was there under an assumed name." Simon fell back in his chair.

"Yes, of course. Sarah Dillon, I believe she went by. Dillon was her mother's maiden name."

Simon's head snapped up.

"Dillon . . . oh, shit." Simon's voice grew taut with concern. "That's the name of the client that Dina was to meet today."

"Good Lord . . ."

Simon reached for the phone and once again dialed the number for Dina's cell phone. He looked up at Philip and said, "She's not picking up. . . . Dina, this is Simon. Do not . . . do not . . . keep your appointment this morning. We—Philip and I—suspect that your Mrs. Dillon is the same person who tried to run you down last week. The same person who killed Blythe. When you get this message, call me at . . ." Simon hesitated.

"Give her my cell phone number." Philip handed him a business card.

Simon repeated the number for Dina.

"Be careful, sweetheart," he said as he hung up, pausing for a second before dialing again. "I should check with Jude and Betsy—damn, the machine picked up there, too."

Simon left essentially the same message for Dina on Betsy's answering machine, then returned the cordless phone to its base.

"What now?" Philip asked.

"Now I head north. If I hear from Dina, I'll meet her wherever she is. If not, I'll continue on to Wild Springs."

"I'm going with you," Philip said as he pocketed his phone. "I can make some calls along the way. I can try Betsy again. Dina, too. And I can try to get in touch with Carolyn Decker as well."

And if they needed to bring in some high-level law enforcement, Philip thought as he followed Simon through the front door, there was an old friend he could call. . . .

"She still hasn't called." Jude stood at the open front door as Simon and Philip came up the walk. "We're at our wits' end with worry. We haven't heard from her all day."

"I don't suppose you know anything about this client that she was going to meet?" Simon asked, on the outside chance that Mrs. Dillon just might be a legitimate customer.

"Only what Dina said this morning. That Polly told her that this Mrs. Dillon had come into the shop yesterday asking for Dina. Said they were looking at a property outside of town and wanted an estimate to restore the gardens." Jude leaned against the newel post at the foot of the stairs. "Hello, Philip. I'm sorry, I didn't mean to ignore you—"

"Don't apologize, Jude. It's all right. I'll save my 'it's good to see you again' for a better time." Norton stepped forward and kissed Jude's cheek gently.

"I forgot that you two have met," Simon noted, then belatedly introduced Betsy.

"It's been years since we've seen each other," Norton said as he extended his hand to Betsy. "We, however, have not met. It's my pleasure."

"Thank you." Betsy took the hand he offered. "Do you have any thoughts on what could be keeping Dina?"

"We keep going back and forth between being paranoid and thinking that something has happened to her and thinking that maybe we're just a couple of mother hens who are worried over nothing." Jude sat on one arm of an overstuffed chair.

"It's still early." Betsy moved to the window and looked out. "Perhaps we should give her a little more time."

"It's eight-thirty." Simon glanced at his watch.

"It's not like Dina to not keep in touch. She never goes anywhere without that phone in her hand." Jude's forehead creased with worry.

"I think we should give Polly a call and see what she can tell us about Mrs. Dillon," Simon suggested.

Simon lifted the phone from the table nearby and handed it to Jude. "If you wouldn't mind . . ."

Jude dialed the number for Polly's house and, when Polly answered, explained that she would be passing the phone to someone who was trying to help them get in touch with Dina. Betsy leaned over and hit the speakerphone button.

"Polly, my name is Simon Keller. We're trying to catch up with Dina, and it seems you were the last person to speak with her today."

"No, actually, I didn't speak with her today. I left a voice mail message for her late yesterday afternoon."

Polly paused, then asked, "Has something happened to Dina?"

"We're hoping not," Simon told her, taking pains not to unduly alarm the woman. "We're hoping that it's nothing more serious than a dead battery in her phone and that she's on her way home. But in the event that that's not the case, we need to know where she went today. We know she went to meet with the customer you called her about, Mrs. Dillon. Do you happen to know where the property is, the one that Mrs. Dillon was looking at?"

"She didn't say. I . . . I didn't think to ask. . . ."

"What can you tell us about Mrs. Dillon? What did she look like?"

"Oh, she was maybe in her late forties or her early fifties. It was hard to tell. She was petite and blond and quite well dressed. Very attractive. She came in and asked for Dina. Said she had some work she wanted Dina to look at, that she'd heard that Dina was good. She left a number for Dina to call. . . ."

Simon and Norton exchanged a long look.

"Do you happen to have the number?" Simon asked.

"It might still be at the shop. Do you want me to go down and see if I can find it?"

"Yes, that would be very helpful. We'll call you back in five minutes at the shop." Jude switched off the phone, then studied the faces of the two men.

"Who?" she demanded.

"This Mrs. Dillon isn't really a customer, is she?" Betsy asked softly.

"We don't think so." Simon reached for her hands.

"Is she the person who tried to kill Dina?"

"It's very possible."

"Do you know who she is?"

"We believe we do."

"Who?" Jude repeated.

"Sarah Decker," Simon told her.

"Who?" Betsy frowned. "Who is Sarah Decker?"

"Sarah *Hayward* Decker."

"Graham's daughter?" Jude gasped. "Graham's *daughter* . . . ?"

Norton nodded.

"How do you know this?" Jude's knees began to quiver, and she backed into the sitting room and folded into the nearest chair. "How can you be sure?"

Simon related his theory.

"She killed Blythe, and now she wants to kill Dina," Betsy said. "We can't let her. . . ."

"We have to call the police." Jude started for the phone when he'd finished. "They—we—have to start looking for Dina now. Right now. . . ."

"On the way up I called Sarah's home, but no one answered. I then called her mother's home in Rhode Island, but the housekeeper told us that Celeste was in D.C. at her son's home. When I called Gray's, the nanny told me that Gray and Jen took Celeste to dinner and the theater for an early birthday present."

"Was Sarah with them?"

"She was expected but never showed up. Julian is at some must-attend function at the Academy, and the nanny said that they assumed that perhaps Sarah got her nights mixed up and went with Julian, but that after the Haywards left for dinner Julian called Gray's to see if Sarah was with them."

"I'm calling the police." Jude reached for the phone.

"And tell them what, Jude?" Philip reached out and took her wrist gently.

"That Dina is missing and that we think Sarah Decker is trying to kill her."

"That's a serious charge to make, Jude, when we don't know for certain," Simon told her.

"I think that you must decide exactly what—and how much—you want the police to know before you make that call," Norton cautioned. "Remember that the press—"

"I don't give a damn about the press. I don't give a damn about who knows what. All I care about is Dina's safety."

"Jude, believe me, we're all concerned about Dina's safety." Simon stood and took the phone from Jude's trembling hands. "But first things first. Before we call anyone else, we need to call Polly back. If she's found that phone number, the police will need it."

"You're right. Besides, Polly's been waiting for way more than five minutes, and she must be getting quite anxious. Especially since she has no idea of what's going on." Jude's fingers flew over the phone's keypad, punching in numbers. The conversation was brief.

"Polly can't find the slip of paper with Mrs. Dillon's phone number on it." Jude fought back the panic that was threatening to engulf her. "I told her to call back if she locates it. She was going to go look through the trash bag in the back of the store, but she's not sure that the trash from yesterday wasn't already picked up."

Norton stepped forward and touched Simon on the arm. "I want to borrow your car to drive to Gray's. I want to be at the house when they arrive home from their evening out."

"What are the chances that Celeste knew about Sarah killing Blythe?" Simon asked.

"That's one of the things I plan on asking her."

Norton turned to Jude and said, "Jude, I know how distressed you are, but you need to be very careful about what you tell the police at this point. If there's a way out of this without telling all, I think you should consider taking it at this point. Once the truth about Dina's parentage is out, there will be no taking it back. Her life will never be the same. I think this needs to be played very, very carefully."

"Assuming she's still alive when they find her," Jude snapped.

"For what it's worth, I agree with Philip," Betsy told them. "I say we not give away anything that Dina may not want made public, unless and until we have to. This needs to be her decision. Besides, supposing we're all wrong and Mrs. Dillon was legitimate and Dina just got distracted somewhere. How do you think she'd react if we called the local police and told them everything?"

"Do you really think that Dina's just distracted?" Jude snapped.

"No. No, I don't, Jude," Betsy replied. "But I think that we need to consider that it is a possibility when we have no facts."

"Jude, can you call the police in Henderson and tell them merely that Dina went to meet a prospective client at a property and hasn't been heard from all day?" Simon asked. "See what they suggest?"

"Yes," Jude agreed. "And I can call Linda Best; she's a realtor down there. She'll be able to pull up a list of all the properties that are for sale in the area."

"Particularly the vacant ones," Betsy added.

"Do it." Simon pointed to the phone; then to Betsy he said, "We'll need a description of the car Dina was driving. License plate number . . ."

"I'll get that for you." Betsy turned her chair on a dime and wheeled down the hallway.

"Simon, if I could take your car . . ." Philip stepped forward.

Simon tossed Norton his car keys. "Keep in touch, Philip."

Norton caught the keys with his left hand. On his way out of the room he turned back to Simon and said, "I agree with Jude that some law enforcement involvement is called for. I'd like to speak with an old friend at the FBI. I can assure you that this can be done discreetly. It wouldn't hurt to have a few agents in the area and on call, so to speak."

Simon nodded. "Do it."

"Consider it done." Norton disappeared through the front door.

"Here's the information on the Jeep that Dina took this morning." Betsy returned to the room moments later.

"Then let's get on with it. My realtor-friend has agreed to put together a list of properties and fax it over to the police department," Jude told them. "I also spoke with Tom Burton; he's with the Henderson police. He's going to radio all of his patrol cars to look for the Jeep that Dina was driving, though I could tell he thinks she's just having a beer with a few friends someplace. He also suggested that she might have stopped for dinner somewhere with this client. I guess that's a possibility, isn't it, Simon?"

Jude's eyes pleaded. She wanted so badly for Dina to be out of harm's way someplace, wanted to believe that there was a logical explanation for the fact that Dina had not been heard from all day. That Mrs. Dillon was in fact a client. That very shortly Dina would be walking through the door, annoyed that her phone wasn't working but bubbling over about the new job she'd lined up that day.

"I don't think it's likely, Jude."

"I can't lose her, Simon. She's my child. She's my everything," Jude whispered, momentarily frozen to the spot where she stood.

"*We* can't lose her," a somber Betsy chimed in.

"We're all in agreement then. We won't lose her." He turned to Betsy. "Is there a car we can use?"

"I have Dina's car," Jude told him.

"And I have a van. It's equipped with a lift for my chair," Betsy said.

"Then we'll take the van, Betsy, if you don't mind driving, and we'll head down to Henderson," Simon said. "Though I don't know what we can accomplish in the middle of the night."

"Anything's better than being here not knowing what's going on down there." Jude nodded.

"Let's go, then," Betsy said from the doorway. "Simon, you can navigate. Jude, you pray. . . ."

Chapter Twenty-Four

"Jude, I still think you're overreacting." For the second time in less than an hour, Tom Burton began his lecture. "I still think she's met up with . . . someone"—Tom paused, making a distinct effort to be as tactful as possible—"Could be a friend, could be a boyfriend, and just lost track of the time."

"An entire night, Tom? Anything could have happened. Her car could have gone off the road into a ditch; she could have been attacked by someone who might have been hiding out in one of those vacant barns."

"Jude, no one ever said you lacked imagination." Tom shook his head but at least had the good sense to not smile. "How old's your daughter? Old enough to spend a night out without checking in with her mother?"

"Yes, of course she is. And I'm sure there have been times when she's done just that. But this time, since we were staying with a friend in Pennsylvania for a few days, she would have called, Tom." Jude pointed skyward. "In case you hadn't noticed, the sun is up. I want to find my daughter before it sets again."

"I understand that. And the best way to make that

happen is for you to give me and my officers a chance to see what's what."

"That's your way of saying go home and get out of your hair. You think she just had a wild night, don't you?" Jude's anger and frustration flared. Her fisted hands rode her hips. "You think that Dina is shacked up someplace with some guy she met in a bar. Well, she isn't. I know she isn't."

"Jude, I'm not trying to make light of the fact that your daughter didn't come home last night. But young people do—on occasion—stay out all night and, for whatever reason, forget to call home. It happens all the time. Now, I understand that being her mother, you don't want to hear that . . ." Tom began, then backed off when he saw the fire in her eyes. "Oh, hell. Fine. We'll make a tour of all the farms that are for sale. Give me that list that Linda Best faxed over and we'll take a look at some of these places."

Jude studied the list as if to memorize it before handing it over to Tom.

"Now, why don't the three of you go get yourself some breakfast and give us a little time to work here."

"All right." Simon nodded. "I'll just take these ladies right across the street to the Henderson Café."

"Good enough." Tom held the door of the police station open for Jude, Betsy, and Simon.

"How can you eat at a time like this?" Jude poked at Simon.

"I can't. But I would like a cup of coffee for the ride."

"What ride?" Betsy asked.

"Jude, where do you think the police will look first?" Simon took Jude's arm as they walked to the pedestrian crossing.

"My guess is that they will start at the places closest to town."

"Then we'll start at the places farthest from town."

"Good plan." Betsy nodded her approval. "Jude, you run into that café and get the coffee. Simon, let's get the van. I don't want to waste any more time than we have to."

"Don't you dare leave me," Jude warned Simon.

"Well, since I don't know where we're going and I'm not familiar with the controls in that specially equipped van of Betsy's, that's one worry you don't have. It's all for one and one for all, as far as I'm concerned. Now, you go on and get the coffee; we'll bring the van around and pick you up right here."

Simon had to quicken his pace to keep up with Betsy's chair, which fairly raced to the van they'd left parked at the end of the street.

"Hurry, Simon. I don't like the feel of this," Betsy urged him on. "I don't like the feel of this at all. . . ."

By noon they'd driven a total of seventeen miles and checked out three of the properties on the realtor's list. All three were occupied, and none of the owners reported any interest in their farms over the past week.

"Jude, are you hungry? We never did get that breakfast." Simon leaned over from the passenger seat and patted a weary Jude on the arm.

"I have no appetite, Simon, but if you and Betsy want to stop someplace, that's fine with me."

"I could use something cool to drink," Betsy admitted.

"We passed a convenience store on our way out to this last place. I can run in there and see what they have to offer."

Simon made his quick stop, pausing to use the pay phone to catch up with Philip, once again cursing the fact that he hadn't replaced his own cell phone when he lost it amid the paper debris of the Hayward book research. While he had no good news to relate, he was gratified to hear that the FBI already had several agents heading toward Henderson.

"All you have to do is let me know when and where you want them," Philip told him, "so I suggest you touch base with me frequently and let me know where you are."

"Must be some powerful 'friend' you have," Simon said dryly.

"Indeed," Philip murmured as he hung up.

"You must be getting tired," Simon said to Betsy as he returned to the van with an assortment of bottled water, soda, and iced tea. "Up all night, no sleep."

"Could say the same for you."

"Yeah, but I'm young and tough." Simon twisted the cap off of Betsy's bottle of water and handed it over to her.

"And I'm old and cranky." Betsy drew a long swallow from the bottle of water. "Even so, today's not the day to get in my way."

"I wouldn't dream of it," Simon assured her.

Betsy was every bit as tired as she looked. More tired than she'd been in a very long time. But there would be no rest. For years she'd prayed that the day would come when her sister's daughter would seek out her Pierce heritage. To Betsy's way of thinking, Dina had been snatched from her family as a child. Betsy wasn't about to let anyone or anything—not even death—snatch her away now that she'd returned.

And then there was the matter of unfinished business with the person who had been responsible for Blythe's death. Betsy had never stopped praying that the day would come when the fates would allow her retribution.

It was beginning to look as if that day had finally arrived.

Betsy patted the deep inner pocket of her jacket, felt the outline of the small handgun she'd tucked inside—just in case—and turned the key in the ignition.

Sleep could wait until the end of the day, she told herself. Until the job was done. One way or another.

On to property number four . . .

Chapter Twenty-five

"They make this look so damned easy on TV."

All of Dina's fingers bore nicks and slices, and it took all of her concentration to hold on to the piece of glass that was now slippery with blood. All the while, she listened for the sound of tires on the drive.

She'd been working at the rope for what had seemed to be forever, her efforts slowed by the fact that she kept dropping the glass and would have to relocate it again each time. But finally, she had made enough of a cut to loosen the ties and slip free.

"Hallelujah!"

She rubbed her wrists with bloody fingers and bloody hands, hoping to speed up the return of circulation.

"Guess you critters will have to party without me tonight," she said as she went to the door and attempted to open it.

The door was bolted from the outside. No amount of pounding or jiggling on the doorknob made a bit of difference.

"Oh, damn!" Angered and frustrated, Dina kicked at the door, her patience at last exhausted.

Commanding herself not to give in to the panic that threatened to overwhelm her, Dina looked around for an alternative way out.

Without something upon which to stand, the window was too far beyond her reach. The hole in the siding was far too narrow for Dina to fit through.

Dina almost missed it, the sound was so faint, but there, she heard it again. The sound of tires crunching on stone, a car door slamming. Footsteps on dried earth. Had her captor returned? Or had someone else come along? Dina stood stock-still, weighing her options. Should she yell for help? Or should she wait to see where the footsteps led?

The footsteps came nearer.

As quietly as possible, Dina slipped into the corner opposite the door. Perhaps if she stayed silent, her captor would be inclined to unlock the door to check on her.

One could only hope. . . .

"How was your night? I trust you had lots of friends to keep you company?" The voice was light and cheery. "Nothing quite like a good party, is there, Dina?" She paused, then called, "Dina?"

Open the door. Come on, open the door. I'll take you down in a heartbeat. . . .

There was no answer from within.

"Dina, for heaven's sake, I know you're in there, and you know that I know you're in there. So stop playing games. We've things to talk about, you and I."

But still, there was no response.

Open it. You know you want to. . . .

"You're really trying my patience; you know that, don't you?"

Silence.

"Look, you can stay in there until you rot for all I care."

Tentative footsteps made their way around the shed, as Dina's captor seemed to be circling the small building and studying it as if it were a puzzle.

Hesitation. Confusion.

The footsteps retreated.

"Well, that was effective," Dina muttered. "I guess I showed her, all right. . . ."

Dina processed the little information that she had. Her captor was apparently a small woman, judging by her light step. Though hungry and thirsty, Dina was otherwise strong and in excellent physical condition. Adrenaline made her stronger still. She felt confident that she could take her captor one-on-one. Unless, of course, she was armed. . . .

Was she armed?

Dina heard the sound of a car engine, tires squealing as if making a tight U-turn.

Then, nothing.

Silence had apparently been the wrong approach.

Dina paced the small room, rubbing her wrists with hands from which the blood still ran in places and dripped onto the floor. The air was close and stale, and the temperature was beginning to rise.

She looked around for something she could use to break out another pane of glass to permit more fresh air into the dusty confines of the shed, but there was nothing. She took off one shoe and jumped up to bang it against the glass, then tried to shield her face from the splinters that rained down.

"Damn," she muttered, gingerly shaking glass from her hair. "If I keep this up, I won't have to worry about what weapons she might have. I'll just bleed to death."

With the end of her T-shirt Dina mopped up the blood from several slices on her right cheek that had been made by falling glass.

"All in all, worth it," she said aloud as she examined the shirt. "At least now there's a little more air in here."

Dina jumped up again at the window, hoping to break out at least one of the upper panes, but found them beyond her reach. She put her shoe back on, then went back to the window to look out.

The window itself was set high in the wall, too high for Dina to see much beyond the trees that bordered the fields. She knew the property only by reputation but knew it was a very large tract. The house had been empty for at least six months, and it was unlikely anyone would be making a social call anytime soon.

Dina gritted her teeth and kicked at what appeared to be a soft spot in the wood. The clapboard bent softly but did not break.

Okay, maybe over here where the boards were broken . . .

But even her most ferocious kicking left the boards intact.

Damn.

What she wouldn't give for that bottle of Deer Park spring water that sat in her bag in the Jeep.

Dina tilted her head, listened, and smiled. The car had come back. A car, anyway. Too bad the window looked out over the field instead of the road. She'd just have to wait to see.

But yes, the footsteps drew closer. Her captor had returned.

"Okay, Dina. Here's how it's going to be. I'm going

to give you one last chance—that was *one*—to tell me where Jude is. I suggest that you speak up."

The woman's voice paused. When Dina did not respond, she asked slyly, "Don't you want to know the 'or else' part?"

"Sure. What's the 'or else'?"

"I knew you couldn't resist." There was a soft chuckle. "The 'or else' is or else I'm going to set fire to your little home."

"I don't suppose you're going to let me out before you strike the match?"

"I don't suppose I will."

"What could you possibly want with Jude?"

"She's the last big piece of the puzzle. After you, of course. And that pesky reporter, but first things first. And as things turned out, you would be first." The voice held an undercurrent that was both smug and sure.

"What's the puzzle?"

"A puzzle that can never be put together."

"Oh, wait, you mean this whole Blythe Pierce/Graham Hayward thing?" Dina forced a touch of derision.

The woman on the other side of the door fell silent.

"You think that *Jude* is the last person who knows the truth about that? Ha!" Dina taunted her. "Surely you can't think that you can get away with killing everyone who knows about their love affair."

"It wasn't a love affair! It was just a fling for him. He never loved her. Blythe Pierce was nothing more than a young tramp who tempted him because she wanted to be able to tell her friends that she'd slept with the President."

"We both know that's not true," Dina said softly. "We both know he was in love with her. Deeply in love with her. Enough that he was willing to give up everything—even being President—to be with her."

"It's not true! It isn't. He wasn't in love with her," the voice insisted, somewhat more shrilly. "Don't dare say that he was. He did not love her."

"He loved her so much that he was going to leave his wife—"

"*No!* He never would have left my mother! Never! He loved my mother! He loved me!"

Ah! Dina smiled in spite of her predicament. At last she knew who her captor was.

"Sarah, you know he was going to leave—"

"No. No. *He* said he was going to leave her, but my father never would have done it. Never. *He* was lying."

"Who was lying?"

"Miles. He told me, told me that I should talk to my father. That he'd listen to me. He'd listen. He'd forget about her if I asked him to. Miles said he would. . . ."

"So you talked to your father about Blythe?"

"Are you crazy? I just wanted her gone. Then things could be the way they were supposed to be again."

"So you killed her."

"I told Miles I'd call Daddy, but I called her instead. It was easy enough to get her number. I told her I needed to see her. That maybe if I met her I wouldn't be as confused about things. I asked her not to tell my father because I just wasn't ready to have that conversation with him just yet."

"Laid it on real thick, did you?"

"You betcha. She bought every word. I told her I'd pick her up across the street from her apartment."

"That's why she was crossing the street," Dina said almost imperceptibly.

". . . and she was so easy to kill. She never even saw it coming. Not like you. You ran like a jackrabbit."

"How could you have done that? How could you have taken her life—"

"She was a problem. When you have a problem, you find a way to deal with it and move on."

Dina's stomach churned at the callousness of the words, but still she had to ask.

"Did you know about me then?"

"Do you think I would have let you live? I didn't have a clue. Not until Miles told me. Stupid Miles. Told that stupid reporter. Well, I couldn't let him tell anyone else. I'm sure that even you can understand that."

There was the sound of paper being torn, then silence. Then the smell of something that Dina couldn't quite put her finger on. . . .

"What is that?" Dina leaned against the door.

"Lighter fluid."

The footsteps were moving around the shed.

Seconds later, brittle laughter faded with the footsteps.

The dry grass outside the shed caught quickly. Within minutes, smoke began to seep through the wall and the floor. The rotted wood smoldered, then took to flame as it dried with the heat. Trapped, Dina dropped to her knees, frantically looking for a way out. Coughing, seeking air, she crawled to the door and pounded on it. Flames licked at her arms and her feet as the floor began to burn.

"I'm not going to die like this," Dina said through clenched teeth. "I will not . . ."

She ran at the door and hit it with her shoulder. The

bolt held. Again. And again, the bolt held. Once more. Nothing.

The flames were too close to the door now. She felt the intense heat and smelled the pungent smell of burnt hair. She reached up and felt the singed strands on the left side of her head. Back onto her knees, Dina watched the flames lick at the door.

Just another minute, she told herself as she lowered her face to the floor to seek out any pockets of fresh air that might still linger. *Just another minute and the frame that the bolt is attached to should be burned through. . . .*

A piece of ceiling fell, and Dina knew she could wait no longer.

She sprang forward, using all of her remaining strength to charge the door.

Mercifully, it gave way. Her lungs tortured by acrid smoke and her head pounding from effort and lack of oxygen, Dina crawled forward from where she landed when she'd blown through the burning door, then lay in the grass, gasping for fresh air, until the buzzing in her head subsided. She pulled herself up, stood on shaking legs, and looked back as the shed fell in upon itself.

"Why can't you just die?" The question was presented softly, matter-of-factly, with a touch of curiosity but absolutely no emotion.

Dina turned to look upon the face of her captor.

Her half sister.

Sarah stood less than six feet from Dina, a small handgun in her right hand, a slight smile playing at the corners of her mouth as she slowly raised the hand holding the gun.

Driven by sheer instinct and the will to survive, Dina lowered her head and drove into the woman, who, on contact, was thrown backward. She landed on the ground with Dina astride, stunned, the wind knocked from her lungs. Dina grabbed the woman's wrist, searching for the gun, but it was gone, apparently thrown into the high brush.

Dina sprang to her feet, her thoughts on reaching the Jeep. It was farther away than she'd remembered, and she prayed with every step that the keys were still there.

Breath coming in ragged spurts, sweat running in dark streaks down her sooty face, Dina ran on shaking legs without looking back.

The first shot took her completely by surprise.

The second grazed her left shoulder with startling sharpness and left a trail of heat in its wake.

But still Dina ran. A third shot hit the ground to her right; a fourth pinged loudly off the Jeep's front bumper.

Dina reached the Jeep and pulled herself into the driver's seat, her right hand seeking the keys in her purse even as it shook almost uncontrollably, but yes! There they were. She need only start the engine.

Clutch, she reminded herself. *Remember the clutch. . . .*

The car jerked ahead and stalled.

Another shot struck the passenger-side door. Dina ducked, wondering just how many bullets had been in that small gun. . . .

She turned the key again, then downshifted into neutral, held the clutch, and gunned the engine. In what Dina would later recall as a sort of slow motion, the Jeep lurched forward.

And struck the figure that had seemed to come from nowhere directly into the path of the accelerating vehicle.

The thud had been unexpected. The tires bumped as the Jeep ran over some solid thing, and it was a moment before Dina realized with sickening clarity exactly what it was that was tangled beneath the vehicle.

"Sweet Lord." Dina jumped from the Jeep and crawled on her hands and knees to the body that lay between the front and back wheels and looked into the upturned face, the blue eyes that stared into her own. "Sweet Lord, she's still alive. . . ."

"Okay, this is number seven," Simon said as Betsy pulled up a long straight driveway as directed by Jude and sat in front of the rambling Queen Anne–style farmhouse. "And it looks as if someone is still living in this one as well. We haven't done so well in tracking down these deserted places."

"There are five more on the list, Betsy, so turn around and head back out to the left." Jude appeared to study the landscape, as if trying to remember something. "Take the next right," she said, pointing to the upcoming intersection. "It seems I did hear about a property that was coming up for sale on Henderson Creek Road, but it's not on the list. Slow down now, Betsy. I think it was the old Matthews place."

Betsy leaned forward and squinted. "Is that smoke I see back behind those trees?"

"Looks like it." Simon nodded. "Where is this property?"

"There, over to the right, there's a FOR SALE sign."

Betsy slowed, looking for a road. "Where do I turn?" she asked.

"I don't know. Maybe farther down the . . . yes, there, by that crooked tree. Turn there."

The road was pocked with holes, but its dry surface bore recent tire marks. Maybe, with any luck . . .

"Look," Betsy spoke up. "Over there, by the barn. And there, see that shed? There's the source of the smoke. And there, that's my Jeep. . . ."

The woman on the ground looked up at Dina even as she struggled to breathe.

Dina fumbled in her bag for her cell phone, punched in 911 before realizing the battery in her cell phone had gone dead.

Sarah coughed, hacking spasms that left her all but breathless.

Dina leaned down and sought the woman's pulse, found it faint, erratic.

"Maybe the adapter for the phone is in my purse. . . ." Dina stood up and took a step toward the Jeep just as the van raced into view.

"Don't . . . bother . . ." the woman whispered as she closed her eyes.

"Dina!" Simon called as he slammed on the brakes and leapt from the van.

Dina looked up at his approach. "I tried to call nine-one-one for an ambulance, but my phone is dead. I don't think she's going to make it."

"Oh, sweetheart, thank God you're alive!" A tearful Jude embraced her daughter. "Thank God. . . ."

"I swear I didn't mean to hit her. She just came at

me, at the Jeep, and slammed into the front of it, fell under the wheels . . ." Dina began to shake as the realization of what had happened began to sink in. "I didn't mean to hit her. . . ."

Simon reached for Sarah's wrist to search for a pulse. There was none.

"She said she killed Blythe."

"She did," Simon told Dina. "Sarah Decker. Graham's daughter."

"She was my half sister," Dina whispered. "She was my half sister, and she tried to kill me."

Dina looked up as Betsy wheeled across the dry dirt road.

"I'm sorry," Dina said as if in a fog. "I broke your headlight. I dented your car. And it's all shot up—"

"I'm sorry I wasn't driving it myself," Betsy said, her face stony. She looked up at Simon and asked, "Is she dead?"

Simon nodded. "It's over."

"Do you have an adapter for your phone?" Simon asked Dina.

"I was just going to look for it," she replied blankly. It was clear to Simon that she was going into shock. "My bag is on the front seat."

"Blankets?" Simon asked Betsy.

"In the back of the van." Betsy nodded. "Are you going to call the police?"

"Not yet," Simon said as he ran toward the van.

He returned in moments with two blankets and a bottle of water, which he handed to Dina.

"Sip at it," he reminded her as she lifted the water gratefully to her dry lips. "Don't guzzle."

He placed one blanket over the woman who lay motionless on the ground, her eyes open to the sky. The other he handed to Jude to wrap around Dina; then he returned to the van.

When he finally rejoined the three women, Dina looked up and asked, "Will an ambulance be here soon?"

"Yes. But it may take a while."

"I think it will be too late," Dina said.

"Maybe for her, but not for you." Jude bit her lip, gingerly holding on to her daughter's bloody hands.

Simon knelt down and searched for the source of blood on the back of Dina's shirt.

"It stings." Dina winced.

"Looks like you were shot," he said, moving to look at the wound from the front.

"I guess that's why it stings." Dina nodded and forced a weak smile.

"It appears that the bullet only grazed your shoulder, though." Simon looked up as several black cars sped into view.

"That's not the Henderson police." Jude frowned.

"No."

"Who are they?" Dina asked as several men got out of each car.

"FBI. They've been looking for you. I called Norton, told him where we were, and he directed them here."

"How can he do that?" Dina was becoming slightly groggy.

"He apparently has friends in high places. Now, listen to me. I want you to let me do the talking. We're going to tell them that you're in shock, which won't be a lie. But you must listen very carefully to what I say.

You will have to be able to repeat the story later. Do you understand?"

"Yes, but—"

"Listen very carefully," Simon insisted. "It's very, very important that you know exactly what to say. . . ."

Chapter Twenty-six

From the evening news . . .

Sarah Hayward Decker, daughter of the late President Graham Hayward, Sr., and sister of Rhode Island congressman and rumored presidential candidate Graham Hayward, Jr., died early this afternoon of injuries she sustained in what's been described as a freak accident. According to Sgt. Thomas Burton of the Henderson, Maryland, Police Department, Mrs. Decker was meeting with a landscape designer at a property she and her husband, a retired navy Admiral, were thinking about buying when she was accidentally struck by a vehicle driven by the landscaper. Congressman Hayward declined comment, requesting privacy for his family. Calls to the home of former First Lady Celeste Hayward were unanswered.

No charges were filed against the driver of the vehicle in connection with the accident.

In other national news . . .

Chapter Twenty-Seven

"Hi." Simon poked his head through the door and looked around the small shop. "I was looking for Dina."

"Oh." The woman behind the counter smiled. "You must be Simon. Dina said you'd be coming by this morning." She walked toward him with her hand out and took his when it was offered. "I'm Polly. I've heard a lot about you."

"Oh?" Simon grinned. "All good, of course."

"Of course. You're the white knight who saved Dina from the bad guy."

Simon laughed. "I'd love to take the credit, but the truth is that Dina didn't need much saving by the time I got there. She's a pretty amazing lady."

"That she is. Now, to find that amazing lady, you'll go out this door and down the path that leads through the trees to the greenhouse."

"I know the way. Thanks, Polly. It was good to meet you."

"I'll see you again, I'm sure."

Polly pulled the curtain aside and watched until Simon disappeared through the trees.

"Nice," she said aloud, nodding her head in approval. "Very, very nice . . ."

* * *

The door to the greenhouse swung open and Dina stepped out, a flat of low-growing plants in her arms.

"Hey!" Simon called to her.

"Hey, yourself!" she called back.

She was wearing jeans that were just a bit snug and a tiny bit dusty and a tank that fit her torso like skin. Her hair cascaded over her shoulders and down her back, and it was all Simon could do to keep from sinking his fingers into those dark curls.

"You think you should be lifting that?" Simon stepped forward to take the flat from her hands. "Weren't you just shot a few days ago?"

"It's not at all heavy," Dina told him as he drew closer, "and it wasn't much of a wound, though I will admit that my shoulder's a bit stiff."

She let him take the flat from her hands. "I'm glad you called. I was hoping you would."

"I wanted to give you just a little time to catch your breath."

"I've caught it." She smiled, and something deep inside him twisted and turned.

"Good. You're feeling all right, then?"

"I'm fine. No permanent damage."

"I'm glad." He nodded. "Glad you're okay."

"I was just thinking about taking these seedlings out to the field. They need to be hardened a bit before we can offer them for planting in the ground. Want to take a walk? I'll show you around."

"Sure."

Simon carried the flat for her, then placed it where she directed, on the ground in the shade.

"Shouldn't they be in the sun?" he asked.

"These are young plants. They have to get used to natural light and temperature," she told him. "A little each day. Otherwise, if they go right from the greenhouse to someone's garden, they'll die."

He nodded as if he understood when, in truth, he was so dazzled by being this close to her again that he could barely comprehend a word she'd said.

"Want to see the lake?" she asked, holding out her hand for his.

"Sure."

They walked through fields still muddy from last night's rain, Dina pointing out what she'd planted here and there, Simon barely listening. All of his senses seemed to jumble. All he really knew for certain was that he was here with her and there was no place else he wanted to be. Ever.

". . . and next week we're going to film a piece for the local TV station," she was saying, "about drying hydrangea. I thought I'd let Polly do that, though she doesn't know it yet. She's so good with the dried flowers."

"Uh-huh," Simon responded because he thought a response was expected at that point in the conversation, though he couldn't have repeated what she'd said.

"We're thinking about doing a little more with the fruit trees this year. We pruned better last fall, and we're thinking that we might just do a pick-your-own thing this summer if we actually get any fruit. You know, where you let people come in and pick what they want and just pay by the basket, or whatever."

"Sounds like a good idea."

Dina nodded. "I hate to see all those apples and

peaches go to waste. Unfortunately, neither Polly nor I have time to deal with them."

"Is Mulch-boy still working for you?"

Dina laughed. "You mean Will? Yes, but he'll be here only through the end of the summer. Then he'll be off to college. Some of the fruit matures in the fall, and he won't be around then to pick."

"Maybe I could give you a hand. You know, be your new Mulch-boy."

"That would be one hell of a commute." She led him down toward the pond. "From Arlington to Henderson just to sling a little mulch and pick a few apples? I don't know how long that old Mustang would hold up."

"My lease is month-to-month, and I wasn't planning on renewing. There's nothing to keep me there," he said pointedly. *Nothing to keep me anywhere but here . . .*

"Where would you go?"

"I was thinking a nice old fixer-upper in a nice, quiet small town might be nice."

"Plenty of those around." She sat on a fallen log overlooking the pond and tugged on his hand to join her. "Nice place to live while you're writing that story."

"Which story would that be?"

"The one that brought you to Henderson in the first place." She no longer smiled, and her eyes focused on something across the pond.

"Oh, that story." Simon sat down next to her, his hands dangling between his knees.

"Ummm."

"When I first told Philip what I was on to—Blythe, Graham, then you—he asked me to consider what would happen to the people involved if the story was printed. What would happen to your lives."

"And . . . ?"

"Well, at the time, I couldn't understand what had gotten into him, that he'd ask me to put a story aside. It made no sense to me at all. I'm a journalist. I find the story, I write it. I was taught—by Philip, incidentally—that nothing was more important than the truth."

"I sense a 'but' in here somewhere—"

"But . . . I look at you—at all of you—and I see so much damage. I see Celeste Hayward, haunted by the truth of her husband's infidelity and broken by the death of her daughter. I see Gray wrestling with all that he's learned about his family, knowing that if he runs for office he will have to either lie and perpetuate the myth about his father or reveal some truths that some—you included—do not want revealed. I see Jude, whose biggest sin was to love you enough to want to keep you safe at any cost, enough to tell you the truth even when she knew it could turn you away from her. And at the center of it all, I see you. It all revolves around you. . . ."

Simon seemed to struggle for words. Finally, he said, "I just don't think it's the right time for this story to be told. Maybe someday . . . but not right now."

He turned her face toward his and for a long moment looked into her eyes.

"How could you give it up?" she asked. "*Why* would you give it up?"

"Because I don't want to be responsible for what will happen to you once the full story is told. I think you've had enough to deal with for a while. You've had your life turned upside down, found out you weren't who you thought you were. You've been hit over the head, locked in a burning building, shot at—"

Dina smiled weakly. "Don't forget the mice."

"What mice?"

"The mice in the shed."

Simon's thumb traced the side of her face. "There were mice in the shed?"

"All night long." Dina shook her head. "Party, party, party."

Simon raised a questioning eyebrow.

"Sarah threw some dried corn into the shed before she left me there. Just to make sure I didn't have to spend the night alone."

"That was thoughtful of her."

"It was the longest night of my life." Dina shivered. "And you left out the fact that I was responsible for Sarah's death."

"Dina, there's no one who doesn't know that that was an accident."

"I just never saw her until the last second, and even then, she almost appeared like a shadow. I will never forget what those minutes were like, knowing she was dying, knowing I was responsible for taking a life. Even *her* life. You don't forget something like that easily, Simon. I doubt I ever will."

"No one could forget, Dina, but you can't focus your life on that moment, either. Sarah's death was an accident, and frankly, if anyone was responsible, it was Sarah herself. Her intent in luring you there was to find out where Jude was, so that she could kill her, then kill you, too. Not to make light of the situation, but Sarah Decker wasn't an innocent party. She was a murderer. And while you can't change what's happened, you can try to put it behind you." Simon drew her to him. "You can start over and go on from here. After all, you have a new life, a new family to get to know."

"Will you be part of my starting over, Simon?" She touched his face. "Will you be part of my new life?"

"I hope so. I want to be."

Simon lowered his mouth and kissed her, long and hard, all of the emotions of the past week swelling inside and taking him over. He kissed her again, ignored the pounding in his head and the sweet licks of heat that invaded his body. Her mouth was hot and sweet and all Simon knew for certain at that particular moment was that he was one hell of a lucky guy on this overcast morning.

"Simon." She placed one finger over his lips, her face flushed, her mouth so ripe that he could barely hear her voice for staring at it. "I just want you to know that I do appreciate that you've postponed writing the story. Maybe someday you'll decide to write it, but for now, I appreciate that you've put it aside. I don't have words to thank you. It's a hell of a lot to give up."

Simon shrugged. "Actually, I pretty much gave it up when I gave the story to the Henderson police after Sarah's death. I couldn't very well come back later with something else. Unless, of course, I have a desire to go to prison for giving false statements to the police. Obstructing justice. That sort of thing." He paused, then nibbled at her bottom lip. "I have desires right now, but they have absolutely nothing to do with defending myself in court."

"Well then, why don't you tell me about them?" Dina rose and pulled Simon with her. "You can do that while I show you my carriage house."

"Sounds like one hell of a plan." Simon took the hand she offered and fell in step with her.

"Oh, it is." She closed the gap between them and quickened her step. "I think you'll like it. . . ."

Dina turned over the sign on the greenhouse door to read CLOSED as they walked past. She unlocked the carriage house door and held it open for Simon, then locked it behind them.

"My home," she said simply.

"Strong colors on the walls and the furniture, enough flowers to make it feminine, enough clutter to make it homey. I'd say it reflects you well."

"Thank you." Dina started up the steps. "But I think you should see the rest of the place before you pass judgment."

"Hmmm. You have a point." Simon nodded. "I sure wouldn't want to make any hasty conclusions. . . ."

From the top of the steps, Simon could see into Dina's bedroom—the old four-poster bed upon which an old quilt spread comfortably, the sheer curtains that blew aside in the gentle morning breeze. Dina stood at the side of the bed, her hands pulling back her hair as she watched him pause in the doorway. Every nerve in her body seemed to hum as he walked toward her, his arms opening, then closing her inside.

She sought his mouth with her own, parting her lips for his tongue, easing back against the side of the bed and taking him with her. She backed onto the quilt, leading him with her hands and her kisses, bringing him along, easing his body onto hers.

"How's the shoulder?" he asked.

"A bit tender," she admitted.

"I'll be gentle."

"I'm counting on it."

Her blood pounded in her ears and her breath quickened as Simon's lips sought the hollow of her throat. His hands found the softness of her breasts and her body arched slightly, offering more.

This, Dina told herself, was chemistry at its best.

A sigh escaped her lips and she smiled to herself. This was exactly what she'd waited for, all her life. Exactly the right feeling, exactly the right man. She tugged her shirt over her head, then helped Simon off with his. She felt herself melting slowly into his body even as he entered hers, and closed her eyes and let herself be washed away on the tide that rose between them, coming to rest only when it finally ebbed.

"You were right," Simon said when his brain began to function again and his breathing returned to normal. "This was one hell of a plan."

"I thought so." Dina lay back against the pillow and smiled.

"Hey, maybe you could give me that job picking apples. You could close down the greenhouse every day around this time."

"I have to admit it's tempting, but I think that Polly might start to get suspicious after a while."

"Would it hurt so much to keep her guessing?"

"Maybe not for a time." Dina shifted her legs slightly, then asked, "Were you serious about looking for a place to rent in the area?"

"Yep."

"What are you planning to do?"

"Work-wise?" He rubbed his chin thoughtfully. "Well, I found I enjoyed writing the book on Hayward.

I want to finish my own book, then maybe do another book or two. Actually, I have several other projects in mind that I'd like to work on."

"Why here?" She suspected but wanted to hear him say it.

"Well, because after all . . . all that happened, after I realized that I would not be writing the story that would take the country by storm, I started to think a lot about what I really wanted out of life." Simon stroked her arm slightly with his fingertips. "No matter what all I put on that list, I just kept coming back to you. I figure if I'm going to win your heart, it would be a lot easier if I'm in the neighborhood."

"I'd love to have you in my neighborhood." Dina kissed the tip of his nose. "And you've already won my heart."

"Even though I ruined your life?"

"My life is far from ruined." She flashed that megawatt smile and added, "As a matter of fact, it's pretty damned great right now."

"So you're not going to blame me for rocking your boat?"

"Maybe it needed to be rocked. Jude's did, anyway. It wasn't right for her to keep that secret for so long. It wasn't right to keep Betsy away for all those years. She's my aunt. We have a right to know each other. Even Jude has come to accept that."

"Oh. Speaking of your family . . ." Simon leaned on one elbow. "I think you may be hearing from Gray in the near future."

"Why?"

"He wants to meet you." Simon watched a cloud pass over her face. "After all, you are his half sister."

"Who happened to kill his sister." Dina bit her bottom lip. "What do you think he thinks of me?"

"Curious, maybe. But I think he might be just as concerned about what you think of him."

"I guess we should meet sooner or later." Dina nodded. "Maybe in a month or so. This whole thing has been so overwhelming, you know? And I still have so many questions."

"Like what?" Simon raised himself up on one elbow.

"Like how did Sarah know about Blythe?"

"The best Philip and I can piece together from what we knew, and from what you told us about your conversation with Sarah while you were in the shed, is that Miles told her thinking that Sarah would go to her father and cry and beg him to give up Blythe and that Graham would feel so bad that he'd end the affair."

"Why would Miles do that?"

"Because he was in love with Blythe himself."

"So he thought that if Sarah talked her father into leaving Blythe and coming back to her mother, then he would have Blythe all to himself . . . ?"

"That's the best we could come up with. But instead of going to her father—"

"Sarah went to Blythe . . ." Dina said softly.

"Miles had made some comments to me to the effect that he'd never meant for Blythe to die. That it wasn't supposed to turn out the way it did, or something like that. And it all makes sense when you add it all together."

"Hmmm." Dina lay back and pondered it for a few minutes. "She must have hated Blythe terribly," she said after a time.

"I imagine she did," Simon agreed.

"I like to think that my father had Dr. Norton in the wings watching over me somehow," she told him. Before he could respond, she added, "And that reminds me that I need to thank Dr. Norton for . . . well, you know, for what he did after. After . . . Sarah—well, there was a lot that never appeared in any official report that I saw. The fire, for one thing—"

"Philip's 'old friend' at the Bureau turned out to be the director. And it's amazing what a call from the director of the FBI can do, isn't it? Your local police didn't even seem upset when the Feds took over everything. Your chief seemed almost happy to have them involved."

"Biggest moment of Tom's life, I do believe. All he had to hear was 'matter of national security' and his lips were sealed. I didn't even see a mention of the gun in the report." Dina paused, then asked, "What do you suppose happened to Sarah's gun?"

"What gun?"

"You know what gun. The gun Sarah shot at me with. Shot up Betsy's Jeep with. The gun she had in her hand when she died."

"There was no gun in her hand when the ambulance arrived." Simon shrugged. "And there was nothing on the report about any damage to the Jeep."

"Are people really that powerful, that they can hide things like that?" Dina half sat up.

Simon raised an amused eyebrow. "You have to ask me that? Sweetheart, they managed to hide you for almost thirty years. . . ."

"Do I look all right?" Dina had the car door half-opened, her legs poised to settle on the ground, an anxious look on her face.

"You look beautiful," Simon assured her. "You have nothing to worry about. Just be yourself."

"What if this doesn't go well? Or if they don't like me?"

"Hey, what if you don't like them?" Simon took Dina's arm and led her up to the front door of Jen and Gray Hayward's Rhode Island home. "Now's as good a time as any to find out. Come on."

It was almost three months since Sarah Decker's death, six weeks since Simon Keller had found the perfect bungalow to rent on a road right outside of Henderson. One month since he'd moved in and one week from the day that he'd started working on his first novel, the story of a young reporter who was tracking a dream of a story.

Jen Hayward was the first to greet Simon and Dina, and she did so warmly.

"Come in, please. Gray's out back with Dr. Norton." She escorted them through the house and out onto the patio. "Gray has been pacing all day, waiting for you to arrive. . . ."

The congressman from Rhode Island stepped forward and shook Simon's hand, all the while looking beyond him to Dina.

"You must be Dina," he said.

"Yes." Dina wasn't sure if she should offer her hand and was happy when Gray offered his.

"Did you have an enjoyable trip?" If anything, Gray appeared more nervous than Dina.

"Yes. It was a nice drive. I haven't been in this part of the country before. It's beautiful." Dina nodded.

"You'll have to see the view from the cliffs." Gray turned toward the sea. "It's spectacular."

"I'll be sure to do that before we leave."

"Let me get you something to drink." Gray gestured to the small bar where Philip Norton stood, watching the interaction. "What would you like?"

"Whatever white wine you have on hand would be lovely."

"I have just the thing." Gray patted her shoulder. "Simon? Your pleasure?"

"A cold beer would be fine."

"Philip." Simon nodded a greeting.

"Simon." Norton nodded back. "Dina, it's a pleasure to see you again," Norton said as he took her hand in his own and held it.

"Dr. Norton, I'd been hoping for an opportunity to thank you for all you did for me. For all of us."

"It was merely a matter of keeping a trust, my dear." Norton leaned toward her, so that no one other than Dina could hear. "As I promised your father I would always do."

Dina folded her arms over her chest and studied the older man who stood before her. Simon had been right on the money. Sean Connery without the accent. Definitely . . .

"Might we have a few minutes alone?" Gray handed Dina a glass of pale wine that sparkled just slightly.

"Of course." Dina nodded, then looked up at Norton. "If you'll excuse me. I know there are other things I'd like to talk to you about."

"Whenever you're ready, my dear."

Dina squeezed Simon's hand for luck and said, "I'll be back."

"I'll be here."

Dina followed Gray into the cool of the house.

"How about here, in the den?" Gray held the door for her, and she smiled tentatively.

"That's fine." Dina followed him into the room.

"I'm so grateful that you agreed to come here today, Dina. I've been wanting to meet you ever since . . . well, since . . ."

"I'm surprised you'd want to meet me at all." Dina looked up at him. "Since I am, after all, responsible for your sister's death."

"My sister took your mother's life." Gray met her gaze head-on. "And, from what I understand, tried her best to take yours. My family and I were stunned. Never in a million years could we have imagined that Sarah would do such things. None of us were prepared for the truth, especially my mother. Sarah had been . . . very ill . . . emotionally . . . on and off as a young girl, but she'd received the very finest treatment. We'd been assured that her illness was far behind her. None of us could ever have guessed that it was still there, under the surface. Dr. Norton thinks that Sarah found out about you from the tape she stole from Simon's apartment—we found it in the glove box of her car—and apparently, the discovery triggered a relapse. . . ."

"But no one had noticed any change in her behavior?"

"Actually, yes, Julian had. He'd spoken to my mother about a month earlier, about Sarah's mood swings and sudden bursts of anger. He'd tried to get her to return to the doctor, but she refused. Julian was hoping that Mother could convince her to go."

"I'm assuming she declined."

"She did. Unfortunately, no one realized just how deeply ill she was."

"How is your mother doing?" Dina asked gently.

"She's not been at all well since Sarah's death. It's all been such a horror for her. To find out that her daughter was a murderer, that she'd harbored such a terrible secret for so many years . . ."

"I'm so very sorry."

"I appreciate that. This has all been too much for a woman of her age to deal with." Gray appeared to swallow hard. "It's been too much for all of us. Sarah deeply hurt so many people. Her children. Julian. Even his sister feels betrayed. You've heard, I suppose, that Sarah'd been driving Carolyn's car the night of the accident. Sarah told her that she'd hit a deer on one of the back roads around the school. Finding out what really happened has been a terrible shock to everyone."

"Why did you invite me here, Gray?"

"Because I felt that we needed to meet, at the very least. Because I felt you were due an apology on behalf of my family. Because I think my father would have wanted me to know you. And because there is the matter of needing to know how much information you're comfortable with ultimately being shared with the public."

Dina sat back on the arm of a wingback chair placed to one side of a small brick fireplace, Gray sat on the arm of the chair facing hers.

"None," Dina said adamantly.

"You mean you're not planning on going on *Oprah*?" He tried to force a smile.

"No. As a matter of fact, I'm not planning on telling anyone."

"You could make a great deal of money from this."

"Are you crazy? Do you know what would happen to my life?" Dina stood, horrified at the thought.

"Yes. You'll be invited onto all the talk shows; you'll have people falling all over themselves to help you write your book."

"Stop it." Dina glared at him as if he were a madman. "That's the last thing I want."

"Well, that makes it easy," he said softly.

"To do what?"

"I'm sure that Simon has mentioned that I've been thinking about running for the presidency."

Dina nodded.

"If I do, my party will expect me to remind the public that my father was the embodiment of morality, just as Simon's book would do. I haven't yet decided if I can, in good conscience, do that." He looked up at the portrait that hung over the mantel. "At the same time, I have to know how you feel about having the truth come out."

"I don't want it to," Dina said bluntly.

"Then I will honor that. You've made this decision much easier for me"—he smiled at her—"since I do not believe I can run for that office without being truthful to the voters. I thank you for being honest with me. I know now exactly what I have to do."

"I'm not sure I understand."

"If I run, I will have a very difficult time not telling the truth about my father. He was a wonderful man, a wonderful President, but he was not perfect and he was not a saint. I cannot run for that office and pretend that he was. But at the same time, I cannot make this story public without bringing you into the fray. Since this affects your life, too, I feel you are entitled to decide whether or not you want your privacy invaded. I will respect that at any cost."

"Are you saying that you would give up an opportunity to be the President of the United States?" Dina's jaw dropped.

"My father took this secret to his grave. Maybe that's where it should stay."

"Gray, I'm so sorry. I don't know what to say. This is a tremendous sacrifice to make for someone you don't know."

"My family owes you much more than our silence, Dina. So much was taken from you." Gray tried to smile. "And besides, we may not know each other, you and I, but we are flesh and blood. That needs to be honored. We share the same father. Whatever else has come to light over these past few months cannot take away the fact that he was a wonderful father. I loved him very much."

Gray's eyes clouded, teared. "I had the privilege of knowing him. You were denied that. I'd like to tell you about him, if you'd care to hear."

"That's very, very generous of you," Dina whispered, touched deeply by Gray's effort.

"I understand that he loved your mother very much." Gray stood and looked out the window.

"So they tell me."

"He loved mine, once, too," he said softly.

"Then we have that in common." Tears formed in Dina's eyes without her realizing it.

"That painting, there over the fireplace, was done only weeks before he died." Gray turned and pointed to the portrait.

"You look like him." Dina looked up at the painting of the handsome man with the silver hair and the direct gaze and the smile that tilted the left side of his mouth. So like his son's.

Gray went to the desk and opened the top drawer, took out a small wrapped package, and offered it to Dina.

"I thought you might like to have this."

Dina unwrapped the tissue paper and removed the picture frame within, turned it over to find a photograph of the late President. He wore a polo shirt over a plaid bathing suit and looked back over his shoulder from the prow of a handsome sailboat.

"That was taken the first year that my . . . our . . . father was in the White House," Gray told her. "I figured he would have met your mother around that time. . . ."

"It's a wonderful picture. He had a wonderful face." Dina could no longer keep the tears back. "You are a thoughtful man, Gray. I cannot even begin to tell you how much your kindness means to me."

Dina reached out and took his hand. "Simon tells me that everyone says you are so much like your father. If that's so, he must have been quite wonderful. History says he was a great President. I think you should think twice before you decide not to follow in his footsteps."

"Thank you, I appreciate that, but I think it's best for everyone that I let the chance pass me by." Gray patted her hand, then let it go.

"How will your wife feel about losing an opportunity to be the First Lady?"

"She'll be one hundred percent behind my decision. She understands me, knows me well enough to know that I can't stand in front of the press and say things I don't mean. Besides, I'd like to see if, over time, you and I could get to know each other. I don't know how possible that would be if I were living in the White House." He looked up and smiled. "Some roads are better off not traveled, Dina. This feels like one of them."

"Not many people would be so honorable. I admire that you're willing to stand behind your convictions. It can't be easy."

"And not many people would give up a chance for fame and fortune—after all, for the rest of your life, you'd be known as the daughter of a President. Who knows? They could end up making a movie about your life."

"Ugh." Dina grimaced, and they both laughed. "But if we are going to get to know each other, I guess that mutual respect is a good place to start."

The door opened and a young boy with dark hair and darker eyes stuck his head in.

"Oops. Sorry, Dad." He backed away.

"It's all right, Son. Come in. I'd like you to meet Dina. She's . . . a friend. . . ."

How'd it go? Simon mouthed the words as Dina and Gray returned to the patio area where Norton was talking about the book that he and Simon had collaborated on.

Very promising, she mouthed back as she joined the group seated around a low table of glass and bamboo.

". . . and so I'm not certain what the future of the book will be," Norton concluded.

"Why is its future uncertain, if I might ask?" Dina

stood behind Simon's chair, her hand resting on his shoulder.

"Well, the intent of the book was to lay the foundation for Gray's run for the presidency," Norton reminded her. "Should Gray choose not to run, we might have to reconsider whether or not to go forward with it."

"Now I hope that wasn't an attempt to influence my decision," Gray said.

"Not at all, son. It's not just a matter of economics. A book such as this would generate greater interest, greater sales, if Gray were running," Norton told them. "But there's also the matter of not appearing to capitalize on the current situation. Some might feel it's insensitive to publish such a book immediately on the heels of Sarah's death. For some that might not be an issue. However, for me, given my long association with this family . . . well, let's just say I'm in no hurry right now."

"If you'll excuse me—I think the caterer is here." Jen looked towards the drive and the van that had just pulled in. "I thought I'd have dinner brought in tonight, rather than cook, so that I could devote my time to my company. I'll just show them where to set up."

Jen disappeared through the gate.

"Simon, can I get you another beer?" Gray asked.

"No, thanks." Simon stood. "But I do think I'd like to share that view of the sea with Dina before dinner."

Simon took Dina's hand and, with a backward glance at the bar where Philip was scooping ice into his glass, turned her toward the vast lawn that lay between the patio and the sea.

When they were out of earshot of the patio, Simon asked, "So all went well? You're okay being here?"

"Well, I admit that I felt intimidated at first, but Gray has been incredibly kind. He gave me a wonderful photograph of Graham. He's a most extraordinary man, Gray is. I don't think I've ever met anyone like him."

"I couldn't agree more. Gray is exceptional. I've never known anyone like him, either."

"I think in time we could be friends. I want to be his friend." Dina thought about it for a moment, then said, "Maybe someday I could even think of him as my brother. Maybe."

"I'm glad that it went well for you." Simon draped an arm over her shoulder. "How do you think Jude will feel about that?"

"This is hard for her, but she will need to adjust. I think she'll come around. She really only wants the best for me. I know in my heart that that's all she ever wanted."

"I'm sure it's difficult for her, as your mother, to deal with a lot of what's happened. It's fortunate that you are so understanding of her."

"I love her." That was all the reason necessary as far as Dina was concerned. She closed her eyes and lifted her face to the sun, then asked, "Do you think Celeste knew that Sarah killed Blythe?"

"I've wondered about that myself."

"Gray said that his mother is just devastated about what happened, that she was shocked to hear about what Sarah had done, but . . ."

"But you have to wonder if she hadn't known all

along and covered up for her. After all, she did whisk Sarah out of the country and to a clinic in Switzerland very shortly after Blythe's death," Simon noted.

"Maybe Jude wasn't the only one keeping secrets for the sake of her child," Dina whispered.

"I doubt we'll ever know for certain." Simon leaned the side of his head against hers.

For a few long minutes they stood close together, drinking in the salt air, basking in the warmth of the sunshine, lost in the roar of the surf from below.

"Tell me about Dr. Norton's wife," Dina broke the silence. "What exactly happened to her?"

"She committed suicide."

"Oh, my God! How terrible!"

"It *was* terrible. She'd lost her son some years before—he'd been kidnapped when he was young. She didn't leave a note, but everyone pretty much thought that she just could not face one more morning of not knowing what happened to her son."

"That's just horrible." Dina shivered. "Was he their only child?"

"Actually, he was *her* son. She'd been married once before and widowed. She had a daughter, too, but I lost track of her over the years. Someone told me recently that she's a composite artist, you know, a sketch artist? She must be in her early thirties by now. But Elisa and Philip had no children together."

"That's so sad, Simon. Sad for her, for her daughter. Sad for him . . ."

"He's never really recovered from it. He's never been the same."

They came to the edge of the cliff and looked out

across the vast expanse of water. Waves below crashed lustily against the rocks.

"This is incredible. Look out there, Simon; look at all the sailboats. Doesn't it look wonderful?"

"It does. Did you ever sail?"

"No. I'm one hundred percent landlubber, I'm afraid. Jude's never been much for water sports."

"Maybe you can get Gray to take you out one of these days."

"I just might do that."

"What did Gray have to say about . . . well, about all that's happened?"

"He wanted to know how I felt about making the story public." Dina laid her head against Simon's shoulder. "I told him I'd be happiest if we just all went on as we were."

"And he'll honor that?"

"He'll decline the nomination for the presidency if he thinks he can't run honorably."

"He told you that?"

Dina nodded.

"I hope he keeps his word."

"He will."

"How can you be so sure?"

"I trust him, Simon. I think he's a very sincere man."

"Not to say that he isn't, but that's what they always said about his father."

"I guess it's hard to reconcile the man who swore he'd never lie to the American people with the man who sure enough did lie to his wife."

"Funny thing about Graham Senior. I do think that for most of his life, he acted from the highest moral standards. I think maybe the only time in his life that he slipped was in his relationship with Blythe. I think maybe his love for her was so strong, so overpowering, that he just didn't have the strength to turn away from her. I think it was bigger than anything else in his life."

"That doesn't make it right," Dina said softly.

"No. But I have to admit that I'm starting to understand how he felt. How love can be so strong and so all-encompassing that you'd give up anything for its sake. While I agree that what Graham did wasn't necessarily right, I'd be lying if I said I didn't understand how loving someone that much can change you. Can make you do things you never thought you'd do." Simon nipped at her ear. "For example, I never thought that rising at dawn would ever become part of my everyday routine."

"You don't have to get up with me," she laughed. "I've told you that you could sleep—"

"Ah, but then I'd miss out on loving you into the new day." Simon kissed her. "Not to mention that great coffee that you make."

"Oh, so it's my coffee that keeps you hanging around."

"That and your many talents." He whispered a few of his favorites in her ear, and she laughed again, the sound of it carrying down to the sea.

Simon stood behind Dina, his arms around her in a close circle, as they faced out to the sea.

"So, then, are you glad you came?" He nuzzled the side of her face. "All's well that ends well?"

"Yes, I'm glad I came. I never had a sibling and it's still hard now to think that I do. I want to get to know him better, and his family, too. Maybe see a bit more of Graham Senior through his son's eyes. But I don't want you thinking for a minute that this is the end, Simon Keller."

Dina turned in his arms, her arms encircling his neck.

"Oh, no, love. *This* is only the beginning. . . ."